About the au

Richard's early working life was as a construction engineer, a career that also took him abroad to work in Zambia and Jordan. Returning home, he joined a major Japanese corporation, administering large civil and industrial projects in Europe, Africa and the Middle East. A career change to run a small family business and read for a Masters Degree in Maritime Studies led to him writing his first novel, *A Cast of Hawks*, published in 2010. The sequel, *Batsu*, was followed by *Shadows in Sunshine*, set in Madeira. *In Treacherous Waters* is the fourth book in the Ian Vaughan thriller series. Away from his writing, Richard is a keen sailor when generous friends have deck space available for him.

Also by Richard V Frankland

A Cast of Hawks

Vanguard Press 2010
ISBN 9781843866077

Batsu

Vanguard Press 2012
ISBN 9781843868590

Shadows in Sunshine

Vanguard Press 2015
ISBN 9781843869689

IN TREACHEROUS WATERS

Richard V Frankland

IN TREACHEROUS WATERS

Vanguard Press

A CIP catalogue record for this title is
available from the British Library.

ISBN 9781784657 20-8

*Vanguard Press is an imprint of
Pegasus Elliot MacKenzie Publishers Ltd.*
www.pegasuspublishers.com

First Published in 2020

**Vanguard Press
Sheraton House Castle Park
Cambridge England**

Printed & Bound in Great Britain

Dedication

To my daughters Caroline and Victoria.

Acknowledgements

First of all I would like to thank my wife, Sandra, for her tireless support and encouragement during the long months of writing this novel, and for providing thorough initial proofreading and plot sanity checking, in addition to a busy working life of her own.

No publication is complete without professional editing and I thank Natasha Orme for her valuable work in improving and sharpening my text.

I also want to thank Jonathan Temples for his excellent work on the cover design.

Finally, I wish to thank my readers for their reviews and kind messages that ring as clearly in my mind as the applause would do to an actor taking a bow.

Thank you all.

CHAPTER 1

Ian Vaughan stepped off the running machine and waited while the nurse removed the ECG pads from his chest.

"Um, one hundred heart rate; any pains?"

"No."

"Let me take your blood pressure, come and sit over here."

Vaughan sat and waited as the nurse took the readings.

"I'll come back in twenty minutes and take it again."

Vaughan stood and wandered across to the comfortable chairs in the corner of the room, looked down at the scar that marked where the hospital in Madeira had extracted his appendix and a 7.62 mm bullet, then sat hoping that he would be released in time to get to his ex-wife's cottage in Derbyshire to take his daughters up to Cumbria for some pony trekking.

Several minutes had passed when Dr Veronica Appleyard entered, walked across to Vaughan and sat beside him, "The Commodore has been telling me about your latest little exploit Mr Vaughan. Tell me, how did you manage to get involved in exposing a coup in Madeira when you were sent purely on a diplomatic mission to befriend a Tunisian political leader at a four nations conference?"

Vaughan sighed, "Do you really want to know?"

"Yes, I do."

"I simply helped a young boy who was stranded on a sailboard a couple of miles out at sea."

"And?"

"Oh, his widowed mother was playing host to her Brazilian uncle who was part of the group organising a coup."

The doctor looked at Vaughan steadily waiting for him to continue.

"Well, this uncle of hers escaped arrest initially but could not get off the island and eventually found his way back to her apartment where he was cornered and tried to use her as a shield and hostage, but he made a mistake and in the scuffle that followed a Portuguese soldier shot him from behind and the bullet went through him and was 'caught by my appendix'."

"You make it sound like a cricket match with you fielding at silly mid-on."

"It was hardly cricket and yes very silly to shoot a bad guy at close range with a rifle when a good guy is standing the other side of him."

"What about your real mission?"

"Oh, that went okay."

"Oh, just okay."

Vaughan nodded.

The nurse approached again and took Vaughan's pulse, "Ooo, seventy – good recovery."

"Can I look at the test results please?" asked Dr Appleyard.

"Yes, Doctor, do you want the X-rays as well?"

"Yes please."

While Dr Appleyard looked through the test results and studied the X-Rays she gave Vaughan a summary of his condition, "For a man of your age you are remarkably fit, good liver function, which for someone in your line of business is unusual, normally your colleagues have spent a lot of time in bars. Kidneys appear to be functioning okay and your ticker is sound, in fact, considering what you have been through I am amazed."

"Can I take your blood pressure again, Mr Vaughan."

Vaughan walked back to the nurses' desk and sat whilst she did the test and wrote down the result.

"Out of interest what was it?" asked Vaughan.

"One hundred and ten over seventy," the nurse replied, not really believing what she had just recorded.

Half an hour later Vaughan was saying goodbye to the Sister and nurses who had been looking after him at the clinic, "I will miss you all, really, you have been wonderful. Thank you, thank you very much."

Sister Mitchell walked with Vaughan to the main entrance of the clinic, "You are very, very lucky to be alive, Mr Vaughan, and I have made that very clear to your superiors." Vaughan looked at her and frowned with curiosity. "This is not the first time that you have chosen to get involved in gun play so I am told, a trait that has some worrying aspects concerning your mental outlook on life."

"Believe me I don't suffer from suicidal tendencies, Sister, in that situation I had to make split second decisions and on this occasion I am very confident that I made the right one, but thank you for your concerns. Goodbye, I promise that I will try to avoid troubling you again."
Shaking her head, Sister Mitchell watched Vaughan go down the steps to the waiting hire car and drive away to catch up with his daughters.

***

Anna-Maria Patterson slowly descended the stairs, her silk tai chi outfit, cool against her tanned body, comfortable in the air-conditioned chill of the riverside villa that stood in the centre of Luanda's most affluent area. At the foot of the stairs she turned and strolled towards the stoep that overlooked the pool, garden, and beyond the high wall, the river. Sliding the stoep door open she stepped outside into heat and clammy humidity of a typical Angolan day. As she walked across the iroko hardwood decking a blue tailed skink, hunting for insects, scurried out of her path to the edge of the stoep then turned to stare defiantly at her. Entering the mosquito netted tent, suspended over the bare wooden table, she took a seat and waited for Emmanuel to bring her breakfast, the one meal in the day she looked forward to, because she could eat alone, her mother and stepfather preferring the chill of the air-conditioned dining room.

Staring unseeingly out across the river she considered again submitting her application for the post of assistant lecturer at the university's English Language faculty. In fact, it was more than just that, she was at last considering her whole future.

People taken in by Anna-Maria's outward appearance of being just a very pretty young, but rather vacuous woman, would be very surprised by the quick intellect hidden behind the dreamy eyes, and the strength and fitness hidden by the languid movements. Born in Lisbon, Anna-Maria Ronaldo, to a Portuguese father and half Portuguese half South African mother, Anna-Maria enjoyed a childhood surrounded by wealth, receiving with that a good education. Speaking perfect English and French in addition to her native tongue, and with well-connected friends,

15

her future in high circles seemed assured until the day her father was killed in a car accident near Porto. Anna-Maria's mother, never feeling quite at home in Portugal, insisted they move to Cape Town, where she met businessman, Jan Vermeulen, marrying him after just six months. Two years later Vermeulen's business interests meant that the family moved to Luanda, where, at a party, Anna-Maria met David Patterson, introduced as an English geologist assisting the Angolan Government on natural resource assessment. Anna-Maria, twenty-three at the time, found in Patterson the soul mate she had sought ever since leaving university and in Anna-Maria, Patterson found someone to match his intellect. A whirlwind romance led to the two marrying and setting up a home of their own in Luanda.

Three years of complete joy followed and despite her husband's many absences, Anna-Maria remained blissfully happy with her life and completely unaware that her husband was an SIS agent, planted in Angola by the British Government to hunt down illegal arms traders. When he was shot and hacked to pieces whilst on a visit to Cabinda Province his death was blamed upon the FlecPM separatist movement, but she had always felt that there was more to it than her David being in the wrong place at the wrong time.

Emmanuel entered the tent with her breakfast and they greeted each other. He informed her that overnight the garden boy had become a father again to a son. He left her now idly wondering how a poorly paid garden boy could afford to raise a family of five children and deciding how much money she should give him for the child's clothes when her musings were interrupted by her stepfather shouting.

"The bastards! Shit, shit, shit! Carla! Carla! Get in here!"

Anna-Maria's whole body gave a nervous jerk and she strained to listen. Immediately she heard the clatter of Carla's shoes on the villa's ceramic floor tiling as the girl hurried to his office. Her stepfather was waiting for Carla at his office door.

"I want you to get on the phone straight away and…"

The door to his office closed with a bang, shutting out any chance of learning what crisis had occurred. She waited, nervously wondering, would he summon her. Had he discovered what she had been up to? Was now the moment to go to her room and grab the pre-packed suitcase hidden at the back of her wardrobe. Only now did she consider how to get it to her car and drive off before Jan Vermeulen's men stopped her.

Inside the villa, Carla Correia had found Vermeulen standing at his office door staring at his mobile phone with what could only be described as an expression of fear on his face. He was a tall man with broad shoulders and to Carla's eyes not very good looking at all, and definitely someone you would not want to argue with. At this moment however, he looked strangely rather small, as if he had shrunk and his normal commanding glare was replaced by an almost pleading expression.

"I want you to get on the phone straight away," he said as the noise of the office door slamming behind them reverberated down the passageway, "and get air tickets for myself, Karl, Pieter, and you had better get one for my wife as well, on this morning's eleven o'clock flight to Lagos."

Carla turned to leave. "And when you've done that tell my wife I want to see her urgently," he added.

"Is there something wrong, Senhor Vermeulen?" she asked anxiously, noting her boss's shortage of breath and the unusual sight of perspiration on his face.

"Yes, so hurry, we must get that flight, we can't risk missing it, so go!"

Vermeulen's eyes were still focused on the screen of his mobile on which the tip-off message had appeared, his mind in turmoil; how did the British get onto the deal and trace it to him, who was the bastard who grassed him up. Despite the coolness of his air-conditioned office he felt hot, claustrophobic and had a ridiculous desire to run out of the house and just keep running. Frantically, he fought to calm his thoughts and plan a way out; he would need more cash funds and that meant a visit to Elmoctar, the only one of his recent clients who had not made the final payment due on a shipment; use of credit cards was out until he could reach London and the Docklands flat that he kept in the name of Henri Vanderkloof. A distant police car siren had him staring in terror out of his office window at the driveway, sitting upright and motionless until the sound drifted away into the distance leaving him looking around his office as if he were expecting policemen to spring from behind his filing cabinets. After a while the silence surrounding the house slowly brought him a sense of relief.

When Lucia, his wife, arrived Vermeulen was brief, "Very urgent business has cropped up and I need you to join me, so get packed, usual limit for air travel. We leave in one hour."

"Ooh, where are we going Jan? Somewhere exciting?"

"First stop Nigeria, then maybe a couple more stops depending on flight availability, now hurry I have a lot to do."

"How long will we be away?"

"Quite a time, why?" He would tell her the truth later, now was not the time; he could not waste time answering questions when the net could close in at any moment.

"If it means me sitting in hotels for hours on end waiting for you to finish your meetings I would like Anna-Maria to come as well, for company, Jan," Lucia replied, a little haughtily, aware from past experience what such trips entailed.

Vermeulen thought for a moment or two, "Yes, maybe it would be better to have her along, tell her, then tell Carla to add her to the list would you, dear."

When his wife had left he got up and went across to his safe and on opening it took out his and his wife's South African passports and a second Dutch/EU passport in the name of Henri Vanderkloof. As he turned to his desk he caught his reflection in the glass of the full height trophy cabinet and stopped. Where was the lean, fit looking man of six years ago seen smiling back at him from the framed photograph, holding the Van der Bijl rifle shooting trophy? He held in his expanding stomach then shook his head, his life with Lucia had been too comfortable, what will she say when he tells her that they must leave all this for good.

***

Lucia found her daughter finishing her breakfast on the stoep, "Anna-Maria darling, Jan has asked me to join him on one of his boring business trips, would you be a dear and come along as well? I just can't bear all those hours sitting on my own waiting whilst he has meetings or goes off to visit his customers' work places."

Reluctant at first, Anna-Maria finally accepted, now reasonably sure that, as she had not been immediately summoned, her spying activities had not been discovered. The trip could also offer the chance to learn more about her stepfather's illegal businesses and clients, if she could just hold her nerve. Leaving the stoep with her mother they both went to their rooms to pack unaware that Vermeulen was frantically emptying his filing cabinets of all documents and carrying them out to the garden incinerator. A final check around his office then a hurried packing of a suitcase was completed just as the taxis arrived.

"Lucia darling, you and Anna-Maria go in the first car with Karl, Pieter and I will follow in a few minutes, we will see you at the airport. I have just two more things to do."

On hearing that Vermeulen's minders were joining the party Anna-Maria started to doubt the wisdom of her agreement to join the trip, Vermeulen would only have his minders along if he thought thug protection might be necessary and neither man had travelled with him and her mother on their previous trip to Russia.

As the first taxi pulled away Vermeulen turned to Pieter, "Hey, go to the garden store and get the can of petrol out, then set light to all the stuff in the incinerator while I deal with Carla and Emmanuel."

Later in the day the Angolan Police would find Carla's body slumped over her desk and a bullet hole in her head. There was now no way that she could tell them where her boss had gone, that would take several more hours to find out by which time it would be too late. Emmanuel's body was found in the dining room in a pool of blood, Vermeulen had never liked his wife's choice of servants and Emmanuel had an air of superiority about him that Vermeulen detested. Switching on computers brought up a demolition derby game behind which was running a virus corrupting the hard drive.

As the two men got into their taxi Pieter said, "The incinerator was almost white hot, boss, what were you getting rid of?"

"Oh, just tidying up the office, you know, old paperwork, stuff I no longer need."

"You gave Carla the day off?"

"What?"

"I said, did you give Carla the day off, she usually comes out to the car when you leave."

"She was busy."

At the airport the party had only just checked in when their flight was called which meant that Vermeulen and his wife were out of breath on arrival at the gate. The last minute booking meant that they were all separated on the flight and in the chaos at Lagos airport it took time for them to become reunited again. Anna-Maria had expected someone to be at the airport to greet them and was surprised when Vermeulen bought tickets for a flight to Dakar leaving her wondering why he had not asked Carla to book the onward flight. There was thankfully only a short time to wait before boarding for the Dakar flight was called, which cut down the nuisance approaches made by officials and black-market currency touts falsely accusing them of taking the local currency, Naira, out of the country.

The very uncomfortable flight from Lagos to Dakar arrived in the early evening and here they were met by Abdoulaye Niang, the tallest African Anna-Maria had ever seen, who, in a convoy of cars took them to the Radisson Blu overlooking the vast Atlantic. She knew that Vermeulen had money but was surprised to find herself sharing a top floor luxurious suite with her mother and stepfather.

Given only a short time to freshen up and change, however, Anna-Maria and her mother then found themselves dining alone while Vermeulen sat the other side of the hotel's Little Buddha restaurant talking to Niang, both men closely protected by their bodyguards.

"I did not realise that Dakar was such a dangerous place," said Anna-Maria looking across the restaurant at her stepfather, her slender fingers toying with the wine glass held close to her lips.

"It does not appear dangerous to me," replied her mother not linking Anna-Maria's comment to the direction of her eyes.

"It obviously is for Jan, Mama, look at the bodyguards he and his friend have around them, but apparently not dangerous for us, or maybe we are of no consequence." Anna-Maria had noted the haunted look on her stepfather's face during the journey; had something happened exposing his illegal activities. Her stomach lurched and the sense of fear returned strongly.

Lucia Vermeulen looked at her daughter sharply, "I'm sure he considers us of great importance."

"Really, Mama?"

"Yes, really, Anna-Maria."

"Or is it that only he has something to fear?"

Her mother looked at her questioningly but did not reply, she had also noticed the change in her husband's demeanour.

As their meal progressed Anna-Maria studied her mother, who she frankly had never quite understood, she being always very close to her father whose intellectual prowess she had inherited. Lucia Vermeulen was still, at the age of fifty, a very attractive woman retaining a good figure, slim legs and beautiful skin. Why a woman of her looks and personality had been attracted to Jan Vermeulen, an ugly bull of a man, Anna-Maria frequently wondered, surely it was not the sex. The thought brought a mischievous grin to her face.

The next afternoon they left Dakar on a flight to St Louis in northern Senegal where, after a quick visit by Vermeulen to the left luggage lockers, they were bundled into a hired Mercedes minibus where Vermeulen announced, "We're not stopping here, we're crossing the border into Mauritania to complete a deal, after that I don't know yet, but it has to be somewhere away from Africa."

His wife's face turned pale, "Why, Jan, why? What's wrong?" Her voice now edged with panic.

"Someone in my organisation has chosen to betray me, someone who now has a very short life expectancy," Vermeulen replied menacingly, his paranoia now taking over his thoughts and reactions.

Anna-Maria's heart missed a beat and she fought to keep her expression of confusion and panic mirroring that of her mother's. Karl and Pieter, the two minders, looked at each other and both shrugged their shoulders and shook their heads, "It ain't nothin' to do wiv us, boss," Pieter the driver said indignantly. Working for ten years with Vermeulen had taught him just how dangerous the man could be and the implied threat had obviously made him nervous; he was also still wondering why Carla or Emmanuel had not seen them off from the house, normally Carla would carry her boss's briefcase out to the car or taxi for him.

Vermeulen turned in his seat and looked at the two men thoughtfully for a couple of seconds making them both feel very uncomfortable. "Here, check the contents in these," he ordered, passing two black holdalls over the seat to Karl.

"What is there to betray, Jan?" Lucia Vermeulen asked, now suspicious, confused and scared by the tone of his threats.

"My main business is arms trading and some loose-tongued individual has informed the British, who still think that they bloody well govern Africa. They then told the authorities in Luanda but fortunately I have friends."

Vermeulen's disclosure of his real business interests brought a gasp from his wife, while Anna-Maria with her hands covering her face had time to compose an expression of shocked outrage. The sharp sound of a zip made Anna-Maria look round at Karl and she instantly realised why Vermeulen had visited the airport's left luggage lockers. Even in the subdued light of the vehicle she recognised that Karl was holding a machine pistol in each hand.

"Let me out!" she screamed, "Let me out! I don't want to be anywhere near you. How could you, how could you; my poor David was massacred by that Cabinda group armed by people like you." Her tears were real enough; the death of her husband was still very deeply felt.

"You are staying where you are, you little airhead. Do you think that I will let you go screaming your head off at a time like this!"

Anna-Maria's mother gave a shriek. "How dare you speak to Anna-Maria like that, how dare you," she cried. "How could you have deceived us like this? You are to let us go right now."

Vermeulen just turned his back on her and instructed Pieter to go faster.

"Jan, you are to stop this vehicle now and let us out! Do you hear me, Jan, we want to get out! Jan, Jan you are not listening, Jan!"

Her protests continued until Vermeulen turned and screamed at her, "If you want to live you will shut up! Now, do you hear me? Shut up!"

There was a stunned silence in the vehicle following Vermeulen's outburst, everyone realising that he meant every word. For Anna-Maria though, the episode had been a relief, Vermeulen had called her an airhead, a fair indication that he did not suspect her as the cause of his problems.

***

According to Senior British Agent, Leonard Staunton, who was in Angola at the time of David Patterson's death, sources suggested that Patterson had changed sides and was working for the arms dealer and was killed, along with his men, for trying to swindle the group by selling them defective equipment.

Devastated by her husband's death, Anna-Maria moved back to live with her mother and stepfather where things would probably have returned to some form of normality had she not been contacted nearly six months later by an Englishman named Alexander Campbell, purporting to be her late husband's uncle. They met in a Luanda hotel where Campbell revealed that rather than being an uncle he was her late husband's boss and the true reason for her husband's frequent visits to Cabinda. He also firmly stated that he believed Anna-Maria's stepfather or his employees were the ones guilty of her husband's murder, not the FlecPM rebel group.

Campbell had timed the meeting to take place when her mother and stepfather were away visiting Moscow and St Petersburg, giving Anna-Maria a period in which to consider this shattering information and give careful consideration to his request for her to act as an informant against her stepfather; with her stepfather away she was able to search his office and it did not take her long to find out the truth and bring about a redirection of her anger and bitterness. Her immediate feelings of rage quickly moulded into a cold anger and calculated desire for revenge, a change that made her a very willing and capable spy into her stepfather's affairs.

Returning from Russia, Jan Vermeulen found his stepdaughter apparently unchanged in her manner and attitude towards him, they had never really liked each other. To her mother the new coolness that she detected she took to be her daughter's lingering grief at the loss of her husband. Wisely, Anna-Maria kept the knowledge of her stepfather's real business dealings to herself fearing that her mother, if told, would warn her husband, after all how could a wife be so unaware of what was going on. The only real change her stepfather experienced shortly after his return was the ambushing by government forces, of a shipment of arms destined for a Liberian rebel movement. The next two shipments intended for the FlecPM had also been flagged up to London by Anna-Maria, but this time they were just tracked through to the town of Dinge, where the trade was allowed to go through, but those involved were identified by David Patterson's replacement for later arrest.

Based on the reliability of her information Alex Campbell had returned to Luanda for a further meeting with Anna-Maria, during which he gave her his direct contact details and told her that it was to be the only route for future information. It would be some time before she would discover the importance of the selective contact route.

A period of quiet followed until Anna-Maria's spying revealed a plan for the supply of weapons to Senegal for use in Western Sahara by a militant section of the opposition, based across the border in Mauritania.

At this point Campbell had decided to act against the group in Cabinda and information was leaked to the Angolan authorities in the hope that the arrest of Vermeulen would also disrupt the Senegal arms' shipment.

***

Campbell's tip-off to the Angolan authorities coincided with Vaughan's return to duty following his convalescence at the private clinic used by SIS. After signing in at the discreet offices of DELCO Publishing in London's Chelsea district, Vaughan made his way to Lieutenant Penny Heathcote's office.

"Good afternoon, Lieutenant."

"Good afternoon, you look a lot better than when I last saw you. The Commodore is studying your medical report at the moment, it seems as if you have made a good recovery."

"So I've been told," replied Vaughan. "Is there anything on for me here?"

"Not that I'm aware of."

"Oh," replied Vaughan, puzzled.

He studied the redheaded Lieutenant whilst she shuffled a heap of paper on her desk into order. Beneath the tidily combed and clip-held red hair was a very pretty elfin face with piercing blue eyes that revealed a sharp brain. She was slender but not thin, and in fact had a good figure. Vaughan liked her a lot and respected her cool professional attitude towards him. Rumour had it that she had been close to a field agent before who had unfortunately been killed while on duty.

He was about to ask why he had been summoned when Heathcote said, "How are the girls?"

"Remote," he replied simply. Heathcote looked up and stared at him questioningly. "Clare and Louise both seem to be totally taken with Sarah's new friend Evan, who I must say seems to be a nice chap, what little I have seen of him. I went up to Derbyshire last weekend and took both the girls up to the Lake District horse riding, well ponies, that's their latest craze, neither wants to go sailing anymore."

"Is that Rebecca still in touch with your wife?"

"That devious bitch; no, she seems to have disappeared off the scene. She probably hasn't got through the money that she and Jerry got for the cottage that I was required to buy for Sarah."

"Part of the divorce settlement?"

Vaughan nodded.

"Has this Evan, moved in with her yet?"

"I'm not sure, I haven't wanted to ask the girls that type of question and I have been telling myself it's no longer something that I have any control over. If he is it would make my bank balance a lot better off if they got married, I know that."

The intercom buzzer sounded. "The Commodore will see you now."

A few minutes later Vaughan knocked on Campbell's office door. "Come in. Ah, Vaughan, good to see you. I've just finished reading your medical report, you're damn lucky to be alive let alone recover the way you have."

"So Sister Mitchell went to great lengths to point out, Sir."

"Good to see you back," said Campbell, carefully sliding a folder into his briefcase. "How is the family?"

"Well, thank you, Sir. Sarah apparently has a new romantic interest who the girls appear to have taken to."

"Umm, how do you feel about that?"

"Disappointed but not surprised, the type of pressure that her parents and her friend Rebecca exerted made the chances of us getting back together again next door to nil anyway, so I've been trying hard to switch off my feelings for her."

"I'm sorry, Vaughan, it seems so bloody ridiculous the way she reacted to the Murata affair."

"Well, it is what it is, Sir, and I can't see a way to turn back the clock, as much as I would like to."

Campbell stood up, walked across to the window and pulled a face as he looked at the rain pouring down outside. "At the present time we don't have anything that suits an agent of your specific talents, but there is the possibility of a cloud appearing on the horizon, so I would like you to return to Madeira and get your yacht ready as soon as possible."

"Right, Sir."

Just then there was a knock on the office door. "Come in." Heathcote entered the room. "Yes, Lieutenant, what is it?"

"I thought you should know straight away, Sir, that Luanda report that the person you identified for them has left the country and they think he has travelled to Lagos, but there was no official record of him arriving."

"On entry he probably used a false passport, I doubt if they were able to have crosschecked with the passenger lists. We need a detailed check on the complete boarding list from Luanda."

"Right, Sir."

The Lieutenant left leaving the Commodore staring out of the window deep in thought, while Vaughan sat silently studying a photograph of an aircraft carrier's flight deck and Campbell in the uniform of a Commander saluting the Queen.

"Lieutenant Heathcote will issue you with some additional charts which may come in useful," said Campbell, breaking the silence, "But for the purposes of communication you are to use this, and only this, number."

Turning back to his desk the Commodore handed Vaughan a slip of paper.

Memorising it Vaughan handed it back. "Only to that number it is, Sir."

"That is my direct number, ensure that you use number withheld if you make a call and should any voice other than mine answer it, end the call immediately."

"Understood, Sir."

When the meeting was over Vaughan collected the charts and air ticket from Heathcote and, leaving the offices, walked around the corner to spend the night in the Firm's hotel, a select apartment block complete with doorman and desk porter.

"Good afternoon, Ballard."

"Hello, Mr Vaughan, nice to see you back, sir," said Ballard, opening the door into the reception area.

Nodding to the desk porter, Vaughan walked over to the retina reader and placed his hand on the palm scanner as he looked at the camera lens.

"That's fine, Mr Vaughan, I've put you in room eighteen again. Dinner is at seven."

"Thanks, do you want to look at these?" replied Vaughan pointing to his luggage.

"Yes, sir, if you wouldn't mind."

Vaughan smiled at the porter's politeness; there would have been no way he could have got further into the building without having his luggage thoroughly checked.

Later, sitting in his room he thought about the meeting with Campbell and in particular the insistence associated with communication. '*Why the Commodore's direct line when there was apparently nothing immediate for me to handle? There was something else during that visit, a definite tension or atmosphere. The whole office was hushed with everyone's heads down seemingly working but not communicating as freely as they had done in the past. I got some odd looks as well when I walked through the general office especially from the sector four people, something is not right but I haven't got time to worry about it now. What was it that Sergeant Instructor McClellan said? Ah yes, obey the last order, and the last order was return to Madeira and prepare to put to sea.'* With that thought Vaughan got into bed.

***

It was late morning when the ferry nudged the North bank ramp of the Senegal River crossing point at the town of Rosso. The women were glad of the darkened windows that hid them in part from the teeming mass of foot passengers pressed up against the side of their vehicle aboard the dilapidated vessel, many of them peering in and some trying the door handles. To Anna-Maria's amazement once ashore they were met, and without undue bureaucracy, in fact just a few handshakes, were waved through Africa's most corrupt border post. It was only then that she realised the powerful web her stepfather had established. Until that moment she had assumed he was a small-time crook, but no longer; for white people to cross this border with such apparent ease proved that Vermeulen was seriously big time.

Their passage through the town was slow, the streets full of people reluctant to move out of the way. Lumbering bullock carts drawn by malnourished long-horned cattle were everywhere, together with herds of long-eared sheep all trampling their way along the dust-covered road littered with refuse of all kinds. The buildings, typical of that part of Africa, were run down and in poor repair, old broken air-conditioning units dangled from the walls of a few buildings that had once been the smart new venture in town. Everyone seemed to be covered in dust, their clothes shabby and the shoes, worn by a few, were down at heel. The smell of dust and sewage pervaded everywhere, even within the recycled air-conditioning of the minibus. On the outskirts of the town they turned right along a rutted track between a mixture of hovels and more substantial dwellings to eventually turn into the high walled courtyard of an Arab style building.

"Wait here," ordered Vermeulen, sliding out of the vehicle and cautiously walking towards the house, preceded by Pieter, who was looking about nervously. Karl also got out and stood beside the minibus, machine pistol held beneath his jacket out of sight.

"What is to become of us, Anna-Maria? I am so scared. Believe me, darling, I had no idea that Jan was really like this."

"Really, Mama, really? You are telling me that you had no idea how he made all his money."

"No, darling, I didn't, he always said that business was business and home was home so I never really asked. Please, Anna-Maria, please believe me, I honestly knew nothing of this. Oh! How could I have been such a fool."

Anna-Maria had not looked at her mother; her eyes were locked onto the scene outside. "It's all right, Mama, I believe you." What was the point, she thought, in rowing with her mother now when both of their futures were in the balance; they could be shot at any moment and their bodies disposed of with ease here. She was trembling with fear and tried hard to calm herself and think clearly.

The shabby double doors at the front of the building opened and two heavies appeared, each carrying guns.

"Nice to see your boys carrying the goods," said Vermeulen to a tall thin Arab-looking man now stepping out to stand between the two heavies. "What do you think of those Heckler and Koch MP7s, eh?"

"They will do the business," the Arab replied nodding and laughing. "No problem at the border?"

"No, the crossing was easy. Thank you for your efforts." Vermeulen took a few paces nearer to the house. "I have brought my wife and stepdaughter with me, they needed a holiday."

The Arab looked surprised. "You brought them here, to Rosso?" he laughed incredulously and shook his head in amazement.

"Just taking a break before going on."

"I will arrange some food and drink," said the Arab, as demanded by his cultural tradition of hospitality to travellers, and turning to one of the heavies gave some instructions.

The man hurried off and the apparent stand-off continued in silence for a time with Vermeulen and Pieter trying to look relaxed and confident but obviously feeling exposed in the middle of the courtyard.

"Bring them inside," the Arab said at last.

Anna-Maria's legs were like jelly as she got down from the vehicle, the heat hitting her like a punch after the comfort of the air-conditioning.

Her mother grasped her arm tightly. "Stop squeezing me, Mama, you are hurting me."

"I feel sick with fear, Anna-Maria, what will he do with us I keep wondering."

"When he is in a safe place he will let us go, Mama," she replied, not actually believing what she was saying.

The Arab's minder, standing by the doorway, gave Anna-Maria a lecherous stare and smile, making her shudder, but she kept moving, stepping out of the dazzling sunshine into what at first appeared to be absolute darkness as a bead of perspiration trickled down her spine causing her to shudder again. She removed her sunglasses and stopped to let her eyes adjust; the interior of the house in the dim light appeared surprisingly clean and tidy, an amazing contrast to the dusty courtyard they had just left. A young woman wearing a brightly coloured mulafa beckoned to her mother indicating that they follow her. The highly patterned ceramic floor tiles and heavily shaded windows gave the house a coolness that made the environment almost tolerable.

They were taken to a room at the back of the house, where Anna-Maria noticed the surroundings to be less elaborate, the floor tiles here were a plain dull fawn but everywhere was clean and tidy. There was a low table in the centre of the room surrounded by cushions and the woman, pointing to them, indicated that they should sit; bowls of water were brought together with hand towels. Washing their hands, Anna-Maria and her mother watched as a roasted goat on a bed of rice was brought in by the woman who then sat at the table with them. Having indicated that they should start to eat, she pulled some meat from the bones and served it and some rice onto their plates then, serving herself, dextrously massaged some rice into a ball and ate it.

"Eat only with your right hand, Mama, this is obviously a Muslim household."

"Obviously, I am not that daft that I do not know such things."

Anna-Maria glanced at her mother and saw how close to tears she was. "I am sorry, Mama, I was just saying…"

Anna-Maria, now anxious to divert attention away from her mother, asked the woman whether she was the wife of the house owner, using French, guessing that it would be understood in Rosso.

"Oui, Madame," the woman replied.

Slowly they learnt that they were in the Elmoctar household and that her husband's name was Harel Elmoctar, a trader. When asked what he traded in they were told that it was mainly rice and ground nuts from Senegal; another family probably unaware of the evil trade that really supported them.

At the end of the meal the woman left them alone and they could hear her excitedly telling someone in a nearby room all about them and the strange way they spoke. When she returned both Anna-Maria and her mother were becoming desperate to use the toilet facilities. After their experience during the journey to the border where they had been forced to urinate at the side of the road guarded and watched by the leering Karl, the Arab style toilet seemed quite civilised. Anna-Maria had just got back to the room when her mobile chirped, and taking it from her handbag she looked at the message then hurriedly tapped in a reply in the hope that the friend from her gym club would be able to help in some way.

"Who was the message from?" asked her mother.

"It was Lynn, she asked why I wasn't at the gym this morning."

"What did you say?"

"I told her where I was and that we were in deep trouble and desperately needed help."

"Can she do anything?"

Anna-Maria shrugged her shoulders, "I don't know, Mama, I just hope she can."

The door opened and Pieter, with a jerk of his head, said, "We're leaving."

Anna-Maria and her mother looked at each other, both seeming unwilling to move.

"Hey, come on, we have a long way to go and the boss is waiting."

Reluctantly the two women got to their feet and followed Pieter through the house and out to the minibus, with Anna-Maria wondering how to get away; but where could she go? In Luanda she knew of several people who would have helped her, even hide her, but here she knew no one, no one at all. Panic was seizing her and she was tempted to chance her arm and just run from the courtyard; she measured the distance with her eye, no, it was too far, she would never make it, and if she did they would soon track her down. Her mother! What was to happen to her mother? It would take far too long to explain how she became involved in the exposure of her stepfather. Again the question of where to run to entered her mind; then she remembered her tablet and the small memory stick giving a list of David's "relatives" which "Uncle Alex" had given her, and was now hidden in her luggage.

Vermeulen, with Karl beside him, was talking to Elmoctar, who as always, was attended by the two heavies; she looked around, now was her chance, with Karl and Vermeulen isolated and Pieter distracted by his bodyguard duty.

Anna-Maria pointed to the back of the minibus, "I need to get something from my case."

Pieter looked at her for a moment, checked that Vermeulen's conversation with Elmoctar was still amicable then, not taking his eyes from his boss, opened the rear door.

Heaving her suitcase up on top of the others she opened it and took out her washing and make-up bags, slipping her tablet under the two items whilst Pieter wasn't looking. Closing the case she said, "Pieter, could you put the case back for me, it's a bit too heavy for me, I seem to have hurt my arm putting it up here." Without thinking Pieter stepped forward, picked up the case and slid it back into the gap, giving Anna-Maria time to take both bags and the tablet into the vehicle and close the door without him noticing the subterfuge. Checking that Pieter's concentration was elsewhere she said, "Tell me when Jan has finished his chat, Mama," as she tore the lining of the make-up bag and took out the memory stick.

Turning on the tablet she inserted the stick and waited while the list loaded. "Come on, come on please hurry… oh, at last, now let's see." After reading through it three times her heart sank. "The nearest 'cousin' lives in Nouakchott. Oh God, that's more than two hundred kilometres from here."

Her mother glanced at her, confused as to what her daughter was talking about, then nudged her, "He's coming."

Pulling out the stick Anna-Maria slipped it back into the bag, switched off the tablet and put both bags on top of it again as Pieter climbed into the seat behind her. Karl was now driving, and with

Vermeulen at his side they drove out of the courtyard where Karl went to turn left, back towards the main road.

"No," shouted Vermeulen, "Turn right and go a couple of blocks and turn right again. I trust Elmoctar about as far as I can spit."

Anna-Maria noticed Pieter, behind her, turn round and keep a steady watch out of the rear window.

"One of his men is watching and reporting, Boss."

"The bastard wants his money back. I thought as much. Well he ain't going to get it today."

"You reckon, Boss, sure he would have held out when you asked him for it or took it by force as we were leaving."

"No, Pieter, that would have been against his Arab culture, he would not harm a guest whilst they were under his roof, but you wait, now we are off the premises."

At that moment Karl threw the minibus into the right turn narrowly missing three women carrying water jars on their heads.

"Go three blocks then right again," ordered Vermeulen, thrusting a long magazine into the base of his machine pistol handgrip.

Three crossroads further on, Karl almost had them in the front wall of the corner property as the Mercedes, almost on two wheels, rounded the corner, a near miss that had both Anna-Maria and her mother screaming. As the minibus accelerated down the narrow track, Vermeulen opened his side window and leaned out, gun in hand. One crossroads, then two, then three were passed without any sign of pursuit and Anna-Maria was just beginning to think that Vermeulen's fears had been unfounded when at the next junction a battered Toyota pick-up truck pulled out in front of them and skidded to a stop. Vermeulen and Pieter opened fire immediately but inaccurately due to the bouncing of the vehicle on the rough road surface. The return fire however was on target and in moments their windscreen had been hit several times before they smashed into the pick-up truck pushing it sideways into the opposite wall just as Karl made a loud coughing noise. Pieter, smashing the side screen out, fired directly into the Toyota's cab, killing both men before shooting a third man as he tried to escape leaping over the truck's tailboard.

"Shit! Karl's been hit. Pieter, climb over and give me a hand getting him out of the driver's seat. Quickly!"

Anna-Maria got off the floor where she and her mother had been sheltering. They were both dazed and terrified by the shooting. She tried to open the door but saw that the truck was pinned up against it. A yelp of pain from Karl told her that at least the man was still alive and she watched in horror as Pieter hauled him between the driver's seat and the double front passenger seat then heave him like a sack of potatoes over onto the seat behind, blood pumping from a chest wound. As soon as Karl was pulled clear, Vermeulen was across and, gunning the engine, reversed the minibus away from the wreck of the truck to the sound of screeching metal.

"Incoming!" yelled Pieter as he looked up to see a second truck hurtling towards them down the side road.

Again Anna-Maria ducked down, kneeling on the floor and making herself as small as possible.

There was something in her way and pushing it to one side she realised that it was her stepfather's briefcase that had been dragged through the gap with Karl's body, it was open and some of the contents had fallen out. A black notebook attracted her attention and she grabbed it just as bullets hit the side of the vehicle. Anna-Maria heard her mother gasp and saw her fall across the seat, blood oozing from a gaping hole in the side of her head. At that same moment the minibus cleared the wrecked pick-up truck and the side door sprung open. As Vermeulen let the clutch in to charge the minibus forward Anna-Maria was thrown out onto the dusty road as the vehicle took off, clipping the truck, before charging through the gap and away down towards the main road, its front wheel arch panel hanging off and flapping like a wounded bird's wing.

Hidden by the cloud of dust thrown up by the wheel spin as the Mercedes accelerated away, Anna-Maria, with her handbag over her shoulder and still clutching her tablet, washing and make-up bags, plus the notebook, hid behind the wreck of the truck to remain unseen by those in the pursuing vehicle as it bore down on the crossroads.

Vermeulen had gone no more than one hundred metres when Pieter called out, "She's gone, Anna-Maria, she's gone, and your wife has been shot in the head."

Vermeulen slammed on the brakes, skidding to a stop and looked at his wife as she lay staring blindly at the back of his seat. Looking up he saw the second truck rounding the corner, and side slam the wreck before taking off again in their direction, "Pieter, shoot the bastards!"

As the minibus pulled away again, Pieter opened fire. Three bullets came through the Mercedes rear window but neither man was hit, then with only two more crossroads before the main road, Pieter got lucky, killing the driver of the pursuing truck, which, after bouncing off the wall of a house, roared out of control across a junction and smashed headlong into the house on the opposite corner.

Meanwhile, Anna-Maria was cautiously getting to her feet and trying hard not to look at the dead bodies in the truck, one of which was hanging half out of the vehicle, his lifeless arm on a patch of bloodstained ground, his assault rifle nearby. She could hear the shooting as the second truck pursued the minibus, and prayed that they would succeed in killing the man who had caused her such heartache and pain, then she heard a crash and the shooting stopped. Was he dead, oh please let him be dead.

A gentle touch on her shoulder made her leap in fear and she turned to find herself looking into the tender eyes of an African woman, who beckoned her to follow. Unsure, she hesitated, but only for a moment, before hurrying after the woman who, after a short distance, turned into an alleyway that led to the next cross street. Here, the woman paused and, peeping round the corner of the wall, checked that all was clear along the road before ushering Anna-Maria across the street and into a house. After the loud engine noise, screeching tyres, gunfire and the horrendous noise of the crash, the quiet of the house seemed quite eerie.

Anna-Maria hardly noticed the distressed interior of the property with its peeling paintwork and cracked floor tiles on which wooden boxes took the place of seats and tables, all her senses were looking for it being a trap. The woman, however, appeared to be calm and almost serene as she placed a worn cushion onto one of the boxes and indicated that Anna-Maria should sit, saying in heavily accented French, "You are safe here, Madame, I will not harm you." The shock of the last five or six minutes were now taking effect and, shaking uncontrollably, her knees on the point of giving way, Anna-Maria sat down and immediately burst into tears.

As they had made their way along the alley there had been another burst of gunfire, closer than previously, that had Anna-Maria staring back in terror, then there was silence again. Now in the stillness of the house she was aware of the woman standing quietly alongside her, the smell of cheap soap reminding her of Emmanuel in Luanda and she was, for the first time in years, aware of her own natural body odour. She heard the sound of an approaching vehicle and stood again holding her breath as she stared at the narrow gap between the window shutters and watched as the battered minibus slowly moved into view and stopped. She turned and looked at the street door as fear gripped her, wondering whether Vermeulen or Pieter would kick the door in and she be handed over to them, but then after a second or two, the minibus moved off again.

"It is all right, Madame, they are gone."

"Are you sure?"

"Yes, Madame, I am sure, no one got out of the car, Madame." The woman stretched out a hand seeking to comfort Anna-Maria but she moved away frightened of the woman's intentions. "My name is Nandini, Madame, please believe me, I mean you no harm."

***

Vermeulen had ordered Pieter to close the side door that Anna-Maria had fallen from, as soon as the second truck had been stopped.

"Your briefcase is down here and a load of your stuff is all over the floor, Boss."

Braking hard, Vermeulen brought the vehicle to a halt and leapt out; grabbing his briefcase he hurriedly checked its contents and picked up the items on the floor. "Christ man, my notebook is missing, it must be on the ground back there somewhere."

"Anna-Maria is also back there, Boss. We should go and look, eh."

Turning the vehicle round, Vermeulen drove back along the track to where the second truck was buried in the rubble of the house. Pieter got out cautiously, there was no sign of life in the wrecked truck, the body of one man lay on the cab roof, his head crushed by the impact with the building, the bloody remains scattered over the cab roof and walls.

Pieter fired at the three bodies in the cab to make sure they were all dead, recognising one man as one of the heavies in the courtyard.

"Elmoctar will have to find a replacement for Faris," he said, when he got back in the minibus.

"Huh, they'll be queuing up for the job, Pieter. Just you look out for the notebook."

"What colour is it?"

"Oh, black."

Vermeulen drove on more slowly, both men looking at the ground for the notebook; back at the junction where Anna-Maria had escaped they got out to search, but found nothing. The shooting had emptied the streets and any houses with doors and shutters had them all firmly closed.

"She got out here. We had better look around for her, she won't have got far." Vermeulen stood still in thought for a second or two. "Maybe she took the notebook, she was sitting that side."

"Why would she do that, Boss?"

"I don't know, maybe she just grabbed it with her bloody make-up kit."

Their search of the surrounding side streets and alleys drew a blank and with the increasing risk of another attack from Elmoctar's men, Vermeulen now settled on another plan of action.

"I'll phone my police contact here and tell him that his friend, Elmoctar, tried to kill me. I will also tell him that my stepdaughter has escaped with enough information to have him put in prison for the rest of his life."

The call to the local assistant police chief ended with the offer of a reward for the safe return of Anna-Maria and "all" her possessions. A second phone call, made out of earshot of Pieter, was to have unexpected consequences for both Vermeulen and Anna-Maria as he failed to mention the loss of his notebook.

As Vermeulen got back in the vehicle Pieter asked, "What do we do with your wife's body, Boss?"

"We'll have to take this wreck as far as we can out of here, and torch it."

"What about the bodies?"

"What about the bodies?"

"You mean burn them as well?"

"Of course I bloody do. You think I'm going to go looking for a funeral parlour in Rosso with Elmoctar wanting a slice of me?"

With time rapidly running out for Vermeulen and Pieter in Rosso they headed out of town to a place where they could dump the vehicle and set it on fire.

White men hitching a lift in that part of Africa was a rare sight, but eventually a lorry stopped for them, and for a price, took them all the way to Nouakchott.

***

Anna-Maria would remember for the rest of her life that she owed her survival that day to the young Mauritanian woman called Nandini. After an hour or so she had recovered enough to begin carefully and slowly telling Nandini of her plight and her urgent need to escape from Rosso.

"Nandini, my name is Anna-Maria Ronaldo. I was a prisoner of some bad men who sell guns to people who want to cause trouble. I desperately need to get to Nouakchott where I have a friend who will help me."

"It is very difficult for a woman to travel there alone, Madame."

"Will you come with me? I will pay," replied Anna-Maria.

"No, Madame, I cannot go with you." Nandini looked away obviously deep in thought. "Maybe my man, Lamin, will take you to the market at Nouakchott when he returns with his lorry from across the river."

The thought of the journey alone with a man she did not know was terrifying to Anna-Maria but there was, at that moment, no alternative and the sooner she left this town the better, not only for herself but also for Nandini.

Nandini pointed at Anna-Maria's trousers, "You cannot safely walk here in Rosso dressed like that. The bad men will learn where you are in a very short time, Madame."

Nandini was right, Anna-Maria would attract immediate attention anywhere in Mauritania, there was no way she could wear such clothes, dusty or otherwise, and not be immediately recognised, but how and where could she obtain suitable clothing in Rosso.

Her rescuer crouched down in front of her, "It is all right, Madame, please do not worry, we will fix this tomorrow."

CHAPTER 2

As the Vermeulen party's ferry had crossed the Senegal River to Rosso, applause was ringing out aboard TAP Flight TP0347 as it touched down at Madeira's Santa Caterina Airport. In seat G3 Ian Vaughan eased his cramped legs, stretching them out into the aisle and circling his feet.

"Excuse me, but why does everyone clap?" asked the rather timid looking young lady in the seat next to him who, apart from a flickering smile when taking her seat, had kept her head buried in a book until that moment.

"Santa Caterina Airport has one of the trickiest final approaches in the world. Crosswinds from the sea or down draughts from the mountains mean that the pilot often has to sideslip the aircraft with great precision to get it to touch down exactly on the threshold and central to the runway; only pilots qualified to land here are allowed on this route and every one of them has had to practice making this approach many times with an empty aircraft before becoming qualified to bring in passengers."

"Goodness, I had no idea," she replied. "Had I known that I wouldn't have come."

"You didn't seem very concerned until I explained the reason for the applause."

"Yes, but had I known before, I…" her voice trailed away as her shyness re-exerted itself.

Vaughan chuckled. "Ground control here know what conditions make the approach dangerous in which case they would then instruct pilots to land at Porto Santo, which doesn't have quite the same problems."

"Is that far away?"

"No, it's only a little over forty miles away, aircraft can wait there until the winds die down and then make another attempt, it's no real problem."

As the plane came to a standstill on the airport's apron the normal scrum ensued with almost everyone intent on being the first to pass through immigration and customs. Vaughan stood up and stepping to his right blocked the aisle with his muscular frame and indicated to the young lady to leave her seat and go in front of him.

"You're blockin' everyone's way, mate," said a short man dressed in a loud patterned shirt, baggy trousers and with a cheap panama hat, one size too small, perched on his head.

Vaughan turned and looking down at the man said, "How long are you staying on the island?"

"What?"

"How long are you staying on the island?" Vaughan repeated.

The short man was about to tell Vaughan where to go then looked up into those cold blue eyes and made a wise snap decision, "Er, two weeks."

"Then being polite and waiting two minutes is not exactly going to spoil it for you is it."

"Oh, er, yeh, alright, mate." But still couldn't resist adding, "She gonna be long?"

Just then the short man's wife prodded him in the back, "'Ere, why you always so bleeding impatient, other people want to get off this plane as well as you. Can't you see she's doin' 'er best to 'urry up."

Her husband turned round, glowering. "Oh shut up naggin' will yer. All I'm sayin' is that I don't wanna spend all my 'oliday on this bleeding airplane, alright!"

"All you ever do, Jack Collins, is moan. This ain't right, that ain't right. Gawd I don't know why I came 'ere with you when Marcie wanted me to go with 'er to Cyprus."

"Excuse me, sir, would you mind moving forward, you're holding everyone up," said the flight attendant.

Turning forward again Jack Collins saw that all the passengers in the front eight rows had left the aircraft.

"Now it's you that's 'olding everything up," said his wife. "Get a move on."

On the bus that made the short journey from the aircraft to the terminal building Vaughan watched with mild amusement as the couple continued bickering. The queue at immigration moved forward very slowly, it was only six weeks since there had been an attempted coup on the island and the authorities were still nervous. Clearing customs, Vaughan went straight to the taxi rank.

"Take me to the marina in Funchal please."

"Sim, Senhor, you been to Madeira before yes?"

"Yes."

"Where you from?"

"England. Tell me is everything quiet now after the coup?"

"So so, Senhor. The army is still here but not so on the street like at first. The authorities, they seek those who supported the rebels. They look hard for a Russian man Reshnovic or something like that."

"I think you mean Reshetnikov," prompted Vaughan.

"Sim, Senhor, that the name. They no find him, so I think maybe he left island and maybe back in Russia by now, eh."

"That's quite likely."

At the marina Vaughan paid off the taxi and made his way to the marina office.

"You return, Senhor Vaughan. We get message from British Consul that you are injured and go back to England. She say she not know how long you are away so we moved your boat to spare finger pontoon berth."

"Thank you, that was very good of you. I must owe you a lot of money."

"Oh no, Senhor. We have order from municipal office to say no charge."

Vaughan was taken aback. "Really, that is very generous of them."

The marina attendant shrugged his shoulders and, putting out his arm to direct Vaughan, said, "I show you place we put your boat."

"Thank you. By the way has anyone been asking for me?"

"Oh shortly after you left some newspaper men they come and ask where you are."

"What did you tell them?"

"I say you back in England."

Vaughan placed a fifty euro note into the man's shirt pocket. "If they ask again I am still in England, understood."

Vaughan's tone of voice was enough for the man to nod and say, "Sim, Senhor, I understand."

Then after a couple of seconds he said, "If the lady comes here again do I give her the same answer?"

"Which lady is that?" Vaughan asked.

"She say she is Senhora De Lima."

Vaughan added a twenty euro note. "Yes, the same answer."

"Really, she very beautiful, you sure?"

Vaughan smiled, "Yes I am sure."

They had reached his yacht and having swung his bags onto the side deck Vaughan stepped back and looked at the weed growing on the hull below the waterline. "It looks like she needs a haul out and a scrub to get that weed off. Do you know where I can get that done quickly?"

"They no longer do it here, Senhor, maybe you must go to boatyard at airport. Good place there under the runway."

"Do you have the phone number?"

"You call by office, I get it for you."

"Thanks, I'll just stow my kit and change and I will be over."

Climbing aboard *"La Mouette sur le Vent"* Vaughan went below and hurriedly checked that no one had entered the cabin. The false bulkhead aft of the anchor locker was as it should be and lifting the quarter berth mattress and baseboard revealed that his service 9mm Browning was where he had left it. He checked the yacht's safe and under the floors then gave the engine space a thorough look over.

Satisfied, he unpacked, made some coffee, then changed into shorts and a tee shirt and waited for the coffee to cool.

'So the press want a word do they, damn, publicity is the last thing I need at the moment. Also, what do I do about Amelia? If I contact her, where could our friendship possibly go; as an SIS agent, what future could I offer her, as much as I like her and yes, feel for her. No, the quicker I get out of here the better.'

Swallowing the coffee he returned to the marina office and made arrangements for his yacht to be hauled out of the water the following day. Back on board he retrieved the Browning and spent ten minutes or so stripping and cleaning it ready for return to the DELCO armourer. On his to-do list was a visit to the British Consul to collect the Browning's replacement, a Glock 26.

His next job was to fill up the fuel tank which meant a tricky time manoeuvring the Saltram 36 round to the fuel dock; having a long deep keel is a great advantage crossing oceans but made close quarter manoeuvres in marinas, a very nerve-wracking experience. Finally, back on his berth Vaughan checked the engine oil levels and cooling water flow before cleaning himself up ready to go for a meal.

Leaving the yacht and wishing to stretch his legs a bit after the flight and work aboard the yacht he took a brisk walk along to the seventeenth century Fortaleza São Tiago at the eastern end of the esplanade. On his return he was about to make his way down the pier steps on the marina's eastern sea wall on his way to the Marina Terrace Restaurant, when he saw Amelia talking to the marina official who, Vaughan was pleased to see, was shaking his head and shrugging his shoulders.

One sight of her, the hair, perfect figure, immaculate dress and he knew only too well the beautiful face had him tempted for just a moment to hurry down and greet her, *"No, definitely no, no distractions, no delays, that's what got you wounded last time you were here."*

How he became involved with Amelia and the dark world of her Brazilian uncle, Olavo Esteves, was through her son and his playing truant from school in order to go sailboarding. The boy's relative inexperience and a new board, a gift from Amelia's uncle, had somehow got the boy a long way offshore and becalmed on a hot summer's day. Vaughan, motor sailing towards the island, under cover as a maritime author, came across the boy and, rescuing him, brought him ashore from where the lad was taken to hospital. The following day Senhora Amelia de Lima had come to thank Vaughan for saving the life of her son and a friendship developed during the course of which Vaughan was to learn of her concerns regarding her uncle and his friends who were eventually exposed as leaders of a plot to overthrow the Portuguese Government.

Amelia's uncle had escaped immediate arrest and had been on the run before returning to Amelia's apartment and then cornered by Vaughan and a Portuguese Army Lieutenant. Using Amelia as a shield Esteves had tried to escape, shooting dead the lieutenant, and in a struggle with Vaughan being shot himself. The bullet that killed Esteves

44

however, also wounded Vaughan and was the reason for his hurried repatriation to the UK and specialist treatment at a private clinic.

Taking one more look in Amelia's direction, as she turned away from the official, he slipped into the crowd of tourists and hurried back towards the old town to find a restaurant in which to hide himself amongst other diners.

***

In London Lieutenant Penny Heathcote printed off the three passenger lists and, checking down each one, used a highlighter to mark some of the passenger names. After a final check she picked up the telephone and started ringing round hotel reception desks in Dakar. An hour later she left her desk and made her way up a level to the Commodore's office and knocked at the door.

"Come in," the firm but friendly voice of Commodore Alexander Campbell always brought a smile to Heathcote's face. She liked her boss.

"I've finally got the passenger lists from the airlines, Sir. I've gone through them and highlighted names of interest."

"Thank you, Penny." He had taken to using her Christian name rather than her rank when there was just the two of them in the office, a habit that had crept in after she had been a bridesmaid at his recent wedding.

"Both Vermeulen and his wife appear on the passenger list from Luanda to Lagos but then he seems to disappear, and eventually I found her on the list of a flight to Dakar."

Campbell looked up and knew from his lieutenant's expression that there was more, "And?"

"They were travelling with his minders, Pieter Scheepers and Karl van Rooyen. When I couldn't find him on any onward flight for that day I thought at first that it was only his wife who had gone onto Dakar, but his two thugs were listed on the same flight and I then discovered that a Henri Vanderkloof was in the seat next to Mrs Vermeulen."

"Oh, well done, Penny. What did I say? I said he had entered Nigeria on a false passport. So now he is hiding out in Dakar is he?"

"No, Sir."

"There is more?"

"Yes, Sir, I checked around the most likely hotels and found that a booking was made in the name of Vermeulen for just one night at the Radisson Blu, I have requested full details which I am hoping will come in overnight. I have also requested passenger lists from Senegal Airlines, which I hope to have before I leave this evening."

"You think he is moving on and so do I. Had he been dropping out of sight in Senegal he would have done so straight from the airport. He either has business there, or Lagos was just a dogleg to put pursuers off the scent."

"I'll leave the lists with you, Sir."

"Thank you, Penny, I'll take a closer look later."

It was eight o'clock in the evening when Campbell next glanced at his watch. Standing, he picked up the files on his desk and locked them away in the filing cabinet then cleared the rest of his desk and locked the drawers. Taking the hard drive from his computer he opened the wall safe and put the disk inside and locked the safe again. His evening ritual completed he was just about to gather up his coat when there was a knock at the door.

"Come in. Ah, Sir Andrew to what do I owe the pleasure?"

"I've just heard that your man Vaughan has reported back for duty."

"Yes, Sir Andrew, that's correct; he reported in a couple of days ago having been given a clean bill of health by the clinic."

"You know I really think we should let him go, he hasn't got the background we really need for the type of work that we are engaged in."

"And what background would that be, Sir Andrew?"

"Disciplined."

"I don't fully understand what you are saying."

"I know you had good reason to consider Vaughan, particularly after the business at Yealmstock Head, but I'm afraid the way he went off mission in Madeira gave myself and his controller serious doubts as to his real suitability."

"As you know, Sir Andrew, I have little respect for the views of Senior Agent Staunton."

"Alex, you know, I wish you wouldn't keep up this thing of yours about David Patterson's reputation; Staunton has proved himself again and again on missions for other sections."

"I'm puzzled by your comments concerning Vaughan, Sir Andrew, the man not only formed a strong link with a leading North African politician, he also presented valuable information that no one else managed to glean from the conference. Given the way in which foreign observers were excluded from it Vaughan worked something of a miracle of diplomacy and intelligence gathering."

"Then he started messing about in the internal politics of Portugal," retorted Sir Andrew Averrille angrily. "The PM may think that was a good idea, but it has caused many ripples and I for one hope that that particular pond calms quickly."

"Are you suggesting that the British Government should stand by and watch rather than warn a friendly nation of an attempt to overthrow its government? Damn it, Sir Andrew, Portugal is our oldest ally!"

"Now calm down, Alex, all I am saying is that Vaughan acting like he did on his first mission demonstrated to myself and others that he is likely to be a loose cannon just as the report, by Jeffery Marshal at The Manor, indicated was possible."

"Marshal covers his backside with that phrase on almost every competent agent that has been through training there."

"I'm not going to argue with you anymore on this subject, Alex. Tell me, where is Vaughan now?"

"In Madeira, I sent him there to recover his yacht. We chartered it from him for the mission and the agreement included return to the UK, as you and I agreed before he went."

"I see, well I want him out the door the day after he gets back, Alex, and that is final."

With that Sir Andrew turned on his heels and marched out of Campbell's office and down the corridor towards the lifts.

***

In Rosso, Anna-Maria had barely slept at all that night, what with the memory of her mother's death and the fear of Vermeulen or Elmoctor's men searching for her. During the following day she relaxed a little though her anxiety soon returned when Nandini left the house to buy material for mulafas, the simple length of brightly coloured cotton that Mauritanian women wind around the full length of their body and over their head. When Nandini returned with two brightly patterned orange and red lengths of material Anna-Maria could have kissed her, such was her relief. During her time spent there, as Nandini showed her how to wear the garment, the two women formed something of a bond as Anna-Maria's mistakes and failures brought humour to the situation. There followed hours with Nandini working at an ancient sewing machine fashioning a suitable undergarment. The results, though not fit for the catwalks of Paris, were ideal for the pre-dawn walk through the streets of Rosso.

It was as Nandini's sewing machine was clunking away that Anna-Maria's phoned chirped again and, expecting it to be her friend Lynn with news, she took it from her bag full of hope only to read "The rains are about to fall. Uncle Alex": the coded message telling her to get out of Africa immediately.

Informed only that Jan Vermeulen, his wife and minders had left Angola, London had assumed that Anna-Maria was still safely at home; what triggered the warning was her name and picture appearing on a leaked US list of British agents operating in Africa posted online by one of the so-called "freedom of information" sites triggered by Vermeulen's second phone call from the back streets of Rosso.

She looked at it despairingly, what use was that warning now, she knew full well that she had to escape. Tears welled up in her eyes. Then she realised that London may not have known about her sudden departure from Luanda and quickly sent back a message explaining what had happened following the visit to the Elmoctar household and that she was now trying to reach David's "cousin" in Nouakchott, having stolen Vermeulen's notebook.

Whether it was the making of her disguise or the confidence she had gained in Nandini coupled with exhaustion, but Anna-Maria slept deeply on that second night. Woken early but still half asleep she washed and dressed herself in the dim light of a paraffin lamp and now stood as

Nandini wrapped her in the mulafa, taking care to cover Anna-Maria's straight hair and face except for her dark brown eyes.

"There, Madame, when we leave here we will look like sisters."

"If I make it out of here to safety I will adopt you as my sister, Nandini, and I will feel blessed to have a sister as brave and kind as you."

"We must go now, Madame, Lamin will be waiting."

The crystal dome of stars shed a silvery light but no colour onto the back streets and alleyways of Rosso as they started their walk towards the ferry landing and lorry park, but as they walked, the stars dimmed as the sun's rays brought hard form and colour to their surroundings. By the time they reached the parking area and found Lamin it was full daylight with the sun already heating the cool earth.

Lamin, like Nandini, was very dark skinned and to Anna-Maria's surprise looked younger than his partner. It took a stressful amount of time for Nandini to explain to Lamin what was required but at no time did he look annoyed or reluctant. All the while Anna-Maria tried hard to make herself invisible, her heart missing a beat every time anyone so much as glanced in her direction.

The dialect and speed of the local pigeon French was too fast for Anna-Maria to fully grasp what Nandini said, except that great emphasis was laid upon the fact that men with guns were chasing her. Eventually, expressing her heartfelt thanks and pressing dollars into Nandini's reluctant hand, she climbed up into the huge lorry's cab, carrying all her possessions in the rather tatty plastic bag in which her mulafa had been supplied. After a few words of parting between Nandini and Lamin he started the engine and so began the eight-hour journey to Nouakchott.

To Anna-Maria's relief Lamin appeared to be a little overawed by her and when he spoke it was always very respectful, starting each conversation by addressing her as Madame Ronaldo.

Once clear of Rosso the thin band of irrigated farmland soon turned to sparse scrub on a reddish sand desert, and away from the river and vegetation the air was dry and the wind rushed like that from a blast furnace through the open windows of the cab. Behind them trailed a cloud of the red dust that seemed to cover everything in that country.

They had travelled several kilometres when Anna-Maria asked Lamin to slow down, she had seen on a track some distance ahead and to the right of the road, a burnt out minibus with a body shape remarkably similar to that of the Mercedes.

Anna-Maria pointed towards the wreck, "Can we stop please, I wish to look at the vehicle over there."

Lamin looked about suspiciously, wondering whether this was a trap for him and the load he was hauling. Anna-Maria understood his concern, "I promise it is safe, I just need to see if that is the vehicle I was taken away in two days ago."

The track was wide and led up to a distant ruined compound, and Lamin, still looking about nervously, drove the lorry along it to a point just beyond the wreck where he turned it round stopping a short distance from the burnt out minibus.

"It is the one, Lamin, it is the minibus he used to bring us here from St Louis."

"Can we go now, Madame Ronaldo?"

"No, please, Lamin, I need to look inside to see if any of my things have survived the fire."

She jumped down from the cab and walked towards the vehicle, the bullet holes in the tailgate and the bullet-riddled bent side panel clearly visible. What she was not expecting was the sight of two charred bodies covered with flies left inside the vehicle. Turning away from the sight she was promptly sick. Spitting the last remnants of vomit from her mouth she heard the lorry's engine rev up and saw it start to move forward. Rushing onto the track she held up her arms beseeching Lamin to stop and with no more than a metre to spare the lorry came to a standstill. Walking shakily round to the driver's side she shouted up, "The body of my mother is in there, they have set fire to the vehicle and burnt her. Please, I need to bury her, will you help me?"

Lamin looked down at her from the cab, very unsure of the safety of being near a vehicle with obviously recent bullet holes in it.

"They are gone, Lamin, the men who did this are gone. Please, please help me."

Cautiously he got down from the lorry and, taking a shovel from the tool rack behind the cab, followed her to a point not far from the wreck.

"Here seems to be a good place, pass me the shovel, please."

He watched silently as she started to dig into the red gritty sand, throwing the grit towards some loose stones not far from where Lamin stood. She had almost completed a trench the length of her mother's body when she saw out of the corner of her eye a movement between the spoil heap and Lamin. When married to David they had frequently camped out in the bush, an experience that had given her a trained eye for the dangers of wild Africa. In one swift move she swung the shovel in a large arc over her head bringing it down no more than half a metre from Lamin's foot to sever the head of a horned sand snake that the digging had disturbed.

"Are you all right, Lamin?" she asked, anxious to know whether she had acted in time.

"Yes, Madame, thank you, Madame, I am good, Madame," he replied, wide-eyed with fear and searching the ground around him for signs of any further dangers.

The sound of her digging again brought him back to the task in hand and taking the shovel from her he started to make the grave deeper. It took them two hours to dig deep enough to discourage wild animals from exhuming her mother's remains, and by the time they had finished both were covered in sweat, and exhausted.

The time had come to move her mother's body, and seeing Anna-Maria's distress at such a prospect, Lamin went to the lorry, returning with a blanket from the pile on his sleeping bunk, and wrapping the charred body in it carried it to the grave. She couldn't bear to watch as Lamin buried her mother's corpse and lay heavy rocks on top of the grave, but once the task was completed she stood at its foot and said a prayer. They marked the grave with a crude cross then returned to the minibus to see if any of her possessions were recoverable. Forcing the rear door open she found that her suitcase had been opened along with her mother's, guaranteeing the destruction of all the contents. Had he been looking for the black notebook she wondered to herself as with a sigh she turned and walked back towards Lamin and the lorry.

Anna-Maria, now beyond the point of tears, and grief-stricken at leaving her mother's body buried in the soil of a country far from her beloved South Africa, sat staring ahead at the road, her mind numb as the vehicle moved off in the direction of the capital.

Along the way, several police checks forced Anna-Maria to take refuge beneath the untidy heap of sweat-soiled bedding piled on the bunk behind the driver's seat. At the first checkpoint they questioned Lamin at length, asking about a white woman but at the rest little was said. They passed a mosque, remote but placed there for the benefit of the faithful traveller. Most of the other buildings along the route were in a half-ruined state, and some buildings apparently abandoned altogether, with a goat or two pulling at the leaves on the sparse scrub. Occasionally, they saw a small herd of camels, normally guarded by elderly men or young boys. The heat and glare were unrelenting and made worse by the plastic covering on the seats in the lorry, leaving Anna-Maria sitting in a pool of perspiration.

At last, in the late afternoon, they approached Nouakchott at the end of what seemed to be an interminable journey and Anna-Maria's heart sank still further as she looked out at the squalid city they were entering. Slowly picking their way along the busy streets, where cars and lorries shared the road with the many donkey carts, they eventually stopped a little south of the centre in the area called El Mina. Lamin drove the lorry off the road and parked it between two similar vehicles on an area of dusty ground.

"You must now hide again, Madame. It is best you stay in the back until it is dark, then it will be safer for you to reach your friend."

"Will you stay with me until then?"

"I must fetch water for engine, Madame, I will return soon, then I will stay."

On his return Lamin found Anna-Maria looking desperate. "Lamin, do you know how I get to Rue Lumumba and is it far? The battery on my tablet is dead and the charging unit was in my suitcase."

"Madame Ronaldo, it is far and very difficult for me to show you how. Can your friend come here to collect you because in this country a woman must not be seen walking alone at night without a man and I must stay with my lorry or I will lose my work?"

"What would happen to me if I was seen?"

"You would be beaten, Madame, and maybe men would, er, use you."

"What am I to do then? I cannot remember the phone number, only the address."

Lamin thought for a few moments then started to look in a box under the bunk. "Ah! Here, Madame, here is a map of the city centre, it is old but I think not so much changed."

Though creased and grubby the map was still legible and soon she found the street name. "How far is it to this street, Lamin?"

"We are maybe about here, Madame," he replied, his finger off the map itself, resting instead near the bottom of the street index. "You should wait until after evening prayers, Madame, the streets will be quieter then."

Whilst there was still light they studied the map and Lamin showed her the safest route.

"Madame Ronaldo, there will still be many people between here and the place you wish to get to, so you must go this way," he said pointing towards the coast. "Then go through the Sebkha area here on the map to cross the big road. Only then can you go straight to the place, but that last part will be the most dangerous."

When the time came for her to leave, Lamin walked with her until they cleared the busy area and reached poorer and quieter streets.

"I must return to my lorry, Madame, you go in that way for two kilometres then turn north until you get to big road."

"Thank you, Lamin, thank you for everything you have done for me. Helping me dig my mother's grave, I could not have done it on my own." Her words seemed to her trivial and almost childish but she knew that only simple words would be correctly understood.

"It is a good thing we did, Madame."

She left, pressing one hundred dollars into Lamin's hand, and expressing her gratitude again.

Following Lamin's warning, her route understandably took her from shadow to shadow, picking her way along side streets and alleyways, hiding in doorways or behind parked cars when either a car approached or she heard voices nearby. How far she walked that night she had no idea except that it had taken her four hours and she felt weak from nervous exhaustion as much as from the physical demands of the journey. Once she had crossed the wide road that Lamin had referred to she could at last locate her position on the map and navigate her way to the house. Finally, running across the deserted Rue Lumumba she reached up and grabbed the high iron railings, then with scrambling feet and tired arms pulled herself up the shoulder high wall then over the railings themselves. Looking around cautiously she then quietly lowered herself down onto the front courtyard of what she believed to be the home of Lars Van der Rykes. As a cloud crossed the thin crescent moon the dark figure of Anna-Maria slipped from the shadow of the wall and ran across the open paved area to the front door of the house and pressed the bell push. Angry barking came from the rear of the house and before she could even take a step back towards the high railings she had climbed over, two Dobermanns blocked her way, growling and showing their teeth.

"Down Pascal! Down! Carmen, heel!" The dogs instantly obeyed the loud command from the squat, hard-faced man illuminated by the bright security lighting that had come on, standing arms akimbo at the front corner of the house. Neither animal moved, then, after several seconds in which neither had taken their eyes off him, he pointed back along a side path and shouted, "Hus!" Immediately both the Dobermanns loped off around the side of the building.

"What do you want?" asked the man, his South African accent clipped and harsh.

"I have come to see a Mr Lars Van der Rykes," replied Anna-Maria, her voice quavering nervously.

The man moved his position slightly trying to get a better view of Anna-Maria who was still cloaked in the mulafa. "You have found him. Who are you, eh?"

"I am Anna-Maria Patterson," she replied removing the headdress and praying that London had made contact.

"Ah, I 'eard you may be coming this way. What name are you travelling under?" asked Van der Rykes, his guttural accent emphasising the 'tr' of travelling.

"Anna-Maria Ronaldo," she informed. "Who told you that I may be coming here?"

"London sent a message," replied Van der Rykes. "Your 'usband is dead I 'ear."

Anna-Maria nodded, trying hard not to show the sadness she still felt, but grateful for the coded confirmation that the man was actually Van der Rykes, the man listed on the stick.

"You 'ad better come in. Do you have any luggage?"

"No, only this," she raised the old plastic bag. "I had to leave in a hurry."

"I 'ave told my wife that maybe the daughter of an old friend of mine who is trying to get away from a cruel husband may need my help," said Van der Rykes, quietly, "I'll leave the details for you to fill in if she asks."

He led her round the side of the house and up some steps to the terrace which overlooked a small garden surrounded by a high wall. An old cast iron streetlamp lit the terrace and there were two smouldering dung coils placed next to a sun lounger, their wisps of smoke helping to repel the swarms of mosquitos.

A tall young African woman stood alongside the sun-lounger, her arm returning to her side from having just zipped up the long dress she wore over an otherwise naked body.

"Blessings, my dear, can you bring us some drinks please."

A slight smile flickered across the young woman's face before she turned and walked into the house, with a grace of movement rarely seen outside of a traditional finishing school for young ladies. Van der Rykes' politeness surprised Anna-Maria, as did the bra strap poking out from under the lounger cushion.

"I will introduce you to my wife in a moment," said Van der Rykes, as he gathered up the cushion and the underwear in one smooth movement and took them inside the house. "Have a seat," he called back over his shoulder.

Van der Rykes and Blessings returned together, Blessings carrying a tray with wine glasses and a bowl of cheese pastry twists.

"Blessings, meet Anna-Maria Ronaldo who has come all the way from Brazil to see us." Then turning to Anna-Maria he said, "This is my wife, Blessings."

"I am very pleased to meet you," Blessings said, in a voice more English than African, offering a slender well-manicured hand, which, Anna-Maria noted, had perfectly varnished nails.

***

While Anna-Maria had been hiding in the home of Nandini, Vaughan had sailed *"La Mouette sur le Vent"* round to the Repmaritima Boatyard; fortunately the yard was ready for him and the lift-out was performed with the minimum of fuss. On learning that he could not sleep on board the yacht, he packed some overnight things and walked up to the airport and got a taxi back into Funchal. The summer season being well underway meant hotel rooms for single occupancy were hard to find, but finally he found a room at the Albagaria Dias Hotel, the back entrance to which was on the Rua de Santa Maria. Checking in, Vaughan went straight to his room, showered, changed and then went down to the bar. The other guests appeared to be mainly from Holland and generally a very jovial group of people. Finishing his beer, he decided on a stroll and dinner at the Casa Portuguesa, a short walk away; the area in which the hotel was situated was close to the Monte cable car, the Fortaleza do São Tiago and numerous bars and restaurants. Leaving by the back entrance, Vaughan stepped out onto the cobbled Rua de Santa Maria and strolled down to the steps that led to the cluster of restaurants and Annabel's, the nightclub where he had sat observing Kazakov and the assassin weeks before.

The scene before him in the warm early evening was one of bustling waiters and brightly dressed tourists all accompanied by a hubbub of conversation and laughter, so the sight of a smart grey suit stood out a mile. *"What the hell are you still doing here, Staunton? I thought you were supposed to be on the mainland tidying up the loose ends from a previous operation."*

Senior Agent Leonard Staunton had been Vaughan's "Controller" during the mission that had first brought him to Madeira. The relationship between the two men had not gone well with Staunton being unfairly critical of Vaughan's handling of the mission, despite the fact that it was considered by many in London to have been a huge success.

Vaughan stepped back into a shadowy corner from where he could watch Staunton who was talking earnestly to a giant of a man seated opposite him. The shadows cast over the bar where the two men sat hid the face of Staunton's companion throughout the conversation but when the man stood to leave, Vaughan instantly recognised him as being the minder who had worked for the murdered Russian arms dealer, Sarkis Kazakov. Vaughan had no knowledge of Staunton's previous missions so was now very curious as to the connection between the two men. The way in which the minder turned to leave suggested that the meeting wasn't exactly over, there was no handshake or salutation suggesting a parting of the ways so Vaughan decided to stay watching Staunton for a while to see what developed.

The big Russian crossed the square and with surprising agility for a man of his size ran up the steps a few metres away from him and walked briskly uphill towards the house on the cliff edge where Kazakov had lived. Staunton, meanwhile, poured himself another glass of wine and sat looking very pleased with himself as he eyed passing young women.

Twenty minutes or so later the sound of a vehicle approaching from the opposite direction to the one the minder had gone hardly attracted any attention from Vaughan until the black Range Rover drew up at the top of the steps and sounded its horn. Immediately, Staunton drained his glass, got up from the table and walked briskly towards the steps. Vaughan, not wishing to be seen, particularly by Staunton, turned and walked down the hill away from the Range Rover, glancing back once and catching sight of Staunton getting into the vehicle.

"What would Staunton be doing in the company of someone who once worked for an arms dealer? Or is that part of your loose ends work, Staunton? If so it gets you pretty close to the attempted assassination of Walid al Djebbar, and the shooting of Kazakov for that matter." As the vehicle roared away up the hill, Vaughan continued down the road taking a turning on the right to the Casa Portuguesa and the evening meal he had promised himself.

Over the course of an excellent dinner he pondered on what he had just witnessed. *"Kazakov was not involved with the coup plot as far as I know and Staunton was not impressed by my involvement in exposing the coup. Could that be it, was Staunton playing support for the coup, and if so was it sanctioned?"* Vaughan considered for some time what advantage there could be in the British Government's support of a coup in Portugal. *"Had it been successful it could probably have precipitated the collapse of the European Union and there were many in Britain who would like to see that happen. All of the information coming out of Government however suggested quite the opposite. Was that why Staunton was given the job of being my Controller so that he could keep me fixed only on the North African Conference and Al Djebbar while he did what he could to further the coup leaders' ambitions? Or was I given the job as a new boy in the hope that I would stand back and let the assassins succeed in taking out Al Djebbar, which would mean that the British Government wanted the North African crisis to continue; no that can't be right. Theory one is the most likely I think, but does it mean that Staunton's work was sanctioned?"*

That still did not explain why Staunton was meeting with Kazakov's ex-minder. *"Had he made contact with Reshetnikov who apparently had some connection with the coup it would be understandable. What is the link between Kazakov and the coup? None, as far as I can see, and for that matter I find it difficult to see why Kazakov would have involved himself in North African politics, other than for the supply of weapons to whichever faction had the money."* The question that really bothered him was how far to go with these thoughts and whether he should raise the question regarding a possible British involvement in the coup with the Commodore. He decided to let the dice roll a bit longer. In any event a call to Commodore Campbell was required if only to be told to butt out of Staunton's activities. On leaving the restaurant he went straight back to his hotel room and phoned Campbell.

It rang only twice, "Yes, Vaughan, what is it?"

"Sorry to trouble you, Sir, but I have just seen Senior Agent Staunton here in Funchal meeting with a man I recognise as having been the minder to Sarkis Kazakov."

"Go on."

"They were meeting at a bar in the old part of the town, then the minder went and got Kazakov's Range Rover and Staunton hopped aboard and off they went. Sadly I couldn't follow them."

"Interesting, Vaughan, very interesting. I don't want you to waste too much of your time trying to find out what Staunton is up to, nowadays he receives his orders from Sir Andrew Averrille." There was a moment's pause, then, "When will you be ready to leave?"

"The work on the boat will take two days, Sir, then I will be all set."

"That's good, Vaughan, a situation is rapidly developing that may well require your talents as a yachtsman, we may well need you to pick up a friend of ours whose situation is becoming, shall we say, difficult."

The Commodore, having received Anna-Maria's response to his coded warning message, had been working hard to notify all of his West African contacts. The resources available were, however, very limited, a rescue mission would take too long to reach her and would have a very high risk of failure now she was on her own; the best Campbell could do would be to get Vaughan in a position to help if the young woman managed get to a British contact on the African coast.

"Where from, Sir?"

"That needs to be confirmed, I am still awaiting final news about your potential passenger and will let you know as soon as I can," said Campbell. "Oh, try not to bump into Staunton if you can, I would rather nobody knew your whereabouts at the moment."

"Right, Sir, I will do my best to avoid him."

When the call ended, Vaughan tossed his mobile onto the bed and looked out of the window, down towards the hotel pool. Some guests were sitting around chatting and enjoying drinks and he idly wondered whether he would ever again be able to relax like them with friends and family. His mind drifted back to the days when he had worked for a civil engineering company and the team he had worked with during the early years of his marriage to Sarah. *"What are they up to now I wonder, how many of them stand divorced and alone in a foreign land and facing uncertain survival. Oh snap out of it, Vaughan, you joined, they didn't force you into this."* Reaching for his jacket he left the room and made his way down to reception, then left the hotel by the front entrance and walked up the hill and took the first turning on the right. At the end of the street there was a small grass area from where one could look down over the main harbour. It also looked onto the rear of the Kazakov property where a few room lights shone through the shutters. Turning downhill again towards the harbour, Vaughan reached the wrought iron gates that gave access to the front garden of the house and, stopping to look in, saw a young girl sitting on the elaborate stone steps leading down from the verandah. At first she didn't seem to notice him looking at her but then she turned her head slightly and looked straight at him. Vaughan smiled and waved and the girl smiled and waved back, before standing and wearily turning, climbed up the steps to the verandah and disappeared inside the house. It was a curious moment in which Vaughan felt an affinity with the young girl who seemed to radiate a sad loneliness similar to his own. Turning away he continued downhill to the Bar Barreirinha where he ordered a beer and found a seat from where he could keep watch on the house. An hour must have passed before he noticed an upstairs light coming on, spilling a glow over the front garden briefly before the occupant closed the shutters. There had been no sign of the Range Rover returning, or of Staunton, so paying the bill, Vaughan returned to his hotel.

***

The following morning he was back at the boatyard, lifting the yacht's floors and cleaning out the bilges and giving the engine a rapid service. By late afternoon he was exhausted but there were still things that had to be attended to, and leaving the yard that evening, Vaughan trudged up the hill to the airport building to get a taxi back into town and the home of the Honorary British Consul.

Her husband answered the door, "Good heavens it's you, Mr Vaughan, come in, how are you?"

"Fine thanks, I can't stop if you don't mind, I have rather a lot to do, I was just calling to see if your wife has received a package for me?"

"I'll go and check, won't be a moment," Henry Bevington replied.

He returned holding a sealed pouch, "Susanne is in the shower but told me to hand you this and get you to check the contents and sign for it."

Breaking the seal, Vaughan put his hand in and pulled out two boxes of 9mm ammunition and a further box containing the pistol, spare magazines and shoulder holster. "Looks like it's all here," he said, then looked up to see the shocked expression on Henry Bevington's face. "Sorry to have this delivered via you but this type of thing causes problems at airports and London don't want the local authorities to know who I actually work for."

"Oh, quite."

"The pouch will go back to London but I should appreciate a carrier bag if you have one."

"Of course, you can't walk through the streets here carrying those items for all to see."

While Bevington went to find a bag, Vaughan signed the receipt slips and put them back into the pouch.

It was Mrs Bevington who returned with the bag. "Is this suitable?" she said, handing Vaughan a bag from the market place in Praco do Columbo

"Yes, that will be fine, thank you, Mrs Bevington. These bags seem to be very popular, a neat way of recycling restaurant coffee bean bags, the young lady that makes them is very talented."

"Yes, she is, no need to return it to us I have several more."

Vaughan turned to leave.

"I had hoped that after being shot you would give up this SIS business and find some nice young lady to marry and settle down with."

"I suppose you have someone nice in mind?"

"Well, I know Amelia de Lima is very keen on you."

Vaughan shook his head and sighed. "I have a job to do, Mrs Bevington, and I have the feeling that it is quite an important one, which brings me to ask whether you have ever spoken to the authorities about the attempted assassination of Walid al Djebbar by the man who killed Sarkis Kazakov?"

"Yes, actually I have, they didn't appear to know much. The identity of Kazakov's assassin remains a mystery, but as he was also killed nobody seems of a mind to find out anything about him. Why?"

"It's just that I saw Kazakov's minder yesterday swanning around in the black Range Rover, then last night saw a young girl sitting on the front steps of Kazakov's old house."

"Ah, that would be his daughter I believe. She was left an orphan and I am led to believe that the minder and his wife are acting as her guardians. I feel very sorry for her as I understand that she cannot speak."

"You mean a mute."

"Yes."

"No wonder she looked so sad and alone when I saw her," said Vaughan gently, his eyes staring into the distance.

Suzanne Bevington smiled, "Seeing that softer side of you is why I think you should find a wife and settle down before the sewer you agents operate in saps the nice guy out of you."

Shortly afterwards they said their goodbyes and Vaughan walked back to the hotel arriving rather later than he had hoped. It was too late to eat a meal, so he turned in for the night.

***

On arrival at the DELCO offices the morning after Anna-Maria's arrival in Nouakchott, Campbell had asked Lieutenant Heathcote to join him, "Penny, I've heard from Van der Rykes, Mrs Patterson has made it as far as his house, but Vermeulen has men watching the port and airport and of course we have got the problem of that damn website."

"There is no chance of the RAF flying in to pick her up then?"

"No, not all the while she has that spy tag attached to her, and the Navy hasn't got anything close from which we could launch a Royal Marine operation to get her off from a beach."

"Is Van der Rykes very resourceful, Sir?"

"I really don't know, Penny, he has been on our lists for a long time, but has been little used other than to gather the political dirty washing. I just pray that he has got talent."

"It is too far away for Vaughan I would think, unless of course Van der Rykes can hide her for a week or so."

"He didn't seem too keen on that idea, Penny. His wife has several friends that call at the house and that would create too much of a risk he thinks, and the last thing I want to do is put them in danger as well as Mrs Patterson."

"I hate to say this, Sir, but is Mrs Patterson that important, I know she has been good with the stuff on Vermeulen, but he's now a wanted man and there is a good chance that he will be picked up."

"You're forgetting Vermeulen's notebook that she mentioned, if he is as big as I am beginning to think he is that book could uncover a lot more about the goings on in African arms trading than we could learn in five years."

"Ah, I see it is not just about David then."

Campbell gave Heathcote a sharp glare, "No, it is not and never was, my concern is about the future of Africa and its people. All the while the Vermeulens' of this world are allowed to trade death, many innocent people suffer. I am also aware that had we picked up the name of A. Patterson on the passenger list from the Luanda to Lagos flight sooner, we may have got a warning to her at Dakar or St Louis."

"I'm sorry, Sir, I was wrong to mention David Patterson, and I am also to blame for missing Anna-Maria's name on the flight lists, it was just that she had never travelled with Vermeulen before and frankly I cannot understand why she did this time."

"Yes, yes, Penny. Look, I should have explained this to you before. My gathering information as it seeps out regarding the death of David Patterson is because I do not believe that he had turned arms trader."

"But what about the Staunton report, Sir, and the initial report from the Angolan government enquiry, they had him down as an arms trader and promptly stopped any Brit from taking up advisory rolls there."

"I think the Angolan government were led by the nose, and as far as Staunton's report goes that was more suitable for The Man Booker Prize than a report we should take seriously."

"Sir Andrew praised it to the skies, Sir."

"Yes," replied Campbell sourly.

CHAPTER 3

Blessings woke Anna-Maria shortly before dawn. "Lars wants to take you to the port later, he knows a fisherman who may be able to take you across to the Cape Verde Islands, he has gone there now to talk to the man."

Blessings went across to the window and drew back the curtains letting in the thin pre-dawn light. "Come through when you are dressed, I have made some food for you." She then left, leaving Anna-Maria with her stomach churning, wondering how safe this next step of her journey would be; she could not bring herself to believe that the fisherman would be as kind and respectful as Lamin had been.

The last time she had looked at her watch it was three o'clock now it was showing five o'clock , she had only had two hours sleep. In the shower she turned the control to the coldest setting in an effort to wake herself up; she was exhausted, both physically and emotionally, feeling permanently close to tears at the loss of her mother whose image in death continuously flashed across her mind. Dressed, she dragged herself downstairs to the dining room.

"Anna-Maria, please excuse my prying, but what has your husband done to you for you to run away like this, obviously in fear of your life?" asked Blessings, almost as soon as Anna-Maria had sat at the dining table.

"It is what I have done to him," Anna-Maria got up and walked over to the window. "I discovered that he makes his money from illegally dealing in things that destroy people's lives. I could not live with someone so wicked so I reported him to the authorities, but he found out and left the country before they could arrest him and he now knows I am the one responsible for informing. If he finds me I am sure he will kill me, he has a very bad temper."

"Does he know that you are here in Nouakchott?" Blessings asked nervously.

"I am not sure; he has many friends in Africa who I think will be asked to look out for me."

Blessings walked to the window and closed the curtains.

When Van der Rykes arrived back he waited for Blessings to go to the kitchen to prepare his own breakfast before delivering the bad news. "Your 'husband' has got men watching the port," he said, pouring himself some coffee, "My man there tells me that many people, including the police, are searching for you, both here and at Rosso, so we must think of getting you out from somewhere else."

Anna-Maria was not sure whether to feel relief or further anxiety. "I was not looking forward to a voyage on a Mauritanian fishing boat."

"Well, there is no chance of you flying out from this town, is there," Van der Rykes said, looking at her in surprise, before realising that she would be unaware of the latest news. "Of course, London may not have been able to tell you, your name and picture have been leaked by someone exposing a US security data list of British agents operating in Africa."

"What, but how could that be? I am not employed as a spy by anyone."

"Maybe not, but you have been passing very useful information that has exposed a number of criminals who now fear for their future, including Jan Vermeulen. You have rocked a very dangerous boat, young lady." Anna-Maria buried her head in her hands. "One thing is very strange, and that is why you appear on a US list at this particular time."

"What do you mean?"

"Well, your escape is being directed by British SIS not American CIA and it is being controlled by a very small group, which tells me that you are very special indeed to the British, but the Americans? Why them?" Van der Rykes shook his head, "Unless of course the British have someone leaking information."

"I do not know of any American link, in fact I don't think that I have done anything very special other than tip off London about some of my step… er husband's plans." Only then did she remember the notebook in the tatty plastic bag hidden by her dirty and crumpled western clothes.

She was about to mention the notebook to Van der Rykes when he said, "I received a message this morning to get you out at all costs, so what you know must be top deal intelligence. You are safe here for a day or two maybe, but the sooner we get you out the better."

"Oh my God, I am so sorry."

"It's not your fault. Africa has far too many people wanting to start wars for their own profit, if by getting you out it will close down some of those bastards so much the better."

"But my being here is putting you and Blessings in danger."

Van der Rykes looked at her but made no reply.

The term "top deal intelligence" had hit Anna-Maria in the pit of her stomach. She knew very little that had not already been passed to London so what was it that made her so important. But of course London knew about the notebook so it just had to reach them. These thoughts were beginning to overload her mind and seeking a change of subject she asked, "Why did you tell your wife that I am from Brazil?"

Van der Rykes smiled, then, looking to check that they were alone said quietly. "Blessings is beautiful and I could not live without her, but she is a little naïve and likely to tell people more than they need to know. If by chance she told someone that you are Anna-Maria Ronaldo from Angola they would easily put two and two together."

Anna-Maria looked at him aghast, "Really, you think so?"

Van der Rykes nodded and Anna-Maria felt fear gripping her again at the thought of such a simple thing bringing about the downfall of her escape.

As Van der Rykes left for his normal day's work at the airport, Anna-Maria went to her room, saying that she was tired, and spent the next hour studying the curious and unintelligible lists and notes written on the pages of the black notebook. No way could she begin to fathom out the real meaning of the notebook's contents but she guessed that someone in London would be able to work it out. Her escape was now no longer for her alone, but for David, her wonderful David, her mother and the continent that she felt so sorry for.

"I must do this and get the notebook to Uncle Alex," she said out loud.

As it turned out the journey was to be sooner than any of them expected, as Van der Rykes arrived back from the airport only two hours after leaving the house.

"You are in luck," he called from the lounge. "My guys working at Nouadhibou Airport in the North say they can't fix the problem they have been sent to sort out, normally I would talk them through it but this time I said I would drive up. On the rare occasions I do this, I always take Blessings with me for her safety and make sure the house is fully secured, my neighbour feeds the dogs. So, you will have some female company and women's clothes will not look out of place if the camper-van is looked into." Anna-Maria had hurried from the bedroom and now stood facing Van der Rykes. "Also it will not give Blessings the chance of gossiping to others," he added quietly and winked.

"How far away is it?" she asked.

"Oh, about five hundred kilometres, but I suspect that the departure lounge is being watched so don't get your hopes up." He saw the look of despair on Anna-Maria's face, "Don't worry, we'll find a way to get you out."

It took a good two hours to get everything ready during which time Blessings provided Anna-Maria with a better wardrobe. It required Anna-Maria to forsake her comfortable trainers for platform soled high heeled sandals to avoid her tripping over the garments' hems. The advantages of that were to make her look several centimetres taller than she actually was, and alter the way she walked. That, together with an improved head covering, lessened the chance of a casual recognition.

Van der Rykes appeared at the bedroom door. "Let me have your passport, Anna-Maria, the one you are travelling under, I'm going to see if I can provide you with a believable false entry."

"I haven't used this one since before I married David," she said handing an unmarked Portuguese passport over, "and I used my married one for the journey to Senegal. No one asked for passports at Rosso."

"Okay, that is good; I should be able to show you flying in and out of here a few times to make it look as if you are semi-local."

The passport, when returned to her, looked much more travel-worn than before, and she noticed with surprise how well travelled she was in West Africa, Europe and islands like the Canaries and Cape Verdes. "How did you get all of these entry stamps put in?"

Van der Rykes gave no reply, just tapped the side of his nose and grinned.

In the camper-van, Anna-Maria tried out the cramped hiding place beneath the double berth in the rear of the van, cushioned from the hard floor by a thin duvet and concealed by the berth base and mattress. The only ventilation to the space was a small grill through which she could just about see down the length of the van to the driver's seat. She struggled to get out as quickly as she could.

"I hope I don't have to spend long in there."

"Hopefully it won't be necessary but we must not take any chances, not in this country anyway." Van der Rykes lowered the base and mattress back into place. "Normally we keep spare bed linen in there, the airport can get very cold at night."

As the time came for them to leave, Anna-Maria lay on the berth rather than under it, with the curtains of the camper-van drawn closed. They were some distance clear of the town when Van der Rykes called for her to come forward and sit beside Blessings. Along either side of the road was featureless desert, windblown sand occasionally covered the road making it hard to follow and with so little traffic to leave guiding tracks Van der Rykes was frequently having to gamble on the safe route to take.

After nearly six hours of driving they were approaching Nouadhibou when Van der Rykes interrupted the women's conversation. "Anna-Maria, get in the back and hide, quickly, keep down as you go to the back." Anna-Maria crawled as fast as she could, and lifting up the mattress and base board scrambled into her hiding place.

To Van der Rykes' keen eye there was something not right about the police vehicle partially blocking the road and the two officers that flagged the camper-van to a halt. The sign-writing on the side of their vehicle was not quite correct and the lighting frame on the roof was not right. Unlike Anna-Maria's journey from Rosso they had not experienced any police checks on the road from Nouakchott and Van der Rykes was suspicious of the one set up here. As one officer came to the driver's side, the other went round to the nearside and tried the door. The one looking up at Van der Rykes had obviously been snorting something quite recently as his eyes were more than a little glazed.

"What do you want?" asked Van der Rykes in heavily accented French. "I'm in a hurry to get to the airport to fix the radar."

"We need to search your vehicle."

"What for?" said Van der Rykes, holding up his Mauritanian Government airport pass.

The van swayed as the second officer tried again to pull open the nearside door.

"Will you stop your colleague from trying to pull the side off my vehicle."

"He has to search your vehicle. Now open the door."

Normally the police would have accepted his government airport pass as sufficient to allow immediate onward travel, the uniformed man standing alongside obviously didn't appreciate the authority that the pass carried.

"I said, open the door!"

Van der Rykes, leaving the driver's seat, walked back through the camper-van to the side door and flicked the lock. Immediately the door was slid open and an angry looking man in a badly fitting police uniform glared at him.

"Why you not open the door straight away?" said the man.

"Tell me what you are searching for," said Van der Rykes, stepping back to allow the man in.

"That is police business," replied the man looking around. "Who else is travelling with you?"

"Just my wife, why?"

The man moved towards the back of the van and opened the toilet door.

"I said there's no one else on board, so why are you poking around?"

"I am searching," said the man, now opening the wardrobe and rifling through the clothes hanging inside.

Next he lifted the seat in the sleeping area and peered into the void below as Van der Rykes stepped across to the bedside cabinet. Turning, the bogus policeman reached down to lift the mattress when Van der Rykes hit him with a rabbit punch, catching the man as he fell. Snatching the pistol from the bedside cabinet drawer, Van der Rykes turned and shot the second policeman in the head as he stepped up into the van, the impact throwing the body back onto the roadside. Grabbing the limp body of the first man, he dragged him to the door and tumbled him out firing two shots through the man's torso to ensure that he was dead. Only then did he take notice of the men's shoes; even in Mauritania the police wore issued boots, both of the bodies on the ground were wearing worn down cheap black trainers.

"I should have killed you both the moment you came near," he said as he jumped to the ground and ran across to the men's truck where his hurried inspection confirmed the paintwork on the truck to be a rough spray job and the lighting frame to be a botch-up; the headlining dumped on the back seats, along with the men's normal clothes.

Getting back into the camper-van Van der Rykes drove away at speed. "Blessings my love, can you go back and tell Anna-Maria that she must stay hidden until I have checked out the airport."

Blessings was still wide-eyed with her hands over her mouth in shock. "Those two men were police, Lars."

"No, my dear, they were criminals, bad men, I think working for Anna-Maria's husband. The police will be pleased to see them dead, believe me." Van der Rykes gave his wife a gentle push. "Now hurry and tell Anna-Maria to stay where she is until I fetch her."

At the airport Van der Rykes walked across to the terminal's check-in area and spent the next half an hour walking round watching for anyone not in uniform but loitering as if searching for someone and studying the few passengers who arrived. Three soldiers ambled around, their weapons held casually and the expression on their faces one of sheer boredom. Satisfied, Van der Rykes went to the airline desk and bought a return ticket on the evening flight north to El Aaiún Airport for his "sister-in-law" then returned to the camper-van and a very anxious Blessings.

The shooting had also terrified Anna-Maria who squealed as Van der Rykes lifted the mattress and base board concealing her.

"Here is your ticket for the evening flight to El Aaiún Airport in Western Sahara. It's an open return ticket to make it look as if you are planning to come back. I will arrange for either Cecil Boyd or Marc Allian to meet you at the airport, you will be safer in Laayoune with them until London can organise your onward journey."

"Are you sure no one is watching the airport?" asked Anne-Maria nervously.

"As sure as I can be. I don't know whether the army soldiers that act as security here are briefed to look out for you but I doubt it, they showed no sign of studying passengers as they arrived."

Anna-Maria was trembling as she reached for the suitcase Blessings had provided. "Hey, sit down and drink this," said Van der Rykes handing her a glass with what looked like a treble whisky in it.

As the three of them left the camper-van and made their way across the car park it looked as if Lars and Blessings were there purely to see Anna-Maria off on holiday, giving her the normal kisses and hugs, and waving as she made her way to the check-in. The check-in went smoothly and Anna-Maria was beginning to gain confidence when at passport control the official, having inspected her ticket, asked her to confirm her name then took a long time looking through her passport.

"Why do you wish to visit Western Sahara?"

"I am meeting a friend there, he has only a very short time to visit Africa and our only chance of meeting is at Laayoune," Anna-Maria replied.

"Show me your ticket again."

Anna-Maria reached into her handbag, trying hard to control the shaking of her hands and, taking out the ticket, opened it and held it up for the official to read. After a cursory inspection he nodded then stamped her passport and handed it back to her. At the security area the arch was not working, so Anna-Maria had to endure being padded down by a woman who was rather too thorough for comfort. It was then just a matter of a short walk to the uninviting departure area where she stood rather than sat, occasionally strolling around, needing to stretch her legs and move about after suffering the confinement beneath the camper-van's double berth, and also hoping to walk off the effects of the Scotch. Finally, a uniformed member of the ground staff announced that the flight was ready for boarding, and after a ticket and boarding pass check, led the passengers out across the concrete apron to the aircraft steps.

The flight was only half full and duration relatively short but it was well after sunset when the aircraft touched down at El Aaiún Airport and taxied to the nearest stand on the apron next to the terminal building. There it stood in splendid isolation for twenty minutes, awaiting the tractor-pulled steps and baggage train to arrive.

An hour later Anna-Maria walked out of the customs area to see a short podgy man holding up a piece of white card with her name on it.

"I am Anna-Maria Ronaldo," she said, looking at the man and wondering why in the apparent cool of the terminal building he was perspiring so profusely.

"Cecil Boyd, your husband is dead I hear," came the languid reply. "You will be staying at my apartment for a night or two, then London wants me to take you to the fishing port."

Anxious to return to the chill of his air-conditioned Peugeot, Boyd turned on his heels and waddled rather than walked away leaving Anna-Maria to pick up her case again and hurry to catch up with him.

She caught up with Boyd as they reached the exit. "Have you lived here long?"

"Too long, my dear, far too long. Let me see, it must be thirty years now and frankly I am sick of it."

"What business are you in?"

"Shipping," came the brief reply, then, "Oh God, the heat, this perpetual bloody heat," he shouted as they stepped out from the cool of the terminal building and turned towards the small car park.

It was a short drive from the airport into the town and Anna-Maria noted the pronounced Moroccan influence, not only in the architecture but with the tidiness of the place compared to Nouakchott and what little she had seen of Nouadhibou.

The apartment above a shop on the Boulevard El Kairaouane, not far from the Mosque Moulay Abdel Aziz, also served as Boyd's office; a fact that went part of the way to explaining the man's obesity and detestation of all outside activity. The other factor in relation to his size was his mastery of cooking and acquisition of excellent French wines. Anna-Maria had not eaten so well since the family had moved to South Africa, all those years before.

***

The morning after her arrival Anna-Maria was receiving breakfast in bed, while Vaughan, having made an early start, was purchasing stores for the voyage from the central supermarket in Funchal. He estimated that he would need enough for two people for a month at sea, so it was a laden taxi that took him down to the boatyard. He arrived in time to watch, with interest, as the antifouling was applied and when the work was finished he started the laborious job of climbing up and down the ladder loading the stores, followed by the equally laborious job of stowing them. He had almost completed the task when his mobile chirped into life.

"Yes, Commodore?"

"Are you ready for sea yet?"

"Almost, Sir, she will be relaunched early tomorrow morning."

"Good, you will get a coded message giving you your instructions at 0900 hrs tomorrow. We have been unable to arrange another safe escape route that is, er, convenient, so we are relying on you to get your passenger back here asap, understood?"

"Yes, Sir."

"Good luck."

The phone went dead and Vaughan was left considering the phrases "er, convenient" and the final "Good luck" which had been said with a tone of hopefulness rather than confidence. "*I wonder whether a compact Glock 26 is going to be up to it for this job,*" was his first thought as he slipped the phone back into his pocket.

Later that afternoon Vaughan obtained the permit required to make a landing on the Selvagens, not that he was planning to make the visit but purely to maintain his cover as a maritime author. Two hours later he was dining again at the Casa Portuguesa having paid the boatyard bill and arranged the relaunch for eight o'clock the following morning. He had also settled his hotel bill and in both cases had used his personal bank card to pay them rather than the Firm's. If someone outside of the Commodore's loop wanted to know his location, his use of the Firm's credit card would make their job easy.

Getting into the taxi at the hotel the following day Vaughan felt sad to be leaving the island; its friendly people, pleasant climate and majestic natural splendour had made a huge impression on him. *"There is also the very desirable Amelia. No, Vaughan, she has suffered enough without you playing with her emotions, assuming of course that Suzanne Bevington is to be believed."* He had to admit to himself that he had been very tempted to contact Amelia again.

"La Mouette sur le Vent" was already on the hoist when he arrived and after one last check of the hull he climbed the ladder to get aboard and waited for the hoist operator to finish his early morning coffee break. As requested by Vaughan the yacht was immersed in the sea but still held on the hoist strops until he had de-aired the stern gland to the pro-shaft, an important task that ensured the non-leak status at the point where the prop shaft passed through the hull. Finishing the task he replaced the access panel to the shaft tunnel, scrambled backwards out of his quarter berth and went on deck to signal that he was ready to leave. Once the lifting strops were clear he motored away from the shelter of the stub quay and turned the yacht's bows southwards, wanting to clear the land before the promised telephone orders were due. At exactly nine o'clock he heard his mobile ring, and connecting the auto helm he hurried below and sitting at the chart table snatched the phone from the rack. It was a voice mail message from DELCO delivered in a measured manner that enabled him to write it down. Anyone hearing the message would assume it was from a relative passing on some family news about a house move and a child's new school. His short text response message was simply, "Thanks for letting me know".

Returning to the cockpit Vaughan adjusted the auto helm to bring the yacht head to wind and hoisted the mainsail, and a second adjustment had the yacht turning to starboard allowing the wind, now on the beam, to unfurl the jib and staysail as he winched in the sheets. Then easing the mainsail a little to balance the yacht on a course of one five zero degrees, Vaughan waited for a few minutes to ensure there was no excessive auto helm activity to drain the yacht's batteries. Checking that all was clear around him he went below to recover his hidden code book from the space behind the false bulkhead in the forward cabin and to pick up his notebook from the chart table.

Back in the cockpit, checking date and time, he selected the section in his code book and set to work; twenty minutes later he sat looking at the message.

"Make to position thirty degrees zero seven minutes North by fifteen degrees fifty-two minutes West. Await Western Saharan flagged fishing vessel licence No 11-331 ETA zero one hundred

hours, twenty-three August. Take on board passenger and proceed to port Gibraltar HM Dockyard. Report arrival.

Passenger is Anna-Maria Ronaldo, use phrase 'I hear your husband is dead' as ID. Approaching destination text 'Landed large tuna fish today,' as soon as in mobile range of land."

Returning below, Vaughan looked at the small scale chart of the area and saw that the rendezvous was to be southeast of the Salvage Islands, in Portuguese the Ilhas Selvagens, then pulling out a large scale chart of the area Vaughan shook his head. *"Oh, thank you Commodore, you could have picked a less tricky area for this. Reefs, rocks and a warning that some positions marked were subject to inaccuracy. At least it will fit my cover."* After a careful study of the chart he marked a waypoint on it and set the fix on the yacht's GPS.

As *"La Mouette sur le Vent"* cleared the wind shadow of the island she heeled a little more, and gathering speed, driven on by the northeasterly trade wind, was now tramping on at a little over seven knots. Now was the time for Vaughan to start his lone sailor activity/rest routine of twenty minutes on watch, twenty minutes rest or sleep. He noted the time as being 0950 hours, giving him enough time to plot his course and estimate the ETA before his rest period.

Allowing twenty-seven hours for the voyage would get him to the Selvagem Grande waypoint at around 1300 hours the next day, thirty-six hours ahead of time, but with the necessary advantage of slipping down the western shore of Selvagem Grande in broad daylight. It also gave him enough time to acquaint himself with the island's wardens to maintain his maritime author cover. He now carefully checked the chart to ensure that there were no islets or rocks to hit between his current position and the Selvagen Grande waypoint and set the course on the GPS. *"This all depends on the wind staying at a constant force 5 and from the northeast. We will soon be downwind of those high forbidding cliffs of the Deserta Islands, I wonder if they will affect progress, even twelve miles away their height may cause a wind shadow or change of wind direction."*

Another check on his AIS and a visual lookout showed that the area was clear of other vessels, and moving forward from the chart table, Vaughan stretched out on the starboard settee and closed his eyes. It had been two months since he had last worked his solo sailor routine and he found it difficult to fully relax in the way that he had previously, but if he was going to get his passenger to Gibraltar he would have to get back into that routine, and quickly.

**

As Vaughan had received the message from London, Senior Agent Leonard Staunton had stopped his hire car at the side of the road, and taking a pair of binoculars from the glove compartment trained them on the yacht. An hour earlier he had walked from his hotel to the marina and learnt that Vaughan had moved the boat two days earlier. The news had cheered him somewhat until the berthing attendant had informed him that Senhor Vaughan had only sailed to the Repmaritima Boatyard situated beneath the airport runway. Cursing, he strode back to the hotel, got into his car and drove out to the airport just in time to see Vaughan set off, but where to was the question. Staunton knew that travelling south away from Madeira was not going to take him back to the United Kingdom and he was now very curious as to where Vaughan was heading. Taking the road under the runway he then made an illegal left turn to get onto a roundabout and a road leading up to higher ground. Stopping the car again he watched the progress of the yacht for the next hour before making the call.

At the third ring a hushed voice answered, "Lenny darling, what is it? I'm at work."

"Vaughan has left Madeira heading due south. Find out what's going on."

"I'll try, Lenny. When are you coming back, darling? I'm missing you terribly."

"Can't talk now. Call me as soon as you've got anything."

Staunton didn't hear the "Bye, Lenny darling, love you," as he had already ended the call.

After one last look through the binoculars, he got back into the car and drove to Kazakov's house for further negotiations with Boris. This was the third meeting between the two men regarding some "assets" of the late Sarkis Kazakov that were stored in the cellar of a derelict house at Paul do Mar on the western side of the island. So far Boris had not divulged the location of Kazakov's "assets" to Staunton, but had told him that he was in competition with a Russian.

Nearing the property Staunton parked the car at the western end of the Rua do Lazareto and walked the rest of the way, keeping his eyes open for plain-clothed police or Portuguese secret service people watching the building. His caution was understandable as Kazakov had been linked to the assassin, Takkal, who weeks earlier had attempted to kill the Tunisian politician, Walid al Djebbar. Takkal was also the man responsible for the death of Sarkis Kasakov, a strange situation that was only resolved by the written statement given by Kasakov's mute daughter.

Magda, the housekeeper, let Staunton into the lower hallway where he waited somewhat impatiently for her to fetch Boris from the garden.

"You are early," said Boris.

"Unlike you, I am a busy man," Staunton replied, irritated that his timing should be challenged by a minder, now gardener.

Boris just stood looking back at Staunton cooly, obviously waiting for Staunton to explain why he had requested the visit.

"My associates are interested in making a better offer but they need me to verify that the stock you hold is what you claim it to be and that it is in good condition."

"The other party is prepared to accept my word after seeing the samples and the same list that I showed to you." The big Russian replied knowing the risk he would run revealing the location of the arms cache to this particular man, he had the smell of a government agent about him.

"The other party being Ulan Reshetnikov?" said Staunton, noting the slight movement of Boris's right eyelid that confirmed his guess was the correct one. "There is an international warrant out for his arrest, it's very unlikely that your 'other party' will be able to complete on the deal, and I have no doubt that steps have been taken to freeze all of his bank accounts."

Deciding that the meeting was going nowhere, Boris stepped past Staunton and opened the street door.

"You're sure that you don't want to do business with us?"

Boris said nothing, he just stood holding the door open.

Staunton shrugged and stepped out into the street. "When the situation changes and I'm sure that it will, you have my number."

Walking back up the hill and along to his car Staunton was seething with anger at Boris's treatment of him and was now more determined than ever to eliminate the competition. Since the coup, both the Portuguese army and police had been searching for Reshetnikov who had been associated with those fronting the coup attempt, but so far they had not found where he was hiding and now it was becoming accepted by the authorities that the Russian had probably managed to leave the island. Staunton, however, now knew almost for certain that Reshetnikov was still in Madeira as Boris had shown the man samples from the weapons cache once owned by Kazakov. If he could find where the Russian was hiding and deal with him, that would take out the competition nicely and mean that the original offer made would stand and his cut of the profits much larger. The question was how to find Reshetnikov, could Boris be the key to that? Staunton sat in his car for a good half an hour trying to work out a way of keeping track of Boris, on the assumption that further meetings with Reshetnikov would be required before their deal could be completed.

As Staunton had guessed, Reshetnikov's bank accounts in Portugal had been frozen and though he could complete the weapons' deal from other sources outside of the country, it meant that he now relied for the payment of day to day living expenses on the earnings of his mistress Sonia's escort business. After the coup Sonia had, for a time, been reluctant to openly run the business directly and had promoted Jacinta to the trusted position of introducer and collector. Sonia's choice of Jacinta for the task was based on the knowledge that having been "slapped" once by Ivor for doing business on her own account, Jacinta would be in fear of any further "correction". Now, after a few weeks during which time none of her girls had been questioned or even approached by the authorities on official business, Sonia had decided to use Jacinta for local clients and resume her role of introducer for new clients and visitors to the island; her latest new client being Leonard Staunton who, after his brief conversation with the pretty and compliant, Petty Officer Alice Morgan, realised his need for female company.

The meeting that evening between Sonia, Monica and Staunton was at a bar in town not far from where Monica had her apartment. The payment made and the two hours enjoyed, Staunton asked Monica whether Sonia was ever available, to be told that, "Ulan would never allow that."

Staunton had not known that Sonia was Ulan Reshetnikov's mistress, so the name Ulan came as a shock to him, but quickly he realised that it was unlikely that the name would be common on the island of Madeira. Staunton, now able to recognise Sonia, guessed that she would be a regular visitor to the bar where they had met; it would only be a matter of following her to see if the trail led back to Reshetnikov's hideout.

Back at his hotel, Staunton went straight to his room and showered, then considered phoning Alice as he was finding himself to be on some strangely unusual guilt trip. He was just about to pick up the phone when it rang.

"Yes?"

"Leonard?"

"Yes."

"Jan Vermeulen."

"Have they picked up your stepdaughter yet?"

"No, I haven't heard a damn thing about her. After the trouble with that bastard Elmoctar, getting information from Rosso was limited, but I think she may have got back across the border," replied Vermeulen. "Can you arrange to have her name taken off that spy list? I guessed it was you who got it put on there."

"Why? She knows nothing that is serious and if they pick her up it won't take long for them to realise that they have a dud, and you will know where she is. I'm sure she will be pleased to see you."

"There is a chance that she has my black book."

Staunton felt a chill in his stomach. "How the fuck did she get hold of that? You bloody idiot, I told you carrying that notebook around was dangerous."

"When Elmoctar's men were chasing us, my briefcase fell open and some things dropped out onto the floor of the minibus, either it fell out of the vehicle when she did or she took it and jumped, I don't know."

"You went back and searched?"

"Of course I bloody did, but in Rosso white guys don't spend a long time walking around the back streets."

"Jesus, what a bloody mess."

"The black book is not a mess, Leonard, what is a mess is why the Cabinda men got picked up and I got fingered."

"I've been wondering the same thing, Jan," said Staunton. "Someone in your set-up has got a loose tongue, unless your little stepdaughter is brighter than you think. She did well at university and Patterson was not into airheads."

"You reckon eh? I don't, she's just like her mother, no idea of the real world."

"If she has got the book, having her name taken off the US list is a priority. Leave that with me."

"What about finding the girl? I'm no longer in Africa."

"I'll make enquiries. Where are you now?"

"Lanzarote, staying with your friend, Maurice."

"Do you feel safe there?"

"Oh yes, safe enough."

As soon as the call ended, Staunton dialled Alice's number, and after ten minutes of uncharacteristic charm, followed by a few minutes of erotic suggestions, he started on the real purpose of the call. "I have just been speaking to the man that sent you those sparkling earrings of yours, sweetie, he's got a bit of a problem and has asked for our help."

"You know I will do what I can for you, Lenny darling."

"I know, sweetie. Can you carefully find out if Campbell's team are trying to pull someone out of the field, probably West Africa?" Then as a thought struck him he added, "It may also be linked to what Vaughan is up to."

"That's going to be very difficult, Lenny, and I haven't seen any of Vaughan's traffic for weeks, I had the feeling that the Firm didn't have any work for him at the moment."

"Have a snoop around, sweetie, I'm sure that he is doing something, as he is now heading in the wrong direction if he was supposed to be following normal orders."

Leaving Alice promising that she would try her best, and enjoying another few minutes of pillow talk, Staunton brought the conversation to an end.

His next call was to the States and his naïve political activist friend whose website had released the falsified CIA spy list. Staunton, using the name of a fictitious CIA informant, made profuse apologies for a terrible mix-up and after a further fifteen minutes of half-truth and innuendo conversation about politics and probable sex scandals about to emerge, received assurances that three of the names, including that of Mrs Anna-Maria Patterson had now been deleted from the site's grand exposé.

When the call was finished Staunton relaxed a little hoping to spend the rest of his waking minutes thinking of Monica and wondering about the glamorous Sonia when his mobile rang again.

"Leonardo?"

"Yes."

"I hear you have some heavy goods to ship."

"Ah, Kallenberg, at last, yes, I expect to have the deal sorted in a couple of days then we can arrange the rendezvous. I think it will be best done on the western side of the island. I've got your number and we'll fix details."

"I'll await your call."

***

In London the following morning Lieutenant Heathcote received a call from the Web Surveillance Team, "WST, Cooper, here. You asked us to put a flag on the Free Zone site that posted that spy list."

"Yes, I did, is it making any more stupid claims?"

"No, it is just that I noticed that the list had got shorter and on checking saw that the names Bowden, Langhorn and Patterson no longer appear."

"Interesting, thank you very much. Can you keep the flag in place, I would like to hear of any other little gems of farce that that little creep is being fed," replied Heathcote with an edge of venom in her voice.

At that moment Lorna Parker-Davis, DELCO's receptionist-cum-gatekeeper entered the office.

"Yes, Lieutenant, of course I will. How about dinner tonight?" asked Cooper, hopefully.

"Sorry, my boyfriend is taking me out."

"Damn, jammy sod."

Heathcote put the phone down, shaking her head.

"When did I have the sex change?" asked Lorna, frowning.

"Twenty seconds ago, when spotty faced Vernon Cooper from WST invited me to dinner."

"Ah, right. You're still on for this evening though, I've got the tickets."

"Wouldn't miss it."

"Unless that God of a boss you worship wants you to work late."

"Hark who's talking, you're just as bad," Heathcote replied picking up the phone and dialling the Commodore's number. "Just to let you know, Sir, Mrs Patterson's name no longer appears on the Free Zone website list."

When Heathcote had put down the phone Lorna said, "Six-thirty then and don't stand me up."

"As if I would, Larry." The buzzer sounded. "Got to go, our God is calling for me."

"I'm not too sure I want to take you now," Lorna said, feigning hurt pride.

Heathcote giggled and getting up, made for her office door.

As Heathcote entered the Commodore's office she found him staring out of the window, "You wanted me, Sir?"

"Yes, Penny, I've arranged a meeting with Sir Andrew and will be going across the river shortly. While I'm away I would be grateful if you could quietly enquire about the recent movements of Senior Agent Leonard Staunton. Vaughan has seen him recently in Funchal and I would like to learn about what he was doing there and I don't think that Sir Andrew will want to tell me."

"Are you lunching together, Sir?"

"No, apparently he is meeting the Home Secretary at twelve."

"At the Home Office, Sir?"

"I believe so, why?"

"That would be the best time for me to have a chat with Celia Marsh."

"Ah yes, good thinking, Penny."

"Is there anything else, Sir?"

"Yes, I estimate that Vaughan will have Mrs Patterson delivered to Gibraltar in about ten to twelve days' time. What I would like is for you to arrange with the RAF to get her from there to our safe house in Chislehurst. You had better act as her escort for the journey, especially as you knew her late husband."

"It will be interesting to see who he dumped me for."

"Pardon?"

"I said that it will be interesting to see who it was he dumped me for," repeated Heathcote. "Is that the safe house that the Vaughans were put in after his initial run-in with Murata and his mob?"

"Yes that's the place, she will be well protected there and well feed if I know Ruby Finch," replied Campbell, "I didn't know that you and David Patterson were a, oh what is the term?"

"An item?"

"Yes, an item. I thought it was purely platonic. "

"No, it was the big thing, for me anyway, but that was, oh, over five years ago now. Lorna said it would never work out and she was right."

"I'll send someone else, if you can just sort out the RAF side of things."

"No, Sir, I'll go, it's perfectly all right, I was over it a long time ago."

"You're sure?"

"Yes, Sir, I'm sure," Heathcote replied in an emphatic tone. "As I said I was over it a long time ago."

"Okay, Penny, that's all for now I think."

"Oh I almost forgot, Sir, our check on the Binter Canarias flight from Nouakchott to Las Palma had Pieter Scheepers and Karl van Rooyen as being on board."

"No Henri Vanderkloof or Jan Vermeulen?"

"No, Sir."

"Interesting. I'll send a message to Cecil Boyd, it shouldn't upset his plans. Oh by the way Lorna Parker-Davis is going on leave soon if my memory is correct. Do you know where she is going?"

"I think she is off to the family's chalet somewhere near the Stubai Glacier in Austria."

"Excellent, would you go and sit at her desk while I have a few words with her."

When Lorna entered Campbell's office he offered her a seat then said, "You are going on leave this coming weekend I understand."

"Yes, Sir, do you need me to change it?"

"No, no, gosh no. It is just that I am anticipating the suspension of DELCO activities at some point in the near future but hopefully not before you go on holiday as I will need you to act as co-ordinator. The trigger will be a call from me using my best Cockney accent. Your main task will be to get Vaughan back to the UK, but there may be other work. You are not to return here until I tell you that it is safe to do so."

Lorna turned a little pale and though wanting to know more knew that this was not the time to ask questions, she trusted Campbell, he was the straightest man she had ever known and like Heathcote, she would walk through fire for him if he asked her to.

"Right, Sir. Is there anything else, Sir?"

"Yes, here's two hundred pounds, go out and buy yourself a new mobile phone and let me, and only me, have the number."

***

At MI6 headquarters Celia March looked up and smiled as Alex Campbell entered her office.

"Good morning, Alex, how are you today?"

"Very well thank you, Celia, and yourself?"

"I'm fine thank you. How is Caroline?"

"She's very well, I left her this morning getting ready to meet her ladies group at the gym. She has been trying to get me to sign up."

Celia March chuckled, "A beanpole like you should stay well away from gyms."

Campbell leaned his head in the direction of Sir Andrew's office door.

"I understand that Sir Andrew is expecting you, so go straight in, Alex."

As Campbell entered Sir Andrew's office he saw the head of the service loading his briefcase with files.

"That looks as if the meeting with the Home Secretary is going to be hard work, Sir Andrew."

"It is to assess the true number of potential Jihadists likely to return from Syria, and you will appreciate how hard it has been to get that put together in twelve hours. You can bet when I get there all he actually wants is a headline grabbing number to make it look as if the Government really knows the problem," replied Sir Andrew Averrille sourly. "But what can I do for you, Alex?"

"You will recall our last conversation, the one in connection with Agent Vaughan."

"Ah, you're going to tell me he is back and out the door, good show."

"No, Sir Andrew, I am afraid I'm not, in fact I am here to tell you that circumstances have arisen that required me to send Vaughan on a recovery mission."

"What?"

"Some months ago I visited Angola in response to intelligence received and made contact with David Patterson's widow. The intelligence clearly indicated that Patterson was executed by either an illegal arms trader by the name of Vermeulen, or his employees. Vermeulen is Mrs Patterson's stepfather."

"There we are, Alex, that's the link, Leonard Staunton was right, David Patterson had been turned then tried to swindle this Vermeulen character."

Campbell ignored the interruption. "On learning of the possibility of her stepfather's involvement, which came as a complete surprise, Mrs Patterson agreed to spy on Vermeulen and in so doing has supplied us with some valuable information concerning arms shipments. One shipment in particular we needed to stop, but in doing so it meant informing the Angolan Government of a shipment that had gone into Cabinda Province, and exposing Vermeulen."

"And you are using Vaughan to get this woman to safety? Why, what makes her so damned important, she was part of that bloody business."

"No, she wasn't, Sir Andrew, she was completely unaware of the murky side of her stepfather's business activities."

"I find that very hard to believe, Alex."

"We now know that in a gunfight in Rosso on the border between Senegal and Mauritania, Mrs Patterson escaped from her stepfather and managed to take with her his coded notebook, which, I am very anxious to read."

"Can't the RAF or Navy help?"

"We have exhausted those avenues, Sir Andrew. What it does mean is that I was forced into extending Agent Vaughan's employment with us."

"How long for?"

"Probably another month, maybe two."

Sir Andrew sighed, "Well I suppose we will just have to put up with it. I'll let Leonard Staunton know."

"No, Sir Andrew, this is a very very delicate operation. If the least whisper gets out before we can act on the information in that notebook, years of work between ourselves and the CIA could be destroyed."

"And you are trusting Vaughan with this?"

"I have no choice, he is the only person in reach and with the skills to do this and get Mrs Patterson and that notebook back here. Success will be a major feather in our cap, not only with the States, but also in the European Intelligence world if he succeeds."

"I still think Staunton should be in the loop, Alex."

"No, Sir Andrew, if he were to inadvertently make a move thinking to assist Vaughan it may well bring failure. You really must trust me on this one."

There was a long pause before Sir Andrew answered.

"All right, Alex, but on your head be it."

As Campbell left Sir Andrew's office he heard Celia March announce the arrival of Sir Andrew's car and point out that it would be at least a twenty minutes drive to the Home Office.

Needing time to think, Campbell chose to walk back to the DELCO offices. Had he done the right thing in informing Sir Andrew and by so doing risk losing the notebook and placing Vaughan and Mrs Patterson in danger. Where was the leak and why was Vaughan's outstanding achievements in Madeira being so roundly criticised.

When he finally got back to his desk, Campbell saw that there was a message waiting for him. Signing in on his computer he read Cecil Boyd's report on the Rosso incident and learnt that in addition to Anna-Maria's mother being killed, Karl van Rooyen had also been shot dead. He lifted the phone and tapped in Heathcote's extension.

"Yes, Sir."

"Cecil Boyd informs that Karl van Rooyen was killed in the shoot-out at Rosso."

"So Vermeulen used his passport for the trip to Las Palma, neat."

"Neat, as you say, Penny, very neat. On that other matter did you have a chance to speak to Celia March?"

"Yes, Sir. She obviously dislikes Senior Agent Staunton but it appears that he has had very regular face to face with Sir Andrew recently. Currently Staunton is in Madeira assessing the impact of the attempted coup among some of his civil service contacts there."

"Thank you, Penny, I had no idea that he also worked for our Foreign Office, but I suspect that it is connected with Sir Andrew's concerns about Vaughan's actions."

CHAPTER 4

It was early evening the following day when Staunton saw Sonia again, entering the bar; on this occasion she appeared to be meeting a young girl whom Staunton took to be another of her escorts and seating himself behind a group of tourists was able, by moving slightly from side to side, to watch the women's meeting without being seen. Finishing their drinks both women got up and left, Sonia getting into her car and the other woman walking off towards the old town restaurant area.

Leaping into his own car, Staunton managed to pull out into the traffic only three cars behind Sonia, who, after weaving through side streets, took the most direct route onto the expressway to Ribeira Brava. Arriving there, Staunton had expected her to turn left into the town but instead she turned right, driving across the island to São Vicente where she left her car parked at the side of the road, walked up the hill, and along a short broad walkway to a Mercedes four-by-four parked at the end of a cul-de-sac. As Staunton drove past the end of the walkway he caught a glimpse of her getting into the passenger side of the vehicle and turning his car round at the next junction, he headed back to the main road, arriving in time to see the Mercedes turning towards the sea and the road that ran along the north of the island to Porto do Moniz. There were two cars between him and the Mercedes, and by the speed that they were travelling, Staunton felt relaxed and confident that neither Sonia nor her driver were aware that they were being followed. At Porto do Moniz the Mercedes threaded its way down to the waterfront before turning left and stopping outside the Esmeralda Brilhante supermarket on the Rua do Lugar, a one way street.

Sonia was being chauffeured by a tall strongly built man, who Staunton guessed to be one of Reshetnikov's minders. Getting out of their car the man hurried into the supermarket only to emerge again two minutes later to look up and down the street carefully before indicating to Sonia that it was safe for her to leave the vehicle and go into the shop.

Waiting outside, the man employed his time using a chamois leather and duster to clean imagined blemishes from the vehicle's immaculate paintwork; every now and again looking up and taking professional sweeping glances of the surroundings, searching for any potential threat. Staunton was impressed, Sonia's minder knew his job and was doing it very well, therefore would have to be dealt with first for his original plan to work. Staunton's basic idea had been to execute Reshetnikov in order to clinch the arms deal, but the sight of a professional minder, and maybe others, required a new plan which would be to divulge Reshetnikov's location to the authorities.

After half an hour Sonia emerged from the shop and indicated that she needed assistance; Staunton settled himself ready to tail the Mercedes.

This time it was the minder that got into the passenger seat after opening the driver's door for Sonia, and to Staunton's surprise, fondly patting her bottom as she went to step up into the vehicle. Staunton waited for her to reverse out into the road before he started the engine. Seeing Sonia indicate that she was making a right turn at the crossroads beyond the shop Staunton guessed that she would be taking the road that ran along the top of the high ground above the north-west coast of the island. Pulling out from the kerb he accelerated hard before slowing quickly at the crossroads to confirm that the Mercedes was going straight across the next junction. Again harsh acceleration was required to get him in a position to see his quarry's direction of travel along the main road. Reaching the junction he was pleased to find only one car between him and the Mercedes and the driver of it going quickly enough for him to stay in touch through the series of steep climbs and hairpin bends that led away from the town. They had continued in convoy for a few kilometres when the car in front slowed for some distance before taking a left turn, a manoeuvre that opened the gap between him and Sonia's car considerably. Foot hard on the accelerator and doing his best at racing gear changes, Staunton made the junction with the ER110 just in time to spot the Mercedes' tail-lights far ahead on the road that led to Achadas do Cruz. The road ran down the side of a very deep valley before turning sharply right to climb again onto high ground. Keeping a safe distance along the winding road required patience and for a moment he feared that the Mercedes had got too far ahead, before seeing it stopped in a driveway waiting for heavy iron gates to open. Driving past, Staunton kept his eyes on the road ahead, satisfied that he had found the Russian's hideout. Taking the second turning on the right he drove around the upper part of Achadas do Cruz eventually finding a snack bar where he bought something to eat and drink, then drove north-west away from the village centre to the cliff top cable car built to enable farmers to reach their fields far below near the shoreline.

To his surprise he found that he had a mobile phone signal and taking advantage of the opportunity made a call. "Hi, sweetie, any news?"

"Nothing certain, Lenny, but there is something going on as Commodore Campbell has been having lots of face to face with Sir Andrew today."

"See if you can look at the DELCO mobile phone log, there should be a subject title against the call identifier, 'Yachtsman'."

"I'm on at 0400 tomorrow and there aren't many people about at that time so I'll have a better chance but if I get caught I could be in a lot of trouble, Lenny."

"Well, make sure you are not caught, sweetie," said Staunton in a tone that made fun of her fears. "Oh, and I will be flying back via Amsterdam in a couple of days or so and you know what that could mean."

At the other end Alice giggled. "Oh, Lenny, will it be like the one you showed me before?"

"Wait and see, sweetie."

Having set the delightfully obedient Alice Morgan a task that might reveal Vaughan's current objective, Staunton eased the back of the car seat and enjoyed the snack and fizzy drink. The day was working out well, Vaughan was no longer someone to risk bumping into, and he had found the Reshetnikov hideout with amazing ease. A self-satisfied grin spread across his face, now all he had to do was confirm that Reshetnikov was at the property and get a message to the authorities. The arrest of Reshetnikov would not only remove the immediate competition but present the possibility of him revealing the existence of the arms cache. Faced with those chances, Boris would have no option other than to do an immediate deal at a lower price before the police or army came knocking on his door. Staunton's smile widened.

Getting out of the car he opened the boot and lifted the floor, reaching down into the spare wheel space, he removed the night camouflage suit and night vision goggles hidden there. Looking around to make sure he was not being watched he took off his jacket and slipped into the suit. He picked up the goggles then got back into the car and drove off, heading for a track near to the property where he could hide the car. It took three passes before he settled on the best trackway, one which lay approximately half way between the last property in the village and Reshetnikov's hideout. Cutting small branches from surrounding trees, Staunton camouflaged the car as best he could then made his way through the woodland, south of the property. There was no moonlight to help and twice he stumbled noisily as he sought a way through the woodland towards the glow of the house lights in the distance. After some two hundred metres he came to the edge of the trees and was faced with an area of low scrub beyond which was a high wall. Carefully, he studied the wall noting the cameras and security lighting positions that gave a clear message regarding the paranoid state of the occupant. Breaking cover with the risk of being illuminated and identified on camera did not appeal, so Staunton chose the second option of climbing a tree to see over the wall.

Keeping to the wood, he picked his way through the trees until he judged that he was opposite the main sources of illumination from the property, and finding a tall tree some way back from the edge of the woodland climbed up high into the branches. Peering through the light foliage he could see a formal garden on the other side of the wall and beyond it a narrow terrace which ran along that side of an elegantly designed bungalow. The light source was from a room in which sat the woman he knew as Sonia, watching television. She appeared to be on her own, and seeing no other room illuminated, Staunton settled himself in for a long wait. It was more than an hour before the man he was searching for, Reshetnikov, made an appearance, shuffling across the room to turn off the television and wake Sonia. Staunton, with a self-satisfied sneer on his face, climbed down to the ground and made his way back to the car.

Two hours later in his hotel room and wearing latex gloves, Staunton was cutting out words from a newspaper to form a message to Colonel Castelo-Lopez, informing him of the whereabouts of the Russian he was seeking. Addressing an envelope, writing with his left hand, he put the message inside and sealed it, planning to leave the hotel very early in the morning to deliver it.

***

By eight o'clock on the morning of his second day at sea, Vaughan had sight of the highest point on Selvagem Grande, now only some twelve miles away and a little to starboard of the bow. Checking the chart and estimating the effect of the current in the area he decided to wait until he got closer before making any course corrections. During the night he had been passed by the Aida Sol cruise ship making her way from Madeira to the Canaries and a little later the P&O ship Azura passed in the opposite direction; apart from that the ocean was empty of shipping, and after the bustle ashore, a rather lonely place. Earlier in the morning he had come across a pod of dolphins and seeing them race along the side of the yacht he left the cockpit and, clipping his life line onto the jackstay, went forward to watch as they played a game of chicken criss-crossing through the water, narrowly missing the bow as if inviting the yacht to join in the game. One in particular had swum alongside with its head out of the water looking at Vaughan and making a clicking noise which he answered by clapping his hands. The game went on for maybe a quarter of an hour before the pod left as suddenly as they had arrived, leaving Vaughan alone again but enriched by their brief visit. Returning to the cockpit he unclipped the lifeline and went below to mark up the chart and take his rest.

It was now time to plan for his arrival, and looking at the notes he had made concerning the anchorage he saw that holding was not good. The seabed was rather rocky according to a fellow sailor he had been talking to at the yard, his advice had been to find a large rock ashore and tie a chain loop to it on the end of a long warp, so based on that advice Vaughan readied the long kedge anchor chain and warp. His idea was to enter the bay beneath the wardens' house and anchor by the bow then take the chain and warp ashore in the dinghy and search for a suitable rock around which to secure the chain, then row back laying out the warp as he went. Once back on board he could then take up the slack in the shore line to take the load. By setting the small storm sail on the backstay he could hold the yacht away from the rocky shore using the northerly breeze.

An hour later Vaughan noted that the current in the area had dragged the yacht west and with the outlying islet of Palheiro da Terra now bearing one six zero degrees he started the engine and disconnected the auto helm. Helming manually, his fingers feeling the minor trembling of the yacht's rudder from the propeller wash, Vaughan stood up onto the port hand cockpit bench, and holding onto a backstay to keep his balance, concentrated on the sea ahead, looking for shoals. The depth sounder, now in range, showed the seabed to be very uneven the nearer he got to the islet.

His aim was to set the yacht on a course to pass between the islet Palheiro da Terra and the much smaller Palheiro do Mar that he could just see off to starboard of his course. Now, he brought the yacht on a heading of one eight zero degrees which would take it parallel to Selvagem Grande clear of obstacles further down the channel. Though not as high as Grande Deserta the cliffs were equally forbidding and Vaughan marvelled at the seamanship of those who years ago had landed on these hostile shores.

All around him hundreds of petrels and shearwaters were skimming just above the waves in their search for food, confirming the islands' attraction to ornithologists.

Approaching the south-west tip of Selvagem Grande he heaved the dinghy from the stern locker ready to take it forward onto the foredeck where there was room to inflate it, and with the south-westerly point of the island abeam he rounded the yacht up into the wind, rolled in the headsails and dropped the mainsail, then hurried forward to inflate and launch the dinghy, securing it astern before cautiously motoring in, searching for the Portuguese Navy's mooring buoy. As he closed on it the bay opened up and he could clearly see the wardens' house at the head of the slipway. Leaving the buoy well to starboard he entered the shelter of the bay and taking the engine out of gear he allowed *"La*

Mouette sur le Vent" to drift inshore along the line of the slipway, coming to a standstill in some five metres of water where he let go the main anchor and allowed the offshore breeze to gently push the yacht backwards until thirty metres of anchor chain were laid. Putting the engine astern the yacht dragged the anchor a short distance before it bit and Vaughan felt that it would hold sufficiently until he had rigged the long warp shore line. Taking the line ashore in the dinghy and returning to set the small storm sail on the backstay went according to plan and leaving the yacht again Vaughan rowed back to the shore to pay a call on the wardens and discuss pilotage and navigation marks. The exercise was mainly to justify his presence on the island although it might prove useful should there be any problem during the rendezvous. The trip ashore went well and Vaughan found that his visit coincided with a sighting of a pair of Zino's Petrels, a rare bird thought to have been extinct demonstrating the importance of the wardens' presence on the islands protecting these rare and vulnerable species. The wardens gave him several hours of their time discussing the islands, their shores, and the work they do to protect this valuable nature reserve. Armed with a mass of notes concerning the islands' safe passages he returned to his yacht as the sun was setting to spend the evening writing up the information.

***

In Madeira, after delivering the newsprint tip-off, Staunton had taken a leisurely walk along Funchal's redeveloped seafront; until Reshetnikov had been arrested there was not much he could do. He had reached the new lagoon when his mobile chirped and Alice Morgan's message appeared on the screen. Arriving at work earlier than she would have normally enabled her to search the communications records for the call sign "Yachtsman" which gave her access to Vaughan's traffic and the coded message sent without being noticed, then, talking to the clerk that sent the message she saw on the man's note pad the word "Daring". For Staunton it was difficult to decode the message but with knowledge of the rendezvous co-ordinates and the Western Saharan boat identification number, he had even more negotiating clout with Vermeulen, who was only too happy to accept Staunton's deal on the Kazakov weaponry in exchange. The only inaccurate part of Alice Morgan's information was her assumption that the word "Daring" written in the margin of the notepad she saw open on the desk, referred to HMS Daring, one of the Royal Navy's latest destroyers. Staunton, in passing on that snippet of information, unwittingly ensured that the attack would be carried out immediately the fishing boat was found; with the threat of a naval destroyer laying in wait, the quicker the fishing boat was found, dealt with, and Vermeulen's departure from the area achieved, the better.

***

Earlier that morning Vaughan had launched the dinghy over the side of the yacht once more, securing it amidships. The reflected swell in the bay made fitting the outboard motor a tricky operation, but after a struggle he was ready to take the dinghy on a complete circumnavigation of Selvagem Grande to check his notes on navigation hazards and mark up the chart. Returning around mid-afternoon he went ashore again for a final discussion with the wardens, learning more about the islands and their interesting history that included claims of buried pirate treasure.

Returning aboard *"La Mouette sur le Vent"* Vaughan went below for a few hours rest in preparation for a long night. The alarm woke him at midnight and he moved swiftly, making coffee and sandwiches before preparing for departure. With the yacht's engine ticking over, storm jib stowed and coffee cooling, Vaughan was over the side and into the dinghy to go ashore to recover the kedge chain and warp. Speed was essential now as the breeze had strengthened threatening to cause her bow anchor to drag once the shore line was released. Scrambling up the rocky shore he took the loop off the large rock and dumped it into the dinghy. Once in the dinghy himself he hauled on the warp to pull himself back to the yacht where he hurriedly heaved the warp and chain onto the side deck, ensuring that all was clearly inside the guardrails. Boarding the yacht he went forward and hauling in the main anchor, stowed it and, returning to the cockpit, conned the yacht back out to sea. Clear of the Navy's buoy, he let the yacht drift again while he stowed everything away properly.

Throughout his life Vaughan had been both blessed and cursed by a feeling in the pit of his stomach that, invariably was a portent of unpleasant things about to happen; that feeling was as strong now as it had been when he had entered Amelia's apartment on the afternoon of Esteves' exposure and death. It was now the reason why Vaughan decided not to show navigation lights on that dark moonless night, a decision that was probably about to save his life.

***

Almost exactly two days earlier Cecil Boyd had gently woken Anna-Maria, "It's time to go, my dear."

"Go where?" she asked, bleary eyed, having been woken from a deep sleep.

"Down to the port; London has arranged your escape from this godforsaken country. I am to accompany you, I suspect to avoid you receiving too much attention from the boat's crew."

The news that he was to accompany her brought both relief and pleasure.

"Are you coming with me all the way back to London?"

"Oh, I wish, but duty calls here I'm afraid. 'Men at some time are masters of their fates. The fault, dear Anna-Maria, is not in our stars, but in ourselves, that we are underlings'."

Anna-Maria smiled, she had taken a liking to the gay Cecil Boyd. The man was extremely well read and would use quotes from Cicero and Shakespeare to Oscar Wilde and Bernard Shaw, tossing them into conversation like well-judged largess to an appreciative crowd.

About an hour later Anna-Maria emerged from her room dressed in the Sahrawi style, covered from head to foot in a densely patterned bright blue cloth with only her dark brown eyes visible.

"How do I look?"

"You could pass for a wealthier local in the marketplace with ease."

"Thank you for going out and purchasing all this."

Boyd waved away her gratitude with a tut and upward flip of his hands, "We shouldn't be stopped on the way to the port but if we are leave the talking to me, women's voices are not welcomed by officialdom here."

The "hurried breakfast" was a very tasty omelette. "I've thrown a few items of food together for the voyage, God knows what there would be to eat otherwise," said Cecil, pointing towards a sizeable hamper in the kitchen.

It was still dark when they reached Port El Aaiun, the phosphate exporting terminal and fishing port just south of the Moroccan border. The journey had thankfully been uneventful and their Sahrawi driver, a man of few words. Finding Beni Tamek's fishing boat proved rather difficult amongst the huge fleet in port at the time. Eventually, after numerous enquiries they were directed to the very end of the jetty where they found a slightly smarter looking craft than the floating wrecks that appeared to make up the rest of the fleet.

Getting out of the car Anna-Maria gagged at the pervading smell of rotting fish and quickly held her lightly perfumed handkerchief over her nose and mouth in a vain attempt to filter out the odour.

"The smell will not be so obvious once we get to sea, my dear," said Cecil as he guided her to the narrow boarding plank.

Western Sahara's fishing fleet was very much the poor relation amongst the nations along that part of the African coast and did not have access to the Spanish waters surrounding the Canary Islands or those legitimately claimed by Morocco. This meant that their voyage would have to avoid known fishing areas and stay out of sight of land until it reached the rendezvous point. Right of passage, however, could not be challenged and the absence of fishing nets and dismantling of trawl beams made it visibly obvious that Beni Tamek's boat was not engaged in any illegal fishing activity, but was under private charter of some sort. In the tiny crew quarters below it was apparent that great efforts had been made to clean the area and remove the crew's normal possessions, leaving the two bunks available for their passengers.

Beni Tamek was lean in stature with a wizened face and deeply tanned skin; he was much older than his crew – El Ghalia, and the boy, Salem. All of them spoke a form of Spanish that Anna-Maria struggled to understand, but which Cecil Boyd was obviously accustomed to. The introductions were brief and the boat got underway only minutes after their arrival on board.

"Time and tide wait for no man. Beni Tamek wants to be well clear of the coast before it gets light," said Cecil, looking into the tiny galley with its small paraffin stove secured to the bulkhead by a piece of wire. "Just as I thought, at sea these men live like animals, and probably not much better ashore."

As the sun rose, spreading its light across the vast ocean, Anna-Maria and Cecil were invited up into the wheelhouse where Beni Tamek proceeded to deliver a strong complaint about EU and US concessions to Spain and Morocco regarding fishing in Western Saharan waters. Despite words to the contrary, Moroccan fishing vessels still plundered the seas of all fish stocks, leaving the fishermen of Western Sahara with little to catch. Then he launched into a tirade about oil resources and the apparently inevitable theft of such priceless commodities by Britain and America without any advantage to his nation. The complaining fisherman went on for almost half an hour before Cecil Boyd was able to point out that Western Sahara was not recognised as being an autonomous nation, and its neighbours, fearing its government would fall to Jihadi extremism, seriously complicated the situation with regard to the country's status in the world. At that point, Anna-Maria decided that the deck would be a better environment, and leaving the wheelhouse found a shady spot on the port side of the vessel where she could sit looking out over the waist high bulwark at the ocean. The motion of the boat as it rode gently along at just under ten knots soon lulled her to sleep to be woken by El Ghalia sometime later signalling food was prepared.

Under Cecil's supervision, Salem had been tasked with cleaning the galley and when the work had been completed Cecil began preparing a meal. The lunch, comprising a vegetable soup and herb pancakes brought lavish praise from both master and crew.

Cecil had added to Salem's duties with an order for him to clean the boat's ancient sea toilet, summoning the boy back twice to do a more thorough job; the result was that for the rest of the day Salem refused to speak to anyone and spent his time sulking on deck.

By nightfall they were sailing along, unlit, halfway between Morocco and the island of Lanzarote. Apart from two container vessels and a phosphates carrier from El Aaiun, they had not seen another craft, something that cheered Beni Tamek considerably.

The night passed without incident but the following morning they found that they were being shadowed by a Spanish trawler. No attempt was made to communicate and after two hours the trawler altered course southward, away from them.

***

On receiving Staunton's information Vermeulen knew he had to act immediately, and now, potentially, with the knowledge of his stepdaughter's whereabouts, hurried in search of Maurice, his host and new found friend. The Frenchman, one of Staunton's more trustworthy informants regarding the recreational lives of French and Spanish political elite, was in his study receiving the previous night's drug money from one of his young pushers.

"Maurice, I'd like to charter your boat for a couple of days."

The Frenchman waved the boy away and turned his attention to his guest. "Where would you like to go?"

"Leonardo has discovered the location of that little bitch of a stepdaughter I am looking for. He tells me the UK's SIS has arranged a rendezvous near to the Selvagen Islands."

"So she is the one who betrayed you to the authorities, Jan." Vermeulen nodded. "They have chosen a very remote place for the rendezvous, does he know how she is getting there?"

"Yes, she is on board a Western Saharan fishing boat going to a spot near to an island called Selvagem Grande shortly after midnight tonight. Leonardo gave me the number of the boat but we need to find it before they get to the place."

"Why is that?"

"If British Intelligence services are meeting them they will be armed and skilled," replied Vermeulen, not revealing the warning from Leonard Staunton that the rendezvous was probably with HMS Daring. "I don't want to get involved in a gunfight with highly trained men."

***

On board the fishing boat the sea remained empty of shipping until after dark when the lights of another vessel appeared in the distance and Cecil noted that it appeared to be carrying out some form of search pattern. As the hours passed, slowly the vessel came closer though not yet close enough for its radar to pick them out amongst the swell and wave clutter and, without their own navigation lights, an approaching vessel would need to be a lot closer to identify them as a solid target.

Beni Tamek endeavoured to coax more speed out of the old and tired engine and for some time it appeared that they were increasing the gap, until, some four miles from the rendezvous, the pursuing vessel changed tactics and came straight towards them.

"They have seen us, Senhor Boyd. I think they went further south on their last sweep and that meant we show up more big on their radar."

"Can you ask El Ghalia and Salem to get that old dinghy ready and put the outboard on it, I will buy you a new dinghy and outboard, I promise."

Beni Tamek studied Cecil Boyd's face carefully before shouting for Salem and giving him the orders. As the young boy turned to get El Ghalia from below, Boyd could clearly see the fear in the youth's eyes.

"It will be all right, Salem, once the lady is in the dinghy and away from us the people in the other boat will not have reason to harm us."

"They are closing very fast, Senhor."

"So I see, Senhor Tamek, so I see," replied Boyd, unable to think of anything that would give them time. "Keep going and don't alter course, we must get as near to the rendezvous as we can before they reach us."

Boyd could now see through the darkness the bow wash and spray thrown up by the speeding vessel approaching them and hoped that the rendezvous vessel was in range and able to intervene.

"That is too fast and too small for fishery protection vessel, Senhor Boyd," said Tamek, his voice giving away his fear. "I think we have big problem, Senhor!"

Then they were caught like a rabbit in the headlights of a car as the searchlight from the approaching vessel blinded them and the order to heave-to and prepare to be boarded was heard loud and clear.

"We must get you over the side and away now," said Cecil, turning to Anna-Maria.

Anna-Maria looked at Cecil in alarm. "What? We are in the middle of an ocean."

"This is not a fishery protection arrest, Anna-Maria. This is that stepfather of yours. If you are not found on board they will search for you somewhere else, then we can turn back and pick you up."

"How do you know that it's not fishery protection?"

"Neither the Portuguese nor the Spanish fishery protection vessels can reach thirty-five to forty knots and they would always identify themselves by radio first."

"They will find my things on board."

"Get them now and hurry. I will get the crew to launch the dinghy."

Anna-Maria almost fell down the companionway ladder from the wheelhouse to the crew mess below. Grabbing the holdall she looked around to ensure she had left nothing behind that would hint at her having been on board. Unzipping the holdall she checked the contents and realised that Vermeulen's notebook was missing. The stress of the moment froze her brain and she panicked and started to lift the berth cushions frantically. Where was she when she last tried to unravel the codes? She stood still and closed her eyes; yes she was in what passed for a galley when the call went up about a fast moving vessel approaching. Stepping into the narrow space she saw the book on the paraffin stove, and snatching it up she rushed over, rammed it into the holdall and made for the companionway ladder.

"Senhor Tamek. Let them get alongside us but do not stop. I will try and talk to them and keep their attention whilst Senhora Ronaldo gets away," said Cecil, unaware that their identity had been leaked.

Tamek nodded and turned to look forward into the darkness beyond.

"Go out the starboard side and lower yourself down to the deck over the forward rail, you can't use the steps otherwise they will see you," said Cecil.

Anna-Maria kissed him hurriedly, opened the wheelhouse door and with Cecil's help slid out over the rail and holding onto the wing deck frame lowered herself down, then let go to drop the last metre to the main deck. Looking up she saw Cecil leaning out lowering her holdall, and catching it she turned to El Ghalia who was pointing over the vessel's side. As she looked over she could just make out the dinghy bouncing against the boat's side on the bow wash. The crewman placed a loop of rope over her head and she put her arms through and grasped hold. El Ghalia then indicated for her to climb over the side, then nodding to her, he leant forward and lowered her down the vessel's side. When she felt her feet in firm contact with the dinghy she waved her hand and with that he let go and she fell in a heap into the ancient Zodiac dinghy, bruising her knee on the pair of oars and banging her head on the thwart. Her holdall dropped onto her feet with a thud then suddenly the fishing boat was gone and the dinghy was bouncing wildly in its wake.

Looking up she saw the two vessels were now on parallel courses with the other vessel still playing its searchlight on the fishing vessel wheelhouse and the loudhailer barking the order in Spanish for the fishing vessel to heave-to and prepare to be boarded. She could just make out the podgy form of Cecil standing at the head of the port side wheelhouse steps apparently shouting back and buying her that precious time to disappear further into the darkness. Another demand for the fishing boat to heave-to was heard, but still Beni Tamek kept the rusting ancient craft ploughing steadily abeam to the gentle swell of the Atlantic.

Then it happened, a burst of small arms fire from the deck of the searchlight vessel. Anna-Maria gasped, surely Beni Tamek will obey now and soon the searchlight will be sweeping the sea for her. She went to reach for the oars then saw the outboard motor on the dinghy's transom and trying to calm herself she quickly talked herself through the sequence David had taught her on their boat trips up the river.

"Release the air vent to the fuel tank, that knob on the top. Turn on the fuel tap, ah, here I think yes, now pull on the starter cord."

The battered outboard coughed but did not start. She pulled again, this time opening the throttle a little and the outboard fired up then died.

"Oh God, please make it start, oh please," she cried, tears now blurring her vision.

She fumbled for the handle to the pull cord and tried again and again until on the tenth pull the Yamaha sprung into life, and putting it in gear she turned the dinghy and set off on a course at right angles to that of the two boats. As she did so she heard another more prolonged burst of small arms fire. Looking back she saw the stern light of the attacking boat drift away from Beni Tamek's vessel, still illuminated by the searchlight, then there was an explosion aboard the fishing boat followed by another then another. Then the small arms fire started up again, but just in short bursts that suggested to Anna-Maria it was aimed at individuals trying to escape. As the dinghy topped a wave she could see the fishing boat in silhouette on fire, then, after several minutes, the silhouette shape changed as the vessel rolled over and sank. Now she had to hide quietly, so reaching towards the outboard, she cut the engine and lay on the dinghy bottom occasionally looking over the transom at the searchlight as it swept the area where the fishing vessel went down.

She was crying now, knowing in her heart that Cecil, Tamek, El Ghalia and Salem were dead, all because Cecil had been ordered to ensure that she escaped the clutches of Jan Vermeulen. Twenty minutes or so must have passed before she heard the faint sounds of the searchlight vessel's engines as it turned south-eastwards and powered away into the darkness, now without showing navigation lights.

Strangely the silhouette of the boat departing against the night sky brought an immense sense of fear as the prospect of being adrift upon the vast Atlantic dawned upon her. "Help! Help! Don't leave me, help!" she shouted, waving her arms high above her head, before realising the futility of her actions.

The question that now entered her mind was how far away from the rendezvous were they at the moment the fishing boat turned over and sank. Starting the outboard again she tried to motor back to the point where she thought the fishing boat had sunk and circled about in search of wreckage. Disorientated in the darkness she had missed the area altogether then she saw the flash of the lighthouse on Selvagem Grande and then four seconds later another flash, then another and her mind cleared. The island, she thought, aim for the island.

***

An hour earlier, satisfied that all was secure on deck and below, Vaughan had turned his yacht onto a course of one eight zero, planning to go south to clear the overfalls around Baixa da Joana and continue on that course until he reached the latitude thirty degrees zero seven fifty north, then turn to port and stay on that latitude eastward until he reached the rendezvous. He had motored some way south when lights appeared on the eastern horizon, as if someone was conducting a search. Vaughan was about to turn in the direction of the lights when he thought he heard shooting. Putting the engine in neutral he went forward away from the engine's noise to listen. There it was, clearer now, the sound of small arms fire, then two or three flashes then the sound of explosions followed by the loom of flickering light that lasted for only a minute or so before being extinguished.

Ian Vaughan knew that London would need confirmation of the loss of his passenger, his position was just under four miles from where he estimated the source of the gun fire and explosions to be, and aware that he needed to be able to hear clearly any cries for help he decided to sail rather than motor towards that location. Returning to the cockpit he freed the mainsheet, letting the boom swing downwind over the yacht's quarter, then hurrying to the mast, hoisted the mainsail. Back in the cockpit he hardened up the mainsheet and as the yacht started to make way released the roller reefing on the jib and hauled the jib sheet tight enabling the yacht to sail at a touch under forty degrees off the wind. Now he noted the log and compass bearing, estimating that in four nautical miles he should be near where the incident happened. The problem was when to show navigation lights, was it safe or was another vessel waiting in the dark to ambush him? Setting the auto helm, Vaughan went below to get his pistol and a spare clip of ammunition. Returning on deck he felt very vulnerable, he had had previous experience of small arms fire against a fibreglass hulled yacht and knew only too well the consequences. Momentarily in his mind he was back on the Chesapeake watching holes appear through the sides of the Victoria 34 he had been hiding behind. Snapping back to the present and his current strategy, he looked at the log then raised his night sight binoculars to his eyes and scanned the seas ahead. *"Not close enough to the danger zone yet, in ten minutes time maybe."*

Vaughan glanced at his wristwatch and noted the time as 0115 hours, his passenger would have been at the rendezvous early had they not been attacked. He had just passed the exact location, according to the GPS repeater on the yacht's cabin bulkhead, but was maybe a mile away from where he estimated the attack had taken place. Raising the night glasses, he searched the seas again in the hope of picking up the sight of a vessel adrift, but there was none. Ten minutes later he checked his position and noted that leeway and a slight shift in wind direction was taking him south of the desired latitude so he tacked the yacht and in doing so brought himself towards the few bits of flotsam from the fishing boat. It was a piece of timber from a hatch cover which *"La Mouette sur le Vent"* struck, that had Vaughan rounding the yacht up into the wind and furling in the jib.

Plugging in the powerful hand held flashlight to the cockpit socket, Vaughan directed the beam onto the sea surrounding the yacht, spotting almost immediately the body of Boyd, floating face down in the water surrounded by bits of a life ring and patches of diesel. As he looked the body suddenly jerked then the telltale fin broke the surface, making Vaughan shudder, there was nothing he could do to deprive the shark of its meal so he offered up a silent prayer. A wider sweep with the flashlight confirmed that he was alone in the area and satisfied that it was safe to do so he switched on the navigation and deck lights. Going to the mast he dropped the mainsail then started the engine and began slowly circling the area finding El Ghalia's body floating not far away. Vaughan of course was unaware of the bodies of Beni Tamek and Salem aboard the fishing boat that had carried both men down into the deep, trapped in the twisted metal of the wheelhouse. Unaware of their fate and unable to offer any service to the two corpses as they floated on the sea Vaughan carefully motored westward, clear of the area, then hoisted the sails and cut the engine in preparation to head to the Canary Islands. *"Just one more look around then head for Lanzarote and report the bad news."*

Then he heard a faint cry on the wind, was it someone calling, it was difficult to pick up the direction of the sound and it took several sweeps of the flashlight before he saw something like a flag billowing in the wind some distance away. Gybing the yacht through the wind he pointed it northward towards the target and set the auto helm. Making his way along the side deck he opened the port side gate, then returning to the cockpit retrieved the boarding ladder and a heaving line from the locker and taking back manual control of the tiller adjusted his course to come just downwind of what he now saw was an inflatable dinghy with a woman on board. Heaving-to, he brought the yacht to within a few metres of the dinghy and hurrying forward to the gate attached the boarding ladder.

"I'll throw you a line," shouted Vaughan, taking the heaving line and throwing it, ensuring that the heavily weighted end sailed well above the dinghy to avoid it hitting the woman.

Grabbing the line she pulled on it furiously dragging the dinghy alongside, then taking hold of the boarding ladder she said, "Thank God, I thought I was going to die, then I saw your lights but could not get the outboard to start again. Thank God you came."

"What's your name?" said Vaughan, looking down at her.

"Anna-Maria Ronaldo."

"I am Ian Vaughan. Your husband is dead I hear," said Vaughan, feeling embarrassed by the dark introduction phrase. "I have been sent by London to meet you and get you to Gibraltar."

The look of relief on her face on hearing the coded message was unmistakeable. "A man on a yacht! Cecil assumed it would be the Royal Navy sent to the rendezvous," she said, taking Vaughan's hand as she started to climb the boarding ladder.

"Afraid not, you have my company for several days instead."

"As long as I'm away from Africa and that evil man I do not mind whose company I am in."

"Is that all you were able to bring with you?" said Vaughan, looking down at the holdall slung over her shoulder. "What happened back there?"

"The fishing boat I was on was attacked, I think by people working for my stepfather, Jan Vermeulen."

"Let's get underway, you can tell me the details then. There is nothing left in the dinghy?"

"No, everything is here in this bag."

"Right. You go and sit in the cockpit, I better sink the dinghy just in case someone else comes searching."

"Can we search to see if Cecil or any of the crew survived?"

Vaughan looked at her seeing the tears running down her face. "I am sorry, Anna-Maria, I searched among what little wreckage remained on the surface. There were no survivors other than you I'm afraid."

Bursting into tears she stumbled into the cockpit and sat, head in her hands, crying her heart out as Vaughan pulled out his Leatherman and opening the blade climbed down the boarding ladder and cut slits in the dinghy's side tanks and watched as the weight of the outboard dragged it to the bottom.

Anxious to leave the scene quickly Vaughan had *"La mouette sur le Vent"* underway on a course of zero nine zero to windward as soon as he had stowed the boarding ladder and closed the gate. The next task was to get a hot drink inside her and some food for them both, so setting the auto helm he helped her below, sorted her out some dry clothes and whilst she was changing in the forward cabin he prepared the food and drink. An hour later Anna-Maria lay stretched out on the starboard settee in the main cabin snug under the duvet that had lulled Amelia de Lima and her son Zeferino to sleep weeks before. Only then could Vaughan return to his lone sailor routine, but now with the Glock 26 firmly thrust into the underarm holster worn beneath his lightweight wind-cheater. Twenty-five miles east of the point where Vaughan had found Anna-Maria, he tacked the yacht through ninety degrees and headed north, thankful to be on a course that was more indicative of his having set off from the Canary Islands.

The last time he had looked at her, Anna-Maria had been asleep and as he returned below to take his own rest period he was pleased to see that she still lay there, eyes closed and relaxed, the exhaustion of previous days overcoming the horrors of the more recent events.

***

Reshetnikov's arrest at dawn the day after delivery of the newsprint message had Staunton standing on the doorstep of the Kazakov house within minutes of the papers hitting the streets brandishing a copy of the newspaper announcing the arrest.

"Here, read this."

Boris read the article. "So?"

"Reshetnikov will happily trade information to secure his freedom. Think about it."

Boris had already thought about it and knew that Reshetnikov would reveal the existence of the weapons under questioning. Was there an alternative to doing a deal with the man in front of him who he really did not like. They haggled for two hours but finally Boris was forced to agree to the original price and later with Staunton's help, moved the cache to a new location.

Staunton knew that the final shipment of arms to Cabinda Province could wait until things had quietened down and new Cabinda separatist leaders identified. It was therefore a very happy and relaxed Staunton who stood at the hotel reception checking out, in readiness to board his flight to Lisbon.

As Staunton walked out to the waiting taxi his mobile rang. "Hello."

"Leonard?"

"Yes, Jan. Did you get the job done?"

"Yes, it's all okay now. We sank it and dealt with the flotsam."

"Good. Was Maurice able to help you?"

"Yes, he did very well. There will be a bonus waiting for you at Rolf Meijer's."

"That sounds interesting. Is there anything else? I'm just about to leave for the airport."

"No, I will contact you when I get to London and by then you should have been able to plan the shipping."

"Usual bar?" asked Staunton.

"Of course."

Sat in the back of the taxi Staunton looked out of the window but noticed very little of the passing scenery. Kazakov's cache of arms was an amazing bonus on top of closing the loopholes left after the Cabinda mess. Even Patterson's wife was out of the way, not that he thought her to be much of a threat, and with her went Vermeulen's black book, that was if it was she who had picked up the book in Rosso.

"You enjoy your stay on Madeira, Senhor?"

"Yeh, thank you, it was okay."

"You come back someday?"

"Oh yeh, I will come back."

Dropped off at the airport Staunton went straight to the service desk and hired a small locker paying for four weeks rental. Locating the locker he positioned himself such that he blocked the view from the CCTV camera and placed the box containing his pistol in the locker.

***

Over the first two days of the voyage to Gibraltar, Vaughan learnt the details of Anna-Maria's escape and the reasons why she had cause to fear for her life. As he learnt more about Vermeulen and his illegal arms business Vaughan began to realise why Campbell was being as cautious as he was in getting the young woman to a place of safety. *"This guy Vermeulen being tipped off in time to make an escape is no surprise, the chances of him having insiders in the Angolan government offices were a sure bet. The knowledge of the rendezvous however makes it certain that it was leaked from inside SIS. Campbell had communications tight so how come they got hold of the information, is there a mole inside DELCO? There was definitely something not right about the atmosphere. I have to believe that Campbell is on the side of the angels or else I am taking this women into a very nasty trap."*

The distance by the rhumb line on the chart was around six hundred and fifty miles, but most of the way would be with *"La Mouette sur le Vent"* hard on the wind on a port tack pushing against a Gulf Stream current of around one knot. The result reduced the yacht's speed over the ground to just over five knots despite the clean hull. For the most part the winds were fair and throughout the passage there were only two squalls, both of which were accompanied by heavy rain. The other thing that impeded progress was the need to stay out of sight of land until they reached the Straits, which meant turning onto starboard tack that reduced the rhumb line distance gain to only two nautical miles per hour for something like twelve hours.

As the days passed by, the look of fear on Anna-Maria's face every time she came up into the cockpit gradually declined until her hurried anxious scanning of the horizon in search of danger gave way to a casual check on the weather and sea state. The nightmares, however, continued to have her screaming and waking in floods of tears, that and her complete inability to grasp the basics of life aboard a thirty-six-foot yacht at sea soon placed some strain on Vaughan working his lone sailor routine.

When her being awake in the daytime matched his free work periods they spoke, she of her childhood and life after moving to South Africa, and he of his life as an engineer before joining the SIS. In looks she reminded him of Amelia de Lima in Madeira, both olive skinned and beautiful but that was where the comparison ended, for Anna-Maria, born with a silver spoon in her mouth, showed none of the energy that appeared to radiate from Amelia. She was, however, very intelligent and though languid in her movements had an athletic grace that showed a potential for swift action. She could also cook, provided that the yacht was not heeling more than ten degrees.

For Anna-Maria the voyage was in one way calming but in another stressful. Calming in that with each passing day she felt safer and less at risk of being found by her stepfather, but stressful in that she felt to be always in the way, and the harder she tried the less she succeeded in avoiding obstructing him at what appeared to be critical moments.

At just over six foot tall and ruggedly handsome he was obviously at one with the sea and the yacht and she would watch with fascination as his lithe muscular frame calmly moved about the boat with the confidence of an expert. Vaughan, she thought, was a much tougher man than David had been but kind, very kind, but there was a sadness about him that she could not quite understand.

They had been sailing for four days when suddenly she asked, "Did you ever meet my husband David?"

"No, I only joined a few months ago and frankly have been busy abroad ever since."

"Oh, I think you would have got on with David very well."

"What was he like?"

"He wasn't handsome, no male model, but he was just an adorable person, warm, friendly and very brainy. He was a geologist and when I met him worked for the Angolan Government and was supposed to be assessing the county's natural resources. I had no idea what he was really doing. They wouldn't let me see his body before his cremation, they said it would be too awful for me. Then I saw a report when I was being questioned about him being an arms trader, it was so terrible to read, and the man so cruel when he pointed to it saying that was what he deserved."

Hurriedly she raised her hand to wipe away tears. "We were so happy together then it all went terribly wrong and I felt so alone I went back to live with my mother and that horrible man she had married."

"Did you know before that Vermeulen was an illegal arms trader?"

"No! I had no idea, but I suspected that he had something to hide regarding his business so when Mr Campbell made contact and told me what Jan Vermeulen really was, I was more angry than surprised."

"So you have met Commodore Campbell have you? What do you think?"

"I only met him twice and each meeting was quite short, but he struck me as being a good honest man and… You now sometimes when you meet somebody you instantly trust them," Vaughan nodded. "Well, Mr Campbell was one of those."

"You don't meet many like that in this life," said Vaughan, mainly to himself.

There was something in the way that she had spoken of her husband and his death that convinced Vaughan of her complete honesty, whether it was her naivety or the tenderness in the way she had described her husband, he didn't know but it was obvious that she was previously unaware of his true occupation or that of her stepfather's.

They were nearing the end of the voyage when, after sitting on the windward side deck for most of the morning, she came into the cockpit as Vaughan was trimming the sails.

"I keep thinking of Cecil and the fishermen, I can't seem to get them out of my head. I think about that night and wonder if they… no, if I had been ready and got into the dinghy earlier, would they still be alive?"

Vaughan thought for a moment or two, he had considered the same scenario, "No I don't think so. I have a feeling that they knew you were on that boat, so if you had left earlier and they successfully stopped the boat and searched it they would still have sunk it then come looking for you. In their position that is what I would have done. Now they think that as the fishing boat refused to stop and be searched you must still have been on board and by sinking it they have dealt with you as well as any witnesses."

"Would you have thought that way as well?"

"Probably not. I would have wanted to make sure you had been dealt with and not assumed that by sinking the boat I had solved the problem."

Vaughan's cold logic response had the effect of chilling the relationship which, due to her relatively long term presence on board, was becoming very tiresome to him as it was. Apart from Vaughan saying, "Excuse me please" and she replying, "Oh sorry, am I in the way again". There was also her perfume, Vaughan had no objection to a conservative use of perfumes, in fact he had quite liked his ex wife's use of it and indeed Amelia de Lima's choice, but Anna-Maria's excessive use of Givenchy Ysatis was almost asphyxiating when he went below. At some point every day Vaughan had to remind himself that she was a passenger not a companion or crew member, but that did not stop those little irritations from irking him.

CHAPTER 5

In the early hours of day six from leaving the Selvagens, Vaughan closed to within mobile range of the north-western coast of Morocco, with about one hundred miles to sail before arriving at Gibraltar. His text message "Landed large tuna fish today" had Campbell and his small trusted team leaping into action. A request for the RAF to make available an A330 transport aircraft for a return flight to Gibraltar was granted and Lieutenant Penny Heathcote ordered to report to RAF Brize Norton the following morning at 0700 hours for the flight and to act as an escort to return flight passenger Anna-Maria Ronaldo. Confirmation sent back from Brize Norton was, however, intercepted and within minutes Vermeulen was contacted.

"Jan, it is Leonard, I have just heard that your little stepdaughter is alive."

"Don't joke, Leonard, she could not have survived, we were very thorough."

"I'm not joking, Jan, she is being met in Gibraltar tomorrow and flown back here."

"Christ, what can you do? Anything?"

"I'll try and organise an interception, but it will be expensive."

"Do it, if she has my notebook we will all be in the shit."

"I won't be, Jan."

"Oh yes you will, so believe me, it is more than my skin at stake here."

"You bastard, what have you done?"

"Just made a record of our business dealings and your valuable assistance with some necessary disposals."

"I should have known that you would try and stitch me up."

"When you play in the dirt, Leonard, you get dirty. That notebook has a lot of insurance policies in it and I am now making a claim on the one I have with you."

It took Leonard Staunton a full five minutes to calm down and make a plan, the first move of which was to contact Christiano Graciano who was at the time listening to a restaurant owner's excuse for delayed payment of protection money.

**

Throughout the day and night Vaughan had been busy on watch steering to avoid the busy shipping approaching the Straits of Gibraltar and shortly after Heathcote's flight landed had put in the final tack directing the yacht's bow towards the Rock and what he hoped would be the end of his mission.

Three hours later Vaughan had only just completed tying up alongside the pontoon in HM Naval Dockyard, Gibraltar, astern of HMS Sabre, when he saw Lieutenant Penny Heathcote walking towards him along the pontoon in the company of a Commander.

"This is Ian Vaughan, Sir."

"Ah, Mr Vaughan, I am Commander Daniel Frazer. May I see your I.D.?"

Vaughan pulled the badge folder from his hip pocket and flicked it open. "Anything wrong?" he asked.

"No, just form that's all."

"Commander, Lieutenant, this is Anna-Maria Ronaldo, my, er, passenger for the last few days."

Heathcote stepped forward smiling, "I'm Penny Heathcote. Your husband is dead I hear. I am so sorry to hear that," her sympathetic comment taking the edge off the brutality of the coded identification. "I have been requested by Commodore Campbell to meet you. As soon as you are ready I have a plane waiting at the airport to take you to England."

"I'll get transport lined up for you, Lieutenant, it will be waiting for you at the gate," said Frazer.

"Thank you, Sir," replied Heathcote, saluting.

As the Commander walked away Vaughan suggested that they went below whilst Anna-Maria gathered her things together. Once on board, Anna-Maria hurried to the forward cabin whilst Heathcote looked around the main cabin and chart table with interest. Vaughan studied her with mild amusement.

"Is she shipshape enough for you Lieutenant?"

Heathcote nodded. "Um, not bad, does she sail well?"

"Very well, though happier in deep water than creeks and marinas."

Quietly Heathcote asked, "How was your passenger?"

"Obviously not a yachtswomen so was always being tripped over, and if I never smell Givenchy Ysatis again it will be too soon. Other than that she was pleasant and attractive company."

Heathcote nose wrinkled as she sampled the air and smiled, "I see what you mean."

Anna-Maria did not take long to pack, returning from the forward cabin with the small holdall which she placed on the chart table.

"Mr Vaughan," said Heathcote, "I have been asked to instruct you to sail back to Dartmouth and report immediately to DELCO."

Vaughan snapped to attention and saluted. "Yes, ma'am."

Lieutenant Heathcote gave him her best withering look and, picking up Anna-Maria's holdall said, "Are you ready, Ms Ronaldo?"

"No, I wish to say goodbye to Ian."

"I'll walk with you to the harbour wall," said Vaughan.

As they started to walk along the pontoon towards the ramp leading up to the quayside Anna-Maria said, "Ian, thank you for saving my life out there. I'm sorry that I was so helpless on the boat and so much in your way, how you had the patience not to throw me over the side I do not know. So thank you again."

Turning to Lieutenant Heathcote she said, "I have so many people to thank for my being here, my prayers each night are very long for Cecil Boyd and those kind brave men who died on the fishing boat, my prayers are very sad indeed."

"You ran into trouble then," said Heathcote, looking round Anna-Maria towards Vaughan.

"Yes they did," replied Vaughan, "It's all covered in the report I'm about to e-mail to the Commodore."

"Oh, I see. You can't give me details?"

"It would take too long and you have a plane to catch," Vaughan replied.

They had reached the head of the ramp now and Vaughan stopped and turned to Anna-Maria. "Safe journey, Anna-Maria, the Lieutenant will look after you well, I am sure."

"Goodbye, Ian, and thank you again for everything." With that she turned away but after two steps turned back, and rushing at Vaughan, flung her arms around him and kissed him. "Goodbye," she said, giving Vaughan such a sad look as she broke away to fall in step with Heathcote. Then they were gone, walking towards the navy blue Land Rover Defender, parked just inside the archway leading out of the naval complex. Vaughan turned towards the Gibraltar Squadron office and within ten minutes was sat e-mailing his report to the Commodore.

***

On leaving Vaughan, Anna-Maria caught up with Lieutenant Heathcote, falling in step with her as they made their way across to the waiting Land Rover.

"How did you get on with Ian Vaughan?" Heathcote asked.

"Oh, all right I think. He tried to teach me how to sail but I'm not very good at that type of thing so for most of the time I felt in the way, but he was very nice about it. I wish I had not been so stupid and useless."

Heathcote opened the door to the Land Rover's rear seat and directed Anna-Maria to get in. "Slide over, I'll sit alongside you."

"To the airport, ma'am?" said the Marine driver.

"Yes please."

The traffic was not particularly heavy and Heathcote looked down at her watch then tried to work out how long it would take them to get back to RAF Brize Norton and London. "You are booked in at our special hotel in London where you will be safe until we have dealt with Vermeulen."

"You have no idea how comforting that is for me to hear. Since leaving Luanda I have been in fear of my life and then poor Cecil, Ben Tamek and the others all dead, just to get me out of Africa," blurted out Anna-Maria her eyes filling with tears of both sorrow and relief. "Even after Ian rescued me from the sea I felt that at any moment my stepfather or his thugs would appear and kill us."

"How did you end up in the sea?"

"The fishing boat taking us to the rendezvous was attacked by men on board a large powerboat. They were ordering us to stop and be boarded but Cecil ordered Ben Tamek to keep going..."

Distracted by Anna-Maria, Heathcote did not see the black Mercedes as it overtook them, then cut in front dangerously close and braking hard.

"What's this stupid bastard up to," shouted the Marine driver as he slammed on the brakes. "Oh shit, hold tight ladies we've got problems."

Fighting the gearbox the Marine tried to find reverse then saw the second Mercedes tight behind them. "Bugger, we're sandwiched. I'll try and push this bastard forward."

As he spoke, Heathcote saw two men leap from each of the Mercedes and race towards them.

The Land Rover jerked then stalled and as it did so the driver's window shattered and the Marine driver fell forward onto the steering wheel, dead.

Whether it was the shock or the speed that surprised Heathcote she did not know but she then found the door was open and a tall man in a dark suit was grabbing her arm and pulling her from the vehicle, whilst Anna-Maria was being similarly manhandled from the other side.

Struggling, Heathcote tried to break free before being spun round and pushed face first against the Land Rover with her left arm painfully pinned behind her back.

"Let go of me!" she shouted, before a rough hand grabbed her neck from behind.

"Shut up or I will shoot you dead just like that soldier there."

Heathcote was pushed, kneed and punched as they herded her towards the leading Mercedes and roughly shoved onto the back seat beside Anna-Maria with a man either side of them. Groping hands searched both girls for weapons, leaving them both feeling violated and terrified. Then from a seat behind them a man leant forward and slapped a strip of duct tape over their mouths then put thick cloth bags over their heads as the vehicle accelerated away turning left at the next roundabout. Though moving fast at first the driver soon slowed down, obviously trying to avoid attention. It did not appear that they had been driving for long when the vehicle turned sharply to the right and both the women's heads were pushed down between their knees as the vehicle stopped, waiting for something, then moving forward to park.

Dragged from the vehicle they were closely surrounded by the now rowdy escorts all the way into what they soon learnt was an apartment building. Penny Heathcote felt sure that such commotion could not be achieved without someone taking notice and reporting it, but she was wrong. The road outside of the Cormorant development had few pedestrians walking along it and drivers were more focused on the road than on a group of people entering a block of luxury apartments. Now pushed, dragged and kicked they were finally ordered to stand still while their hands and feet were tied and each then forced to lie down on the twin beds in the room. Only then was the bag blindfold removed allowing them to survey their surroundings and get a better look at their captors. There were seven of them, but where they were from Heathcote had no idea, except that they were not French, German, Italian or English speaking. Glancing at Anna-Maria, Heathcote saw the signs of understanding in the young woman's eyes and concluded that maybe the men were Spanish or Portuguese.

Making as much noise as the duct tape would allow Heathcote succeeded in gaining the attention of one of the gang who, stepping across to her bent low, his face inches away from her, said in Portuguese.

"You, shut up, you understand, I do not want to hear a sound from you."

She could not understand what he had said but it was the sneering way in which he said it that produced a reaction from a very annoyed Lieutenant Heathcote. The convulsive movement of her head caught the man completely by surprise as did the eye watering pain as her forehead made hard contact with his nose. The rest of the gang laughed but the injured man took his revenge by delivering two vicious full swing slaps across her face and had he not been restrained by the others he undoubtedly would have continued the attack.

As the rest of the gang herded him from the bedroom he called back in Portuguese, "It is not over you bitch, I will hurt you again, be sure of that."

***

The Glasgow kiss dished out to her abductor by Lieutenant Heathcote coincided precisely with the opening of the Naval Base general office door. Vaughan looked up to see Commander Frazer hurrying towards him with a troubled expression on his face and guessed that something serious had happened.

"Mr Vaughan…"

"Yes, Commander, what is it?"

"Did you know the officer who came to collect your passenger?"

"Yes, I know her. What's the problem?"

"The Royal Gibraltar Police have informed me that they have just found the Base Land Rover with a dead Marine driver inside. It appears that your Lieutenant Heathcote has snatched your passenger."

"No definitely not, that officer is one of the most trusted within SIS, there is no way she is responsible for this incident," Vaughan responded instantly, "Where was the vehicle found?"

"Near the junction of Queensway Road and Waterport Road, in fact right beneath the lettering Montagu Counterguard," replied Frazer. "Are you sure about this Lieutenant?"

"Absolutely sure," said Vaughan firmly, "My passenger was on the run from a very dangerous man who I suspect has excellent contacts here, or just across the border." Vaughan thought for a moment or two, then said, "I doubt if they would try and fly them out from here or for that matter try a ferry across to Tangier, so my guess is that they have either crossed the border into Spain or have a boat waiting to get them across the Straits."

"I'll get the RGP to check all vehicles going through," said the Commander, "Hopefully we will be in time but it's not very likely as our Spanish friends seemed to be working normally today and not causing long delays."

While the Commander got onto the RGP, Vaughan phoned Commodore Campbell.

"It's Vaughan, Sir, bad news I'm afraid. The vehicle taking the Lieutenant and Ms Ronaldo to the airport was intercepted, the driver killed, and both women are missing."

"Damn, this place has turned into a blasted sieve, how the hell did they know about that leg of her journey," replied Campbell. "See what you can do on the Rock, they are maybe being held there."

"Right, Sir, I'll do what I can."

"Vaughan, be very careful, both of those ladies are becoming more important by the minute. There is a very bad smell developing in the air around here and I suspect their safe return could dispel it. As soon as you can, buy a pay-as-you-go mobile and text me the number."

Vaughan sat for several minutes after the conversation taking in the Commodore's warning and considering what was likely to be the abductor's plan other than straight assassination.

"We need to find out if there were any witnesses," said Vaughan, as Commander Frazer put his phone down from a second call made.

"Yes, use my car." Then turning to an able seaman said, "Seaman Robson, here are the keys to my car, take Mr Vaughan and a Marine driver to where the Land Rover was stopped; when you get there see if the police will release the vehicle and tell the Marine to get it back here."

"Yes, Sir," replied the seaman, saluting smartly.

"You obviously are to wait with Mr Vaughan until he is ready to return."

The journey took them less than five minutes and on arrival they found two police cars and half a dozen police officers on the scene.

Inspector Lopez was in charge of the case and after checking Vaughan's I.D. he took him over to the vehicle where the dead Marine Sergeant was still slumped over the steering wheel.

"We have two witnesses who say that two other vehicles were involved, the first stopping in front of this one and the other pulling up right behind to stop this one from reversing. They say two men from each vehicle got out and took two ladies to the front vehicle and then both cars drove away. Only then they saw this man laid like this."

"Did they get a good look at the two vehicles?"

"They tell me that both were Spanish registered, black four-by-four Mercedes."

"When the two Mercs boxed the Land Rover was there any impact?"

"Wait please, I will ask."

Vaughan following close behind as the Inspector walked across to two men and a woman who were standing a few metres away from the Land Rover. "Was there any type of collision between the Land Rover there and the other two vehicles?"

"Yes, the Land Rover driver tried to ram the car in front out of the way."

"Was that before or after the men from the cars approached the Land Rover?"

The man thought for a few moments, his eyes closed trying to recall the sequence. "It was after the men got out of the cars," the man replied, "Yes, I am certain that as the men from the car in front jumped out and started to run towards the Land Rover that is when the Land Rover driver tried to push the car forward."

The other male witness then stepped forward saying, "That is correct but he only gave the car a bump, not so very hard."

Vaughan sauntered over to the Land Rover and peered in the passenger side, then climbed into the rear seat and avoiding gripping the gear stick knob checked its position. Returning to the group he said, "When he went to ram the car in front, the Land Rover was in third gear and probably stalled, that was why the effect was just a bump and not much more damaging."

The Inspector gave Vaughan a surprised look. "Thank you, that would explain it."

"What about the car behind?" asked Vaughan, "Any damage done to that?"

"No, it got very close but I do not think it hit the Land Rover."

"Thank you, if you could wait a few minutes longer, I may have more questions for you," said Lopez.

Moving away from the witnesses he said to Vaughan, "I have asked the border officials if they have seen two such vehicles travelling together, they checked their CCTV records but found nothing," said Lopez

"Damn," replied Vaughan, "It looks like they have either gone to Tangier by ferry or transferred the two women to a fast boat and crossed that way."

Turning to Able Seaman Robson, Vaughan asked, "Can you get me round to the Tangier Ferry Terminal?"

"Yes, Sir."

"Don't leave any rubber on the road, just let's cruise around, eh," said Vaughan, seeing the glint of action in the young seaman's eyes. "I don't want attention put on us unnecessarily, surprise is the key."

"Oh, right, cruise it is, Sir."

They wove their way through the apparent maze of parking bays associated with the flats overlooking the Marina Bay complex then further along North Mole Road all to no avail.

"We could try Queensway Quay, Sir," suggested Robson.

The Queensway Quay development was behind security gates and Vaughan had to flash his SIS I.D. in order to gain entry.

"Often wondered what it was like in here now it's all finished," said Robson.

"Well, now your curiosity is satisfied, Robson, maybe we can move on?"

"Well er, yes, Sir," replied the seaman, showing some embarrassment. "It wasn't just my curiosity, Sir. I just thought it might be a possibility."

When they turned into the Cormorant Wharf car park Vaughan left the uniformed seaman in the car and strolled around looking at the vehicles parked in the area. Making his way casually along Queensway Vaughan looked over the low wall into the Cormorant Quay development at the vehicles parked there. He was near to the far end when he saw what he was looking for, a black Mercedes four-by-four with Spanish plates and a damaged rear bumper, parked facing the apartment block.

Back at the car, he phoned Frazer. "I think we may have found one of the vehicles involved in the incident, Commander."

"Where are you, Vaughan?"

"Cormorant Quay, the vehicle in question is parked up inside the development near the north end."

"I'll get the police onto it straight away, Vaughan."

"No, Commander, I suggest we wait and keep watch on the vehicle. A police search of the apartments may well endanger both women's lives," replied Vaughan, hurriedly.

"Do you think so? Well they are your people not ours."

"Can I get Robson into civvies and hang onto him for maybe a day or two?"

"What does he say?"

"He is sat alongside me nodding his acceptance, Commander," replied Vaughan, "I'll send him back with your car shortly, this job ideally needs a white van and overalls."

"Leave that to us, Vaughan, I'll get my people working on it straight away."

Hanging up, Vaughan turned to Robson, "I need a mobile phone shop, do you know the nearest one?"

"Yeh, there is a couple up the hill in Main Street."

"Get me there quickly."

With two phones purchased Vaughan got Robson to drop him back at the Cormorant Quay then sent the seaman back to the base whilst he texted the new phone number through to the Commodore.

During the wait for Robson's return, Vaughan got close enough to the damaged vehicle to confirm that dark blue paint was embedded on the damaged rear panel of the Mercedes.

Three hours had passed before he and Robson were sitting in a white Renault van parked on the Waterfront restaurant side of Cormorant Wharf car park from where they could keep watch on the apartment complex's vehicle entrance.

"We stay hidden in the back, the one on watch can see the gate to the development by looking through that cut out in the bulkhead behind the central passenger seat."

"Right, Sir. Oh, Commander Frazer told me to tell you that he is in touch with Gibraltar VTS so if we want any small craft monitored by radar, just give him a call."

"We may well need that, Robson."

"You think they are still on the Rock, don't you, Sir," his voice edged with excitement.

"Yes, I do. My guess is that it was not until Lieutenant Heathcote was despatched here that people guessed that my passenger was still alive. The man that desperately wants to talk to her would not be able to safely land at Gibraltar without risk of being identified and arrested, so he will need to talk to my passenger somewhere else, like Tangier."

"Yeh, but there are lots of small boats that shoot over there, they could have gone anytime during the day," replied Robson.

"True, but as he had to use Spanish people to do the abduction I'm guessing that he doesn't have a boat immediately available and would probably prefer to use one from the Moroccan side to avoid too close a scrutiny on return."

"Let's hope you're right, Sir."

"How about we ease up on the formalities. My name is Ian and you are?"

"Me mates call me 'Puncher', I do a bit in the ring see."

"Let's hope you don't have to use those skills on this little stunt, Puncher."

They had been sat in comfortable silence for a while when Puncher, pointing to the yachts' masts in the marina behind the Cormorant Quay development asked, "Why do you think they will leave by car and not just walk round the back to the marina there?"

"Because that marina is for the exclusive use of residents and I am gambling on Gibraltar being a surprise location for Vermeulen requiring him to accept what he is given and work from there. Assuming that he has not struck gold with a boat from here, my guess is that he will have the women taken off from Marina Bay where at night there will be less likelihood of attracting attention."

***

The three-metre-high wall surrounding the half acre of immaculate garden also contained a much renovated and extended head gardener's cottage. This idyllic hideaway on the edge of the New Forest was once the kitchen garden to a large house, demolished forty years earlier after a fire. The current owner of the cottage and the person who had supervised all of the renovation and extension work was ex-SAS soldier Barry Jacobs who, on the morning of Anna-Maria and Heathcote's snatch, was stretched out on a sun lounger drinking coffee.

When his mobile rang he looked at the screen then quickly put the phone to his ear, "Yes, Sir, what can I do for you?"

"Are you busy for the next week?"

"Nothing I can't alter, what's on?"

"Get yourself on the Portsmouth to Santander ferry leaving at 1700 with that removal lorry of yours. You will be met at the other end by the Sousa brothers who will travel with you to Burgau."

"What happens then?"

"You will be asked to collect two high value women and hold them at Burgau until I give you further instructions."

"Right, understood. Will hear from you later then, normal rates?"

"Yes, normal rates plus your expenses of course."

At three o'clock that afternoon Izzard and Sampson International Removal Agent's removal lorry driven by a Barry Jacobs was parked outside the ticket office at Portsmouth's Continental Ferry Port.

"Oh 'allo, you again, Mr Jacobs, you're becoming quite a regular."

"Well, it's all these people wantin' to get back after the Brexit vote, they're scared their pensions won't reach em after the break away."

"It's good for your business though innit?"

"Yeh it is, Debs, it'll keep me going for a fair while. See yer," Jacobs replied picking up his paperwork and walking back to the lorry.

An hour later he was jumping down from the lorry again to make his way up to the bar on board the Santander ferry. It was by now a routine, he would drive from Santander down to either the Algarve coast or Galicia and sometimes Murcia with a load of household furniture, pick up whoever had paid for the ride, then drive back to a pre-arranged marina in northern France where his associates with powerboats would take the human cargo or drugs across the English Channel. His share of the money he had invested eventually on the London Stock Exchange after he had deducted enough to live on. Occasionally he would dispose of the furniture once he had delivered the human cargo and go round the French furniture auctions buying up pieces either for himself or items he knew he could sell on at a good profit. In his years in the army he had learnt a lot from the officer classes and antique furniture was just one of those valuable lessons. What he had learnt from Major Leonard Staunton was that there were less taxable ways of making money than doing a nine to five job when he got back to civi street.

It was unusual for him to be met at Santander; normally he would be sent details of the pickup location and find his own way there. He was however used to taking orders from senior ranks so Jacobs accepted without question the arrangement and soon he was enjoying a good evening meal with a bottle of wine and looking forward to finishing "The Peninsular War: A Battlefield Guide" by Andrew Rawson, in his cabin afterwards. Jacob's family had provided infantry men for the British Army for generations and it was more than likely that at least one of his ancestors had fought under Wellington in the second phase of the Peninsular War.

***

In the apartment in Gibraltar, after bundling the man Heathcote had head-butted out of the room they left just one man on guard outside the doorway to the bedroom. Occasionally he would glance in but seemed more interested in the programme being shown on the television in the corner of the room he was sitting in. Two hours passed and then Anna-Maria started to make noises that had the guard come in and eventually whip the Duck Tape painfully from over her mouth.

"What do you want?" he asked in Portuguese.

"Toilet. Do you understand, we need to visit the toilet!"

The man turned back to the door and said loudly, "They say they need to use the toilet, Christiano."

"Untie them one at a time, but they do not close the toilet door, especially that red headed bitch," replied Christiano, pleased to inflict another form of punishment upon the woman that had dared to strike him.

When Anna-Maria was returned to the bedroom and again tied hand and foot, the guard forgetting the Duck Tape gag moved across to Heathcote and untied her feet and led her away. As soon as the two had left the room Anna-Maria wriggled across her bed to the bedside table and, using her teeth, pulled her handbag onto the bed and nuzzling it open, bit onto the corner of the black notebook belonging to her stepfather, Vermeulen, and lifted it out. Now she wriggled to the head of the bed and dropped the notebook onto the pillow then nosed it over the edge to fall to the floor between the bedhead and the wall. She had only just got the handbag back onto the table when the guard and Heathcote returned.

It was then that the guard remembered the Duck tape and fearing reprisal from the one called Christiano hurriedly gagged her again.

***

Midnight had come and gone with no news from VTS regarding small craft approaching the harbour from across the Straits when suddenly the security gates to Cormorant Wharf opened and the Mercedes swept out turning north up Queensway. The vehicle had hardly disappeared before Vaughan and Robson were out of the rear doors of the van.

"You drive, Puncher, and don't lose them. I'll phone the Commander."

Dialling the number, Vaughan was impressed by the immediate pick up. "Yes, Vaughan, any movement?"

"There is, Commander, the car just left here in a hurry and seems to be making for Marina Bay. Can you organise some armed backup?"

"Certainly, I've got two RHIB's waiting to go, packed with marines and I've just given the nod to the Gibraltar Police."

As Vaughan's telephone conversation was in progress Puncher Robson fulfilled one of his great ambitions in driving at breakneck speed through a city and frequently on the wrong side of the road without fear of having his licence pulled. As anticipated the tail lights of the Mercedes were seen turning into Marina Bay Square and as they turned in and headed towards the corner nearest to the marina walkway they saw the Mercedes abandoned with its doors left open.

"Stay back, Puncher, you're not armed," ordered Vaughan as he leapt from the van and ran towards the walkway flicking off the safety catch on his Glock 26 as he went.

He had just reached the waterside when he saw two men rushing two complaining women along the pier to then be hidden behind the hull of the Sunborn Floating Hotel and Casino. All around him were groups of people and Vaughan, desperate to avoid anyone being caught in the crossfire, weaved his way through them and over the bridge to the pier then along it in search of the foursome. He had passed Sunborn's bow when he saw his quarry in the distance making towards the furthest pontoon arm. Sprinting now, Vaughan threw caution to the wind as he raced in pursuit hoping to get well within range before drawing fire. The four had reached the bridge from the pier to the pontoon when one of the men saw Vaughan coming at them and raised his automatic pistol and squeezed the trigger.

Seeing the movement, Vaughan dropped down flat and rolled to and over the pier edge grabbing hold of one of the mooring bollards to prevent himself completely falling into the water, his feet however, creating a loud splash. Whether the gunman thought he had hit Vaughan he could not tell, but his action was sufficient to bring a halt to the attack. Peering over the edge of the pier decking Vaughan noticed the foursome had moved on and, clambering back onto the pier cautiously, he continued his chase. Reaching the bridgehead he saw one of the men bundling the women onto a fast looking motor cruiser and pushing them below into the boat's cabin. The boat was out of range for the Glock, but, with a gentle easterly breeze blowing he knew that the sound would travel and he fired three shots, hoping that the threat of his presence would delay the men. The response from the more powerful automatics held by the men peppered the small pier-head building as he lay out of sight on the deck. The faint sound of the motor cruiser's engine starting had Vaughan making a run down the bridge ramp to the floating pontoon section and the screen of moored boats. Reaching the T junction he continued walking in a low crouch towards the boat the women had been forced onto. There was no sign of anyone ashore and Vaughan supposed that they were busy securing the two women and preparing for sea.

He was approaching the boat on which the women were being held when he sensed, as much as heard, a movement on the foredeck of the vessel alongside of him, above and to his left. Dropping to the decking and rolling in one smooth movement he felt the closeness of bullets as one plucked at his collar and heard the staccato crack, crack, crack of the man's automatic before he could pull the trigger. The bullet had hit the man squarely in the chest and Vaughan watched as he fell backwards to lay lifeless on the power boat's deck. *"One down and one to go,"* thought

Vaughan as he rolled again and scrambled to his feet eyeing the last boat on the pontoon. There was no sign of anyone on deck nor apparently on the flying bridge above it. In a crouching run he made it to halfway along the vessel, just short of where the cabin windows started, then holding a guard rail stanchion, rolled under the lower safety wire onto the narrow side deck and cautiously got to his feet. The scrape of a foot told him that someone was up on the flying bridge and he was just about to edge back to a point where he could see the person when the thwack of a bullet hitting the deck inches from his foot had him diving forward and rolling across the foredeck as more bullets chased him. Then the engines roared and the vessel powered away from the pontoon as Vaughan saw a man leap into the water. Thrown about on the waves as the powerboat cleared the protection arm formed by the airport's runway Vaughan found it difficult to make his way astern and up to the, now deserted, flying bridge. As he climbed up he found himself caught in the beams of two powerful lights from fast vessels intercepting the boat. Groping for the controls Vaughan closed the throttles and the boat rapidly lost way.

"Stand and put your hands on your head," came the command from the nearest of the two RHIB's now maintaining a parallel course. "We are going to board your vessel, any resistance will be fired upon."

Vaughan did as he was told, experiencing the growing feeling that he had been set up. A jolt as the second RHIB came alongside made Vaughan stagger, then a fresh-faced marine's head appeared, his gun pointing at Vaughan.

"If you reach into my hip pocket you will find my SIS I.D," said Vaughan.

"Oi, Banner, get up here and check this guy's hip pocket will yer."

Another young Marine appeared and cautiously circled Vaughan. "What am I looking for?"

"SIS I.D."

"Oh."

Vaughan felt a hand slide into his pocket and remove the wallet containing the badge.

"Hey!" came a shout from below. "This bloke's got a couple of birds tied up down 'ere."

"Is that true mate?" asked the Marine called Banner.

"No, I came aboard to try and rescue them but now realise it was a blind while the gang got away with the real hostages."

"Sorry, I don't understand you, mate," said Banner, "Wait till the captain gets on board and tell him."

It was half an hour before Vaughan got to question Jenny Grant and Amanda Dodge about their abduction. They had been returning to Jenny's parents' apartment when they were grabbed by a group of four men and gagged. They hadn't seen anything of the journey to Marina Bay as they had been hooded, then when the hoods were removed they were threatened that they would be killed if they resisted during the walk past the Sunborn Floating Hotel. Obviously they complied hoping that someone would realise their plight. It was when they were crossing the bridge that they realised only two of the men were with them. Scared stiff as to what was happening they tried to resist until they both felt gun barrels pushed into their stomachs. Then after being rushed along the pier the taller of the two men had shot at someone following them. A loud splash and the sight of a deserted pontoon had both girls thinking that soon they would be killed.

***

The one called Fidel and two others in the gang entered the bedroom as scuffling was heard in the room where the television was on.

"Stand up, we are leaving."

Anna-Maria stood and picked up her holdall and waited for Heathcote to join her by the door. They could see two girls being held by the one called Graciano, both hooded and, from the muffled noises they were making, gagged. Looking on were the three remaining gang members all casually holding machine pistols. With a word from Graciano the two hooded girls were pushed and shoved out of the apartment and towards the lifts by the four men, leaving Fidel and his two henchmen guarding Heathcote and Anna-Maria.

Several minutes passed then they heard the lift return and one of the gang hurried to hold the doors open as Heathcote and Anna-Maria were herded out to be crammed into the lift with the men. At the ground floor they were taken to the marina side of the building and after much pushing and shoving put aboard a sinister looking powerboat. There they waited, sat under guard in the boat's saloon for almost ten minutes until Fidel's phone rang and he was told that the decoy had worked and he was to leave immediately.

Once clear of the marina Fidel came below and whipped off the gagging tape over the women's mouths, then gave an order to the larger of the three men.

"What did he say?" asked Heathcote.

"He just told this one, called Gregorio, to keep an eye on us."

"Well, at least we are not travelling with the boss boy."

"No, he would not have enjoyed this, I heard him say that he suffers with sea sickness."

"Did you hear where they are taking us?"

"Yes, a town on the Algarve coast called Lagos. Graciano said that someone called Leonardo has made arrangements for us there."

"Is this Leonardo anything to do with your stepfather?"

Anna-Maria shook her head, "No, I have not heard that name mentioned by Jan, but he never talked about business when my mother or I were in earshot. Huh, I used to wonder why, now I know."

They were quiet for a time then Anna-Maria asked, "Do you know Ian well?"

"Why do you ask?"

"Well, it seems strange that shortly after I have been delivered to Gibraltar I am captured and now it appears I am to be handed over to someone called Leonardo."

"You were praising Vaughan for rescuing you yesterday, why do you think he is working for the bad guys?"

"I have been thinking and it seemed so strange now that a sailing boat is sent to rescue me, specially as Cecil thought that your Royal Navy would be sent to such a remote rendezvous. Maybe Ian Vaughan was Jan Vermeulen's back-up plan if I survived the fishing boat sinking."

"If he was he would have shot you on the spot. Besides, I personally know that the Commodore pushed both the navy and the Royal Air Force for assistance but thanks to our bloody incompetent Government we no longer rule the waves and don't have good enough diplomatic relations to secretly have a military aircraft land in either Mauritania or Western Sahara without a load of bally hoo ha."

Anna-Maria was quiet for a while then said, "If I had stayed aboard Beni Tamek's boat and given myself up maybe they would all still be alive and you would be safely at home in London and not here with these horrible people."

"Did they board the fishing boat or just sink it?"

"I, I don't know, at the time I was so scared and had got a long way from Beni Tamek's boat by the time it was sunk. It's still all of a blur," Anna-Maria closed her eyes, and frowning tried to take her mind back to the night when she had escaped the sinking. "I am sorry, I am still confused and too muddled to be sure. I just wondered, maybe Ian Vaughan was Jan Vermeulen's back-up plan to get his hands on me and his notebook again."

"You have Vermeulen's notebook?"

"Not anymore, I dropped it behind the bed last night when you were being taken to the toilet."

"What was in the notebook?"

"It was all in some sort of code, so I think maybe it was very important and as I was not likely to get it to Mr Campbell, then maybe Vermeulen would not kill us when we are handed over to him. I just thought that if he thinks the notebook was just lost in Rosso I, I…" Anna-Maria's voice faded and she just lay on the berth shaking her head in frustration.

"Vaughan has not been with us for very long, but he doesn't strike me as being someone who would get involved with the likes of your stepfather. We know a lot about Vaughan's past and I cannot recall anything that would link the two men."

"What about this Leonardo?"

Heathcote shook her head, "There you have me, but it still doesn't fit somehow, not with his past and how we identified him as being suitable to work with us."

"You are right, Penny, please ignore me. Ian knew about the notebook and was looking through it himself as we sailed here. It would have been easy for him to throw me over the side and just bring the book and hand it over to this Leonardo or whoever was the link."

"I'm pretty confident that Vaughan is on the side of the angels in this, Anna-Maria. For a start why hand you over to me in the first place, why not sail straight into the marina by the apartments and hand you straight to Graciano."

"Yes, of course I am being stupid, it is just all the killing and now it appears that it was all for nothing."

At that point Fidel came down from the boat's flying bridge and ordered Gregorio on deck whilst he took over the watch of the two women.

**

"Whilst your diversion was going on, Mr Vaughan, VTS reported another craft leaving at speed from the marina at Cormorant Quay," informed Frazer.

Vaughan buried his face in his hands. "Oh what a plank, fancy falling for that. They must have seen me eyeing the Mercedes earlier and guessed we were onto them," replied Vaughan, annoyed with himself for obviously having given the game away. "In which direction did it go?"

"The radar tracked it as following the Spanish coastline until we lost it behind cliffs. There apparently hasn't been anything that small crossing the Straits so we think that they are either still in Spanish waters or now moving your people by land."

"We need to find where they were being held in the Cormorant Quay development, Commander," said Vaughan. "There is a chance that they have left some clues; in the meantime I must report to London, God knows what the Commodore will make of this cock-up."

The middle of the night is never a good time to impart the news of failure but though the telephone conversation with Campbell was not a comfortable one, Vaughan sensed that the Commodore understood that he had been outwitted rather than having blundered. "You say that the gang removed the body of the man you thought you had killed."

"Yes, Sir, so it appears. The police could not find any sign of a body and I am quite sure that when he went down he would stay down." Replied Vaughan. "I suspect that he may have been well known which would lead the police to the rest of the gang. Even so they took a hell of a risk as the Gibraltar Police were closing in pretty quickly on the scene."

What Vaughan was unaware of was that the man who had jumped from the powerboat and swum back to the pontoon had, whilst all attention was on Vaughan, found and lowered the dead man's body into the water then swam with it over two hundred metres to a pontoon nearer the shore from where the body was collected just before dawn.

"Stay with it until you are satisfied that nothing more can be learnt from the apartment, assuming that they find it. Inspector Lopez is a good copper, I worked with him on a terrorist case three years ago, he's got a good nose."

"Right, Sir, then sail back I suppose?"

"Yes, Vaughan, I suppose you better had," replied the Commodore, thoughtfully. "For the first few days at sea I want you to keep close enough to the shore to be in mobile phone range."

CHAPTER 6

At his home in Dulwich, Commodore Campbell looked up from his breakfast in surprise. "Sir Andrew, to what do I owe the pleasure?"

"I thought I better come myself to tell you of the decision that has been made by the Prime Minister and I. It is linked to the crisis exposed by agent Vaughan and the ramifications that are following it within certain areas of the EU and the States; also the current operational problem you have caused by utilising one of our most important office staff on a field operation that, I for one, knew nothing about. The upshot of this is that you and members of your immediate team are to be put on, let's call it, 'gardening leave' and be restricted from any contact with each other, the press and anyone in connection with this business."

Campbell slowly put down his knife and fork. "That is very convenient, Sir Andrew, I was getting a little concerned with regard to the hedges and there is always a lot of weeding to be done."

"You're taking this extraordinarily calmly, do you not appreciate what such a sanction implies?"

"I'm well aware of its significance. I am also aware of the forces behind it."

"What 'forces' are you talking about, man?"

"I will not say anymore at this juncture, Sir Andrew, powder is best kept dry in readiness for battle," replied Campbell. "Now if you don't mind, I have some weeding to do."

Sir Andrew Averrille looked at the Commodore aghast. "Is that all you have to say?"

"Yes, I'll come and show you out."

They were just leaving the dining room when Sir Andrew's phone rang, "Yes, what is it?" There was a pause during which Sir Andrew was nodding his head, then frowning. "Wait a moment I will just ask, hold on."

Pointlessly holding the phone to his chest Sir Andrew turned to Campbell, "Whereabouts has your receptionist Lorna Parker-Davis gone for her holiday? Obviously we need to contact her."

"I haven't a clue, Sir Andrew, there was some suggestion of Germany I think but she could well have changed her mind," replied Campbell.

"Do you mean that someone in your section has gone on holiday without notifying you of a place of contact for emergencies?"

"No, it does not. It just means that I do not have that information immediately to hand."

"Well, who does then?" answered Sir Andrew, frustrated and annoyed by Campbell's apparent game playing.

"You could try contacting John Jessop."

Sir Andrew put the phone to his ear again, "Apparently you should contact DELCO section's office manager/cashier." There was a somewhat brisk reply that brought a furious frown to Sir Andrew's face. "What, he's on leave as well!" The frown turned to puzzlement as he listened to the response. "Oh, yes, he was the first on the list. Well, get over to his home then and wait for him. Do I have to do all of your thinking for you?" With that Sir Andrew Averrille pocketed his phone and strode down the hall to the front door. "An inquiry panel is being briefed later today and you will probably be called towards the beginning of next week," he said, turning back towards Campbell.

"I will look forward to it, Sir Andrew. You will notify me of course as to the panel members."

"Is that normal procedure?"

"It is at this level, Sir Andrew."

As Campbell turned after closing the front door, his wife, Caroline, emerged from the study. "I couldn't help overhearing the conversation, Alex. I know you have been expecting something but I never thought it would come to this."

"I thought it might eventually, darling, but in fact it has happened sooner than I expected and I was almost caught off balance," Alex Campbell replied, putting his arms around his new wife and kissing her tenderly. "I think we are moving towards the end of a bit of internal skulduggery that has been festering for some months."

"What is it that poor Ian Vaughan has done that is so terrible?" she asked, before immediately saying, "I'm sorry I shouldn't have asked that question, I was wrong to even think that you could answer it."

"Come on, get changed into some suitable clothes for a walk in the country, I'm on 'gardening leave'."

***

Three hours later they were enjoying lunch in the "Old Station Tea Rooms" at Holmsley on the New Forest, having first confused their followers among the shops of Winchester.

They had just ordered their meals, when Alex Campbell got up. "I'm just going to the gents, darling, won't be long."

Stepping out of the restaurant he walked past the tea and ice creams kiosk then round the back of the building to the gents' toilet, passing two middle-aged men in incongruous dark suits sitting at one of the outside tables. On his return Campbell stopped at the table and turning to the two men said, "In your report you should mention that we are both starting with the mushroom soup, then my wife is having the salmon and I went for the braised steak. We haven't made up our minds yet as to whether we will have desserts."

The older of the two smiled. "All right, Sir, don't rub it in, we are just carrying out orders."

"I know you are, but a bit of breathing space would be nice."

Returning to the table Caroline greeted him with a wide smile, "I saw you talking to those two men outside, I assume that they are our tail."

Alex nodded, "Yes, probably not the only ones though. Have you got one of those pay-as-you-go mobiles handy? I'll make that call to Lorna now while our two tails are too embarrassed to peer through the window at us. Hope this act works as I bet there is someone monitoring phone calls for this location."

Putting in Lorna Parker-Davis' number he waited.

"Hello, darlin', I got a gardening job for a week or so, so it don't look as if I can join yer now," said Campbell into the phone, starting to speak before Lorna could say any more than "Hello". Her response made him smile and with a wink to his wife he ended the call with, "Don't yer get up to nothin' with him or I'll be real upset. I'll giv' yer a bell when I can, just to hear how you're getting on like. Cheers, luv."

Caroline sputtered with laughter, "That's the first time I've ever seen you do that, it was brilliant, you should be on the stage."

"If this goes wrong, that is a career I might have to consider, my love, but don't let us get downhearted, not yet anyway," replied Alex Campbell.

The message was the trigger for Lorna Parker-Davis to make contact with Vaughan, but the last part was a clear instruction to stay away and wait for further instructions.

They skipped the desserts but lingered over coffee then leaving the restaurant crossed the road to the car and changed into their walking shoes. Taking the path along the permanent way of the old railway line they strolled hand in hand for some two miles before sitting on the bank making plans for a short holiday in the Lake District.

Switching the subject Alex Campbell turned to his wife and said, "You have been incredibly relaxed about all that has happened, Caroline."

"When I overheard Sir Andrew's initial statements it had my stomach churning and I wanted to burst in and order him from our house, but you seemed so calm," she replied. "Your calmness told me that you were expecting something like that to happen and knowing you from when I was just your driver, I knew you already had a plan."

Kissing her he got to his feet and gave her a hand, "Come on I have done all I can do today, let's go home and see what Mrs Craven has cooked us for supper."

"Do you think that the mobile phone is far enough into that rabbit hole, Alex?"

Campbell turned and putting his foot up onto the bank pretended to tie up a shoe lace whilst looking into the rabbit hole in question. "I can't see it and it's switched off, so a chance ring won't reveal it, I didn't think you saw me do it."

"I just caught a glint of metal as you tossed it in, just as you sat down, then I knew why we had stopped so early on a walk."

"You are not just a beautiful lady, but I have known that for some time."

"Oh, thank you, kind sir," Caroline replied, curtseying theatrically but giving Alex Campbell a, "don't patronise me" look.

Starting to walk back to the car, Caroline, looking ahead said, "I don't see our tail anywhere."

"There is another pair way up on the rise behind where we were sitting," replied Campbell. "I would think the other two have been taken off the job. Let's change the schedule and give the new team something to consider."

"What do you have in mind?"

"A trip to a boatyard and a brief enquiry with a yacht broker."

Caroline chuckled, "That will have Sir Andrew in a quandary."

At Berthon's Yard in Lymington the broker could not have been more helpful, "Forty to forty-five foot modern cruising yachts are at the upper limit for a couple to handle without crew, but if, as you say, you have friends available to help on long passages then either of those two yachts would be ideal for your needs."

Mr and Mrs Campbell walked away with full details of two yachts that would, according to the broker, be ideal for a Mediterranean cruise. As they crossed the car park Caroline said, "You sounded as if you were genuinely interested, Alex."

"Funny you should say that because on the drive across the forest I got to thinking how nice it would be if you and I could get right away from time to time," replied Alex. "So by the time we got here I was quite excited by the prospect of owning a yacht. What do you think?"

"Hmm. I would have to try it with someone who I know, knew what they were doing, Ian Vaughan for instance."

"Yes of course, darling, I wasn't thinking of rushing into anything." He paused for a moment or two. "I bet you anything that Ian Vaughan has been given his marching orders by Sir Andrew, so the chances are that he will be back in the UK before long."

As they got back into their car, Alex Campbell said, "Parked outside of the gates is a Ford Fiesta, can you get its number and write it down."

"Our new tail?" she asked as they approached the entrance.

"Yes, but something a little more interesting, I think."

Caroline glanced at him, then turned to ensure that she got the number. "Got it, Alex, by the way a car some way back has just pulled out behind us."

"Yes, I saw it. If my guess is right that is the official tail and the Ford is, shall we say, part of the real problem."

"There was nobody in it to follow us, Alex."

"No, she was in the brokerage subtly finding out what our interests were," Campbell replied. "She was writing down the name of the Oyster we were looking over. I saw her hurry through between it and the Amel alongside. Time to use the other phone I think."

As Caroline reached into her handbag, Alex handed her his phone. "On there is Jackson's direct number, phone him and ask him to do an immediate search on that Ford and hold on for the reply."

Hurriedly Caroline dialled the number, praying that it would be Jackson who answered.

"Jackson."

"Chief Inspector, I am glad I caught you. It is Caroline Campbell, Alex Campbell's wife."

"Oh, what a nice surprise, er, how are you both?" The "er" was because before becoming Mrs Campbell, Caroline was Caroline Tucker, a police driver who frequently drove the Chief Inspector and Commodore Campbell, this meant that Jackson was now unsure of how he should address her.

"Very well thank you. We have a favour to ask. Can you do a search on a vehicle registration for us?"

"Yes, of course, I hope you have not been involved in an accident."

"No, it is nothing like that, it was just a matter of ownership." Looking down at her note she gave Jackson the number.

"Shall I call you back?"

"No, I will hold on, if you don't mind, it is rather urgent you see."

"Oh, er, yes of course."

It only took a matter of two or three minutes before she could hear Jackson put down a telephone and pick up the one she was on. "The car belongs to a Ms Alice Morgan. I hope that is what you were looking for, er Mrs Campbell."

"I'll just check," Caroline replied.

"He said it belongs to a Ms Alice Morgan, Alex."

"Thanks, Brian," Alex Campbell said loudly. "When I get back from holiday we must meet up for lunch."

"Tell him I will look forward to it, and enjoy the rest of your holiday."

"Thank you, Chief Inspector. I must go, we are just about to arrive."

Goodbyes said, Caroline slipped the phone into the car's glove compartment.

"Well done, darling, you handled that perfectly. Brian of course will be wondering what the hell it is all about but I know he won't discuss it with anyone else, five years of working with him taught me that I can trust him."

"Did the name mean anything to you, Alex?"

"Yes, she is one of the Communications Room staff, and the one that Penny Heathcote has had doubts about. I wasn't sure when I saw her at the boatyard."

Alice Morgan had seen and understood the significance of the instruction to break all contacts with Commodore Campbell unless specifically ordered to. She was also aware that Leonard Staunton had taken over Campbell's desk, so when she conveyed the information regarding Campbell's outing to the New Forest and lunch location she found herself being sent on a mission to find out where and what Campbell was up to. After a high speed journey down the M3 she had caught up with the Campbells as they were returning from their walk and had trailed them to the boatyard.

"Is this to do with whatever it was that Ian Vaughan was doing?"

"Sorry, my darling, I can't tell you anymore."

"Oh, Alex, I am sorry I shouldn't have asked, that's the second time today I have had to say that."

"I'm going to pull in for petrol at Fleet Services, would you mind driving the rest of the way home?"

"No, of course not, it will be just like old times. Are you going to sit in the back?" Caroline replied giggling.

Alex Campbell sputtered and laughed. "No, I much prefer being near you."

She reached across and stroked his arm, "I like that, my love."

"Getting back to sailing," he said and continued, "When I was full time RN, I went on several sailing courses at the Joint Services establishment at Gosport. It was leadership skills stuff wrapped up with some good sailing. Les 'Jumper' Cross was one of the instructors; the first time I went out with him he nearly had me doing cartwheels with the yacht in order to drum into us the 'Man Overboard Drill'. I used to thoroughly enjoy those trips. It is sad really how easily work gets in the way of enjoying life a bit, as it did when I was pulled into Anti-terrorist Command." Caroline looked across at him, waiting. "There was a big plus side too though, I met you."

At Fleet Services Campbell topped up the fuel and returning to the car found Caroline adjusting the driver's seat to suit and checking the mirrors. "Another Ford Mondeo parked over by the air and water," she said, as he settled in the passenger side. "Here's the phone."

Campbell smiled, "I hope they don't guess why we have switched over."

Back on the M3 Caroline successfully got three or four cars between them and the tailing Mondeo. "They are a few cars back, Alex, they shouldn't be able to see you making a phone call."

Campbell tapped in the number. "Jackson."

"Sorry to bother you again, Brian, but I have another favour to ask and I don't want to go the direct route."

"What do you need to know, Alex?"

"Can you give me the name of the person in charge of the team tracing terrorist group funding?"

"Yes, that's easy, I was talking to her only this morning, it's Margaret Hutchinson, you know, tall skinny and a tongue like a razor."

"Yes, I do know, excellent. She was damn good on that South African Krugerrand exchange case. Thanks, Brian, that's brandies to follow."

An hour later as the car entered the driveway of their home the front door opened and Mrs Craven was seen standing in the doorway.

"Oh dear, I wonder what has happened, every time I have arrived to that welcome it has heralded bad news," said Alex Campbell.

"Can you put the car in the garage tonight, Alex."

Campbell looked at his wife for a moment, "Security you mean?"

"Yes, Alex, that is exactly what I mean. So please will you set the garage's independent alarm system before you come in."

"Yes, I think you're right, we are going to have to be very careful."

Caroline waited for her husband while he put the car away then they walked together towards the front door and Mrs Craven.

"Problem?"

"Someone has been in the house while I was out at the shops," Mrs Craven said quietly.

Holding a finger to his lips as a sign for everyone to keep quiet, Campbell stepped backwards out onto the garden path and led them to the driveway.

"When was this, Mrs Craven?"

"Just before lunch, sir, so I would say between eleven, when I left, and twelve thirty when I got back."

"Anything obviously missing?"

"No, sir, nothing taken," then turning to Caroline she said, "I hope you don't mind but I checked your jewellery box and dressing table."

Caroline smiled, "No of course not."

"I didn't call the police, sir. I thought it best to wait till you got home."

"Quite right, Mrs Craven. Don't let us cause unnecessary fuss," replied Campbell, looking down thoughtfully at the ground. "We will just carry on as if I am er, say, retired."

"If they didn't take anything, darling, I assume that they left something," said Caroline.

"Yes, dear, probably some listening devices."

"Oh well, if they want to listen to my boring conversation, they can," she replied with a shrug. "What delights have you got for us tonight Mrs Craven?"

"Fish pie, Mrs Campbell."

"Suddenly I am very hungry," said Campbell, rubbing his hands together enthusiastically.

"Retirement hasn't changed you then, sir," said Mrs Craven, sparking a shriek of laughter from Caroline.

***

143

It was around eight o'clock in the evening when the Gibraltar Police found the apartment they were looking for. While officers were questioning third floor occupants they were told by one family that they had heard what they thought was a domestic fight going on in the neighbouring apartment the previous afternoon. When the apartment was entered it was obvious that a disturbance had taken place in one of the bedrooms as there was furniture damage and traces of blood on the bedroom floor and in the bathroom.

By the time Vaughan arrived on the scene the forensic team were there taking fingerprints and conducting a thorough search.

Inspector Lopez was sitting on the floor outside the apartment, a cigarette dangling from his mouth, his eyes squinting through the trail of smoke at a black book. "Anything of interest?" asked Vaughan.

"Yeh, this. They found it under the bed, not sure whether it's connected as I can't make head nor tail of it as it's all in some type of code," the Inspector said.

"Mind if I have a look?"

"You'd better glove up first, the boys inside said they wanted to do some tests on it."

Vaughan waved to one of the forensic team and indicated a request for gloves.

"Okay, here is a pair but please do not handle it too much as it will damage evidence."

Vaughan held out his gloved hand flat, palm up and Lopez carefully placed the book on it. Vaughan then studied the leather cover. "Did you see these teeth marks on the top corner of the spine?"

Lopez nodded. "I guess that if it was one of the two ladies we are looking for, she had to pick the book up with her teeth in order to drop it to fall under the bed."

"That was my immediate thought," replied Vaughan. "I know that the Lieutenant is extremely bright and the other young lady is no fool either. I'm also sure that the little bunch that took them would have made absolutely certain that they were tied up to keep them out of mischief." Vaughan sniffed the notebook, "Yes, this has almost certainly been in the hands of Anna-Maria Ronaldo, it has her perfume signature all over it."

Using just his thumb on the corner of the book he opened it, then carefully selected a page at random. "Wow I see what you mean about code; a job for GCHQ I think, I'm sure their boys and girls would love to have a look at this."

"We would like to bag that now, Sir," said the forensic guy who had issued the gloves.

"Sure, here we are," replied Vaughan, closing the book and sliding it into the evidence bag held open for him. "I know you guys are good but that book needs to get to GCHQ in the UK in a hurry as they have all the tools to unlock what's in there."

Behind him Vaughan heard the lift door open.

The forensic guy turned to the Inspector. "Is that okay, Inspector Lopez?"

The Inspector nodded, "Yeh, do as he says get that book on its way by the fastest means possible, Grayling."

"I'll handle that for you," said a voice behind them.

Vaughan turned, "Senior Agent Staunton, to what do we owe the pleasure?"

"Cleaning up your mess again, Vaughan." Then turning to the surprised Grayling he flashed his SIS badge and said, "I'll take that now," and almost snatched the bag containing the book from the young man's hand. "Have you found anything else of interest that I should know about?"

"I'll get our team leader to talk to you," said the rather annoyed Grayling as he turned and went back into the apartment.

Staunton had arrived straight from the airport having successfully persuaded Sir Andrew Averrille that he should be the one to dismiss Vaughan and take over the search for the two missing women.

As the man disappeared Staunton turned back to Vaughan, "London has directed me to inform you that you are dismissed, fired. You are required to hand over to me your SIS identity badge, weapon and all issued equipment immediately."

Vaughan almost reached for the Glock pistol he was carrying in the thigh pocket of his trousers.

"Oh, so you've finally got your way have you, well, you can have the equipment but not the weapon. The armorer at 'The Manor' gave me strict instructions that I am to return it only to him," replied Vaughan angrily.

"I am relieving you of that duty, Vaughan, without SIS identity, carrying of that gun is illegal, so hand it over, with the rest of the stuff."

"You're unarmed aren't you," said Vaughan, realising why Staunton had listed the weapon separately from the other equipment that he had been issued with. "Because you were travelling by air and not allowed to disclose your security status to airport staff, you have had to leave your weapon behind. Are you planning on shooting someone while you're here?" continued Vaughan, with a knowing smile that brought an immediate expression of anger to Staunton's features.

"As your superior, I demand that you comply with my orders. You are finished, Vaughan; career, yacht charter, the whole lot, it's over for you, so just get the damned equipment and weapon, and hand them over now."

"The charter does not end until the yacht returns to its home port of Dartmouth. That's the agreement, check with Lorna or Commodore Campbell, they will confirm it."

"They have been suspended from duty awaiting the outcome of an enquiry into the handling of the coup affair and this latest stunt Campbell has involved you in."

"What did you say, Commodore Campbell suspended? What the hell's going on?"

"That is no longer any of your business."

These weren't your real orders, Staunton, I'll be bound, otherwise Campbell would have warned me. When you have pushed a little harder I will hand you over the Browning, but you're not going to get the Glock without a real fight."

Vaughan gave Staunton an angry glare, "Well, the record of the charter will be at DELCO's offices," he replied, trying to sound both indignant and concerned at the same time. *"So you've managed to organise a coup inside SIS have you, Staunton, I wonder how many other little maggots you have on your side?"*

146

"Oh, stop buggering about and get the damned equipment and hurry. I have a lot to do."

"You had better come with me to the boat then, it's all there," replied Vaughan.

"What! Your weapon is sitting on board your boat in a situation like this?"

"Yes, I didn't think that working with the Gibraltar Police Department I would need to be armed."

"Of course, you are the idiot who, unarmed, took on an armed and dangerous man who was physically holding a woman hostage."

"Yep, and the guy ended up dead, but had I waved a gun at him, both she and I would have been shot."

The police car that had delivered Staunton to the crime scene took them back to the quay where Vaughan's yacht lay. There they were joined by Commander Frazer and Seaman Robson.

"I understand from Mr Staunton that you will be er, leaving us," said Frazer, obviously aware of the situation and embarrassed by it.

"Yes, I see that you have been brought up to speed, Commander. Thank you for all your assistance. If Seaman Robson could give me a hand casting off in a few minutes I would be further obliged," replied Vaughan.

"Of course."

Leaving Staunton talking to the Commander on the pontoon Vaughan went below and reached under the quarter berth mattress, lifted the plywood base section and took out the Browning, neatly packed in its box, the three full ammunition clips but leaving the unopened box of ammunition from the bag and put them with the weapon on the chart table, covering them both with a couple of charts. He then went forward and accessed the false bulkhead to remove the compressed air powered grapple and line together with a radio microphone set, recorders and finally the shoulder holster for the Browning. Selecting an old grey sailing holdall, he put the equipment into it and returned to the main cabin and added the pistol and loaded clips to the haul. Opening the cupboard beneath the chart table seat Vaughan opened the safe and took out his equipment issue sheet, then, carefully locking everything again, he pulled open the second chart table drawer and took out a small brown envelope. Hoisting the bag onto the quarter berth he quickly took the Browning from its box, stripped it down and removed the firing pin, before reassembling it and putting it back in the holdall. *"I must be losing my touch, I almost gave that bastard a weapon that could be quickly loaded and fired. Slack, Vaughan, very slack."* Putting the firing pin into the envelope he slipped it into the Browning's box then placed the pistol in the holdall to be hidden by the small tubular grapple compressed air reservoir.

Heaving the holdall out onto the yacht's side deck, he said, "There you are, Staunton, that is everything I signed for, except to report the loss of a spare ammunition clip during the Al Djebbar incident."

Then stepping up alongside the bag he held out the equipment list form and said, "Sign the bottom and print your name and number."

"Piss off, I'm not a stores clerk."

"Well, you don't get these then," Vaughan replied, putting the holdall back down into the cockpit, out of Staunton's reach.

"Oh for Christ's sake, give me that damn bit of paper."

Vaughan picked up the holdall and stepped down onto the pontoon handing the equipment sheet to Staunton.

Muttering under his breath Staunton signed the form as requested and handed it back to Vaughan. "Satisfied?"

"It will do, until I return and report in."

"Didn't you hear, you're fired, out of it, not wanted."

"The game is far from over, take my word for it. It still has a long way to go."

"Bullshit," replied Staunton stepping towards Vaughan and grabbing his shirt front pulling him close. "Get that old barge and yourself back to England by the end of the week. I want you out from under our feet soon, understood."

The impact of Vaughan's left foot onto the arch of Staunton's right foot caused enough instant pain for Staunton's head to jerk forward to receive what is known as a "Glasgow Kiss" aimed at the man's nose but hitting his right cheekbone and eyebrow.

Staunton staggered backwards then went to move forward again only to discover that the pain from his right foot would not allow it.

"Grab me again like that, Staunton, and you will find that I have broken more than a couple of bones in your foot. Now go crying back to London before I change my mind and deal with your arms and legs here and now."

Grabbing the bag Staunton rummaged for the gun.

"Stop that now! The pair of you!" shouted Frazer. "Mr Staunton, you come with me. Robson, see Mr Vaughan safely away please."

It was a reluctant Staunton that turned away to hobble beside the Commander along the pontoon towards the quay feeling a rapid swelling in both his right foot and around his right eye.

"Nice one, Ian, if you don't mind me saying, but watch your back, that little bastard wants to kill you," said Robson quietly.

"The feeling is mutual I assure you."

Robson went to walk away to start the process of casting off then stopped and turned back to Vaughan. "The Commander was told that a boy in those apartments knew the name of the boat that they think did the runner with the women you were searching for, it was called Corredor Rápido."

"He was sure?"

"Apparently so, Ian. I didn't hear him but Frazer was told it sounded kosher, though your mate Staunton reckoned the kid was just trying to appear big."

"When did they say all this?"

"Frazer got a call while you were below, I overhead what they were saying."

"Thanks, Puncher, that is the most useful bit of information I have heard in days."

***

Two hours before Vaughan had got to the apartment in Gibraltar Jacobs had driven off the Santander ferry and been met at the port entrance by the Sousa brothers, both skilled craftsmen, instructed previously by Leonardo to prepare Jacobs lorry ready to take both hostages in secret across borders. Leaving Santander they directed him down past

Salamanca to a farm near the small town of Arapiles. On seeing the place name as they approached the town Jacobs showed signs of excitement.

"Arapiles, well I'm buggered, I was readin' about this place on the way over on the ferry, cor I've wanted to get here for years."

"You know this place?" said Carlinhos Sousa, the brother with the better understanding of English.

"Yeh, well no, but I know of it."

"Why you know such small town?"

"Well in 1812 this place was the centre of the Duke of Wellington's first great victory over the French Army under Marshal Aguste Marmont. Twenty-second of July it was, and us and you Portuguese fought together as allies. In fact I think we are your oldest ally going back way beyond that war."

At the farm, while Jacobs went with the farmer to view the fields over which the battle had been fought, the brothers unloaded the furniture and proceeded to measure up the inside of the load area.

On his return Jacobs was confused to find the furniture spread over the yard and the farmer's wife pointing to items she wanted taken into the house.

"Ere what's goin' on?"

"Leonardo he say we dump these things and measure for secret compartment inside."

"Oh he did, did he, well he can bloody well pay to have it taken out again when I gets back home, cheeky bastard, who the bloody hell does he think he is." Looking across at the farmer's wife Jacobs said, "Is she gonna pay for that lot?"

"She give us free meal tonight and bed to sleep in and food for tomorrow, it will be good deal."

"Well, tell her that the big fridge has got to go back on the lorry as that is for someone else."

The following morning they left early crossing the border into Portugal at Vila Formoso then turned south arriving in Burgau on the Algarve coast at seven o'clock in the evening after having stopped for the legally required driver breaks and to collect the materials for the secret compartment.

Soon after passing through the town the brothers directed Jacobs to turn right away from the sea, up a steep narrow road and over the brow of a hill, then left up a very narrow track, climbing further then descending into a hollow where a large house lay.

"Yeh, good location this, no neighbours can see us," observed Jacobs, having given the area a sweeping, but professional, glance. "Whose car is that?"

"It is my car," said Carlinhos, "We travelled to Santander by bus from my brother's home."

"Oh, right. You gonna open up then or do we sit here all night?"

***

In Gibraltar, Staunton sat waiting to have his foot X-rayed at St Bernard's Hospital, and took the opportunity to put a call in to Vermeulen.

"Hello."

"Jan, good news for you, I have your notebook and your stepdaughter."

"Where?"

"I am in Gibraltar at the moment and due to fly back to London in the morning."

"What about Anna-Maria?"

"She is on the way to Lagos in Portugal, after that she and her companion may be having a change of career."

"Employed by your Turkish friend I take it, like nosy Maria."

"Something like that, Jan. I'll be busy for a few days as I have to rub out another name on the page, I suggest you use the sailing option crossing the English Channel and give me a call when you have arrived, don't rush, as I said I will be busy for a while, tone up that suntan of yours for a week."

***

As Staunton was speaking, Commodore Alex Campbell in England was strolling down the garden of his Dulwich home. At the bottom of the garden was his tool shed and behind that a loose panel in the fence that gave access to Douglas Furlew's house behind. Moving the panel to one side Campbell slipped through the gap and checking that all was clear hurried up the garden path and entered the property via the back door. Making his way immediately to the alarm panel he tapped in the code before settling himself in Furlew's study and dialling Vaughan's personal mobile number.

"Hello," said Vaughan, not recognising the number of the caller.

"It's Campbell, Vaughan, what's the news?"

"I'm just leaving Gibraltar, Sir, in the faint hope of tracking down a powerboat named '*Corredor Rápido*' which left here last night with Lieutenant Heathcote and Ann-Maria Ronaldo aboard. I tried calling you earlier but your phone was switched off I think."

"Yes it was, Vaughan, I can only receive during restricted hours at the moment and have had to ditch that phone."

"I see, Sir. By the way I have just been fired by Senior Agent Staunton who turned up here all of a sudden and has walked off with a black notebook belonging to Vermeulen that the Gibraltar Police found in the flat where Anna-Maria and Lieutenant Heathcote were held," replied Vaughan.

"How the hell did Staunton get to know about this operation, he is supposed to be in Portugal on other business that Sir Andrew wanted tidied up," replied Campbell obviously shocked by Vaughan's information. "This is very serious and makes it clear to me why events today have taken the turn that they have. Anyway back to the name of this power boat, '*Corredor Rápido*' you say, is that intelligence reliable do you think?"

"Commander Frazer here took it seriously."

"Vaughan, I will be frank with you now. When I assigned you to the Madeira Conference mission, I was seriously pressured into allocating Staunton as your mission controller. At the time I had grave doubts about the man as he was involved in the operation in which Anna-Maria's husband was ambushed and killed. I think that this current situation is linked to that failed operation, but thus far I have only vague pieces of information to go on and if that is Vermeulen's notebook I think it may well be the key to revealing why a very capable agent was lost." There was a pause before Campbell said, "You know that DELCO has been closed down and the staff suspended awaiting an enquiry as to its future. Under current circumstances I can only be contacted through this number between 2200 and 2230 hours for the next three days. Then I will have to find another safe place to call from."

"Staunton said that you and the DELCO team had been suspended but he blamed that on my revealing the coup plot in Madeira."

"Yes, that was one of the excuses that Sir Andrew Averrille mentioned, but that is not the real issue, there is a lot of unpleasant politics going on here and it has been going on for some months. Things now are coming to a head and that places a great deal of importance on the safe recovery of Lieutenant Heathcote and Ms Ronaldo. I am trying to establish communication routes so you may get a contact from Lorna Parker-Davis, who I am hoping will be able to act as a message hub for us, provided that Sir Andrew Averrille's bloodhounds don't reach her and order her into silence," replied Campbell. "Vaughan, what else did Staunton say?"

"Nothing really, he was more interested in my handing over all the equipment issued to me, particularly my weapon, he was so mind-bent on getting hold of that he forgot to take my SIS I.D."

"So you are unarmed but still have I.D."

"According to his paperwork I am, he got the Browning 9mm that I was due to return having been issued, via Madeira, with a Glock."

"So you are still in the game. Good," said Campbell. "For God's sake watch your back, Vaughan, Staunton is an efficient killer. One final thing, only call on this new number for the next three nights, after that, well, I will see what I can arrange through Lorna. I had better get back to the house, Vaughan, otherwise any watchers looking towards my garden shed will start wondering what I'm up to."

"Right, Sir. I will try contacting you tomorrow night on this number, goodnight."

Slipping the phone into his pocket, Vaughan focused his thoughts on getting out into the Atlantic and northwards toward Cadiz.

***

The head of the Portuguese Servico de Informações de Segurança, the equivalent of Britain's MI5 had endured another long day questioning those coup members arrested weeks earlier in Funchal but now imprisoned in Lisbon. Coups are rarely staged for the benefit of those who present the public image and Natanael De Lacerda was determined to discover those powerful backers who would, for obvious reasons, wish to remain anonymous.

His mobile bleeped and glancing at the screen he frowned not recognising the caller's number. "De Lacerda."

"Natanael, Alex Campbell here, how are you, my friend, busy I suspect?"

"Alex, it is good to hear you, do you have any more earth-shattering news for me?"

"No, not this time. I am phoning to ask a favour."

"Ask away."

"This is a very special operation and I would appreciate you using only this number on which to contact me."

"I see, it sounds that, like me, you are sailing in a leaky boat. Of course I will keep this only between the two of us, how may I help?"

"I am looking for a powerboat named *'Corredor Rápido'*, my information is that it was involved in a snatch of two rather important people."

"Where did this happen, Alex?"

"Gibraltar."

"Gibraltar! You think they came all this way. Why not just across the bay to Spain?"

"You are right, Natanael, that would be the obvious direction and I have put feelers out there as well, but I have a gut feeling that your shores are the real destination."

"I see, Alex, I will make some immediate enquiries for you. I can easily cover it under another search we are conducting."

***

At first Vaughan's progress into the Straits of Gibraltar was good but as he reached the narrowest part the constant eastbound current made sailing progress slow. Starting the engine he set the yacht up to motor sail under control of the auto helm then went below to write up the log starting with the phrase "Blackstrapped", a term coined in the days of the Georgian navy, when ships entering the Mediterranean took on barrels of a dark red rough wine for their crews. Molasses, the product of the third boiling of sugar cane and known as "Blackstrap" in the Caribbean, soon shared its nickname with the coarse wine issue for ships in the Med. The term's relevance to Vaughan's log was the fact that as soon as the Georgian sailors saw the wine being loaded they knew they were heading for the Mediterranean, and the prospect of years away from home, at the end of which they faced days, or even weeks of hard sailing with little progress as they forced their passage through the Straits and back into the Atlantic.

It took four hours of motor sailing against the current before *"La Mouette sur le Vent"* rounded the Punta de Tarifa O Marroqui to then point hard on the wind in the direction of Punta Camarinal and Cape Trafalgar; and when in sight of the Cape he tacked the yacht to get closer to the shore where the current running south, that also impeded his progress, was slightly less. At seven o'clock in the evening Vaughan brought the yacht round into the Bay of Cadiz and sailed across the harbour entrance to El Puert de Santa Maria where he anchored between the marina and the training wall of the Rio Guadalete. As tempting as marina facilities were, Vaughan wished to avoid appearing on marina registers, preferring the comparative anonymity of the anchorage. By 2210 hours he had dined and cleared away leaving himself free to make the call to Commodore Campbell from the yacht's cockpit where he could be sure to avoid unexpected interruption should some observant official wish to come from the shore to check his papers.

Dialling the number Vaughan didn't hear it ring before Campbell's voice was heard. "Vaughan?"

"Yes, Sir, I am at anchor on the eastern side of the Bay of Cadiz."

"Slow progress then."

"Well, as you know it's a bit of a struggle getting out of the Med. and it has been northerly winds all the way," replied Vaughan, for some inexplicable reason, feeling that his excuse seemed a little lame.

"Never mind, I learnt from Inspector Lopez that the man you killed was one Christiano Graciano, leader of an enforcement gang that has connections with the town of Lagos on the Algarve coast. His body was found in the back of a car as the driver tried to leave Gibraltar this afternoon."

"Did they learn anything from the driver?"

"No, except that the body was to be taken to his family in Lisbon," replied Campbell. "I understand that when the police started asking what was in the box the man got very nervous, so they opened it up and found the body sealed up in several layers of polythene."

"Does that get us any nearer to finding Ms Ronaldo and Lieutenant Heathcote, Sir?"

"Enough for me to take a gamble and ask you to set sail immediately for Lagos. I have asked for the port to be watched."

Vaughan went below and looked at his large scale chart. "At a guess that is a full day's sail, Sir. I had better leave the boat here and go overland."

"No, Vaughan, don't do that, I am going to inform my contact in Portugal's Servico de Informações de Segurança about who you are, with the request that it goes no further. Do the best you can sailing there, Lagos would be a likely port of call for you to take on supplies or do repairs."

"Right, Sir, I will up anchor now and get underway."

"Call me this time tomorrow evening, Vaughan, if you can. Oh and buy yourself a few more pay as you go mobile phones. I don't want any communication risks."

"Right, Sir, till tomorrow."

Taking the back of the phone off, Vaughan threw the battery, SIM card and phone separately into the sea. *"This is becoming bloody expensive, I hope Campbell gets reinstated otherwise my expenses form submission will be a waste of time."*

Half an hour later *"La Mouette sur le Vent"* was heading out to sea again under full sail, charging along comfortably off the wind now that Vaughan was able to set a course of two nine five degrees giving a wind angle of more than sixty degrees.

***

The following morning as *"La Mouette sur le Vent"* romped along with Vaughan below stirring porridge in the galley, Jacobs was inspecting the handy work of the two brothers.

"Neat, yeh very neat, you've done this before I bet."

The brothers had worked solidly throughout the night building the two bunk compartment behind the driver's cab. Two thick skins of thermal insulation sandwiching thick reflective foil surrounded a marine plywood accommodation box complete with bunks and a chemical toilet. Ventilation was through the roof and could be closed off during periods of vehicle inspection. The only weak point was that it reduced the internal length of the load area by a metre and a quarter, something that a sharp eyed vehicle inspector might notice.

"Once or twice, yes. Senhor Graciano he sometime needs to help people who do not want to be seen," replied Carlinhos, his chest a little puffed up with pride at Jacobs' recognition of their skill. "You will see that it is well insulated so thermal cameras will not pick up a heat source."

"And you get in and out of it via my sleepin' berth above the cab, yeah that's good, I might even use it myself cause those bunks look a bloody sight more comfortable than what I've got."

"We are finished now, yes?"

"No, mate, your friend Leonardo wants you two to stay here and cut down all of the weeds and plants around the house and up the slope, nothing to be left over the width of your hands high."

"That will take all day, Senhor."

"Don't worry you'll get well paid, if anyone comes and asks, say you are working for the owner, right, meantime, I've gotta go and pick up a couple of people."

"Who is the owner?"

"I don't know, phone Leonardo and ask him."

Jacobs patted Carlinhos on the back and, sliding behind the wheel of the lorry, started the engine, "See yer later, dump everything out of sight over the top of that bank."

CHAPTER 7

Jacobs reached the outskirts of Lagos and as planned refuelled the lorry at the one and only fuel station on the road. After paying for the fuel he parked the lorry up and was just about to make his way to the onsite café when he saw a tough looking man in his mid-twenties walking towards him.

"Senhor Jacobs?"

"Who are you?"

"Fidel."

"Fidel who? What's your other name?"

The man sighed, "Fidel Castano."

"Where is Graciano?"

"He dead."

"Wait while I check this out."

Jacobs flicked through his phone list and rang Staunton, "You heard anything about Graciano bein' topped?"

Staunton's answer was quite brief. "Yes, he got sloppy."

"Oh shit right, I've got a Fidel Castano standin' 'ere, is he kosher?"

"Yes, he's all right, anyone else?"

"Dunno, 'old on."

Putting the phone to one side he said, "Fidel, you got someone workin' with you?"

"Si, my friend Gregorio, he guarding women at apartment."

"Did you 'ear that?"

"Yes, I heard, he's a right bloody hoodlum. They are both to be used until you get the women back to Burgau and locked up, then I want those two taken out. Neither of them are bright so they are a risk as the police now know that the Graciano gang is involved."

"Are they looking around 'ere?"

"No, they are still chasing their tails in Gibraltar."

"Let's 'ope you are right, speak to you later, Sir."

Jacobs put his phone back on the dashboard rack. "What 'appens now?" he said to Fidel.

"You follow me to apartment, we put women in back with Gregorio to guard them. The one with red hair is big problem."

"She won't be for long. You lead the way then," then remembering just in time Jacobs called, "Oi, Fidel, if anyone asks we are deliverin' a refrigerator to this place, you understand."

"Si, I understand, we deliver refrigerator."

The development of luxury apartments lay behind a manned gatehouse and Jacobs now realised why Staunton had arranged the escort as even Castano had to argue with the man in order to gain entry.

Opening up the back of the removal lorry Jacobs untied the refrigerator and loaded it onto his sack trolley and with the help of Fidel got it to the lift and up to the apartment.

"Where we put this?" asked Fidel pointing to the refrigerator.

"We don't, we are seen deliverin' this one and taking away the old one, got it?"

"Ah, yes I understand. Ah here is Gregorio, Gregorio meet Senhor Jacobs."

Gregorio, who was older than Fidel, sported two nasty recent scratches across his face.

"You look as if you've 'ad some trouble from the two ladies you've been looking after."

"The one with the red hair, she fight like a cat, so I smack her."

"Sounds like what she needed. Well, let's 'ave a look at them."

Fidel led the way through to a bedroom overlooking a quiet side road. Both women were tied and gagged and were lying on the two single beds in the room. Jacobs' eyes went straight to the redhead's face.

"So you smacked her eh. Christ, a broken nose and black eye is some smack. Your Leonardo will not be very pleased about this," he said before moving closer to look carefully at Anna-Maria and seeing the look of fear come across her face, smiled, the type of lecherous smile women fear most.

"Right, ladies, get up, we are going to a new 'otel for a few days."

Anna-Maria responded straight away making an urgent sounding noise and nodding her head in the direction of the partition wall.

"Ah Miss Glamour wants her make-up and toilet bag," said Fidel mockingly.

"Go with her," said Jacobs, who then turned and looked down at Heathcote.

"Oi, you get movin' as well you little cat or I will give you a smack and I won't be as gentle with it as Gregorio 'ere."

Painfully, Heathcote stood and Jacobs guessed that she had many more bruises on her than those on her face. Slowly she shuffled across to join Anna-Maria who was now waiting with Fidel by the door to the apartment.

"Fidel, you and Gregorio here follow me down and whisk these two into the back of the lorry, I'll be waitin' in there to make sure they don't give Gregorio any trouble on the journey. Make sure you are not seen."

Jacobs had only just got the refrigerator off the sack trolley when Anna-Maria stumbled up the lorry ramp pushed by Gregorio. "Stand her over there against the side," he said pulling his double-edged Commando knife from its sheath beneath his right armpit. Cutting her wrist bonds he quickly and securely tied her wrists to the horizontal load restraint battens that ran along the side of the load area, as Heathcote shuffled across to stand alongside her.

"Now you, hold still or I might cut more than you would wish." Heathcote's head hardly moved as he issued the sinister threat, instead she just stared down at the floor, her resistance for a while at least broken. "Good girl, carry on like this and you and I might get along."

"Are you sure you need me along, Senhor?" said Gregorio.

"Yeh, better be safe than sorry, I'm told that these two are high value so they better not come to any more harm."

As the ramp was raised and rear doors closed Gregorio made himself comfortable on the sofa rejected by the farmer's wife and now tied to the battens opposite the two women. For most of the journey he looked at Penny Heathcote with something of an air of satisfaction as with each turn in the road and bump she moaned in pain. Only one woman had ever dared strike him before and she had been beaten then thrown out through a fourth floor window.

The journey taken at a slow pace lasted just under half an hour with Fidel in his sporty Seat trailing along behind. The track leading off the side road was the worst part of the journey and Heathcote was on the point of passing out by the time the lorry came to a stop outside of the house.

When her bonds were cut Heathcote almost collapsed onto the floor of the lorry but fortunately, Anna-Maria, having been freed first, was there to support her and shuffle with her as they were herded into the house. The climb up the stairs was agony for them both as the ankle tethers cut into their flesh and despite the threats, the climb took a full five minutes. Once on the landing they were separated and wrist tethers fitted again.

When Jacobs got to tying Anna-Maria's wrist tether he took her holdall from her, "I'll put that in the bathroom for you, now hold out your 'ands."

They were then put into different bedrooms neither of which had either carpeting or furniture and with the external shutters closed and the doors locked both found themselves in complete darkness.

Outside Fidel and Gregorio were lounged against Fidel's car watching the Sousa brothers hard at work when Jacobs came out of the house. "Thanks for your help, I will pass on your apologies for damaging some of the goods, Gregorio." Then, pulling a silenced pistol from his pocket, shot both men in the head before either had a chance to move.

"Carlinhos, get your arse over here and give me a hand."

A little confused and curious Carlinhos Sousa put down the saw he was using and strolled across towards Jacobs stopping in horror when only five metres away at the sight of the two dead men.

He looked at Jacobs aghast and was about to turn and run when he saw the slight movement of Jacobs' right hand holding a gun.

"Leonardo's orders, mate. Come on we have to get rid of these two. You give me a hand getting them into this car then follow me down the road to a point where we can torch it."

On unsteady legs Carlinhos approached as Jacobs opened the front passenger door, then bent down and reaching under the armpits of Gergorio hauled his body and sat it alongside the passenger seat.

"You grab that side of him and I'll take this and when I say lift haul him up into the seat."

It took several minutes to get the big man into position and fit the seat belt and both men were breathing heavily when finally Jacobs slammed the car door closed.

"Bloody hell he weighed a bleedin' ton. Right now let's get his mate into the back seat."

Fidel's body was a lot lighter but still a struggle to handle into position.

"When we gets to the place and it's all clear we'll have to put old Fidel here into the driver's seat then hopefully the police will think it was nasty accident."

"Graciano will kill us for sure, you are crazy to do this, for order of Leonardo or no," said Carlinhos finally finding the will to speak. "Graciano he very powerful man and very quick temper, he will soon know and we will be punished."

"No you won't, mate, 'cause Graciano is dead, Fidel told me earlier and I checked with Leonardo. He's as dead as those two are."

"You are sure?"

"Yeh, positive. I think the only reason that these two carried on with the deal is because Fidel there had illusions of takin' over Graciano's territory. Fat bleedin' chance a little punk like him would have had."

Carlinhos, still looking troubled, turned and went to walk back to join his brother.

"Where are you going?"

"You want to do this now?"

"No, 'cause I don't, but we need a can of petrol, 'ere's a few euro, five litres will do. And get some milk and breakfast cereal, oh and coffee. Here, there's another fifty."

Again Carlinhos went to walk towards his brother, "Oi your car's over there, Bento can carry on with the clearing job while you're away."

Reluctantly, Carlinhos walked towards his car, his hopes of taking his younger brother, Bento, with him dashed. It was only his loyalty to his brother that had him returning an hour or so later having completed all of the errands.

As he unloaded the food stuff onto the kitchen table Jacobs asked, "What have you done with the petrol?"

"I left it in the back of my car."

"Did you have enough money?"

Carlinhos nodded. "I bought some wine as well."

"Yeh, nice one, that'll be good with that cheese we was given, good idea," Jacobs looked up at Carlinhos and noted the rather scared expression on his face. "By the way, you did good this afternoon, I know you two didn't sign up for all of this bit down 'ere. I'll make sure Leonardo gives yer both a good bonus, I promise."

***

Considering a waterline length of just over twenty-eight feet, the yacht's performance over the distance of one hundred and twenty-five nautical miles was impressive and proved that the hull cleaning in Madeira had been worthwhile. Six hours after Jacobs had taken the women from the apartment in Lagos to Burgau Vaughan reached the Marina do Lagos in the city centre, tying up to the arrivals' pontoon just to the seaward side of the footbridge. Checking in and paying for a two night stay he was allocated a berth at the very end of one of the long pontoons. Returning to his yacht Vaughan warped the yacht along the pontoon to the fuel pumps and spent time filling the fuel tank and after paying cast off again to enter the marina, motoring behind two other yachts forming a neat line astern as they passed through the lifting footbridge that formed a type of gateway to the marina pool. Tying up at the berth, he then walked into town via the footbridge to purchase some food and the mobile phones before sauntering around the marina in search of the powerboat. He had almost given up the search when he finally spotted the boat moored between two large "Gin Palace" style motor cruisers. Instantly, he could see why the boy in Gibraltar had noticed the boat, it was very sleek and painted in matt black instead of gloss finish giving the vessel a decided stealth image. Vaughan walked along the pontoon towards the boat and on passing it had a long enough look to be confident that no one was on board. Walking back along the pontoon he stopped and gave the vessel an even closer inspection, before leisurely strolling back to the pontoon where his own yacht was moored. He was about to turn and walk along to his boat when he saw them, two men in suits standing by his boat, one talking on a mobile phone. Turning back, Vaughan hurried to the nearest bridge to the quayside and walked up it then along the line of restaurants and yacht broker offices to a point where he could watch the men without it being obvious. The man holding the phone was looking into Vaughan's yacht gesticulating as he spoke, while the other man looked about as if searching for someone. After a few minutes both men turned and walked back towards the quayside, the man with the phone going into the Oasis Cafe from where he could keep an eye on Vaughan's yacht, and his partner walking away in the direction of the car park.

Vaughan needed to know who the men worked for as somehow they didn't fit the image of either gangland thugs or police, now that they were separated he had the opportunity of making an approach on level terms and keeping close to the buildings he walked briskly towards the café. On entering he saw the man immediately, walked straight towards the table and sat opposite him.

"What is so interesting about my boat?" he asked.

As Vaughan had entered the café the man had been startled, but now Vaughan had spoken the man looked more relaxed. "I am Agent Ascensao of the Servico de Informações de Segurança, we were sent here to look for a powerboat with name of '*Corredor Rápido*', but we arrived too late to help those your boss is interested in. We then received order to stay and give you assistance."

"Do you have a badge?"

"What?"

"Do you have any identification that you belong to Servico de Informações de Segurança?"

"Oh yes, here," said Ascensao, handing Vaughan the leather fold holding his I.D. "You are Senhor Vaughan, yes?"

"Yes I am. You have made enquiries at the Marina Reception obviously," said Vaughan.

"Yes, they tell that the owner, who lives in Lisbon, had no knowledge that his boat had been taken and used. The owner he now has reported this crime to the police in Lisbon who are now making enquiry."

"Who is this man?"

"His name is Leonardo de Oliveira, a high level banking official in the Banco Salvadore Tesoureiro. It is a private bank for the very rich and powerful."

"Does that make him untouchable?"

"No, it does not, but we have been on board his boat and it was obvious that the locks had been broken and the engine start electrics were pulled out, suggesting that they started the engine without using a key."

"So, he is off the list?"

"Yes, he is off the list."

"Were there any witnesses to the boat's arrival here the day before yesterday?"

"We have been asking around and are following up some possible leads, that is what my colleague is doing now."

"Unlike in the UK, I did not see one CCTV camera around here," said Vaughan.

"This is a peaceful place, Senhor Vaughan, not so much crime, only a few people that party too much."

"My information was that the people involved in this are well known local criminals."

"That is true for Christiano Graciano but he is now dead and we have not too much information regarding the rest of his gang, we are checking with the local police and will probably be knocking down a few doors before long."

"Ah the soft approach eh."

Ascensao laughed. "Yes, it is called gentle policing."

Just then Ascensao's phone chirped. "Ascensao," he said, then sat listening intently to the caller. "Have they brought her in?" there was a short pause then, "I have just met Senhor Vaughan, we will come straight away."

Putting the phone back in his pocket Ascensao looked across at Vaughan. "They have found Graciano's girlfriend. Let us say she is co-operating," Ascensao said. "Would you like to hear what she has to say?"

"Most certainly," replied Vaughan. "Let's hope she's not just complaining about the loss of her meal ticket."

They drove north from the marina through the outskirts of Lagos to the N125 and turning left onto it crossed the river passing the football stadium then, at the next roundabout, Vaughan saw the smart new Police Headquarters in front of them. At the reception they were told that the girl was being interviewed in room "B" by a local police inspector and

165

they were shown to the adjacent observation room, where a young detective sergeant brought them up to speed.

Ascensao then took over interpreting for Vaughan. "Apparently she was due to meet Graciano when he returned from the job and was standing on the footbridge waiting when the boat came in, but she could not see him on board. Then three men and two women came across the bridge and she recognised one of the men as a man who worked for her boyfriend and she asked him where he was. Now as you see she is crying so we have to wait awhile."

It took several minutes before the girl could be persuaded to continue and when she did Ascensao took up the translating again.

"She is saying that she was told that her boyfriend had been shot dead by a British secret service agent and she should go far away, but she had nowhere else to go as all her family are here in Lagos. She was arrested when she returned to her parents' home after wandering the streets for two days and nights asking friends for help."

Vaughan immediately wondered how Graciano's men would know that he was a British secret agent. "She obviously didn't make many good friends then," he said.

"Her friends did not want to get involved when they learn her boyfriend he die in a shooting."

"Good point I suppose. Can she describe the two women?"

"Please wait, I will ask."

Vaughan waited patiently while the question was relayed.

"She says that she thinks one had red hair but she did not take much notice as she had been told bad news."

"A redhead, that sounds as if they were the two women I am searching for. Did she see where they went?"

"She is explaining now. Apparently Graciano's accomplice gave her some money to leave the area and she followed them back across the bridge thinking maybe to take a bus and go to another town but then she felt too scared. She now say that the women were put into a car and driven away."

"She is going to need protection," said Vaughan. "The people her boyfriend were working for are very dangerous men with links to arms trafficking in Africa and I suspect in other parts of the world. I doubt if she or they are aware of that, as I think this little snatch job was organised in a hurry."

"What makes you say that?" asked Ascensao.

"They would have had little time to react to the arrival of their target and I would bet that the power boat left from here in a hurry three days ago," said Vaughan.

"We will make enquiry if you think it important." "It would confirm the urgent response nature of the snatch," Vaughan replied. "While you are making enquiries can you also find out whether the boat owner has property here?"

"And if he has?"

"I would like you to get a search warrant."

"Huh, you are a very suspicious man, Senhor Vaughan. Of course I will need to get approval for such action."

Ascensao gave Vaughan a lift back to the marina and promised to have answers to the issue of property and a search warrant by morning. Boarding his boat Vaughan made a quick meal which he picked at, his mind piecing together the events that had occurred since leaving Madeira. *"How did Staunton appear like the rabbit out of the hat in Gibraltar if my little operation was to be a small team affair? I have a link between Staunton and Kazakov's minder, which could mean a link to Vermeulen, then of course there was the link between Anna-Maria's husband, Patterson, and her relationship to Vermeulen. Was someone else on that failed Angolan operation still in the loop and feeding Staunton information, if so it would confirm the Commodore's doubts about Staunton's part in that stunt. With Kazakov dead the minder is in prime position to deal with any stock holding so it could be simply that Staunton has been tasked to find out where Kasakov's assets are hidden. "The other bit that is a mystery is why there was so much fuss made over my revelations concerning the Madeira coup. Maybe our Government wanted the coup to succeed and that was why Staunton was so keen to stop me following the Reshetnikov link with Olavo Esteves and the coup. What was it that they told me on my initial training, ah yes, 'There are times when your orders might offend your moral principles.' Well that type of situation would, that's for sure."*

At 2215 hours Vaughan phoned Campbell's number and brought the Commodore up to date with the situation, then sought his advice. "If this guy Leonardo de Oliveira does have property here but a search warrant is refused, do you want me to make an unofficial visit?"

Campbell thought for a moment or two.

"Yes, maybe he is bankrolling Vermeulen," replied Campbell, "But remember you are no longer a member of SIS, I.D. or no I.D., so if you get caught you could well end up in a Portuguese jail with not many people wanting to help you."

"Understood, let's see what Agent Ascensao brings in the morning," said Vaughan, before moving the conversation onto his other concern. "Commodore, tell me, why was there so much fuss made of my role in revealing the coup, surely the British Government would not actively support such a thing?"

"According to Sir Andrew Averrille, it was the fact that a British agent got involved operating outside of his mission brief in a way that interfered with another nation's politics. He claimed that had the coup been successful and Portugal had left the EU, it would have presented a different European political dynamic, which may have been an advantage to Britain, but interference, though in this case helpful, may have been quite the reverse."

"I see, stick only to the task set."

"In a nutshell, yes, though personally I think that as Portugal is our oldest ally you did the right thing. It was those thoughts, I think, that led to my suspension and the closure of DELCO. So you see, Vaughan, sometimes our masters move in mysterious ways, their wonders to perform, leaving us floundering as to the reasons why," answered Campbell. "Why do you raise this now by the way?"

"Oh just the way Staunton got heavy about the coup when he gave me the sack, suggesting that he was having to clear up my mess when there was nothing to clear up from what I could see."

"Maybe his meeting with Kazakov's minder was following through on the man's links to the assassin and he just threw in the coup for good measure."

"Why should he do that and not leave the Kazakov problem with the Portuguese?" replied Vaughan, "And why refer to the coup when the assassination attempt was in connection with the North African conference and Walid al Djebbar?"

"He could well be operating under orders, Vaughan, possibly the FCO want it followed through your contact Charles Stanthorpe-Ogilvey."

"Charles didn't mention anything about a follow-up when I met him back in London," said Vaughan. "I'm sure he would have done, as he had received the full story from Walid."

"You met Stanthorpe-Ogilvey on your return?"

"Yes, Sir. In fact we had lunch together just before my meeting with you."

"Go careful with information there, Vaughan."

Vaughan was tempted to ask why but thought better of it. He had noticed previously that the Commodore was not a particular friend of Charles Stanthorpe-Ogilvey. "Of course, Sir," he replied.

"Is that all, Vaughan, as I have got other calls to make? Lorna Parker-Davis will be acting as link between us, you will get a call from her later."

"Right, Sir, I think that is all, goodnight, Sir."

The call ended and Vaughan sat worrying about the link added to his chain of command as it would inevitably delay response. It was obvious that the Commodore was under surveillance and probably his every move under scrutiny. Vaughan was still baffled by the reaction to something that struck him as being very minor on Commodore Campbell's part, which indicated that there was much more driving the situation than his straying from a set task and the Commodore's support of his actions.

Half an hour later Vaughan's phone chirped, "Hello".

"Vaughan?"

"Yes."

"It's Lorna Parker-Davis, the Commodore asked me to establish contact."

"Sorry, Lorna, I was half asleep and didn't recognise your voice."

"You've been told about DELCO?"

"Staunton briefly mentioned that it has been closed down when he gleefully told me that I was sacked."

"Where was this?"

"When I was talking with the Gibraltar Police at the apartment where Lieutenant Heathcote and Ms Ronaldo had been held."

"How did he get to be involved?"

"Apparently London issued his orders, which, as the Commodore is suspended, means Sir Averrille."

"This is serious, Vaughan."

"Yes I know it is, Lorna, you don't have to tell me."

"No, that's not what I meant, Vaughan. It means that the Commodore has no access to a higher authority so he must work outside of any official support system, whilst that sneering ape Staunton gets his feet firmly under the Commodore's desk."

"Surely he is not next in line, Lorna."

"I'm afraid he is, despite the fact that he has only been in the Service for four years."

"Where was he before?"

"Army, Afghanistan, possibly SAS."

"I see, well he has lost a lot of his fitness and reactions in that time."

"What do you mean?"

"He grabbed my shirt and threatened me shortly after I handed over my equipment. He is now walking with a limp and can be identified by a black eye."

Vaughan heard Lorna gasp then giggle. "Remind me to give you a big hug when we next meet."

"Um, yes I will."

"What are you up to now, Vaughan?"

"I'm waiting for two agents of Portugal's Servico de Informações de Segurança to get back, hopefully with a search warrant."

"You are onto something then?"

"It's just an idea. A witness in Gibraltar gave us the name of a boat that could have been used in the snatch operation. It has been traced here to Lagos on the Algarve and the owner has property here as well but lives and works in Lisbon," said Vaughan, "He apparently is working for a private bank."

"There had to be big money in it somewhere."

"Hopefully we'll find out tomorrow, Lorna. Oh, by the way can I call you on that phone you are holding?"

"I'm not using a mobile, this is a call box and I will use a different one next time."

"I'm impressed that you can find one that hasn't been vandalised."

"It has been a bit of a hunt, but then I went into a hotel foyer."

"I always knew you were smart."

"You've already earned your brownie points for the day, Vaughan, don't overdo it."

Vaughan chuckled, then, serious again, said, "Getting back to DELCO, does it mean that the whole of that set-up has been suspended?"

"Yes, it does, and I am led to believe that we all have to re-apply for our posts in two months' time. I was speaking to John Jessop earlier, he told me those glad tidings."

"Did you tell him where you were?"

"Good God no. I even used a friend's phone and number withheld from a point an hour's flying time from here, he said that he was suspended by one of the latest arrivals, a bumptious little irk called Housmann."

"Haven't heard of him."

"No you wouldn't, he went through the Manor shortly after you and was placed under Staunton at Babylon-on-Thames."

Vaughan laughed at her description of the Vauxhall Cross building design that housed MI6.

"A Staunton man eh, well this is beginning to look more like a coup at every twist and turn."

"That was my assessment as well. We must all watch our backs very carefully from now on. I haven't officially received the news yet and when my leave is up in two weeks I have been told by the Commodore to stay away until he gives the order for me to return. Let's hope it's sorted by then and Staunton put back in his place."

"I suppose that Staunton inherits all of the Commodore's workload."

"Yes, but don't worry about him, he is famous for dumping the real work onto others while he runs up the air miles to arrive back in time to collect all the glory. He calls it 'blue sky thinking' the older group under him call it 'brown nose lurking'," replied Lorna acidly. "The only person that appears to have any time for him is Sir Andrew, God knows why."

"Interesting, Lorna. It does seem strange that without any real team support he has got that far up the greasy pole of promotion."

"Yes, doesn't it. Anyway I will call again tomorrow on that number you have there then after texting me your new number you had better ditch that phone. Goodnight."

***

"Natanael Raimundo de Lacerda, virtually our top man, had the search warrant issued in minutes of my request," said Ascensao. "He obviously has a great interest in this banker."

Ascensao had arrived at Vaughan's yacht at seven o'clock in the morning waving the envelope that contained the search warrant.

"De Lacerda wants you to accompany me and the search team, as you may identify something that will make the link."

"He is hopeful that there is a link then," replied Vaughan, feeling a buzz of excitement. "I wonder whether our banker has crossed your boss's path before?"

Ascensao shrugged his shoulders. "Maybe, Senhor Vaughan. I hope there is a link for all our sakes, for, if the place is clean, I am sure Leonardo de Oliveira will make a great fuss and I will lose my recent promotion."

"Well, let's go and have a look and see what we can find."

The apartment was not far away from the mouth of the river and by the time they arrived the forensic team were already there awaiting the burglar alarm service engineer.

"What happened to the idea of knocking down doors?" Vaughan asked with a wry smile.

"That is reserved for the not so well off," Ascensao replied, returning Vaughan's smile. "They normally do not have loud burglar alarms to arouse the newspapers."

The forensic team's lock expert had already cleared the deadlock on the door so when the burglar alarm engineer arrived it was only a matter of a few seconds before they gained entry led by two armed response officers who confirmed that the apartment was empty. The forensic team then started their work and, suitably overalled, Ascensao and Vaughan joined them with Vaughan asking immediately he crossed the threshold, "Are either of those two ladies in your team wearing Givenchy Ysatis."

Both women shook their heads, one saying, "I wish".

"You recognise that scent?" asked Ascensao.

"Yes, Anna-Maria Ronaldo appeared to bathe in the stuff; the smell still lingers in the forward cabin and the heads on board my boat," replied Vaughan, "But that doesn't mean she has been here, it does however raise the possibility though."

"In here, Sir!" called one of the search team from a doorway leading from the reception hall of the apartment.

Vaughan and Ascensao hurried over to see what had been found.

"We just pulled back the curtain and found this," said the man pointing towards the window. "Look at the back of the curtain."

Ascensao pulled the curtain across the window and stepped behind it. "Clever, yes very clever, come and look at this, Senhor Vaughan."

Vaughan stepped behind the curtain and saw that someone had used what looked like beetroot juice to write the words, "Help get police" on the blackout curtain lining.

"Nice try but obviously nobody took it seriously, assuming of course that someone would have looked all the way up here from the street."

"Here is what they used, Sir," said another member of the search team holding up a slice of beetroot that he had just picked off the carpet under the bed.

Ascensao turned to Vaughan, "It seems that we have found where they were being held but where are they now?"

"We need to question the neighbours, hopefully they will be able to tell us something," said Vaughan, "A few words with the owner of the apartment might be a very good idea as well."

"I will leave the banker to Senhor de Lacerda to do the honours, he is very keen to disturb those in high places at the moment. I think the recent coup attempt has made him more suspicious of the people in banking circles and the super rich of our country."

"I don't see the immediate link between this and the coup but you never know, there may be something," commented Vaughan.

The interviewing of the neighbouring apartments' occupants revealed nothing of any interest and Ascensao and Vaughan left the building two hours later feeling disappointed and started to walk back out of the grounds to the public highway where they had left Ascensao's car. A gardener was cutting back dead leaves on a fern planted in a large pot in the middle of a grassed area. Ascensao stopped and called the man over.

"Were you working here yesterday?" Ascensao asked, flashing his badge.

"Sim, Senhor," the gardener replied, somewhat nervously.

"You are not in any trouble, we just want to know if you saw two young ladies being taken away from that apartment block?"

The gardener thought for a moment or two then shook his head. "No, Senhor, yesterday I was working over there, behind that building. Please you wait, I come back with my friend."

Half walking and half running, the gardener hurried away, disappearing out of sight down a flight of steps to the terrace area below. Five minutes later he returned with a shabbily dressed young man with long hair.

"He has something to tell you, Senhor."

The young man mumbled something and Ascensao stepped forward, and bending slightly, listened intently. "You are sure about this?" Ascensao said, stepping back a pace.

"Sim, Senhor," replied the young man, quietly.

"Okay, I need your name and the address where you are living."

It took some time getting the full details from the young gardener but with the help of the older man Ascensao was finally satisfied.

"Whether we will be able to find him again I have no idea, but I think he saw your women put into a dark green removal truck yesterday, around midday, that had foreign registration plates and big gold lettering on the side."

"Does he know which country the plates represented?"

"No, but he said they were not Portuguese or Spanish plates," said Ascensao. "He also tell me that one of the women had bright red hair and both seemed reluctant to get in the vehicle."

"Were they just reluctant or did they really resist?"

Ascensao called the two men towards him again and spoke rapidly to the younger gardener.

"He says that they did not want to travel in the back of the truck and had to be pushed."

"Did anyone travel in the back with them?"

"Yes, each of the women were pushed in by a man, then before the door was closed one of the men came back out and left the site in a car, which followed the lorry."

"Did he see which direction it took?" asked Vaughan.

"No, apparently he had a phone call from his girlfriend."

"You don't go in for CCTV on your roads do you," said Vaughan, "So the chances of being able to track this vehicle are nil."

"There may be some CCTV here that we could check on," replied Ascensao looking around.

The only point in the gated complex covered by CCTV was the gate itself and after an hour of searching for the site manager Vaughan and Ascensao sat down to review the previous day's recordings.

"There we are, that's the lorry and there is the driver. Pause it there please," said Vaughan. "Tough looking guy who appears to be on his own. Roll it on a fraction, hopefully we can see more of the cab door."

Whilst the car driver contacted the person controlling the gate he was successfully blocking the view of the vehicle but when he moved away Vaughan said, "Stop it there, we can just see the name of the company on the cab door – Izzard and Sampson International Removal Agents. Right we can look them up on the web I would think, I can't read the registration number though which is a pity."

Ascensao immediately started tapping the details into his mobile phone. "According to this there is no such company."

"Why does that not surprise me," said Vaughan, "I would take bets that vehicle has false floors and hidden compartments in the fuel tank, in fact anything a well organised smuggling operation needs."

"Let's have another look at that driver," said Ascensao. The site manager scrolled back to the point where Jacobs' face was reasonably in focus.

"Ex-military I would say," said Vaughan, "Clean shaven, and doesn't look as if he's driven very far to get here, in fact he looks quite fresh and rested. Not carrying any paperwork, unless that is in the cab. We need to know what reason he gave to gain access."

"The log say that he came to deliver a refrigerator and take the old one away from apartment Christo Columbus 4b," informed the site manager.

"And Leonardo de Oliveira's apartment is on the next floor," said Ascensao.

"Our gardening friend made no mention of a refrigerator being put in the lorry," said Vaughan, "Maybe that was just an excuse to gain entry, I can see why he didn't want the women up in the double cab with him, that would be far too risky."

"Maybe," said Ascensao, "or maybe the refrigerator was loaded before the gardener started to pay attention. It would be a big risk to assume that the gate man or somebody would not check inside the lorry both going in and out."

Vaughan shrugged his shoulders. "True, but to do so would probably have been fatal based on this gang's methods so far, though it's not that important now, but what is, is where the vehicle went to."

The CCTV record of the exit of the little convoy revealed the registration of the kidnappers' car and within minutes the vehicle's registration number had been circulated. "With luck the car followed the lorry to its destination in order to collect the man travelling with the hostages," said Vaughan.

Ten minutes later Ascensao received news that the car had been found that morning at a place called Aldeamento Porto Dona Maria.

"They tell me that it was burnt out."

"And that there were two bodies inside," interrupted Vaughan.

"How did you know that?"

"Whoever is pulling the strings here would have known that Graciano's little team have been identified and that it would be only a matter of time before they were hauled in for questioning. Now they cannot tell anyone where they drove to yesterday."

Ascensao nodded, "Yes you are right, it would have been our next move to round up Graciano's men. We know there is still at least one more out there, the third man on the bridge that Graciano's girlfriend met."

"If I were him I would be asking for police protection right now," said Vaughan, "Or running as fast as my little legs could carry me away from here."

"I think we should go and look at this car."

"Does the location of the vehicle tell us anything?" asked Vaughan.

"It's hard to say except that with both men in the vehicle it indicates that the lorry had reached its destination and the men were supposedly on their way back to Lagos."

Under blue lights and two tone horns the journey to the scene took only ten minutes, two marked police cars were parked up together and the scene of crime van with two men wearing blue overalls standing alongside it.

"Who is in charge?" asked Ascensao.

One of the men pointed down the steep bank towards the blackened wreck where another two blue overalled people were leaning into the front of the wreck through where the windscreen had once been.

"Do we need to suit-up?" asked Ascensao, holding up his badge; both men nodded and one moved to the rear of the vehicle returning with two sets of protective clothing.

Standing at the top of the track made by the vehicle Ascensao asked. "What do you make of this?"

Vaughan looked down at the tyre marks in the verge and studied the first few feet of the vehicle's run down the steep slope. "This car was just pushed off the road not driven, there are no skid marks either on the road or off it and I'm sure there are safer routes to the beach."

"Exactly my thoughts, Senhor Vaughan."

"They were obviously both dead before they took this last ride. A bullet in the head would be my guess."

Vaughan took his time making his way towards the vehicle, carefully looking at the ground as he went. Arriving at the car he was introduced to Dr Monica Quintal and her colleague Francisco Brito.

"Senhor Vaughan here thinks that both men were shot in the head before the car was pushed off the road up there."

"That is exactly what happened, Agent Ascensao, then someone came down here and with petrol from that can, torched the car," Quintal replied, pointing to a discarded ten-litre plastic fuel can in the scorched bush a few metres away.

"Was everything torched?"

"Pretty much I'm afraid. We have gathered up bits of charred and burnt paper that the heat of the fire and wind scattered around, they are under that polythene sheet."

Vaughan sauntered across to the sheet and, squatting down on his haunches, folded it back and started to pick through items that had retained some writing. Shortly he was joined by Ascensao.

"What do you hope to find, Senhor Vaughan?"

"I don't know until I find it," replied Vaughan, "But there may be a receipt for fuel or food that gives us a clue about their journey."

"Okay let us see what we can find."

The offshore breeze that had been blowing gently across the scene during the first half hour that the two men had been searching had at first faltered then died away altogether allowing the smell of burnt flesh to settle in a sickening cloud.

"Try wearing these, it will help," said Quintal handing Vaughan and Ascensao masks. "We have removed one of the bodies and found these remains of a note fold where his hip pocket would have been located. I will ask Francisco to help you separate the contents."

Francisco came down the slope carrying a folding table that he set up close to where Vaughan and Ascensao were working. Taking the note fold from Quintal he selected a pair of tweezers and carefully started to tease the leather fold apart revealing some bank notes and a credit card receipt all scorched and brittle but not completely burned.

"I do not know if this is of interest but it is payment for some food items from the Centro Commercial Supermercado in Burgau. The date is yesterday at just after twelve o'clock."

"That is not long after they left the complex at Lagos," observed Ascensao.

"Where is this Burgau?" asked Vaughan.

"Just a few kilometres west of here," informed Francisco.

"Was that the turning point I wonder or was that much further west."

178

"I think it is about time we organised a GNR helicopter now we know the direction in which they left Lagos," said Ascensao, pulling his mobile phone from his pocket.

Half an hour later they learnt that a search and rescue helicopter was taking off from Montijo airfield just south of Lisbon. "It should be with us in about three quarters of an hour and we have it for two hours max unless there is a search and rescue shout, then it dumps us and goes back to its proper job."

"I am impressed, this boss of yours, De Lacerda, has a hell of a lot of clout."

"And if you mess up, you feel that clout very hard, Senhor Vaughan, so we better get some good result from this."

***

The Merlin helicopter, painted in full dazzling SAR colours, touched down on the road just above the car wreck. The winch man, running out under the moving rotors, issued them with helmets then guided them back, helped them on board, and got Vaughan and Ascensao seated one on either side of the aircraft, and checked their seat belts. As they took off, Ascensao gave instructions as to the search pattern. The only thing they had to go on was the road and the communities along its route. A false alarm at Salema had the aircraft hovering low over the town centre in order to read the writing on the side of a lorry only for it to be recognised as belonging to a local firm and having Portuguese registration plates. By the time they got to Sagres both men fully recognised the enormity of the task they had set themselves.

"This idea of ours is based on the lorry and hostages staying on this tip of the Algarve more than one night," said Vaughan. "They would know that the car job would soon be recognised for what it was and want to get away from this area smartish."

"Smartish?" queried Ascensao.

"Yes, I mean quickly, not wanting to stay."

"I see, we had better return smartish then and think of something else."

"We've done the coastal communities, can we go back a little further inland," requested Vaughan.

The pilot turned the helicopter towards Horta do Tabual, circled the town, then continued east towards Buden, neither of which showed anything of interest.

"You had better take us back to where you found us," said Ascensao to the pilot, who shrugged his shoulders and made a small adjustment to the aircraft's course that brought them back just north of Burgau.

Vaughan, sat on the right-hand side of the helicopter, had not taken his eyes off the scenery below for more than a second throughout the flight and was now finding concentration hard. As the little town of Burgau came into view he looked down at the farm land and a few isolated buildings at the end of rutted tracks.

"Wow, hold it, what is that over there, to our right, alongside the big house in that hollow in the land."

Altering course they flew almost over the property gaining a really good view of a lorry.

"Do you want another look?" asked the pilot.

"No, it's okay," said Vaughan, trying to sound disappointed, "Just drop us back, please."

Ascensao gave Vaughan a curious look but said nothing. On landing, having thanked the aircrew for their efforts, Vaughan and Ascensao followed the winch man clear of the helicopter, both squinting as they cleared the dust storm generated by the rotors.

"What was that about back there? That was the vehicle, Izzard and Sampson International Removal Agents, in huge gold letters on the side?" said Ascensao, with a flabbergasted expression on his face.

"Yes, let's get going before they have time to pack up and do a runner," replied Vaughan as he watched the helicopter take off to fly north back to its base. "I did not want to share information unnecessarily. We need to get back there as soon as possible and follow their every move so that we can call in sufficient back-up."

"You drive, I will call the boss and bring him up to date," said Ascensao throwing the car keys to Vaughan.

If Ascensao's driving had been fast, when getting them from Lagos to the crash site, Vaughan's was so much faster, stretching the SEAT

Leon FR to the limit of its two litre engine. Ascensao had only just got off the phone when they passed the track leading to the property.

"I'll pull over, just up here a bit," said Vaughan, looking for a suitable track way or break in the bank to their right. "This looks good," he continued swinging the car off the road and stopping it behind some low scrub.

"If we cross the road and make our way up that hill, we should have a good view of the property."

"De Lacerda was in an interview room when I called. He was being harassed by Leonardo de Oliveira and an army of his lawyers, needless to say he was glad to hear what we found at the apartment and that we have located the removal lorry," informed Ascensao as they hurried across the road and made their way up the hill through the scrub vegetation and stunted trees.

"Is he sending in the cavalry?"

"I told him to wait until we confirm the lorry is still at the house."

The heat of the day and the steepness of the climb had Ascensao gasping for breath way before they had reached the top.

"You follow on, if the lorry has gone I'll come back straight away," said Vaughan, wanting to confirm whether Lieutenant Heathcote and Ms Ronaldo were still at the house.

As the chimneys of the property came into view Vaughan crouched then switched to a crawl until he could get behind a bush through which he could see the whole layout of the property. After a few minutes Vaughan heard Ascensao trudging up behind him and turning said in a hoarse whisper,

"Get down low," signalling with his hands.

When Ascensao crawled alongside him Vaughan explained what he could see.

"If you peer through the branches here you will see that the house has a clear view of everything around for about one hundred metres. Whoever chose this location did a good job, our only real chance will be under cover of darkness."

"If we surround it with men what could they do?"

"Threaten to execute one of the hostages, and I can assure you that both of those women are very valuable to my boss."

"Ah, but would they?" replied Ascensao, "Often they make threat but with some negotiation all is resolved without loss of life."

"Out in the Atlantic they sank the fishing boat on which Ms Ronaldo was making her escape costing the lives of four men in an effort to stop her talking to us," said Vaughan, "Frankly I'm surprised that she has survived this far."

CHAPTER 8

The amazement of her survival was a feeling shared earlier by Anna-Maria Ronaldo herself who could not understand why she had not been shot on sight when she and Penny Heathcote had been snatched from the Land Rover. The room in which she was now a prisoner was unfurnished and she sat back against a wall, her bottom hurting from hours on the hard wooden floorboards. In the corner was a bucket with a toilet roll alongside it. Her hands and legs were shackled but she had sufficient movement to eat food and attend to the basic toilet requirements. Movement around the room was limited to a painful shuffle as the ankle straps had soon produced painful sores. Since the snatch she had been almost permanently in fear of her life, hungry, thirsty and after meeting Jacobs, in fear of being brutally raped. The rough sea voyage, to where she recognised as being Lagos, had been followed by a night in an apartment there, where she had lain awake terrified and confused, cursing herself for ever thinking of leaving Luanda. The stress of everything from the day she had left with her mother had confused her to a point where she could hardly remember what month it was let alone what day. Then Jacobs had arrived, this really terrifying man, who had ordered them into the back of a removal truck for the short painful journey to this new prison where another night had passed but one in which she had had little sleep.

Early the following morning her jailer Jacobs was sat at the dusty kitchen table eating the last of the pasta salad that the farmer's wife had provided. He was idly wondering what plans Leonard Staunton had for the two women when his phone rang.

"Yes, Sir?"

"Have you got them?"

"Yeh, they are here all tucked up and tidy in separate bedrooms. What do want done with them?"

"I'm making arrangements to have them transported to Turkey to take on new careers."

"Oh, right, how far do you need me to take them?" Jacobs asked with a big grin on his face.

"Montpellier, just over the Pyrenees in France, I'll let you know the exact exchange point."

"Who are you gonna use?"

"Probably Andre Ameaux, he has the right connections for the Greek and Turkish borders."

"Yeh, it's an area I'm not too keen to visit again. Is the ladies' new career the one I think it is?"

"Yes," Staunton replied, "I'm sure they will be a great success. Now if I say be at the changeover in three days' time is that going to be enough do you think?"

"Yeh, I need to get fuel and food sorted as we can't take them out to restaurants en route can we," replied Jacobs already making plans for Anna-Maria.

"Okay, you get that sorted I'll contact you in a couple of days."

Jacobs finished his meal and left the house to find the brothers who were now close to completing the task he had set them, "Oi, Bento, take a break and go to the town and bring some food back here, pizza or lasagne and some fruit, enough for five people. Your Leonardo wants you and Carlinhos to keep watch here overnight then tomorrow morning we move out, okay?"

"Si, Senhor Jacobs, you wish when I get back I help Carlinhos again?"

"No, don't seem much point now that we are due to leave soon." Then as the man walked away he called after him, "Don't be long getting that stuff mind."

"Carlinhos, you're with me, we need to sort out a watch duty roster for tonight, I don't want to spend all night awake like last night."

***

In Anna-Maria's room she was woken from a troubled sleep by footsteps along the landing outside; a key rattled in the lock and as the door opened, assuming the visitor to be Jacobs, a rush of fear swept over her. When the rather nervous Portuguese man who Anna-Maria remembered was called Carlinhos entered, carrying a plate of food and a mug of water, the relief almost made her cry. Putting the plate and mug alongside of her Carlinhos carefully removed the tape from her mouth.

"Thank you," she said squinting her eyes at the light pouring in through the open door.

The previous visit to the room had been made by her thug of a jailer bringing a clean bucket and another toilet roll. He had put them against the opposite wall then just stood looking down at her his eyes slowly wandering over her body whilst on his face was that lecherous smile of his that struck so much fear into her.

"What is the date today?" she asked Carlinhos.

"September seventeenth."

"Thank you. Er, can you tell me what is going to happen to me?"

Carlinhos shook his head. "I do not know, Leonardo will decide, Jacobs says we leave here tomorrow."

"Who is Leonardo?"

"Galician Mafia, Senhora, he a dangerous man, I am sorry I cannot tell you anymore."

"Do we leave with you?"

Carlinhos shrugged, he had heard the stairs creak and guessed that Jacobs was coming so did not want to pursue the conversation. Hurriedly leaving the room he made his way along the landing to where Heathcote was being held. Anna-Maria could remember from her teenage years references to the Galician Mafia and the terrible crimes it was accused of, the mention of it now did not surprise her, nothing would when linked with Jan Vermeulen. A movement in the doorway made her look up to see Jacobs' leering face staring at her.

"Here, Mrs Patterson, as soon as you've finished that, get down to the bathroom and have a bath, you stink."

"Why should that worry you?" Anna-Maria answered, surprising herself by her response.

"Because I don't like to have women that smell, right."

The word "have" made her shudder and she felt a different kind of fear welling up inside her, the kind one experiences looking down the wrong end of a gun barrel, "I don't think I want a bath."

"The decision ain't yours to make, darlin'. You either go by yourself or I drag you by your hair and bath you myself, what is it to be?"

Anna-Maria looked down at the floor.

"Well?"

Putting down the plate she struggled to her feet and shuffled across to the door. Slowly he stepped back out of her way.

"That's better, now get on wiv it," said Jacobs. As she left the room she heard him say to Carlinhos.

"You and your brother stay downstairs until I call yer, understand. Keep a lookout, anyone approaching I want to know about, got it?"

Carlinhos nodded then glanced along the landing at Anna-Maria then back at Jacobs.

"Just do as you are told, chum, and don't ever question me, **right!**" said Jacobs grabbing Carlinhos by the throat and pinning him against the wall.

Wide-eyed, Carlinhos made a limited nodding motion and as Jacobs released his hold said, "Sim, Senhor, we stay downstairs until you say."

Jacobs watched as Carlinhos made his way downstairs then walked towards the bathroom slipping his shoulder holster off as he went, at the bathroom he pushed the door open and saw Anna-Maria, bending over to turn on the taps. Leaning against the door frame he watched as she tested the water temperature. When she straightened up he walked silently across the room and put a hand on her shoulder making her jump then freeze.

"Of course you can't unzip the dress with your wrists tethered," he said taking the zip tag and pulling it slowly downwards to her waist. "There, now for the bra strap, is that better now things are not so restricted."

He took a step back, "Turn round. I said turn round!" Grabbing her shoulders Jacobs spun her round to face him. "You will find that it is a lot less painful if you do as you are told straight away."

Anna-Maria felt that she was going to be sick, the menace in his voice was terrifying and frantically she swallowed and swallowed until the nausea subsided.

"Don't move from that spot or else," he said backing away towards the door. "I will be back in a moment." As soon as he had undone the zip Jacobs had realised that the dress would not fall to the ground unless the wrist bonds were cut. In his haste for gratification he had failed to plan and was furious with himself for spoiling something that he had dreamed of since the first moment he had seen her terrified face in the bedroom at Lagos.

As he left the room Anna-Maria stepped across to the washstand and took her nail scissors from her toilet bag hiding them in her clenched fist. She had just regained her position as Jacobs came back into the bathroom holding the vicious looking double-edged knife.

Turning the bath taps off he said, "Hold out your hands."

The knife sliced through the bonds as if it was a length of cheap cotton thread. Reaching out Jacobs slipped the dress from her shoulders followed by her bra, watching appreciatively as they dropped to the floor.

"Oh nice, very nice. Let's look on this as your apprenticeship for your next career," he said going down on one knee to cut the ankle ties. "There, now it is just the knickers to take down."

Tears were now streaming down her face as she felt the garment being pulled down to the floor. The point of her nail scissors pricked her thumb reminding her of what she must do, but when?

Jacobs was starting to stand, rising so close to her that she could feel his hot breath on her skin as she stood trembling, listening to the raggedness of his breathing until his head reached the top of her thighs and she realised that this was her moment.

Jacobs thought the movement was going to be just a slap, something he had actually looked forward to, too late he felt the sharpness of the scissors as the point pierced the skin of his throat and through to rip a hole in his jugular.

He was dying even as he reached for her hand, falling backwards as his life drained away.

For a moment or two she froze, staring in horror as Jacobs gave a throaty rattle, twitched and then lay still, his lifeless eyes staring blindly at the washstand as a pool of blood spread across the linoleum floor covering.

She heard footsteps on the ground floor and realised that the sound of Jacobs' fall had attracted the attention of the brothers. Stomping her foot on the floor she cried out, "No, no, please, no you are hurting me." Then putting her hand over her mouth continued to make muffled protest as she picked up his knife and ran from the bathroom to where Jacobs had left his holster and gun. She reached it just as Carlinhos had reached the top of the stairs and, pulling the gun from the holster, pointed it at him.

"Senhora, please you put the gun down before you hurt yourself. We come up here to help you."

Carlinhos stepped onto the landing, his hand out wanting her to give up the weapon. Bento then appeared but hung back behind his brother.

"Of the many lessons I learnt when living in South Africa one was how to shoot a pistol. I am a very good shot," Anna-Maria said in her native tongue to avoid any misunderstanding, feeling now more confident recalling that neither of the men in front of her had appeared to carry any weapon.

"Please, Senhora, please you had better give me the gun for all our safety," pleaded Carlinhos who then made the mistake of taking another pace towards her. The bullet went through his left calf and with a look of absolute shock Carlinhos hopped backwards once then with a pained yell fell backward onto the floor where he lay groaning.

"Don't move," shouted Anna-Maria, as Bento went to rush at her, "Or I will kill you!"

Bento stopped, now frightened, staring at the unwavering barrel of the pistol pointing at his head.

"Lay face down on the floor, **now**."

Bento did as he was told.

"Where are the room keys?"

Carlinhos reached into his pocket and held up a bunch of keys.

The direction of the gun barrel switched from Bento to Carlinhos, "Toss them over here."

With a clatter the keys dropped at her feet and crouching she picked them up with her left hand and, retreating to the bedroom where

Heathcote was held, blindly tried the keys one by one, in the lock until she found the one that turned. As the lock worked so the door was flung open and Heathcote appeared staring wide-eyed.

"You bloody hero, Christ you've got no clothes on."

Ignoring Heathcote, Anna-Maria motioned with the gun saying, "Bring your brother in here and no tricks or believe me you **will** die."

Supported by his brother Carlinhos made it into the bedroom leaving a trail of blood behind him.

"What happened?" said Heathcote, locking the door behind the two men.

"That evil bastard Jacobs started to rape me."

"Where is he now?"

"In the bathroom," Anna-Maria replied. "My clothes are in there, but I can't go in there, not now, not after what happened."

Heathcote helped her sit with her back to the wall, "You wait there, Anna-Maria, I'll go and get them."

Anna-Maria hardly noticed the roughness of the wooden flooring on her bare behind, she just felt an overwhelming sense of relief and yes, pride. She had faced up to a dangerous thug and then naked, faced up to two other bad men, and she knew in her heart at that moment that her David would have been so proud of her.

At the bathroom door Heathcote gasped in horror at the scene, "Oh my God, oh my God, Anna-Maria did you do this?" Looking round Heathcote saw Anna-Maria nod. "I don't know how you did it, but that bastard deserved it. Hold on, I'll be back in a moment."

Giving the body of Jacobs a wide berth Heathcote found it hard to take her eyes off the nail scissors protruding from the man's throat. Groping blindly she picked up Anna-Maria's clothes then, backing away to the door, took them back to her, "Where did you get the nail scissors from?"

"My toilet bag, somehow they had got through the tear I'd made in the lining and when they searched it in Gibraltar they missed them."

"Well, they found mine and my nail file, which would have been useful after I broke this nail on that ape Gregorio's face," said Heathcote holding up the middle finger of her right hand. "When you've got that third strong drink in your hand you can tell me what happened."

Hurriedly, Anna-Maria dressed whilst Heathcote spoke loudly through the bedroom door to the brothers, "Push the key to your car under the door and I will go and get a doctor to deal with the bullet wound."

"You take him to doctor please, he loses much blood," pleaded Bento.

"Use the toilet paper and press it against the wounds, I will not be long."

"Please you take him, he will not harm you."

"I don't believe you, so give me the key."

There was a short conversation between the brothers followed by some shuffling then the tip of the key appeared and was snatched up by Heathcote, "Wise move, I will be as quick as I can."

***

On the ridge above the house Ascensao had just finished the call to De Lacerda when they heard the shot. "Oh shit, that doesn't sound good," said Vaughan, "how long do you think before the cavalry arrives?"

"Maybe half an hour."

"You said to meet with us here, right?"

"Yes," replied Ascensao, "I did not want them approaching up the trackway to the house."

"Right, we sit and wait then."

They scrambled up to the ridge and could hear shouting from inside the house then all went quiet again.

"What was that all about, that sounded more like Portuguese to me and a woman's voice," said Vaughan.

"This Ronaldo lady she is Portuguese is she not?"

"Yes, of course you're right, I hope to God that doesn't mean they have killed Heathcote."

"It does not sound good whatever has happened in there."

"I presume you have some marksmen level guys in your armed support teams."

"Yes, normally two men who carry special rifles."

"Let's hope that they will be given a clear shot."

Some five minutes passed during which voices could be heard but not identified then they saw a dishevelled Lieutenant Heathcote peering nervously out of the building's front door.

Vaughan leapt up and shouted, "It's all right, Lieutenant, there is no one else about," as he broke cover to run down the slope towards the house gun in hand.

As he got close to her he was shocked to see the state she was in. Her nose had been broken and her eyes were black, her wrists and ankles had sores and were bleeding and her right hand hung limply at her side. "Who was the bastard who did this to you?" said Vaughan, gently putting his arms around her. "Let's get you sat down somewhere, more help is on its way."

"Anna-Maria is upstairs, go and see if she is all right, I can manage," said Heathcote.

Turning to Ascensao, as the man jogged across the level section towards the house, Vaughan said, "Agent Ascensao, can you take care of Lieutenant Heathcote here and tell your troops that it is safe to come straight in, and bring a good medic with them."

"Sure, Senhor Vaughan."

Carefully Vaughan climbed the stairs alert to any movement.

"Who is that?" said a frightened voice on the landing.

"It is me, Anna-Maria, Ian."

An ashen-faced Anna-Maria Ronaldo peered round the corner at the head of the stairs holding a gun very professionally, her expression of suspicion changing to joyous relief at the sight of Vaughan coming up the stairs towards her.

"Thank God, it's a miracle, how did you find us? I was so afraid that I was to die here," she sobbed, her relief turning to tears.

"Is there anyone else here?" Vaughan asked, "We heard a shot."

"I… I shot a man called Carlinhos in the leg, he is in the locked bedroom just along there," she sobbed, pointing to a door along on the right of the landing.

"Join Penny downstairs, I'll take a look."

"He is in there with his brother so be careful please, Ian."

"Can you make it down the stairs on your own?"

"I think so."

"You will find Penny and Agent Ascensao of the Portuguese SIS waiting down there. More help is on the way."

Vaughan waited until he was sure she was managing the stairs safely then went in search of the men that Anna-Maria had talked about. A bunch of keys hung from a door lock and taking them Vaughan worked his way along the landing opening each of the other doors and checking carefully inside each room until he came to the bathroom and saw Jacobs' body sprawled on the floor and the nail scissors stuck in his throat. *"Jesus wept, I bet that was Heathcote's work, no way was this done by Anna-Maria?"*

Leaving the bathroom he went back to the door where he had found the keys and working his way through them found the one that fitted the lock. Taking his Glock from the trouser holster he readied himself to open the door.

"Afasta-te da porta!" Vaughan said loudly.

"Okay, Senhor," came a rather nervous reply.

Turning the key Vaughan threw open the door standing to one side before glancing in to see Bento Sousa standing in the middle of the room looking fearful and his brother sat in the corner, his left trouser leg rolled up and blood stained toilet paper bandaged round his calf.

The door had swung right back against the wall but Vaughan was still cautious as he entered. In response to a flick of Vaughan's pistol Bento backed off to the other side of the room where, after another signalled command, he turned to face the wall. Vaughan took a few moments looking at Carlinhos, assessing whether the man was capable of causing trouble, then considering it safe to do so stepped over and pushed Bento hard against the wall and padded him down for any possible weapon. Satisfied, he pulled the man round to face him and indicated for him to sit then turning to Carlinhos, Vaughan indicated that he should stand. Painfully, Carlinhos rose to his feet and without instruction turned and faced the wall, allowing Vaughan to search him. As Vaughan turned him back to face him Carlinhos said in English.

"We are not the ones who hurt your friends, Senhor. That evil man in the bathroom did all of the hurt, please we were only here to build a compartment in the lorry, behind the driver's, er cab, but then it all turned very bad when that man say Leonardo need us to clear away the plants from around the house and help him guard the women."

"Who is he, the man in the bathroom?" Vaughan asked.

"He is Englishman called Jacobs. He was sent by Leonardo to transport the two ladies."

"What is his first name?"

"I am sorry I do not know, Senhor. All I know is he is bad evil man even though he say he was some time in British Army. He tell us that many of his forefathers were British Army as well, and he knew much about British Army fighting together with Portuguese Army against the French."

"Who killed him?"

"It was the one with the dark hair, Senhor."

Vaughan look surprised, "Are you sure?"

"Yes. Jacobs, he tried I think to rape her, he is very bad like devil."

'And there was me thinking that she wouldn't have the nerve, well Anna-Maria, hats off to you, young lady.' He could hear a further commotion from downstairs as the backup arrived.

"Where is this Leonardo?"

"I am not sure, Senhor, the last time Jacobs spoke to Senhor Leonardo I think he say Leonardo was in London," Carlinhos replied, now keen to give up all the information he could in the hope that it would make things easier for himself and his brother.

"Do you know this man Leonardo?"

"We meet him in Lisbon a few weeks back, he needed some boxes made for something he and Graciano plan."

"What is he, what does he do?"

"He Galician Mafia I think, but I not really sure, please I am trying to help all I can, Senhor."

"Was he due to come here?"

"I do not think so. Jacobs he say that we were to leave here tomorrow morning and he take the women somewhere else."

"Do you know where they were going to?"

"No, Senhor, I am sorry, but Jacobs he not tell me things like that, he only say they were leaving."

At that point Ascensao's partner entered the room. "Ah, Senhor Vaughan, we can take over from here."

"All right, but I would like to sit in when this man here is questioned. Have you seen the dead guy in the bathroom?" Then pointing to Carlinhos said, "He says that he was an Englishman and his accomplice is believed to be in London at this time, so I could assist your investigation a great deal."

"Who are these two?"

"I don't know their names but this one told me that they were employed by a Senhor Leonardo."

"Who is he?"

"Again, I don't know, but whoever he is I get the impression that this guy is terrified of him and thinks he may be Galician Mafia."

"He could well be Mafia, this is their style."

"Well, organised crime then."

"We must continue this in Lagos, Senhor Vaughan. Our boss Senhor De Lacerda wishes to be there, he will be most interested in what these men have to say."

"The two ladies downstairs need to be safely returned to London as soon as possible, but first of all I need to make the arrangements with the head of my section," said Vaughan, wondering how the hell he was going to make contact with Commodore Campbell. It was then that a thought struck him, Heathcote.

"Excuse me er, sorry I didn't get your name."

"Boquinhas, Agent Boquinhas,"

"Excuse me, Agent Boquinhas, I must talk to Lieutenant Heathcote urgently."

Vaughan hurried from the room and threaded his way amongst the numerous policemen looking around the building. He found Heathcote in the kitchen having her ankles bandaged with a pale Anna-Maria sat alongside her.

"How are you feeling?"

"Not good at the moment, mainly because I was so bloody useless when the chips were down."

"Unarmed, what else could you do," said Vaughan, "Look, I don't want to rush you but do you have Lorna's personal mobile number?"

"It's on my mobile. That bastard Jacobs put it somewhere. I know it's still about as it kept on ringing until yesterday."

"I'll be back in a jiffy," said Vaughan, turning to hurry upstairs to the room where he had seen the single sleeping bag neatly laid out on the floor. The police were searching the room. "Has anyone found a mobile phone? Come on, quickly, has anyone found a mobile phone?"

"Sim, Senhor there are three over there."

"Can I have some gloves?"

A uniformed woman reached into her pocket and handed Vaughan a pair of latex gloves.

"Obrigado," said Vaughan, the woman gave a faint smile and returned to her work of searching Jacobs' jacket.

Rushing back down the stairs to where Heathcote was receiving attention to her face, Vaughan excused himself and asked, "Which one of these phones is yours, Lieutenant?"

"This one," she said, taking the one with the dark blue protective case. "Shall I give her a call?"

"Yes if you would, and ask her to get permission from the Commodore for me to bring you both back to England by sea."

Heathcote gave Vaughan a hard look then nodded. "It probably would be safer," she looked at her phone, "Damn, battery dead."

"I'll hunt round and put it on charge for you," said Vaughan, taking the phone back again.

He found the correct type of charger almost immediately but before returning the other two phones to the police Vaughan went back to where the brothers were being held.

"Sorry to interrupt, Agent Boquinhas, but I need to ask the brothers one more question."

"Go ahead, Senhor Vaughan."

Looking at Carlinhos, Vaughan asked, "Which of these phones belonged to Jacobs?"

Carlinhos looked at both and pointed to the one in Vaughan's left hand.

"What about the other one?" Boquinhas asked.

"It belong to the lady with the dark hair."

"Can I return it to her?" asked Vaughan. "And we need to know what earlier communications were made from this one."

"Yes okay, I think De Lacerda will be more interested in what these two have to say."

Back watching as Heathcote endured the painful process of having a gauze packing inserted into her nostrils. "Fortunately for you, Senhora, your nose was not pushed to one side so you keep this in place until you next see a doctor, maybe keep it there for three to four days, yes?"

Heathcote nodded.

"Once the bone starts to set I think maybe not much change to your lovely face, meantime, Senhora, you put colder padding gently on your nose to help the swelling and I give you some painkillers to help, eh?"

"Thank you, Filipe, you have been very kind."

"My brave patient with the beautiful red hair, it has been a pleasure," said the young medic, "I must now go and see this man with the wounded leg, excuse me please."

When the medic had left the room Vaughan asked, "Did he get your phone number?"

"No, he did not, Vaughan," Heathcote replied indignantly.

Smiling to himself Vaughan switched on Jacobs' phone, "Blast, it wants a password, any ideas?"

"He was definitely ex-military so have a look on his body for any tattoos."

"Good idea, Lieutenant, I'll be back shortly. Oh, Anna-Maria here's your phone, if you ask round maybe someone has the right charging lead."

Anna-Maria took the phone and unsteadily getting to her feet approached two policemen stood in the hallway.

They had covered Jacobs' body with a curtain taken from one of the downstairs windows; lifting it off the torso Vaughan started to inspect the left arm. Rigor mortis had not yet set in making the corpse easy to manipulate. *"Now let's see what we can find. Um, signs that the tattoo on the forearm has been removed and the one on the upper arm. I'm beginning to think that you were SAS or one of us at one time."* Checking the other arm and chest revealed nothing more so Vaughan went through to where Jacobs had set himself up to see what the police had found.

"Have you found anything to confirm the dead man's identity?"

"He had two passports, Senhor, one British and one Serbian."

"May I have a look?"

"Sim, er of course, Senhor, here."

Vaughan opened the British passport, *"Barry Michael Jacobs born Clacton-on Sea on the 12th August, 1980. The question is whether that is your real name."* Opening the Serbian passport he looked at the details, *"Miroslave Nenadovic born Beograd 12th August, 1980 and the same passport picture. Interesting, I wonder what operation you were sent on to have this, or is this access to somewhere you can run and hide if the heat is turned up. Interesting that the next of kin is a firm of solicitors."*

Photographing the pages on his mobile Vaughan returned both passports to the police and went back down to the kitchen.

"Here is something that will interest you, Lieutenant, have a look at these pictures."

Heathcote took a couple of minutes studying the passport details, "Why do you think he is holding a Serbian passport?"

"At first I thought he may have been working for us at some stage or SAS and been sent there on a mission but on second thoughts I think he has a bolthole there that he can run to if something went wrong with his smuggling activities."

"How do you know he was a smuggler?"

"The Sousa brothers were employed to build a secret people smuggling compartment behind the driver's cab of that lorry outside and I am betting that there are other compartments in which stuff can be hidden."

"Were there any tattoos of interest?"

"No, they had been removed some time ago I would imagine."

"Making it more likely that at one time he was with SAS or us," said Heathcote with a sigh. "We train people to do some pretty awful things hoping that they will only use those skills in defence of our country but we are never that sure they will stay clean."

"I'm going to try using his Serbian passport number to open his phone."

He tapped in the first six numbers only to see that they were rejected, then the last six numbers in reverse getting the same result. After the third try using numbers from Jacobs' British passport were rejected the phone was locked.

"Failure I'm afraid, we'll have to get it sent to London via the Portuguese police."

"No, Vaughan, don't do that, I'll take it back with me. I don't want to risk that being conveniently lost."

It took half an hour before Heathcote's phone responded and a very long time before a reply came confirming Campbell's agreement. In the meantime Vaughan, together with the two women, had been driven back to Lagos, and while Vaughan, assisted by a police constable, set about provisioning the yacht, Lieutenant Heathcote and Anna-Maria were being interviewed at the police station under armed guard; no one was taking any chances in view of the snatch operation that had been carried out in Gibraltar.

Dropping the stores off at the yacht Vaughan got the constable to take him back to the police station, where he was asked to wait and meet Senhor De Lacerda. Blue flashing lights and something of a kerfuffle in the main entrance announced the arrival of De Lacerda who had flown down from Lisbon especially to interview the Sousa brothers. De Lacerda was short in stature and rather portly but very upright with dark and darting alert eyes that seemed to be hoovering up every visual detail he saw. After a greeting from the senior staff at the station he was introduced to Vaughan.

"Ah, Senhor Vaughan, I understand from Agent Ascensao that you have been of great assistance, please be assured that I will pass on his praise to my old friend Alex Campbell when he contacts me later. I understand that this operation of yours is very, very delicate."

"Yes, it is, Senhor, very delicate indeed. May I ask if it would be possible for me to get a description of a man called Leonardo who the Sousa brothers seem to think is the mastermind behind the abduction of Lieutenant Heathcote and Senhora Ronaldo?"

"We have brought in the police artist from Faro who is working with them at this moment endeavouring to obtain an image of that very man; when he is finished I would be happy to supply you with a copy," informed the station's chief inspector.

"That is most kind of you, thank you. One further request, would it be possible for me to be in the interview observation room when you start your questioning?"

"Certainly, I will ask Agent Boquinhas to sit with you and translate. Please let us make a start."

The interview of Carlinhos Sousa got underway and De Lacerda demonstrated straight away that he was not always the "mister ultra polite" that he had appeared to be when talking to Vaughan. After some minutes, the interview was interrupted by a uniformed policeman entering with the artist's impression of the man known as Leonardo.

"The artist has also been talking to Bento Sousa so this picture is probably a composite of the two descriptions," Boquinhas said quietly. "De Lacerdo is now asking Carlinhos whether that picture is correct, and he say that it is very close with maybe the face just a little thinner."

"What other features were there about the man?" asked Vaughan.

"Apparently none that he can recall, De Lacerda has just asked that question. Sousa say it is some weeks since they last met this Leonardo."

After ten minutes or so the policeman entered again having got the artist to make the further adjustment to the Leonardo impression. This time Carlinhos agreed that it was a good likeness and the policeman was sent away with the picture to have copies made. After an hour De Lacerda declared that his first interview was over and ordered that the brothers be taken to Lisbon where they would be held for further questioning before being placed on trial.

"Carlinhos Sousa and his brother have been very keen to co-operate with us and his answers reveal a great deal about the workings of the Graciano gang and its part in relieving the equipment stores of our Portuguese Army and that of Spain of a considerable amount of weaponry," said Boquinhas, "These revelations also linked this mysterious character Leonardo to the thefts, which were probably some of the old HK 417 rifles based on the Heckler & Koch G3 that fired the now disused 7.62 bullet."

"Your Army still issues those weapons to its troops, as I painfully found out in Madeira."

Boquinhas gave Vaughan a questioning look.

"I'll explain later. Does De Lacerda need to talk to Lieutenant Heathcote or Senhora Ronaldo?"

"I will ask for you, please wait here."

Five minutes later Boquinhas returned, "Senhor De Lacerda say that questions to these ladies is the responsibility of Commodore Campbell in England so they are free to leave in your care. He is much more interested in learning about this Leonardo and will be asking many more questions of the other Sousa brother arrested today. If this Leonardo is Galician Mafia and their information leads to his arrest then De Lacerda will have maybe shed a light on a very dark corner of our criminal world, Senhor Vaughan."

"According to the older Sousa brother, this Leonardo is in London and he didn't expect him to come here as they were about to move the women somewhere else, where, he didn't know. Tell me, was Graciano's gang part of this Mafia group?"

"We are not sure. There is no doubt that taking out a large part of that gang, including its leader, is very helpful for us and we hope to soon find the last of his team that kidnapped your Lieutenant and Ms Ronaldo, but whether he will be willing to own up to membership of such an organisation as the Galician Mafia is very doubtful," said Boquinhas. "Other than the passport, the Englishman, Jacobs is a mystery, there was nothing to definitely identify him by, either on his body, or in the vehicle he was driving."

"Did your people find the concealed people-smuggling compartment behind the lorry's cab?"

"No, we did not!" said Boquinhas visibly shocked, "Is there such a place?"

"According to the Sousa brothers there is. I would also suggest that you look for other secret compartments as I am sure that people smuggling is not the only illegal business that the lorry was used for."

Ascensao entered the room, "We are having the vehicle brought here for further investigation so I will go now and make sure that these compartments are discovered. Oh, here is the artist's impression that De Lacerda promised you," he said handing Vaughan a brown envelope.

De Lacerda and Agent Boquinhas left shortly after saying their farewells, leaving Agent Ascensao to drive the two women and Vaughan to the marina and see them on board Vaughan's yacht. Vaughan was relieved that it was night-time, which would make their departure much less of a spectacle for idle or interested observers.

"I'll get the footbridge raised for you," said Ascensao, as Vaughan went to step ashore again to see if the marina office was still open.

"Thanks and thank you for all of your support while I have been here," replied Vaughan, shaking Ascensao's hand. "You've been brilliant."

"Ter uma viagem segura e cuidar," replied Ascensao wishing him a safe journey.

"Obrigado, Senhor Ascensao."

***

The river current helped when Vaughan cast off from the pontoon as he saw the footbridge begin to lift. It was only a short distance to the sea and, running before the wind, now under full sail they had soon gone far enough south and clear of the coast to switch off the navigation lights and point the yacht's bow west-south-west on a broad reach to clear the tip of the Algarve, Fortaleza de Sagres.

"Why no lights?" asked Heathcote, who had just joined Vaughan in the cockpit.

"I didn't want anyone second guessing where we are bound for but with clear skies and a half moon a bit later that is a fond hope."

"Yes, it is rather."

"Could you keep a lookout for a few minutes? I want to take a look at that identity sketch of this mysterious Leonardo who appears to put the fear of God into everybody," said Vaughan. "The auto helm is doing the steering so it's just keeping an eye out for other boats."

"I have sailed before, Vaughan."

"It's 'Ian' when you are on board my boat, Penny," replied Vaughan, as he turned to go below.

The envelope was on the chart table and opening it he pulled the picture out and switched on the chart table light. "Good God, it can't be," he exclaimed. *"No, it can't be Staunton,"* looking up into the cockpit he said, "Hey, Penny, take a look at this."

201

Penny Heathcote gave a quick look around then came below to join Vaughan at the chart table.

"What am I supposed to be looking at? Oh heavens above, that is Staunton surely!"

"It surely is, Penny, and it ties in with how and why Staunton appeared like a rabbit from a hat in Gibraltar," replied Vaughan, "Oh, by the way, did you know that we have been suspended? In fact I have been fired altogether never to darken your office door again."

Heathcote looked shocked. "Yes, Lorna told me about our situation but I didn't know about you," she replied, giving Vaughan a rather sorrowful look. "I feel sorry for the Commodore, he has worked so hard to get his section up to speed and now this."

"And according to Staunton I am the main reason, along with the Commodore, for DELCO to be closed down," said Vaughan. "He claims that it's all my fault in involving myself with the affairs of another nation beyond the brief of my assignment."

"When the first reports hit, you were acclaimed as a hero and the PM appeared to be over the moon that the British Intelligence Services had saved a friendly nation's government from being overthrown. Just before I left, however, there were rumblings that several MPs thought your interference was against a democratic process within the EU and not something that the British Intelligence Services should be doing, so applied some pressure on the PM and Sir Andrew Averrille," replied Penny. "I was surprised that Sir Andrew was falling for it but he had received a huge amount of negative reporting about you from Staunton during the period when the Commodore was away on honeymoon."

"Well, this may be the reason for Staunton's negative reporting, as it appears he was supposedly involved with the Galician Mafia."

"Who told you that?"

"I was listening in when De Lacerda was interviewing Carlinhos Sousa, the older of the two brothers."

"And he said that Staunton was associated with this Mafia bunch?"

"No, what he said was that the mysterious Leonardo might be, but Graciano's bunch had links with it, anyway that sketch may not be Staunton, just someone that looks very like him."

202

"Oh, don't spoil it, I was really looking forward to that man getting his come-uppance."

"When is your next reporting time to Lorna?"

"There is no fixed time for that but apparently her contact with the Commodore is very limited."

"Have you got a signal on your phone?"

"I'll check, hold on."

"I'll be in the cockpit, Penny."

On deck Vaughan quickly searched for other vessels then checked the yacht's heading and the set of the sails, trimming the staysail in slightly, he had just finished when Penny appeared. "I've got a signal, do you want me to contact Lorna now? It's one in the morning."

"Yes, even if we have to wake her up, it's important that suspicion is put on Staunton as soon as possible, before he can do any more damage."

"Yes, of course it is, hold on I'll call her now."

"Tell her about the identity picture but also tell her that Staunton was supposed to have been the agent tasked with searching for you and Anna-Maria by Sir Andrew Averrille, he had all the information to start the search that I had, yet he didn't put in an appearance at Lagos. And don't forget to mention Jacobs, and what the Sousa brother told me about his family having been in the British Army for generations." Vaughan thought for a moment or two then added. "Jacobs and Staunton may well have worked together previously; we need a check on both their service records."

Ten minutes later Heathcote had conveyed all the latest information and received worrying news back.

"The Commodore has agreed about you sailing us back but that was about all she could tell us, she will not be in touch with the Commodore until much later today and will convey all of our information. I just hope that he will be listened to when he passes it to Sir Andrew."

"Why shouldn't he be?"

"You won't like the sound of this, but apparently Staunton having taken over the Commodore's office has delegated four agents to search for us."

"How does she know that?"

203

"Apparently the Commodore has been in touch with Celia Marsh, Sir Andrew's secretary. She and his first wife were close friends years ago and I know she has a soft spot for the Commodore."

"If Staunton finds out that you are both with me he will probably also have learnt that we left Lagos by sea. No stops on the way home then if we can help it," said Vaughan. "Is Anna-Maria awake? A thought has just occurred to me, it was something the Commodore said about Staunton being given the role of my controller."

"She was in the heads a few minutes ago, do you want me to fetch her?" asked Heathcote.

"No, Penny, just show her the picture and ask if she ever saw the man whilst she was in Luanda."

A few minutes later Anna-Maria came up into the cockpit holding the picture. "It was a long time ago, Ian, but this man is very much like David's colleague on that last trip to Cabinda Province, do you think he had something to do with David's death?"

"I don't know for sure, I need to find out if there is a link between this man and your stepfather."

"The black notebook, if only I had kept the black notebook," she said, shaking her head in apparent despair.

"Unless you are an amazing code breaker that notebook will be of no use until it is in the hands of our code breaker specialists," replied Vaughan. "Leave the picture on the chart table I'll put it away when I come below."

"Do you want a baguette? I'm feeling hungry."

"Thanks, that would be great."

After the light meal Vaughan and Heathcote agreed a watch keeping schedule of four hours on four hours off, leaving galley duty to Anna-Maria who, Vaughan noticed with a smile, was very relieved not to be included in handling the boat.

"We'll start in six hours' time, Penny, you get your head down, I'll need you to be fully rested for when we round the point and start to beat northwards into the wind."

***

It was four o'clock when Yakov Gorokhin switched off the desk lamp, leant back in his chair and rubbed his tired eyes. He had received the black notebook two days ago and was still no further forward in unlocking the codes it contained. The frustration he felt was due to the fact that the code was obviously consistent which meant that once unlocked it would read as easily as a normal book. Standing, he stretched and walked the two paces to the window and drew back the curtains. The grey dawn over Hampstead did nothing to raise his spirits. In two hours' time Leonard would be in touch, his purring opening to conversations turning to sarcasm and threats when once again he would be told of Yakov's failure. He went to the bathroom, used the toilet, then splashed water on his face in a vain attempt to restore function to his brain, before wandering into the kitchen to put a kettle on to boil. Yawning, he selected a mug from the pile of dirty crockery and swished it around under water from the hot tap.

Back at his desk, a steaming cup of coffee in hand, he switched the lamp back on and looked at the notebook again; reaching across for another clean sheet of squared paper he considered the function of the Greek letters in the context of the overall page. Yakov Gorokhin had just taken the first step through the maze.

CHAPTER 9

At 85 Albert Embankment, London, Staunton limped into the surveillance section of SIS dedicated to the Campbell watch.

"Anything to report?"

"No, Sir, nothing at all, unless you are interested in how much gardening they are doing. His wife looks very tasty in a bikini."

Staunton ignored the remark.

"Phone calls?"

"Nothing of note," said the tracker seated in front of four monitors and wearing headphones. "She chats to her parents every couple of days and places orders with their grocer, that type of thing; it's all in the log."

"What about internals?" asked Staunton.

"Oh, they're a lot of laughs they are. Those two have quite a sense of humour, he's talking a lot about getting a yacht and going cruising. I'll tell you what, I wish my missus was as fond of me as she is of him, cor."

"Keep with it, he's going to make a slip-up sooner or later."

"Do you think he knows we are doing this?"

"Of course he bloody does, idiot."

With that Staunton left the monitoring co-ordination centre.

The tracker turned and went to make a comment but thought better of it. Just watch, listen and record, that is all the job was about; other than keep your mouth shut about what you see, hear and record.

"So that is the new supremo then," said the tracker in the next booth.

"Yeh, bit abrupt."

"A right bastard from what I hear."

"Really? Oh, hold on Campbell's picked up the phone."

He listened intently waiting for the person called to pick up. "Tyrrhenian Yacht Brokerage, Charlotte Beecham speaking."

"Ah, Miss Beecham, Alex Campbell here, how are you today?"

"Very well thank you, Mr Campbell, I am so pleased you called, I have heard from the owner of the Oyster 45 you are interested in, he informed me that it is currently under the care of a highly qualified delivery skipper and two crew and currently heading up from the Med. The yacht in fact should be at Plymouth in about seven to eight days, all being well."

"Terrific news, would you be kind enough to get the owner to contact me when it has arrived so that we can arrange a convenient inspection date."

"Certainly, Mr Campbell, is there anything else I can do for you?"

"No, thank you, that is all for now."

The goodbyes said, the tracker switched off the recorder and put a note in the log.

In the Campbell household in Dulwich, Alex Campbell put the phone down smiling as much at Lorna Parker-Davis' cut-glass accent as at the news she had just conveyed concerning Vaughan's current status.

Back at his desk, Staunton, unaware of the fate of Jacobs and the release of the two women, sat wondering how he could engineer an immediate trip to Burgau to question Anna-Maria Patterson about the code book. His checks on her had revealed that she was in fact a highly intelligent young lady and therefore he thought quite capable of figuring out Vermeulen's code. Why Yakov Gorokhin had failed he was not sure, maybe the man was looking for something more complex and missing the obvious; Vermeulen, he thought, was no genius.

His right foot, encased in a light plaster and boot, was hurting and he swivelled his chair round so that he could put it up on the desk. Six to eight weeks they had said before the plaster could come off.

Once Vaughan was found he would have him killed. He would have happily done it in Gibraltar but for Frazer's presence.

Staunton then checked his mobile again for any messages from Jacobs, thinking that it was strange for the man not to report in to update him following the report of the pick-up.

A knock on his office door disturbed his thoughts, "Come."

Sir Andrew Averrille entered the office looking rather harassed.

Staunton leapt to his feet, "Sir Andrew, how may I help?"

"I have just heard that you have sent Agents Graham, Levens, Housmann and Page to Spain on the hunt for these two women believed to have been abducted. What is this all about?"

"It is in connection with this assignment ordered by Commodore Campbell, Sir Andrew, we believe that the snatch in Gibraltar was conducted by a Spanish gang, so I have sent a team out to try and track them down."

"Why use Agent Graham? The man is a good analyst I grant but definitely not a field operative."

"I sent him to analyse and co-ordinate the activities of the other three, Sir Andrew. I know it is unusual but I thought this type of operation could be a pattern that, with such closer and intensive focus, may prove more efficient than our current long range co-ordination that frequently has personnel availability limitations."

"I'm not fully convinced about this, Leonard, I want to be kept informed on a daily basis."

"Certainly, Sir Andrew, I will."

As the door closed behind Sir Andrew, Staunton breathed a sigh of relief. He well knew of Graham's limitations and far from giving the man the role of analyst and co-ordinator he had split the men into two pairs, each in separate areas of Spain with orders to search for two women who he knew perfectly well were in Portugal.

Looking down at his desk he saw the Cairo mosque file and reluctantly pulled it towards him. He started to read the latest assessment regarding the link to a mosque in Birmingham. Picking up his phone he punched in a number.

"El Keraki."

"Staunton here, have you found out whether Mustafa Khouri flew out to Cairo last month or not?"

"Yes, Sir, it has just come in from Egypt Air, he flew out on the seventh and no return flight booked as yet."

"Let the French and Germans know, we must not be accused of keeping Mr Khouri's holiday plans to ourselves must we."

"No, Sir," replied El Keraki, stunned at Staunton's attempt at humour.

Putting the phone down Staunton checked his watch, he had just enough time to speak to Yakov Gorokhin again before the section heads' co-ordination meeting. He dialled the number, "Anything?" he said as soon as the phone was answered.

"I may have made a breakthrough, Leonard. This man is very clever in formatting the code somewhat like a crossword. It has a series of letters that produce a second puzzle, when I have converted a few more pages it may well produce a pattern that is breakable."

"How long?"

"It is hard to say, maybe two days, maybe a week, I do not know."

"You've got two days, that is all," said Staunton, before slamming down the phone.

He got up and limped across to the window looking down at the murky waters of the River Thames. Staunton hated having to wait and now yet again his future appeared to be on hold. He needed one more nail to put in Campbell's career coffin before he could be sure of keeping this position from which he could wield power.

Staunton glanced again at his watch noting that it was time to join the meeting and taking the briefing notes from his desk, he left the office, limping past his secretary without a glance.

The meeting had been in progress for about half an hour when Staunton felt his mobile vibrate in his pocket. Easing back from the table he pulled the phone surreptitiously into view to see that the caller was Housmann, by far the brightest of the four he had sent on the fool's errand.

"Excuse me, I must take this," he said standing and making for the door.

Outside in the corridor he held the phone to his ear, "Yes, what is it?"

"Housmann, Sir, I'm in Lagos, Portugal, following up on information from Gibraltar and have discovered that Agent Vaughan was here yesterday and according to some low life here who was connected with Christiano Graciano – that's the man Agent Vaughan killed in Gibraltar, Vaughan left here on board a yacht late last night."

"Listen carefully, Housmann, Vaughan has been dismissed and is no longer working for us. If he's doing what I think he is doing we need to have him stopped. You and Graham work your way north along the coast and when you find him report to me immediately." Staunton had almost used the word "eliminated" instead of just "stopped"; elimination would be a job he would give to others.

Returning to the meeting, Staunton sat it out contributing little in order to have it finished as soon as possible. On leaving, he hurried back to his office to contact Sir Andrew Averrille's secretary before she left. "Is Sir Andrew available, Mrs March? A rather disturbing situation has developed in the Spanish operation he and I were discussing earlier."

"If you wait a moment, Mr Staunton, I will check with him." Staunton waited, aware again of Mrs March's use of his surname. Why was it that when Campbell had phoned through she had always called him Alex?

"I'll put you through now, Mr Staunton."

"Well I was hoping…" Staunton had hoped for a meeting.

"This had better be quick, Leonard, I have a meeting with the Joint Chiefs of Staff to get to."

"My team inform me, Sir Andrew, that Vaughan is sticking his nose into this hunt for the missing women. I have asked Housmann to find Vaughan so that we can warn him off. This just confirms the man to be a complete nuisance."

"Don't be too hasty, Leonard, Vaughan may be onto some important lead, tell Housmann to find Vaughan and keep watch."

Staunton took a gamble. "Another thought has come to mind, Sir Andrew, that Vaughan could be acting on instructions from Commodore Campbell."

"No, Leonard, I have just seen the watch report on the Commodore. There has been no sign of any contact at all not even with his DELCO team. Campbell plays a straight bat in these situations, it is a damn shame that he appears to have dropped the ball in sending Vaughan to Madeira," replied Sir Andrew. "I can't stay any longer on this, Leonard, otherwise I will be late, I'll expect an update from you in the morning."

Though not the most positive outcome, Staunton knew that he had planted seeds of doubt in Sir Andrew's mind regarding the Commodore. It was time, he thought, for a bit of relaxation, so leaving the office earlier than usual, made his way to Alice Morgan's flat in Croydon for dinner and compliant sex.

**

By the time Penny Heathcote came on watch *"La mouette sur le vent"* had cleared the point of Fortaleza de Sagres and was now close to Farol do Cabo de São Vicente. "God you look all in," she said, as she climbed the companionway steps into the cockpit.

"It was a long couple of days, Penny, how do you feel? Are you up to this?"

"Oh yes, I slept like a baby and really feel quite rested. You go below; Anna-Maria said she would fix you something to eat."

"Just keep her pointing to windward on this tack, Penny. That will take us well clear of Cape St Vincent and out away from any prying eyes," said Vaughan, "Give a shout if anything changes in wind, weather or shipping."

"Ian, I have done this before, many times in fact, now go below and get some rest, I will look after her," Heathcote replied, patting the side of the cockpit combing affectionately.

Returning from a visit to the heads Vaughan found two bacon baguettes waiting for him and a mug of tea on the galley top.
"Those are yours, Ian, I'm just doing some more for Penny and myself."

"Thank you, how are you feeling this morning?"

"Feeling safe again in your company, you are again my hero. In the house with that evil man Jacobs was an experience I never want to have ever again."

"I imagine he was the guy who gave you the split lip."

"Yes he was, and I think he enjoyed doing it too. To be honest I thought every time he came near me he wanted to rape me, then when he got me in the bathroom and I could feel his breath on my legs…" Her eyes started to water as she recalled the fear and the moment when she had stabbed him. "I'm sorry, but I am not so strong as Penny."

"What you did was very brave and probably saved both of your lives, Anna-Maria, and don't you forget that. According to Carlinhos Sousa,

Jacobs was moving you both in the morning and I doubt that it would be to safety in England."

"Maybe, but Jacobs also beat Penny and look at her today, strong and able to help, whereas I am crying like a child and fit only to fry bacon." She turned away from him fumbling in her pocket for a handkerchief. "Penny has been so marvellously brave, she head-butted the one they called Christiano you know, he was so angry and would have killed her I'm sure had the others not stopped him. Then when that ape Gregorio groped her she lashed out leaving deep scratches on his ugly face. He hurt her badly, that was when her nose was broken."

"They are both dead now," said Vaughan, in a matter of fact way that surprised him. "*Jesus, Vaughan, are you that used to killing.*"

"They are dead?" she said, surprised.

"Yes, Christiano Graciano was shot while leading a diversion that made me miss your powerboat removal from Gibraltar, and I understand that Jacobs killed the other two, probably to silence them."

"Good," she replied, then looked a little sorrowful for having said it. "So many people have died because of me."

"Come on, snap out of that, you will be in England soon and away from all this illegal arms trade horror. Look out, the bacon is burning."

"Oooh!" she said and turned to the galley stove leaving Vaughan to sit at the chart table to eat, before climbing exhaustedly into his berth.

At 1150 hours Anna-Maria gave Vaughan a gentle shake to wake him, "Penny says that it is time for your next watch, Ian."

"Okay, tell her I'll be right there."

Sliding out of the quarter berth, Vaughan visited the heads again and had a quick wash, coming out to find Anna-Maria standing at the companionway steps holding out a mug of coffee.

"Thanks, you are an angel," he said, taking the mug from her and climbing up into the cockpit.

"I take it there were no dramas?" Vaughan said as Penny relinquished the tiller.

"No, it was all very peaceful, she sails beautifully Ian, you must be delighted with her. We have been averaging seven knots over the ground according to the GPS, my father would be very envious, '*Buxom Wench*' puts in five knots at best in these conditions."

"I'll run the engine for a bit to top up the batteries again, hope it won't disturb your rest."

"I doubt it, Ian, I will be glad to lie down again to be honest. I had no idea how exhausted the last week has made me feel."

"In the top drawer opposite the heads you'll find a bottle of aloe vera gel to put on your face and hands," said Vaughan looking closely at Heathcote's face.

"Oh God this red hair, it's just not fair, look at Anna-Maria standing there like a piece of beautifully carved teak, whilst I look like a boiled lobster."

Vaughan smiled and, putting his arms around her shoulders, gave her a hug, "Go below and coat yourself in that gel and when you come on watch again put on one of my sun hats, that baseball cap doesn't shade you enough."

As Heathcote went below Vaughan started the yacht's engine and, disconnecting the auto helm, settled himself to steer her on the course that was taking them gradually further out into the Atlantic under a steady favourable nor-nor east to north-easterly wind. He made a mental note to put in a tack at the 1600 hour watch change, then his thoughts turned to the night's communication with Campbell. *"I wonder whether he's managed to persuade Sir Andrew into thinking that Staunton has questions to answer, also is anyone at HQ checking out this cretin Barry Jacobs? I must mention that the artist impression of the mysterious Leonardo is the spitting image of Staunton, surely that should raise concerns, and given the information available in Gibraltar about the powerboats name why was he not in front of me searching for the women in Lagos?"*

Anna-Maria's lunch was a surprisingly good spaghetti carbonara and Vaughan, not for the first time since they had started the voyage, wondered at the change in her that appeared to be taking place. Slow change yes, but Anna-Maria was at last getting the hang of life at sea, he hadn't tripped over her once since leaving Lagos.

At the next change of watch Vaughan instructed Heathcote to continue the eastward course wanting them to be in mobile range of the coast between 2200 hours and midnight ready to receive Campbell's call.

Anna-Maria woke Vaughan fifteen minutes before his watch started with a sandwich and a mug of black coffee.

"You are a very quiet sleeper, Ian," she said as he sat, mug in one hand and sandwich in the other trying to get his brain in order.

"Really, my wife made a similar comment, apparently it spooked her a bit and if she woke in the night she would put her hand near to my nose to check that I was still breathing."

"You are married? I somehow thought you were single, you have never mentioned a wife before."

"Divorced, don't ask, it is a long tiresome story."

"Do you have children?"

"Yes, I have two daughters who live with my ex-wife."

"Oh, how sad for you, fathers are normally very close to daughters. I was very close to my father and was devastated when he was killed."

"Was he military?"

"Oh no, he was the Commercial Director for a food packaging and distribution company."

"What happened?"

"He was driving to one of their warehouses near Porto when he was involved in a head on collision with a drunk driver who was on the wrong side of the road."

"How terrible for you. Were you very young?"

"I was sixteen at the time. We stayed on in Portugal until I finished school then we moved to South Africa and my mother met Jan Vermeulen." She stood for a moment or two, her lips tight, holding back her desire to shout or scream. "I returned to Portugal to go to university but when I got my degree my mother pleaded with me to join them in Angola where I met David."

At that point, Penny put her head down and said, "I can easily see the sweep of the Sines lighthouse and there are one or two ships about."

"Right, we had better show some lights then. I'll be up in a moment, then you can get your head down."

"Do you want me to be up when the Commodore calls?"

"No, Penny, but can you leave me with your mobile just in case he calls that one."

They were closing the coast near the small port of Sines and were dangerously close in and still Vaughan's phone had no signal.

"Anything on Penny's phone?"

"No, nothing," replied Anna-Maria nervously, picking up the tension in Vaughan's voice. "Twenty metres depth of water here at the moment, Ian."

"Yes at the moment, but as I don't have a detailed chart for this area I'm going to tack and steer parallel to the coast and just pray we pick up a signal further along. Now I see the value of SSB phones on yachts."

Immediately, Anna-Maria moved to the head of the companionway steps out of Vaughan's way.

As the yacht's bow came through the wind Vaughan hauled on the lee side sheets and swiftly applied three turns around both winches before adding a fourth turn on the staysail sheet running it into the self tailer. Checking that the yacht was sailing full and by he put the fourth turn on the genoa sheet and like the staysail ran it into the self tailer. Then starting with the genoa he winched the sail in harder until he was satisfied with its set then did the same with the staysail. When he had completed the task by trimming the mainsail Anna-Maria laughed and clapped her hands.

"How you do that, steering the boat with your buttocks and getting those sails to behave is quite amazing, Ian."

"Years of practice and many moments of embarrassment went into that, believe me. You can guarantee that when you get it wrong there is a huge crowd of spectators watching, all of whom happily point out where you went wrong at the first opportunity they have."

Just then Vaughan's phone chirped, snatching it up from the cockpit seat he glanced at the screen, "Hello."

"Vaughan, I have just been speaking with Lorna who has updated me with your news regarding this man Jacobs and what one hopes is a Staunton look-alike. I hate to think what the outcome will be if it is actually Staunton involved in this. Where are you now?"

"We are currently just south of Lisbon, Sir. It is slow progress north I'm afraid with the high pressure holding as it is."

"Right, well do the best you can and in the meantime I will try and get your information in front of Sir Andrew."

"We showed the sketch of this Leonardo to Ms Ronaldo, Sir, and she thought that the man was the colleague of her husband's when he went on his last visit to Cabinda."

"Well, that is not so surprising, Vaughan, as that would probably have been Staunton who she met but whether they are one and the same man seems to me pretty unlikely really."

"If you could find out about this Barry Jacobs, Sir, you may also find a link to Staunton, they could have served together in the Army."

"I can't make a direct approach, Vaughan, but I know a man who can so leave that with me." Vaughan sensed that the Commodore was going to say something more and waited. "Lorna has told you that Staunton has sent four agents out to Spain in search of Heathcote and Ms Ronaldo."

"Yes, Sir, she has."

"Normally I would tell you how to make contact with them but not on this occasion. Your plan to bring both ladies back in secret by sea is the safest so do your best to avoid contact with the land."

"I'll do my best, Sir. When you are talking to Sir Andrew can you mention that Staunton was given the same information that I was about the powerboat that Anna-Maria and Lieutenant Heathcote were taken to Lagos aboard, but failed to show up in Lagos."

"Yes, I will, though whether Sir Andrew will give that much weight remains to be seen. I am not supposed to be involved in this so I can't reveal that I know the name of the boat but I will think of some way to get the man thinking."

The call ended and Vaughan immediately altered course a little to take the yacht further away from the coast on the starboard tack charging over the waves in her element.

***

Nearing the end of the fifth day at sea during which the watch keeping pattern had been in use, Vaughan recognised that Heathcote was now struggling due to lack of proper sleep.

"Penny, you wait there a moment, I am going to tack east again and head for Muxia, you and I can't keep up this routine all the way to the

UK, so I'm going to put in for forty-eight hours rest. It will also be a chance to get you both fitted out with the right gear, this good weather can't last."

"I'm sorry, I feel I am letting you and Anna-Maria down being such a wimp," Heathcote replied, "You won't be able to use the company card, they would have blocked it immediately you were dismissed."

"Don't worry about that, they can't block either of my personal accounts and if I use the US Dollar one there is even less of a chance."

Heathcote looked at him with surprise. "Get you, Mr Dollar account."

"A reward for services rendered, funnily enough it hasn't been touched since the divorce settlement so it has grown back enough to cover a couple of sets of heavy weather gear and some other clothes for you two."

"If we make it through I promise you will be repaid every cent."

"Hold tight I'm taking her round now, then you can play for a while."

He took the yacht through the tack with the ease born of long experience and now on port tack, heading east he trimmed the headsails and main while Penny looked on in admiration.

"Keep her pointing as high as you can please, Penny. If the wind gets up any more give me a tug, okay?"

Niggled by his mildly patronising instruction she said, "I'll do my best, sir," in a tone that had Vaughan giving her a questioning look. "I said earlier, Ian, that I have done this many times before."

"Sorry, Penny, of course you have."

Towards the end of three hours Penny Heathcote had found herself dozing twice, woken only by the sound of a flapping headsail when the wind angle changed, a problem when trying to point high into the wind using an auto helm. Halfway through the watch Anna-Maria had brought her up a coffee and a chocolate bar but the caffeine and sugar burst had quickly worn off. Again she felt her eyelids getting heavy and stood, working her legs and arms then flexing her shoulders, but five minutes later she had dozed off again and this time the yacht had come up into the wind and almost stopped before she woke and grabbed the tiller, hauling on it attempting to bring the boat back on course.

Woken by the racket created by the flapping headsails, Vaughan was almost halfway up the companionway steps when the yacht came off the wind again and the sails filled with a bang pinned on the wrong tack.

Reaching the cockpit he shouted, "Are you all right, Penny?" as he quickly surveyed the yacht checking for any damage.

"I'm all right but look what I've done to the genoa. Oh Ian, I'm so sorry."

Vaughan looked forward and immediately saw the big horizontal tear in the sail right from the luff to the leach. Freeing the sheets he hurriedly set the staysail to get the yacht moving again on the starboard tack.

"I'll go forward and get that sail down then get the previous owner's original yankee put on, it'll slow us a bit but not by much. Can you hold her for a little while longer?"

Heathcote nodded, "Yes."

The big genoa was a hell of a handful to bring down but finally Vaughan got it safely lashed to the port hand lower guardrail. "I'll keep it there till we get into port, no point in bagging it now it's too much effort, we'll best do it in port before we take it to the sailmakers."

Hoisting the smaller yankee was a much easier task and on completion Vaughan came back to the cockpit and sheeted it in. "Much weather helm?"

"Yes, it is quite heavy," Heathcote replied, looking very sad and annoyed with herself.

"I'll stick a reef in the main, that should balance her up."

When the mainsail was reefed the smaller sail pattern dropped the boat speed to five knots through the water and about four over the ground. "There, all sorted, Penny, now you go below I'll take her in from here. Please don't worry about the sail, it looked as if the stitching had gone, repair won't be too much of a problem. The sail came with the boat and is a good ten years old now, I had planned to have a new one cut at the end of the sailing season."

As she went to go below Vaughan could see tears in her eyes. "Hey, come here," he said putting an arm around her and was a little surprised that she didn't pull away, "These things happen, you are exhausted and I had pushed you too far, so if anyone is to blame it's me, all right, so cheer up."

Heathcote nodded, sniffed, then as Vaughan released the hug she went below and flung herself onto the starboard berth in the forward cabin, leaving Vaughan berating himself inwardly. *"What a pillock I am, thinking that a four on four off would work with both of us exhausted before we started. Why the hell didn't I go straight into my twenty minute cycle and keep Penny rested for emergencies. Prat, prat prat."*

Twelve hours later, *"La Mouette sur le Vent"* slipped alongside the head of a pontoon arm at Marina Muxia. It was dark and Vaughan was by now really exhausted so he decided to wait until the following morning before checking in. Going below he went forward to look at Penny. "Has she had anything to eat or drink since coming below, Anna-Maria?"

"No, she has been asleep all the time."

"While I tidy the shorelines and sort things out on deck, can you wake her and cook something for us to eat, bacon and eggs may be a good idea," said Vaughan, "Oh and toast, you'll find some marmalade in the store under that berth."

***

It was Graham, the analyst, who had worked it out and with some reasonable accuracy had plotted the potential places that Vaughan would call in at on his way northwards up the Iberian peninsula.

They had spent a day waiting for Vaughan in Lisbon before driving north making enquiries at virtually all the marinas up the coast as far as Baiona, where again they waited.

Vaughan was returning from the sailmaker and Penny and Anna-Maria were shopping for clothes when Graham and Housmann arrived at Muxia's marina.

"I keep telling you, Peter, Vaughan is probably fifty miles offshore and heading straight out across the Bay of Biscay," said Housmann, stretching after another long car drive.

"You're probably right but we have to check, if he's not here then he has gone straight for it, though single handed I'm very surprised," replied Graham. "Mind you, he was a tough sod and star when we did our bit at 'The Manor'."

"So I heard from that bastard McClellan."

"You were in the batch that arrived the day after Vaughan left, Mac would still have had sore nuts even then."

They had walked across the car park and were looking out over the basin at the neat rows of yachts moored to their pontoons.

"Let's ask at the office," said Housmann, wanting to get away from the boredom of listening to Graham and join up with Levens and Page.

"No need," said Graham, "There he is, making his way across to the pontoon ramp. Quick get behind that van before he sees us."

***

Had they not made the quick movement, Vaughan would not have caught it in his peripheral vision and thought more seriously about a Portuguese registered car being parked near the entrance. Climbing on board his yacht he unlocked the hatch and went below to fetch his binoculars. Carefully keeping out of sight he used the view from the cabin port window just forward of the galley to look across at the two men.

Identifying Graham, Vaughan picked up his mobile and phoned Heathcote, "Penny, where are you both?"

"In what passes for a sportswear shop, towards the fishing quay, why?"

"We have company in the form of Agent Graham and one other, and I think they arrived in a Portuguese registered car, which means they have been sent to look for us."

"Which section was Graham in?"

"I heard he was sat behind a desk as an analyst, probably a good one from what I could see during my time at 'The Manor'."

"Staunton inspired do you think?"

"That is exactly what I think. I also think that he has sent them to look for me not to find you and Anna-Maria."

"Why do you say that?"

"If they were searching for you two they would have come and made themselves known straight away so that they can report that you are both safe and sound. Instead they are just reporting that they have seen me."

"Where are they at the moment?"

"Standing by the marina offices, Graham is on the phone."

"What do you want us to do, come and introduce ourselves?"

"No, I somehow don't think that would be a safe move. Stay where you are for the moment, I'll call you when I have anything like a plan."

***

By the marina office Graham was waiting excitedly for Staunton's secretary to get him out of a meeting.

"Yes, Graham, what is it?"

"We've found Vaughan, Sir, at the Spanish port of Muxia."

"Whereabouts is that?"

"It's on the north-western most tip of Spain, Sir."

"Whatever you do don't let yourselves be seen by him, just keep an eye on the entrance to the port and report to me when he leaves, understood?"

"Understood, Sir," replied Graham, "Housmann and I will do just that... Sir... Sir?"

"The bastard put the phone down on you. Jesus, I wonder why we signed up sometimes," said Housmann, feeling for the first time some sympathy for Graham who had chosen to share the credit for the find, when in fact he personally had thought to search here was a waste of time.

"He wants us to avoid at all costs being seen by Vaughan, instead we are to keep watch at the harbour entrance and report when he leaves. Over there looks to be a good spot," said Graham, pointing to a car park further along the road with a clear view of the harbour entrance.

"Well, we better get that car out of the way then, you don't see many Portuguese licence plates here. Looking at the map the best thing we can do is go round this inlet and park up on the point over there where we would have an uninterrupted view of the entrance, and not stand the

221

chance of you being recognised by Vaughan," said Housmann, pointing towards the opposite side of the inlet.

"Ah yes, I see what you mean, good idea."

***

On board *"La Mouette sur le Vent"* Vaughan had watched the two men closely throughout the phone call and subsequent conversation, watching with interest Housmann's animated directions. As the two men hurried away back across the car park Vaughan put down the binoculars and went on deck in time to see the roof of their car as it moved away, turning left out of town.

"A stroll up onto the mole with the binoculars is the next thing on the list to see where their monitoring point is." He spotted their car easily noting Graham's sidekick standing beside the vehicle stretching and exercising. Returning to the yacht he tried to work out what plan Staunton had in mind, assuming that the man knew he had Heathcote and Anna-Maria with him. *"If this was legitimate why didn't they make an approach and confirm that they were ordered to take-over the safe return of Penny and Anna-Maria... No this has a nasty smell about it that makes me think that either another snatch is being planned, carried out by someone not connected with British Intelligence, or he thinks I am alone and plans to have me removed permanently by someone other than Graham and his sidekick."*

Taking the mobile phone from his pocket Vaughan rang Heathcote again. "Penny, are you still in that sports gear shop?"

"Yes."

"See if they have any of those waterproof bags in which you and Anna-Maria could pack some clothes and shoes in, and buy some swimwear as well," said Vaughan.

"You have a plan?"

"No, not exactly; just planning for some contingency."

"Are you still being watched?"

"No, not directly, they have moved off to the other side of the inlet, so if you want to come back for some lunch it seems to be okay. On the other hand you both may prefer to lunch ashore," said Vaughan.

"Anna-Maria has been like a cat on a hot tin roof since your last call so I think we will be returning on board."

Whilst Penny had been talking Vaughan's brain was thinking through the permutations.

"No, Penny, on second thoughts stay where you are, our watchers may have friends nearby. I need to have a look round to see if they have," instructed Vaughan. "You get lunch somewhere and tell Anna-Maria that the watchers have moved on and that there is no need to worry."

"Okay, it's your credit card, don't say I didn't warn you."

Smiling, Vaughan put the phone away and, pulling his waterproof grab bag from under the quarter berth, then loaded and sealed it, placing it on the port hand settee in the main cabin where it could be grabbed quickly.

***

In the restaurant, "Saburil", on the corner overlooking the wide-paved promenade and the harbour beyond, Penny and Anna-Maria studied the menu.

"I'm going for the seafood paella," announced Penny, "I haven't tried that for years."

Anna-Maria put her menu down, "I will do the same, Penny." She looked across at her confident companion anxiously, "Is Ian sure that it's safe, us being here and not on the boat?"

"Oh absolutely, he would not have said that had he not been certain that it was okay. Relax, enjoy yourself."

At that moment Penny's phone rang and looking at the screen she saw that it was Lorna. "Can you order for me Anna-Maria, I'll take this outside, it's a bit personal."

"Hello, darling, what can I do for you?" Penny said, standing hurriedly and walking out onto the terrace.

"Penny, the Commodore wants to know where you are, apparently some of Staunton's people have been snooping around Lagos."

"We are in northern Spain at a small port called Muxia, Lorna, and yes Staunton's men have found us but have not made any contact, they are just watching. There is Graham and one other sat in a car some distance away keeping an eye out for our next move I think. Ian is checking now to see if they have left a third person keeping a closer watch."

"When are you leaving?"

"Yesterday I wrecked the genoa on the boat and we had to put in to have it repaired, it shouldn't take long, maybe two days."

"The Commodore tried to go through Jackson at Anti Terrorist Command to find out about this guy Jacobs, only to learn that the man's file was pulled just over two years ago."

"Surely that means he was working for either MI5 or us."

"Exactly, Penny."

"Well, then why was that bastard knocking me about or trying to rape Anna-Maria come to that."

"Tell Vaughan to get out of there as soon as you can, at sea you are relatively safe, sitting there I think you are in great danger."

"Can they find out who authorised the file to be pulled?"

"Jackson is onto that at the moment apparently but is facing a few road blocks."

"I sometimes think we spend more time obstructing ourselves than we do blocking the real enemy."

"Maybe we have an enemy within," said Lorna, thoughtfully.

"Staunton!" they said together.

Returning to the restaurant Penny did her best to remain calm during the meal but was relieved when Vaughan phoned to say that as far as he could see the coast was clear.

"Let's stroll back to the boat, I fancy a little bit of shut-eye after that meal."

Paying the bill with Vaughan's credit card they sauntered back along the promenade to find Vaughan filling two five gallon fuel cans from the pumps near the head of the pontoon access gate.

"When you get on the boat, Anna-Maria, could you put the kettle on for some tea?" said Vaughan. "Penny, I'd be really grateful if you would give me a hand with this trolley going down the ramp."

"Sure, Ian, you go on, Anna-Maria, we'll be there in a minute or two," said Penny, then when Anna-Maria was out of earshot she asked anxiously, "No further signs of our shadows I hope?"

"No but I want you to tuck all of that gorgeous red hair of yours under this sun hat and then go to the boat, from where they are parked they will see you crossing from here to the pontoon ramp but once you are down below the sea wall level you will be out of sight."

"What about Anna-Maria, won't they recognise her?"

"Dark hair like most local women, huge sunglasses and the fashionable wide brimmed sunhat, that I expect I will see on the tab listing your purchases, no they won't. As far as they would know she could be the Duchess of Cambridge."

Glancing at Anna-Maria as she walked along the pontoon towards Vaughan's yacht Penny sighed and said, "Yes, Ian, I see what you mean."

Piling her long red hair onto the top of her head she pulled Vaughan's sun hat over it, "I had a call from Lorna just now."

"What did she have to say?"

Penny relayed all of the message including her own and Lorna's conclusions.

"The very astute 'Puncher' Robson suggested that Staunton intended to kill me, that was after I had stamped hard down on his foot mind. Maybe that's what this is all about, which means that the dirty work will be done by others and not Graham and his mate," said Vaughan. "That in mind, I think we will cross the ria and anchor in a cove on the other side as soon as it's dark. In fact I was already planning to do that anyway. I called in at the marina office just now and was told about a delightful little spot which, according to the guy there, is his favourite rest-day place away from his wife."

"To avoid some much needed household jobs more like, anyway let's get this fuel on board," said Heathcote, unimpressed by the marina staff's attitude.

"You go on in front, I'll follow in a couple of minutes, just in case they're looking."

On board, Vaughan explained to both women what he thought they should pack into the waterproof bags and once that was done, had them put their bags alongside his own.

"Now, Penny and I are going to get some sleep while you, Anna-Maria, keep watch from the cockpit, anyone turning to come along towards us from the main pontoon I want to know about, all right."

"Okay, I'll keep watch."

"Are you a good swimmer?"

Anna-Maria looked at Vaughan a little puzzled. "David used to call me his mermaid," she replied, wistfully, "Why do you ask?"

"We may need to take a midnight dip."

"Oh."

Vaughan waited thinking that Anna-Maria would want to know more, or seek some assurance, but to his surprise she just poured herself another mug of tea and climbed up into the cockpit.

***

As darkness fell, Heathcote cast off the yacht's warps and, clambering back on board, went onto the foredeck to coil the warps then worked her way down the side deck untying the fenders while Vaughan steered and worked at stowing everything as Heathcote dropped it onto the cockpit sole. Pointing the yacht towards the harbour entrance, he looked up to check that the mast head tricolour light was working then concentrated on following the deep water channel outside the marina entrance.

"I wonder if our watchers are still on duty," said Vaughan, as Heathcote stepped down into the cockpit and settled herself comfortably against the cabin bulkhead. "I'll hoist the main in a moment to make it look as if we're really going to sea."

"While you were doing the passage plan below I saw several yachts leave, some with rig not too dissimilar to ours."

"Good, that should confuse them, or at least Graham. He didn't show any knowledge of boats or sailing when Bowen and I were chatting about West Country sailing. Graham was a chess fanatic as far as I remember," replied Vaughan. "We are going to go out to sea a bit then double back on a course that will take us almost directly into the bay. The entrance is a bit narrow and, according to this local chart I got from the marina office, the bottom is rocky but there is a sandy bottom right in the centre where the holding is good in calm weather like this."

As the yacht cleared the harbour Vaughan hoisted the mainsail whilst Heathcote steered, then with a clear course out to sea she brought the yacht off the wind and Vaughan unfurled the yankee, sheeting it in until it set, adding to the mainsail's drive.

"As we turn back I'll drop the sails and we'll go in under motor so will be showing a lower white stern light plus port and starboard ones and no masthead tricolour, from a distance we will look like a small motor boat showing only deck steaming lights."

"Nice move, let's hope it works as I don't really fancy a swim tonight."

"You all right steering?"

"Yes, I'm fine."

"Good, because I want to prepare the kedge anchor."

Ten minutes later Vaughan had hauled his trusty Fishermans anchor from the locker, locked the stock through the shank and set the anchor with its ten metres of chain on the small stern deck. Taking the warp section through the pushpit and leading it back through the port hand fairlead flaking all thirty metres out along the yacht's side deck and putting the loop in the bitter end over the port side genoa winch.

An hour later Vaughan and Heathcote nervously watched the depth sounder as he nosed the yacht into the small cove.

"Okay, Penny, lower the kedge into the water and let it pay out."

The regular clink of chain could be heard as Penny handed it out. "All the chain is away, Ian."

A slight scuffing noise was heard as the warp was slowly pulled along the side deck and out over the side following the chain down to the sea bottom.

"The warp is getting towards the end of its scope, Ian."

"Okay, Penny," replied Vaughan, pulling the throttle lever back to neutral as his eyes switched between the depth sounder and a white painted building on the slope above the centre of the cove.

The yacht gave a very slight lurch as the kedge anchor bit, halting their gentle progress towards the shore. Vaughan hurried forward and let go the bow anchor until it hit the bottom then seating the chain into the anchor winch pawl he returned to the cockpit.

"I'm going to winch in on the kedge anchor while you ease the brake on the bow anchor winch. Give me a shout when we have twenty metres out."

After Penny had called to him Vaughan put the yacht's engine astern and gently opened the throttle.

"It's dug in, Ian!"

Anchored now bow and stern, Vaughan switched off the engine and went below to check on Anna-Maria's progress with the evening meal.

CHAPTER 10

They came shortly after one o'clock in the morning. Vaughan had anchored the yacht exactly in the centre of the cove where a gentle breeze from the northern shore kept the yacht on a perfect line to its anchors. After eating Anna-Maria's excellent cottage pie, Vaughan had spent the rest of his time preparing for any unwelcome visitors. The first job was the defence ring around the side decks comprising of two strips of clear sticky tape with drawing pins pushed through, providing an unpleasant welcome for bare feet and a hindrance if embedded in the soles of shoes. Then came the three thousand candela trigger operated spot lamp designed to take out anyone's night vision for several vital seconds, this being plugged into the fore deck twelve volt outlet. To provide a hiding place he removed the large yankee sail from its furler and laying it along the centre line of the deck in a similar way to a handed on sail, it provided a shadow in which they could hide. Finally, he folded down the spray hood to reduce the windage and remove the obstacle from line of fire. Then he told the women to change into their swimming costumes in case they needed to evacuate in a hurry.

The light breeze from the shore had carried the sound of the car and trailer arriving, and the sound of the trailer's wheels as it was pulled over the fine shingle along the high tide line meant that they would arrive by boat and not swim out. Aware that they would be concentrating on launching the dinghy, Vaughan, leaving the women nervously waiting in the forward cabin, slipped out through the forward hatch and crawling towards the bow lay down in the shadow of the yankee with the spot lamp in his left hand and pistol in his right. The half moon was giving sufficient light for him to clearly watch the two men as they paddled the small rib out, choosing to come alongside the shadowed starboard side of the yacht where their dinghy would be in darkness. A whisper or two were exchanged and a hand appeared over the gunnel, then the head of a man came into view. *"La Mouette sur le Vent"* had a high freeboard making boarding from a small inflatable something of a task requiring agility. The hand moved along to a guardrail stanchion then the man reached for the aft lower shroud and brought a foot and knee up to hook over the gunnel. He hauled himself on board causing the yacht to heel slightly.

It was then that the fun started as the man pushed and pulled himself into a standing position and in stocking feet stepped over the guard rail. His right foot had obviously landed between two drawing pins but his left did not. Letting out an involuntary yelp, he lifted his left foot pulling the drawing pin out only to put it back down on another pin, the reaction to which caused him to lose his balance slightly and correct it by stepping slightly to his right with the other foot and finding another waiting drawing pin. Now he started a strange dance, like a slowly accelerating fandango as he lifted first one foot then the other at which point Vaughan, pointing the spotlight towards the man's head, switched it on. The beam of light hit the man like a punch sending him toppling backwards over the guardrail and down into the dinghy, landing on top of his associate.

Swiftly moving to the yacht's side and taking care to avoid the drawing pin defence lines Vaughan trained the spotlight onto the two men.

"The gun, drop it into the water. Now!" Vaughan shouted, using what little Spanish he had gleaned from a phrase book. The man hesitated and Vaughan fired a shot into the dinghy floor causing a small spout of water to spring up. There was a splash as the man dropped his pistol into the sea. "And your friend's gun."

The man now looked at his associate, who was lying apparently unconscious with his head over the dinghy's transom at a strange angle. "The gun! Left hand and slowly," said Vaughan.

The man reached cautiously beneath his accomplice's left armpit and pulling with just his thumb and forefinger extracted the gun, and after holding it up for Vaughan to see dropped it into the sea.

"Your friend is dead. When you fell on him you broke his neck."

The man understanding what Vaughan had said gave his accomplice a shake in the hope that the diagnosis was wrong.

"If you start rowing now you may make it to the shore before the dinghy sinks."

The man reached for a paddle but Vaughan noticed another movement that was not related to escape. Suspecting an ankle pistol Vaughan was already sighting up his target and the man had barely raised the weapon halfway before he died.

Grabbing the boathook, Vaughan just managed to catch the spray hood of the dinghy and pull it back alongside. Next he fished the dinghy's painter and secured it to the midship's cleat.

"Now let's try and find out who our visitors were," he said, looking back at Heathcote, as she cautiously peered around the edge of the spray hood.

The hip pocket of the man with the broken neck contained a wallet in which a driving licence revealed him to be Alberto Sousa from Porto, his partner wearing a fair length of sticky tape around his feet had no identification on him. Taking the driving licence and a set of car keys Vaughan climbed back on board the yacht.

"It's time for them to go I think," said Vaughan, casting the dinghy adrift. He watched it drift further away out into the cove blown by the breeze and taken by the falling tide, and was pleased to see it clear the rocks and drift further out into the ria.

Vaughan's mistake was then to put the main cabin light on to see how Penny and Anna-Maria were. His action confirmed that he had survived the attack.

"Are you two okay?"

"Not really," said Penny, "But we are alive, and thank God, so are you."

"Hopefully that will be the end of it for tonight, you both go forward and try and get some more rest."

He smiled as he watched the two women turn like a pair of dismissed school girls and without question make their way forward, Penny in her sensible midnight blue one-piece swimsuit, and Anna-Maria in a skimpy red bikini. Both would turn men's heads on any beach but Anna-Maria would be the one that would make them sit up.

Turning the cabin light out again, Vaughan went on deck and started to remove his drawing pin defence ring. Twice he stopped wondering whether he was doing the right thing, something at the back of his mind was telling him that it was not over yet. He saw the dark shadow approaching the entrance to the bay as he was just finishing balling up the last remnants of tape.

"Bugger, the back-up has arrived, and probably in force. This will take more than sticky tape and drawing pins."

Hurrying below he reached for the grab bags then went straight into the forward cabin. "More unwelcome visitors I'm afraid, and this time I suspect in larger numbers. When I have opened this fore hatch fully I want you both to go out through it and keeping as low as possible lie down close to the sail that is laid out along the deck, one either side."

"What then?" asked Heathcote.

"Get ready to slip over the side and swim underwater as far as your lungs will allow to the shore and hide amongst the rocks," replied Vaughan, pushing the hatch fully open. "There you are, it's open, now go, but keep your heads down."

Returning to the main cabin Vaughan, looking over the yacht's stern, checked on the progress of the power boat. It was being handled very cautiously and he could only just hear the sound of its engine. In the moonlight he saw three men make their way onto the starboard side deck, their stance that of men holding automatic weapons.

"Prepare for full broadside, Vaughan, these guys really mean business."

Vaughan had hoped that there would be a challenge and that the boat was official but no challenge came and when it was only ten metres away the powerboat executed a sharp turn and Vaughan, standing just forward of the galley, grab bag over his shoulder and pistol raised, saw one of the men raise his gun. Squeezing the trigger of his Glock, Vaughan caught a glimpse of the man turn and fall as he himself turned and ran forward, scrambling out of the fore hatch as bullets tore into *"La Mouette sur le Vent's"* main cabin.

As the clatter of gunfire started both Heathcote and Anna-Maria had slipped over the yacht's bow. Once on the fore deck Vaughan was considering a response in order to keep the gunmen's focus on the yacht when he heard the sound of something hard land inside the main cabin and rattle along the cabin floor, then another.

"Grenades, bloody hell."

He scrambled forward towards and through the large opening in the pulpit railing, *"One, two, three, four, five, six."*

The first explosion caught him just before he hit the water and as he went down into the cool depths the second came followed by an orange glow surrounding him. The two bulkheads between the main cabin and the bow section of the yacht had protected him from potential injury caused by a pressure wave.

"Anchor chain pull myself down on the anchor chain, hope Penny and Anna-Maria are all right."

In the glow he saw the chain rear up and grabbed at it as he momentarily broke the surface again before pulling himself under and making his way along the chain towards the anchor until his lungs were empty and he was forced to surface. Taking in a lungful of air he looked back then dived again, swimming this time along the same line, the image of his once beautiful yacht sinking beneath the waters of the cove, her mast falling sideways like a felled tree, etched in his mind. Near the shore Vaughan used the rocky bottom to pull himself to a point where a line of rock ran up past the end of the white sandy beach. Still lying in water he peered around a rock and watched the powerboat circle the spot where his yacht had sunk, a spotlight playing on the water littered with debris. In the light of the beam two men gave each other high fives and shouted something to the helmsman. In response the helmsman opened the throttles and turned the boat seawards.

Leaving the water, Vaughan ejected the Glock's magazine and sitting on a rock flicked the bullets out and shook the case to remove any droplets of water. Shaking water out of the barrel he then reloaded the magazine and inserted it back into the handgrip. Hoisting his grab bag back onto his shoulder Vaughan crept up the beach then ran along the narrow road to the car in which their first attackers had arrived, it was empty.

The sound of the powerboat, now safely through the cove entrance, powering up and charging straight toward Muxia stopped Vaughan from opening the vehicle's door. Should any of the crew on the powerboat be looking back to admire their work they would be bound to see the indicators flicker as the door was unlocked.

"Lights, there were no lights on in the house up the road earlier, surely the noise would have woken anyone inside."

Looking up the hill Vaughan could just make out the dark shape of the house against the backdrop of trees, all was in darkness.

"Now let's find those two women." "Penny, Anna-Maria, it's me Ian, make your way to the car above the beach," Vaughan shouted.

There was no response so he shouted again moving away from the car, now fearing the worst. Reaching the beach he walked down to the water's edge and started making his way along it in the opposite direction from where he had left the water. He looked out across the cove, he could see bits of wreckage floating and small fires from the burning fuel dotting the surface. Had they been caught by the shock wave or a stray bullet, the firing was wild enough. Had the men doing the high fives seen bodies floating amongst the bits of flotsam?

Vaughan had reached the rocks on the eastern side of the beach, "Penny, Anna-Maria, are you there? It's me, Ian, Ian Vaughan," he said, speaking normally now, not shouting.

A few seconds passed then a head rose from behind a rock.

***

The vibrating mobile phone rattling on the top of the bedside table woke Alice Morgan. "Lenny, wake up, it's your phone. Lenny, phone!"

"Oh, right," replied a half asleep Staunton, as he rolled over and fumbled for the mobile, catching it just before it fell onto the bedroom floor. "Yes?"

"Leonardo?" asked the caller in a voice with a strong Portuguese accent.

"Sim."

"O trabalho está feito."

"Obrigado," replied Staunton, now wide awake with a satisfied grin on his face. "So the job is done, smart arse Vaughan's out of the game, permanently," he said quietly then, putting the phone down, Staunton turned to Alice.

"Is everything all right, Lenny?" she asked nervously.

"Oh yes, sweetie, everything is just fine," replied Staunton, rolling on top of her and pushing his knees between her legs.

"Oh, Lenny darling, no, I've got to be at work soon, you know I'm on earlies… Lenny, oh Lenny."

The previous evening Staunton's second cosy supper in a row had been interrupted by Graham's call advising him that Vaughan had set sail earlier, putting out to sea. Instructing Graham to return to Lagos and learn what he could about a police raid on an apartment there three days previously, Staunton had turned his thoughts to Vaughan and his night-time departure, concluding that it was possibly a blind. Immediately he had contacted Alberto Sousa, who he had directed to Muxia earlier in the day, and learnt that Vaughan had indeed doubled back towards the northern shore of the ria. Then there had followed strict instructions to Carlinhos's cousin, Alberto, ordering the attack and instilling the need for a good back-up. After the evening meal, while Alice had washed up and taken a shower, Staunton had been plotting how he could use the death of Vaughan to further his interests and his status in the eyes of Sir Andrew Averrille. Now with confirmation that Vaughan was dead, Staunton looked smilingly down at the naked body of Alice Morgan and wondered how much longer would she be of use to him. Their affair would no longer be convenient once he had secured Campbell's position, and just ending it would risk her taking revenge in some way. The last thing he wanted was her telling anyone that he had got her to pass him information.

***

Several miles east of Staunton, Alex Campbell also lay awake but his thoughts were far from triumphant. The previous evening he had received information from Lorna Parker-Davis resulting in him again attempting to persuade Sir Andrew Averrille to conduct a search for information associated with Jacobs. The conversation had been brief, with Sir Andrew thanking Campbell for his thoughts and informing him that he would put the matter in the hands of none other than Staunton. Argument on that matter was deflected by accusations of resentment towards a successor in post and the phone put down abruptly. Having given Sir Andrew the opportunity to possibly uncover Staunton's dubious web of intrigue Campbell had no compunction in using alternative routes to obtain information.

A call to Chief Inspector Brian Jackson from the tenth tee of the golf course was, however, more fruitful in that Jackson had received a similar request from De Lacerda of the Portuguese Servico de Informações de Segurança and promised that any information would be shared via Lorna. The call also revealed that large sums of money had been moved into the Portuguese Banco Salvadore Tesoureiro and that Margaret Hutchinson's team were currently trying to trace the money back to sources believed to be British. Jackson had also learnt that the fraud team were in touch with European and American tax officials in a combined attempt to identify potential Portuguese coup supporters.

Campbell's biggest problem continued to be one of communications and since using the neighbour's house at the bottom of his garden was no longer an option he had now taken to long evening walks in Dulwich Park with Caroline or evening rounds of golf at the Dulwich and Sydenham Hill course, followed by a drink at the nineteenth. As the normal chatter with friends on his contract phone throughout the day and into the evening had continued at the normal rate, the eavesdroppers were becoming somewhat bored. It still meant that response times to any changing situation were far too slow, which meant leaving Vaughan to cope very much on his own. Every day that passed, Commodore Campbell was becoming more and more aware that his career, and indeed his whole future, depended upon a man who was a relatively new recruit into the shadowy world of Britain's Secret Intelligence Service.

***

Arriving at his office the next morning Staunton was surprised, and a little anxious, to find that Sir Andrew Averrille had made a request to see him as soon as he arrived.

"Any idea what this is about, Ann?" asked Staunton, brandishing her note.

"No, Sir," replied Staunton's secretary, surprised that he had actually used her name when asking a question.

"Damn," he said, turning on his heels and leaving.

Along the corridor he knocked and entered the reception area to Sir Andrew's office suite. As usual Mrs March greeted him with that expression of hers that suggested a bad smell had entered the office.

"Take a seat, Mr Staunton, I will see if Sir Andrew is available."

Struggling to be polite Staunton said, "Thank you, Mrs March."

Five minutes passed before Sir Andrew's office door opened and Mrs March invited Staunton in.

"Ah, Leonard, I have a task that I would like you to treat with 'a' the utmost urgency and 'b' the utmost discretion."

"I am at your command, Sir Andrew."

"Does the name Barry Jacobs mean anything to you?" asked Sir Andrew, noting that slight intensity in Staunton's eyes that indicated recognition.

"No, Sir Andrew, I can't say that it does."

"Oh, I thought you might have served with him," said Sir Andrew now wondering whether his reading of Staunton's eyes was in fact correct. "I would like you to trawl through SAS records and see what you come up with and report back to me."

"This is sensitive, Sir Andrew?"

"Yes, Leonard, very sensitive. Your earliest report if you would."

"Certainly, Sir Andrew, I'll get onto it straight away. May I ask what it is in connection with, it may help me narrow things down. I doubt if there was only one Barry Jacobs who has served with SAS."

"I don't want to restrict your search, Leonard. If there were as many as, say, ten, that would be fine."

"I see. Is there anything else, Sir Andrew?" asked Staunton, standing as if to leave. "Oh, you may not have heard yet, Sir Andrew, but that man Ian Vaughan, who we had to dismiss a few days ago has been killed. Our information, though limited I must add, suggests that it was a collision at sea."

"I see, Leonard, that is very interesting information, that changes a few patterns of perception. Thank you, now if you could deal with the Jacobs business."

It was a very satisfied Leonard Staunton that left Sir Andrew Averrille's office that morning. A man in fact who knew personally that the file on 40128165 Sergeant Barry Jacobs had been pulled two years before.

A few minutes later passing his secretary, sat at her desk, he said, "Get me the earliest appointment to view SAS records; then contact Bowen at Kingsbridge and tell him to return immediately to operation Nightjar."

***

On the beach, Vaughan had almost raised his gun and fired.

"Penny?"

"No, it's me, Anna-Maria. Penny is here, but she has been hurt."

Relieved, Vaughan scrambled over the rocks to where the women lay, Penny's head resting on Anna-Maria's lap.

"Where are you hurt, Penny?"

"I think I stopped a bullet in the thigh, Ian. It hurts like hell."

"Right, I'm going to fireman's lift you up to the house on the hill and see what we can do for you there," said Vaughan. "Anna-Maria, you bring the grab bags, here's mine."

Vaughan helped Heathcote to her feet and putting her torso over his shoulder lifted her and picked his way up through the rocks to the road.

"How are you, Penny?"

"Not good, will this take long?"

"I'll get you there as soon as I can."

By the time Vaughan lowered Penny onto the porch bench of the house he was breathing heavily and took several minutes to recover. A careful tour of the outside indicated that the property did not have a burglar alarm system.

Vaughan pressed the door bell and heard a chime sound from inside. Waiting a few seconds and seeing no lights appear he pressed the door bell again. "No one at home, pity, illegal entry it has to be," he said, before leaving the two women again and disappearing towards the rear of the property.

Anna-Maria heard the sound of breaking glass, then two minutes later the front door opened.

238

"We better get Penny inside and close the curtains before we put any lights on," said Vaughan, hoisting Penny over his shoulder again.

Once they were inside, Anna-Maria hurried around closing curtains and internal doors. The small hallway led to the kitchen at the back of the house with a sitting room and dining room either side of it. Vaughan carried Penny straight through to the kitchen and laid her on the large refectory table in the centre, that was covered with a brightly coloured plastic cloth.

"Anna-Maria, you look round in here for first aid stuff, while I look around upstairs."

Vaughan found what he was looking for in the bathroom cabinet, then had some success with a search of the sitting room.

"This should do until we can get you proper attention," he said, holding up a first aid box and a bottle of Vodka. "With tonic Penny?"

Anna-Maria immediately walked across the kitchen and took a bottle of fizzy lemonade from a cupboard. "How about this?"

"I couldn't face a drink right now, Ian, thank you all the same."

"Oh I'm sure you can, Lieutenant."

The switch from her name to her rank had Penny looking at Vaughan questioningly for a few moments before nodding her head. "Oh, why not celebrate our survival."

"That's the spirit, here we are have a good swig of that," said Vaughan, putting a glass with a triple measure of vodka and the same amount of lemonade in her hand.

"We need to get you dry and warm and that means getting your swimsuit off. Can you give Penny a hand when she's finished her drink, while I find towels and some clean sheets and a blanket or two."

"Yes of course, Ian. You wait outside please while we're doing this," replied Anna-Maria, her expression very serious.

Some twenty minutes had passed with Vaughan waiting in the hallway, then the kitchen door was opened slightly and a hand appeared, to take the sheets and blankets. Five minutes later he was waved into the kitchen.

Surveying the scene, Vaughan was impressed with the way Anna-Maria had prepared Penny ready for him to treat. It looked just like the table in a hospital operating theatre with Penny laid face down covered from shoulders to feet except for the wound area.

"Oh neat, nurse Anna-Maria, very neat indeed. Now let's have a look at the damage," said Vaughan, bending over and looking closely at the back of Penny Heathcote's thigh. "Entry wound and no exit wound. On the bright side, though the wound is bleeding it's not pumping out, so no major vein or artery hit, possibly you stopped a ricochet, which may mean the bullet is not in very deep," said Vaughan, almost to himself. "Can you boil some water for me please, Anna-Maria."

As she moved away from the sink Vaughan went across and thoroughly washed his hands and lower arms, then he tore up a clean bed sheet and using pieces soaked in cold salt water delicately cleaned the wound site, the salt extracting a shriek from Penny. Using a clean dry cloth he tried to staunch the bleeding whilst the kettle boiled.

"Find a clean saucepan and pour the water into it and put it on that gas stove and keep the water boiling please, Anna-Maria; then we'll need a sieve," said Vaughan, sorting through the first aid box and selecting a pair of tweezers and small scissors.

Opening his grab bag he pulled out a double edged knife, the sight of which made Anna-Maria gasp, but she said nothing.

Crouching down alongside Penny's head, Vaughan gently brushed some hair from her face and stroked her cheek. "How are you feeling?"

"I'm very scared at the moment and the wound hurts so much I feel as if my leg has been blown up."

"I'm sorry to say that I'm going to hurt you a bit more shortly, but we must see if we can get the bullet out."

Penny bit her lip as tears trickled down onto the small pillow supporting her head.

It was possible that the alcohol was having some effect as Penny hardly flinched as Vaughan, wearing a pair of latex gloves from the first aid box, pulled the wound open a little with his fingers.

"Put the knife in the boiling water as far as it will go, and the tweezers and scissors in the sieve and place that in there as well, would you please," he said looking at Anna-Maria. "Mind the knife, it is razor sharp."

"Are you going to use some of the vodka on the wound to kill the germs?"

"Anna-Maria, you have been watching too many Bourne films, alcohol would damage the tissue and delay healing," replied Vaughan, winking at her and smiling.

"I did not know that," she said somewhat chastened.

"Neither did I until I went into training with SIS," Vaughan replied, "I think it's a common mistake that many people make."

Anna-Maria moved to the sink and again washed her hands and arms, drying them on the spare bed sheet then she took gloves from the first aid box and put them on.

"Ah, are you going to assist, nurse?"

Anna-Maria smiled.

Having given the knife, tweezers and small scissors five full minutes in boiling water, Vaughan lifted the sieve out of the saucepan and handed it to Anna-Maria. "If you could stand that side, facing me."

He then used a fork to turn the knife so that the handle and the rest of the blade were immersed. "We better wait until those things have cooled down."

The knife blade was still slightly warm as Vaughan used the tip to probe the wound and saw Penny's fists clench. "Sorry, Penny, ah, there it is. Anna-Maria can you hold the knife as still as you can, while I try and get it with the tweezers and scissors."

Penny yelled twice but bravely kept remarkably still.

"Got it, fortunately the bullet was not in deep," said Vaughan, great relief apparent in his voice. "Now to stop the bleeding and close up."

Washing the wound again in salt water brought another shriek from Penny.

"Sorry, Penny, but we must make sure it's clean."

Pinching the skin together as best he could Vaughan exerted pressure on the wound, holding it for over a quarter of an hour. "Anna-Maria, can you look in the first aid box and see if there is any antibiotic cream in there?"

Picking up a tube Anna-Maria studied the small print. "Um, this is no good, er this one may be, um no. Ah yes here we go this is the one, and it has not yet been used."

'Okay, we also need that roll of surgical tape," said Vaughan. "Can you cut off three strips about seven centimetres long."

Placing cream on the wound Vaughan again pinched it together whilst Anna-Maria applied the tape.

"I'm going to bring down a mattress from upstairs, Anna-Maria. While I'm doing that can you clean up as much of the blood Penny is lying in as you can, but try not to open up that wound."

When Vaughan had found the cleanest of the mattresses and brought it down to the hall he discovered the kitchen door closed. Knocking he was firmly told to wait until he was invited. When he was finally granted entry he was relieved to find that, thanks to the plastic tablecloth, sliding Penny onto the mattress was easier than he had feared.

"Okay, Penny, you and Anna-Maria try and get some sleep. I'm going to get that car and hide it nearby."

Leaving the house, Vaughan cautiously made his way down the hill to the beach, finding the car still where it had been left earlier. The problem was what to do with the trailer and unable to find another suitable spot he pushed it out into deep water. The Renault was old and reluctant to start at first, but on the fifth turn of the ignition key the engine sprang into life. Driving past the house he saw, further up the hill, a corrugated iron covered shed near the entrance to a grassy field. Turning into the field he parked the car out of sight of the road and walked back to the house.

Anna-Maria was already asleep on a settee in the sitting room and Penny Heathcote lay, eyes closed but awake, on the mattress in the kitchen. Sitting on a chair beside her, Vaughan watched over her as she slowly dozed off, spending the time considering which was the best way to return to England.

They left the house shortly after eight o'clock in the morning and drove in the ancient Renault to Acoruna where Heathcote had her wound checked and redressed at the Teresa Herrara Hospital overlooking the bay. Her explanation that she had fallen on a sharp gardening tool in a friend's garden was readily accepted and she left after treatment, two stitches closing the wound and a course of antibiotics to take; by evening they had arrived at Santander to await the next ferry to Plymouth.

"Penny, get checked in at the Hotel Bahia over there, the other side of the gardens, tell them that the airline will deliver your cases when they have found them. That should pass for arriving with no luggage. I'm going to ditch the car and get our tickets for the ferry, see you later," looking at her he paused then asked, "Are you all right; you have been very quiet since leaving the house this morning."

"Yes, Ian, I'm fine just a bit shaken up that's all, I'm not used to being shot at. I should have thanked you properly for what you did for me and for us," she said pointing to herself and Anna-Maria, "You always seem to know what to do and how to plan."

"Come on get that hotel arranged."

***

Yakov Gorokhin had finally cracked the Vermeulen code at three o'clock in the morning and spent the rest of that day typing the decoded information into his primary computer. It did not take him long to realise that the information held within the pages of the notebook was of immense value to anyone who could decipher it. Names, places, transactions, cupboard skeletons, politicians' weaknesses, it was all there. Ten pages were of particular interest to him personally as they contained information about senior Russian officials and their corrupt activities as suppliers of arms, who would pay a very high price to have the relevant pages destroyed. Maybe they would be able to find his wife and daughter, Gorokhin thought. His escape to the West had been for him a moral decision more than a political one, his stance on certain issues reaching a point where arrest and imprisonment were a possibility. His wife, however, had not shared his views and went out of her way to publicly denounce him the day after he had left. His then two-year-old daughter of course would not know of such things and she had over the years constantly been in his thoughts. He wondered now what had become of her, would she forgive him for abandoning her.

In the eyes of Yakov Gorokhin the content of the notebook was far too valuable to just hand over to Leonard Staunton in return for money. As most valuable of all in the notebook were the two pages that held details of Leonard Staunton, British Intelligence Agent, these he carefully cut out. Aware that Staunton was not the type to negotiate once a deal had been done, Gorokhin decided to edit the information leaving out some of the Russian section and of course the dirt on Staunton himself. These particular edits were to be his downfall, for when Staunton arrived near midnight he had immediately skimmed through the stick Gorokhin had made for him along with the black notebook itself, and knew for certain that some important contact details and backgrounds were missing. He had also seen the minute gap left in the notebook's spine where the two pages had been, which confirmed that the Russian had dangerous ambitions of his own.

"You cheating bastard Russians think we in the West are stupid," said Staunton with quiet menace. "You think that you can sell a car with no wheels and it won't be noticed."

"Why do you say such a thing?" Gorokhin replied, watching as Staunton started to open the desk drawers then move to the corner bookcase. "What are you looking for?"

"There are pages missing from this notebook and names missing on that memory stick," replied Staunton, his anger beginning to build.

"I have put everything on there that the notebook contains, Leonard."

Staunton was pulling out books and checking what was behind them, then shaking them for loose pages as Gorokhin replied.

Picking up a heavy glass paperweight from a shelf Staunton turned. "Do you think that I would accept that without seeing the name of Androv Milakov or Jaska Nikulichev in the index," shouted Staunton, having noted that his own name was also missing.

The desire for revenge against the corrupt political system he had run from and the potential the withheld information contained for news of his daughter and yes, even blackmail, had been too great a temptation for Gorokhin, "Do you want me to make something up?"

Staunton bent down and whispered in the Russian's ear, "No I want you to complete the work... every... last... word," before standing and delivering a brutal blow to the side of the old Russian's head with the paperweight.

Gorokhin couldn't reply. The blow to the old man had caused brain damage enough to put him instantly into a vegetative state, jaw dropped but still breathing unable to communicate.

"Where is the rest?" asked Staunton, almost mildly.

The Russian, now slumped in his chair, was silent, his eyes staring blankly at the floor. Grabbing Gorokhin by the collar of his cardigan, Staunton yanked him to his feet, "Where is the rest of it!" he screamed. "Tell me, where is it?"

Gorokhin blinked, his stale breath causing Staunton to tilt his head away, but the old man remained silent, as Staunton shook him like a rag doll. "Answer me, you little Russian shit, answer me!"

Dropping Gorokhin to the floor Staunton kicked him hard in the chest, then kicked him again, then again and again and again. He knew he had killed the Russian a long time before he had stopped kicking the frail body across the floor. When finally his anger was spent, Staunton returned to the task of searching the house for the missing pages and data, starting with the removal of the computer hard drives. Moving back to the bookshelves his frustration and anger grew again until the search became more of an exercise in trashing the house, but all to no avail.

***

At three o'clock that morning Alice Morgan was woken by Staunton hammering on her front door.

"Lenny darling what is the matter?" she asked, half asleep.

"Sir Andrew has found out that I pulled Barry Jacobs' file two years ago."

"Is that important? I don't understand."

"I've been using Jacobs for odd jobs where a bit of muscle was required, like dealing with Jan Vermeulen's stepdaughter and that redheaded bitch Heathcote, something has happened that got Sir Andrew to ask me to search for Jacobs' SAS file."

"Well?"

"Well, I said that I didn't know Jacobs but now someone else has discovered that I had his file pulled and Sir Andrew wants an explanation."

"Oh. Oh, Lenny why did you do it, what was so important and what has happened to Penny Heathcote?"

"Bloody Campbell's job that's what was so important. All the while he was in Anti Terrorist Command I was making my way up the ladder but he knew I had something to do with David Patterson, his blue eyed boy's disappearance, so when he came back into SIS he started digging. I used Jacobs to remove some of the information for me."

"Is that why you needed to know about Vaughan's movements?"

Getting hold of her arm he marched her towards her bedroom. "Have you got a place where you can hide for a few days?"

"Stop it, Lenny you are frightening me." The shock of what he had just said alarming her. "Why do I have to hide?"

"Because they are currently watching my place and when I don't show at eight o'clock in front of Sir Andrew they will break in and search it."

"Well?"

"The pictures," he replied, "You know, the ones of us."

Alice gasped. "You said you had destroyed those, Lenny. You promised me that you had."

"It's too late now, sweetie, they'll soon know that you were also involved, so get your case packed while I get my flight organised."

"What will happen to us, Lenny, when they catch us?"

"They won't catch us if you get a move on. I have a plan in place so don't worry, sweetie, I have a few of these to cash in," Staunton said, taking a velvet purse from his pocket and dangling it in front of her, "And a few more due when you deliver a little notebook for me to our generous friend."

Fear was now gripping her, "No, Leonard, I'm not doing any more, I'm too scared, Leonard no, you can't make me do any more."

"If you don't, sweetie, it will be jail and for a long, long time. You see there isn't enough in this purse to look after both of us and only you can deliver the notebook."

"Where are you going to be then? Why can't you deliver the notebook or would that risk your precious neck." The threat of being abandoned to her fate and virtually penniless made her hit back with a hostile response.

"Look, I just need to cover up some things in Spain, then we can meet up for a new life together, how does that sound. Just the two of us with more money than we could earn in SIS in a decade," replied Staunton regretting his implied threat and knowing the need to keep Alice on side for just a bit longer.

Alice didn't answer. To her, the new life together rang falsely in her ears as did the promise of wealth. Her thoughts now were more concerned with the immediate future and a safe place to hide. Several seconds passed in which she recalled a cottage near Lampeter that was not in use at the moment, belonging to some friends of her parents.

"What if I don't deliver this notebook thing? What if I just disappear, Leonard, what then?" said Alice, suddenly defiant.

Staunton knew now that it would only be fear that would get her co-operation.

"Well, my generous friend, Jan Vermeulen, will be very angry... with you." The pause in the delivery of his answer sent a chill through Alice from head to toe. She felt more used than ever before and even, yes, violated, by the man she had only the day before been in love with. She shivered, aware of him staring at her waiting for her to respond and knowing that he had the skills to find her wherever she ran to. "Why not just post it to him," she said.

"No, it has to be hand delivered, Alice, as he has to give you a small package, your share of the sparklers."

"What good would they be to me? I couldn't sell them, I would be caught in no time," she replied, stunned by his suggestion.

"You take them to Rolf Meijer's in Amsterdam. I will arrange transport for you. A day's sailing will put some colour in your cheeks, sweetie."

"Sailing?"

"Yes, it's the best way to get into Holland, you might well be identified at a ferry port," Staunton replied, casually. Alice shivered again now knowing that to get free she must get deeper involved in his murky scheme.

Whilst Alice was out of earshot, Staunton secured a seat on a flight to Madeira then stole a glance into the bedroom to see Alice frantically throwing every item of clothing she had into two suitcases together with her most precious personal items, and by the time she had finished she could hardly lift either of them. A hurried trip to the bathroom, and dressing in the clothes she had set aside for the journey, she struggled with the cases to the front door.

Staunton sat on the settee, his concentration fixed on his mobile phone. He was studying a text message sent several hours before from Sir Andrew Averrille. "Leonard I have been asked by Anti Terrorist Command to explain why a file on SAS soldier Barry Jacobs was pulled by you some two years ago. I need that answer from you personally at 0800hrs in my office."

As soon as he had received the message he knew that it was through Campbell that Anti Terrorist Command had become involved regarding Jacobs; for a period Campbell had been seconded to ATC as part of the shared intelligence and resource programme and Staunton was now wondering how Campbell had got to know of Jacobs. He had left four messages on the man's phone and was beginning to realise that something had gone wrong in Burgau that had got to the ears of Campbell; if that was the case then David Patterson's wife and the redheaded cat Heathcote had been found, but that didn't matter now he had the decoded version of Vermeulen's notebook. What was essential was to make use of all that information and to complete the deal for the Kazakov arms cache then get it moved on quickly in order to be in the game for a move into Cabinda Province and takeover Vermeulen's turf before others knew that Vermeulen was basically out of business there.

"I'm ready, Leonard."

"Right, sweetie. How do you fancy living in Chile?" Staunton replied, noting that she had dropped even the mildly irritating "Lenny". However, the omission of the endearment stung him; was she thinking of dumping him?

"We won't ever make it to Chile, Leonard, not together anyway."

"Don't say that, sweetie, it will turn out fine you'll see," he replied, now sure that her usefulness was coming to an end. Just two more favours and she would be en route to Istanbul.

All the way to the airport Staunton worked on a charm offensive, he still needed her to deliver the notebook and collect the stones as payment. It was a cause of mild amusement to him how it was that women were so much more physically suited to smuggle diamonds across borders than men. Once she had got them to his man in Amsterdam would she be any further use to him? Before that night he would probably have kept her for a time, but the switch to "Leonard" sounded rather, well, terminal in their relationship, definitely the Istanbul route from Amsterdam would be best, penniless of course.

***

"We'll get a taxi to Kingsbridge as soon as we can; I have a room there where you both should be safe for a week or so." It was the afternoon following the disappearance of Staunton and Alice Morgan, and the ferry from Santander was entering Plymouth Sound.

"You still keep that room on then, Ian?"

"Yes, I didn't need anywhere else, living on my boat most of the time. Her sinking may well alter that unless the UK Government stump up for a replacement, but as I wasn't working for them at the time, well, we will see."

"It will depend on whether Staunton completes his con trick," said Heathcote. "My advice would be to tell no one that we are here."

Vaughan nodded, "You're right, we keep out of sight until we are sure it's safe."

The taxi ride was a new experience for Anna-Maria who had never seen the English countryside before. "Everything is so green and I love some of these houses, they are so quaint."

"The green grass is thanks to the rainfall but agreed, some of the property in this area of Devon, which is called The South Hams, is very attractive."

"Didn't you have a job down here before you joined us, Ian?"

"Yes, Yealmstoke Head, my last honest days' work."

"Don't let the Commodore hear you say that."

"Why not, I struggle still to find anything solid in what I do now."

"I know that the Commodore thinks you do solid work, so don't you forget it."

Vaughan turned in the seat to look at her and saw the commanding lieutenant look in her eyes, then her expression softened and she smiled at him.

In Kingsbridge, Vaughan knocked at the door to the cottage where he rented the first floor. "Just a minute," he heard through the kitchen fanlight.

When the door opened a rather flustered Miranda Cox looked at them blankly.

"Hi, Miranda, I thought I better knock rather than use my key," said Vaughan.

"Good God, Ian, I didn't recognise you. You are as brown as a berry, where have you been?"

"Oh swanning around, Miranda, doing a bit of this and a bit of that, you know. Let me introduce you to Penny and Anna-Maria."

"Oh, yes er, pleased to meet you, I'm Miranda Cox, Ian's landlady. This is a surprise, Ian, it's been months since I last saw you. Come in all of you, er sorry about the mess I'm in the middle of a project."

In the tiny living room a huge canvas was set on an easel beneath a bright spotlight. The subject was a middle-aged man standing proudly wearing a chain of office.

"The local mayor?"

"Yes, Ian, he is. Counsellor Gilbert Dashwood," she informed. "Would you like some coffee, I need a break from this."

When she returned with a tray of mugs, Miranda asked, "What brings you back to these parts, I was beginning to think you were gone forever."

"Well in fact I'm not back just yet, I have a couple of little jobs to finish first, but I would appreciate it if my two friends could stay here for a while."

Miranda gave Penny and Anna-Maria a closer look. "They are not in any trouble are they, I don't want the police knocking at the door."

Penny gave Miranda a hurt look.

"No they are not in any trouble, Miranda, I assure you," said Vaughan chuckling at the thought. "They just need a place to stay while their flat in London is being refurbished," replied Vaughan, making up the story about the flat on the spur of the moment.

"Oh I see, they'll need another bed put up there, surely you thought of that before bringing them all the way down to Devon?"

"Yes, Miranda, I've got it all in hand."

The flat pack bed and mattress was delivered an hour later and Anna-Maria assisted Vaughan in assembling it while Heathcote tried to contact Lorna, giving up after the twelfth attempt.

They had been discussing where to have dinner when Heathcote's mobile rang.

"Hello," she said cautiously.

"It's me, Lorna, where are you?"

"We are back in England, Lorna, any news?"

"Jackson finally got a response to who pulled the file on Jacobs, guess who it was?"

"Staunton."

"Oh, yes it was, but you didn't know that he apparently did a runner yesterday together with a signal clerk named Alice Morgan."

"So now we know how Staunton got himself to Gibraltar so quickly, he had a pair of ears and eyes in the communications room."

Vaughan gave Heathcote a questioning look, to which she held up her hand as if to say, please wait.

"The Commodore has been asked to return, by the PM no less, and Sir Andrew Averrille's future is under review, or so the Commodore understands. He will get the top job if Sir Andrew goes."

"Any orders?"

"The Commodore wondered whether Vaughan wanted his job back, and if so to report to SIS headquarters as soon as possible."

"He has a job for him?"

"Yes, he is to find Staunton, and a little black book."

"Oh. Tell him he will be on his way in a couple of hours," Heathcote said in a tone that indicated both disappointment and regret.

When she put the phone down Vaughan asked, "What have you just volunteered me for?"

"You are back on the payroll with instructions to report to SIS HQ immediately, the Commodore wants you to find Staunton, apparently he pulled Jacobs' SAS file from records two years ago and has now done a runner together with a communication room girl called Alice Morgan."

"How do you know I want the job back?"

Heathcote looked shocked, "Don't be daft, of course you do."

"I might have got one over on Staunton at Gibraltar but hunting down a trained killer like him is not an attractive job prospect."

"I'm sorry, Ian, I should not have made the assumption, but you are the only person the Commodore can trust, no one knows how far Staunton's tentacles have reached." Again there was the tone of regret in her voice, she paused as if summoning the courage to say something more. "Frankly I don't want you to go but, like the Commodore, I believe you are the one most likely to succeed." Then the tears came, "Sod it, sod it, sod it! It is like David all over again," she said now looking directly at Anna-Maria.

"You mean, my David, don't you, Penny."

Heathcote nodded then sat heavily on the bed, "I, we were, as they say, an item when he joined SIS, then Angola and…"

Vaughan crossed the room and went into the bathroom and turned on the shower, twenty minutes later he emerged to pack a suitcase and found Heathcote and Anna-Maria sat side by side on the new bed, Anna-Maria with an arm around Heathcote's shoulders and the other hand holding Heathcote's. *"I must leave now before I tell the Commodore to go to hell."*

Checking the contents of his case Vaughan checked his pockets then, handing Anna-Maria the front door key said, "Look after Penny please," and left.

CHAPTER 11

At ten o'clock that evening Vaughan swiped his badge across the pad to the side gate on the Albert Road main entrance to SIS Head Quarters, to his surprise the gate slid back letting him through.

"Good evening, Mr Vaughan, can you put your case on here, Sir, and open it for me."

Vaughan complied noting that the man did not look at the case but kept his eyes firmly fixed on Vaughan.

"Now if you would go across to my colleague, Sir, and empty your pockets and check in your weapon, Sir," continued the security officer, "We will check your case and weapon into the reception luggage store, you will need this to collect it on the way out."

The officer handed Vaughan what looked like a hotel key then pointed in the direction of his colleague.

Placing just the pistol on the table next to his wallet and the other items the second officer asked, "And your shoulder holster please, Mr Vaughan."

"I no longer have it I'm afraid, it is at the bottom of a ria in Spain, along with my boat."

The man's expression didn't even flicker.

"Could you take your jacket off, Sir."

Vaughan complied and watched as the man padded it down before rounding the table and padding Vaughan down very professionally.

"Here is your jacket, Sir. You can go up when you are ready; the Commodore is waiting for you in briefing room eight on the fifth floor. Reception is through the security system over there, Sir."

"Thank you, gentlemen."

The main entrance and corridors were not as busy as during the day but there were still a lot of staff on duty. At the door to the briefing room Vaughan knocked.

"Come in." The Commodore sat with a woman and a man both of whom Vaughan vaguely recognised.

"Ah, Vaughan, you made good time. May I introduce our Foreign Secretary, Eleanor Geddings, and Home Secretary Marcus Hatton-James. Have you had a meal?"

"I grabbed a burger from the train's buffet car on the way," replied Vaughan shaking hands with the two ministers.

"Coffee and some sandwiches are on the way, take a seat," said Campbell. "It is Ian Vaughan here who is responsible for not only exposing the planned coup against the Portuguese Government but also exposing a dangerous and corrupting influence within SIS."

"We received some further praise about your work from the Portuguese Ambassador only a few days ago, Mr Vaughan," said Eleanor Geddings, giving Vaughan a wide and friendly smile.

"What we would like you to do, Vaughan, is to take us through this latest operations of yours starting from the day you left Madeira," requested Campbell.

Two hours later, Campbell and the two ministers sat silently looking at Vaughan trying to take in what they had just heard.

"Was it our decision to get her out through Western Sahara, Commodore?" asked Eleanor Geddings.

"No, Minister, it was forced on us by circumstances. Jan Vermeulen had people watching ports and the main airport in Mauritania."

"She was lucky to fly out of Nouadhibou then."

"She was indeed, it was very smart thinking on the part of our local man to get her up into Western Sahara so quickly."

"Who governs Western Sahara now?" asked Hatton-James.

"Basically Morocco, but Algeria continues to make claims. At a recent United Nations C24 colonisation seminar apparently the Moroccan and Algerian delegates came to blows over the issue."

Hatton-James looked at Eleanor Geddings in amazement, "Really, they actually came to blows in the seminar!"

"So it has been reported."

"Good heavens."

"And the UN just stood by and observed," said Vaughan, receiving a sharp look from both ministers.

"Where are Lieutenant Heathcote and Mrs Patterson now, Mr Vaughan?" asked the Home Secretary.

"Safely tucked up in a safe house, Home Secretary."

"But the Lieutenant was wounded."

"She has recovered well, despite my crude surgery. According to Mrs Patterson, the wound is healing well and the bruising subsiding."

"In the attack they actually threw grenades into our boat, as well as firing on it."

"It wasn't the government's yacht, Home Secretary, we thought that Vaughan's cover as a maritime author on the earlier mission was better achieved by the use of his own yacht. During his previous operation in Madeira there was a risk that he may meet someone whom he knew and who would know his boat," explained the Commodore, "The government will of course pay for its complete replacement, Vaughan."

"There are many other expenses I will have to claim; after my dismissal I was forced to use my own funds to cover the expenses for the three of us."

"I'll get one of our accounts staff to go through it all with you, Vaughan, as soon as you wish."

"Thank you, Sir."

"You mentioned that the Portuguese secret service were very keen to question this banker who owned the apartment in Lagos. I don't fully understand why," said Eleanor Geddings.

"We believe that it is something to do with the financing of the arms trade and possibly the coup, maybe leading to exposing details of the individual backers," said the Commodore. "Vaughan here and I discussed this possibility some time ago and the Serious Fraud people are actively searching through what information they can get from the City."

"Isn't this more a Portuguese Government matter?" asked Geddings.

"It is, Foreign Secretary, but it is also ours insofar that British subjects may be involved not only in the illegal arms trading but also supporting the recent coup attempt. If we find the information first it will give us the opportunity of either sorting it out here discreetly, or handing the information over to demonstrate our support and friendship with Portugal," replied Vaughan, closely watching the politicians' reactions.

"Oh God, the Treasury will go bloody mad if there is another banking scandal centred on London," groaned the Home Secretary putting his head in his hands. "Was this rogue agent involved with the coup?"

"We won't know for sure until we have tracked him down but it is a possibility," replied Vaughan, "I would suggest, however, that we avoid issuing an international arrest warrant and instead, once we have an idea where he has gone, send a small team that includes a Special Branch Police Officer to actually make the arrest, that would significantly reduce the spread of information regarding the reasons for the arrest."

"It sounds as if you are volunteering for the job, Mr Vaughan," said the Foreign Secretary, looking at Vaughan intently.

"If those are my orders, Foreign Secretary, I will be happy to carry them out."

"You think you know where he is, don't you," said the Commodore studying Vaughan carefully.

"I have an idea, Sir, yes."

"Get yourself checked into the Firm's hotel and see me back here tomorrow morning at about ten o'clock," said the Commodore. "I'll come with you to the lift."

In the corridor the Commodore stopped Vaughan and said, "I owe you a great debt, Ian, but that debt I am afraid can never be used as a 'Get you out of Jail Card' but it does help in getting you up the promotion ladder."

"I don't play Monopoly, Sir, so I would never have thought of picking up the 'Get out of Jail Card' you refer to," replied Vaughan stiffly, offended by Campbell's insinuation.

"You never struck me as someone who played that game, that is why I hired you. I am sorry that I had to make it clear now, but in this world such matters must be expressed in black and white clarity, grey boundaries create too many problems. Now I must get back and discuss a few more issues with our guests while I have their full attention."

Twenty minutes later Vaughan paid off the taxi in Chelsea, close to the DELCO offices, and walking past them noticed Lorna Parker-Davis standing at the reception desk apparently sorting through a pile of paperwork. At the Firm's "hotel" he was greeted, swiftly checked in and shown to his room.

"What time would you like your morning call and breakfast, Mr Vaughan?" asked the steward.

"Better make it seven o'clock for the call and say seven-thirty for breakfast."

"Certainly, Mr Vaughan, good night."

***

The next morning Vaughan found the Commodore waiting for him in the Albert Road briefing room together with Lorna.

"Good morning, Vaughan."

"Good morning, Commodore, Lorna."

"I want Staunton found first of all and I've deployed a large number of people and organisations in this country to find out where he has gone," said the Commodore, indicating that Vaughan should sit opposite him at the table. "We are also searching for a Miss Alice Morgan recently employed here as one of our communication staff."

"Her flat in Croydon was searched the day before yesterday, Vaughan. Fingerprints and DNA found there indicate the recent presence of Staunton," informed Lorna Parker-Davis. "In his apartment we found some pictures that definitely confirmed their 'close' relationship and Miss Morgan's DNA."

"How many passports did Staunton hold?" asked Vaughan.

"On this Portuguese business authorised by Sir Andrew Averrille he was operating under his own name we believe," replied Lorna.

"Previous ops?"

"We collect in all alias passports on return from each duty."

"Is that just DELCO or this place as well?" said Vaughan.

Lorna picked up the phone and dialled. "Document division...? Good... This is Lorna Parker-Davis acting PA to Commodore Campbell, can you send up the passport issue and return sheet for Senior Agent Leonard Staunton... Fifth floor briefing room eight. Thank you."

"You think he is using a passport retained from a previous operation with which to leave the country?" said the Commodore.

"If that is what he has done, my guess is that he has gone to Madeira, to conclude an arms deal with the minder of the late illegal arms trader Kazakov. He now needs money and a lot of it."

"Of course, Vaughan, the man you saw Staunton talking to in Funchal."

"Yes, Sir. After Kazakov's death the minder became almost by default the guardian to Kazakov's mute daughter, so he would also need the funds available from any cache of weapons Kazakov held, to support her."

"Mute you say?" said the Commodore.

"Yes, Sir, mute, in fact quite a sorrowful looking young girl, when I saw her at Kazakov's old house, who must feel very alone now."

The Commodore looked at Vaughan and could see the man's shared sense of loss and the loneliness it brings, and made a note to grant Vaughan leave to spend time with his daughters.

"Did this Kazakov have any link to Vermeulen?" asked Lorna.

"I don't know but I am sure Staunton does have and I'm sure that he wanted to take that black notebook to use it and avoid being incriminated by it," said Vaughan. "I guarantee that GCHQ never received it."

"Why would they?" asked Lorna.

"Because it was in the most complex code I've ever seen. Agreed I am no expert, but the pages I studied on the passage from the Selvagems to Gibraltar did not reveal anything like a pattern," replied Vaughan.

"Well, Staunton wouldn't have been able to," Lorna said with some feeling. "In my short time here, before I was given the job across the river at DELCO, I was in the next section to his and everyone knew that he passed coded stuff to his assistant to do, even if the stuff was above their STRAP level, because he didn't have a clue."

"Which begs the question why was he so well in with Sir Andrew Averrille if he was that rubbish at the job," said Vaughan.

"That same question has been bugging me for years, Vaughan," said the Commodore.

"Did anyone know of the relationship between Staunton and this Alice Morgan?" asked Vaughan.

"Nobody in the communications room knew of it," said Lorna. "The joke was that the person she was overheard talking to on the phone was a Lenny from Covent Garden Market."

"When it was in fact, Lenny Staunton," said Vaughan. "Are you all right, Sir?"

"The first time I saw that young lady in our communications room was just after the assassination attempt on Walid al Djebbar. I remember saying to Heathcote at the time that I had seen her before, and went as far as having her file brought up but there was nothing in it that presented any problem. Now I have just remembered where I had seen her before, and that was the day after Sir Andrew Averrille had been appointed to the top post and he had thrown a garden party for senior staff and partners. She was there with Staunton, but not with Staunton if you understand me."

"You mean that she was brought along by Staunton to be seen by someone else," said Vaughan.

The Commodore nodded, "Yes, Vaughan, I think that is precisely what I mean."

"Are you thinking what I am thinking?" said Lorna.

"Staunton found a love child of Sir Andrew's and has cashed in his winning Monopoly Chance Card, worth a lot more than the two hundred pounds on it," said Vaughan.

"That is one hell of a leap, Vaughan," said Campbell, frowning.

"In the light of current circumstances, Sir, maybe somebody should put the question to Sir Andrew."

"You are right, Vaughan, but I would be a lot happier to have more than just Miss Morgan's DNA."

"We have it, Sir, both on record and from her flat, we could in fact do a two way match to Sir Andrew, from his records," said Lorna.

"This is not helping us find Staunton though, is it," said Vaughan. "How long does it take to dig out Staunton's document record?"

There was a knock at the door. "This answer your question, Vaughan."

"I hope so, Lorna."

"Sorry it took so long, we had a problem checking it against his operations list."

Lorna, thanking the clerk and taking the list, passed it across the table to the Commodore who carefully studied it.

"Two are missing, the first, EU/Italian was in the name of Leonardo Giovani and the second was South African in the name of Laurens Van Vuuren," said the Commodore, "I don't recall him having worked in Italy."

"Maybe he was just blowing the bloody doors off of something," said Vaughan, in his best Michael Caine mimic.

The Commodore looked up and frowned for a moment then made the connection with the film "The Italian Job". "Oh, yes, very droll, Vaughan."

Stifling a giggle Lora asked, "Shall I get these details out to the airports and ferries, Sir."

"Yes, Lorna, and we better also do the same for Alice Morgan's passport."

"Yes, Sir, I will get onto it straight away. We have already issued details of Staunton's own and Alice Morgan's passport but so far have not heard anything."

"Last night, Vaughan, you again linked Staunton with the coup. This is not just because he mentioned it when you met him in Gibraltar is it?"

"No, Sir, it's that I got the feeling from Agent Ascensao that De Lacerda was linking the banker who owned the boat and the Lagos apartment to his search for the coup backers. I am sure now that Staunton was the organiser of the snatch operation based on his rapid arrival in Gibraltar and the vast amount of time he has spent recently, supposedly, tidying up so called loose ends of a previous operation I suspect is more to do with covering his tracks and others in connection with the coup."

"Mmm, let's keep that thought, Vaughan, and see if we cannot add a little more substance to it."

For the next half an hour the three of them went back over the timetable of events as they knew them starting at the time Vaughan sent his text message from off the coast of Morocco. Assuming that Alice Morgan had intercepted the message and passed the details onto Staunton they concluded that it was Staunton who arranged the snatch. To use the banker's boat and Lagos apartment also clearly indicated Staunton's deep involvement in Portugal's wealthy hierarchy increasing the chances of his involvement in radical political change.

At the end of the discussion Vaughan moved on to a meeting to sort out his expenses, followed by a chance to phone his daughters. He had just put the phone down when Lorna came into the room. "You were right; Staunton flew out to Madeira on his own aboard yesterday's early morning Easy Jet flight from Gatwick. We have people checking CCTV to see if Alice Morgan saw him off."

"What name did he use?"

"Laurens Van Vuuren."

"Right, what next?" asked Vaughan.

"The Commodore asked whether you would be prepared to do the arrest. We will put a man from Special Branch with you to do the formal bit."

"You mean I can't kill him?"

"Afraid not, Vaughan, but accidents do happen," Lorna replied. "Can I take that as a yes?"

"Yes, you can, Lorna. Can you sort me out a good photograph of him; I may need to show it to a couple of people?"

"Certainly, and you are booked on tomorrow's Easy Jet flight, it leaves at 0710 hours."

"How did you know I was going to volunteer for this one?" said Vaughan, frowning at her, then shaking his head said, "I had better pack and get some sleep."

"A car will pick you up at 0400. You will be travelling under your own name, it appears that you are too well known in Madeira to use an alias," replied Lorna smiling.

"Probably yes, and there is not enough time to grow a beard."

***

Arriving in Madeira three days before Vaughan, Staunton had retrieved his gun from the airport locker he had hired then, picking up the hire car he had ordered, immediately drove to the Kazakov household and settled the arms deal with Boris. That done he was intending to lay low in Funchal and leave with the arms shipment to the Cabinda Province of

Angola in a week's time, the luxury of knowing that most of Vermeulen's contact data was in his hands, helped ease his fears of failure over Campbell's position. He was actually beginning to believe that he no longer needed SIS to manipulate those subtle shifts in control that would make him rich and powerful, even the idea of northern Chile being the base of his operation was becoming an attractive dream the more he considered it.

Checking in at the hotel, Staunton, using the name Leonardo Giovani, went straight to his room and unpacked. Picking up his phone he intended to try phoning Jacobs again, then dropped it back on the bed, realising that if Jacobs was being held by the police they would be able to locate the caller. Crossing the room to the writing desk Staunton pulled a receipt from his wallet and on the back of it started a shopping list, the first item of which was hair dye, he then left the hotel and made his way over to the car rental offices before sorting out his change of appearance.

By evening Staunton's hair had gone quite grey and with thick framed horn-rimmed spectacles he looked more like a university professor than the almost unmistakeable government agent of his former appearance. He studied himself in the bathroom mirror, was pleased with what he saw and even surprised by how much his appearance could be changed by such small adjustments.

Returning to the bedroom he picked up his phone and dialled the MV Verlorenvlei's Inmarsat number.

"Kallenberg."

"Leonard. Did Jan Vermeulen contact you?"

"Ah, yes, Leonard. Yes, Jan called, I understand you have a cargo for Cabinda."

"Correct, where are you at the moment?"

"Hamburg until tomorrow then we pick up a cargo from Antwerp."

"When can you arrive off Madeira?"

"Maybe in one week's time. I will be keeping in touch with you to arrange exact timing."

"That is probably best. If you can get here sooner so much the better."

"We will do our best. Is there anything else?"

"No, that's all for now. Don't forget the sooner the better."

***

Unlike Vaughan's previous arrival there was little applause as the landing at Madeira's Santa Caterina airport was quite straightforward. There was no short coach journey to the terminal building on this occasion and passengers were safely guided by ground staff from the aircraft to immigration and passport control. The walk, reducing the chance of being overheard, enabled Vaughan to brief his companion, Special Branch's Detective Sergeant Brian Conway, on his personal status. At Gatwick their introduction had been too brief and too public and with a full aircraft they found that they were separated. Conway looked older than Vaughan had anticipated he would and gave the impression that he had been around the block a few times, a feeling that gave Vaughan some confidence in the man's abilities.

"Just in case the Yard didn't mention it, my cover here is that of a maritime author who came here to research pilotage and shore facilities for inclusion in a new book."

"Yes, they did, mind you it was about the only thing they did tell me," replied Conway. "A Tramps Guide to the Islands of the Atlantic."

"That's the one, Sergeant. Oh, you had better call me Ian by the way, we are supposed to be two guys who just got talking to each other at Gatwick," said Vaughan.

"Okay, I'm Brian, first names it is."

Clearing immigration and customs Vaughan walked with Conway over towards Carlos who greeted Vaughan like a long lost friend.

"Brian this is Carlos, he will take us to the Pestana Grand Hotel. I have to look up an old friend once I've checked in; maybe we could meet up this evening for a beer?"

Conway looked surprised. "That sounds good, Ian."

Carlos led the way several paces in front with the trolley, allowing Vaughan to explain the reason for delay in searching for Staunton. "The last time I was here I should have made contact with the lady that was involved with exposing the recent coup attempt. It was a stupid omission on my part and is something I should try to put right."

"I was briefed with most of the arms smuggling information and abduction but it's the first time I've heard about your involvement in the coup, Ian."

"This is just my suspicion and something I have to confirm as soon as possible, but I somehow think that this man Staunton may have had some connection with the coup, not just the illegal arms trade."

On the way into Funchal, Vaughan gave the Sergeant a brief history of the island and its people.

"You seem very fond of Madeira, Ian."

"I am, particularly the people, they are really rather special."

"I must say the road system is a hell of a lot better than I expected."

"The amount that Portugal is having to pay back to the EU though is very rough on its inhabitants. Fortunately, the trouble in Egypt, Turkey and Tunisia has meant that a lot of tourists are returning here for their holidays, which can only be a good thing for the island, as it does not have much to export."

At the Pestana Grand, Vaughan paid Carlos and having checked in, both men went to their rooms. Swiftly unpacking, Vaughan changed into lighter clothes, then leaving his room walked out of the hotel grounds and up the hill a short distance to the Real Canoa restaurant.

The owner, Bruno, was standing on the pavement alongside the menu board. "Mr Vaughan, welcome back, it is good to see you again. Are you lunching with us today?"

"Yes, if you have a table free. The name is Ian by the way."

"Of course we have, please how about that one there," Bruno Silva said, pointing to an outside table close to the main restaurant window.

"That is great, thank you, sorry I mean, obrigado."

"Amelia will be very surprised to see you back here again, she was very upset that you left without visiting her, she saw your boat had gone and when she asked she learnt that you had returned and then gone away."

Vaughan and Amelia had become platonic friends. Vaughan, still hoping for a reconciliation with his estranged wife, had suppressed any feeling of attraction he had for the beautiful Amelia and would have ended the friendship earlier had she not expressed her concern about her uncle's secretive meetings. Following their exposure of the coup plot the two had spent a lot of time together whilst they endured seemingly endless questioning from the military, who had imposed temporary martial law on the island. When Vaughan was seriously wounded, SIS had him flown back to England, then, not making time to see her again when he returned to collect his yacht he had obviously caused hurt.

"Sadly it was all very much of a rush, I am afraid I was unable to call at her office."

"That is a great pity, Mr Ian, because shortly after you left she was attacked in the street by two men and badly beaten. She was in hospital for some days and now she only working half day and is still suffering much hurt from people."

"That is terrible, Bruno. Have the police found out who made the attack?"

Bruno shook his head, "No, Mr Ian, and I think maybe they do not try so hard."

"Why not, it is obviously connected to the coup and that blasted uncle of hers. Maybe some of those people who would have supported the coup."

"Or, Mr Ian, those who believe she was part of the coup."

"Are there many who believe that?"

"I think yes, there are. She gets shouted at occasionally when she is out in the street and her son, Zeferino, he now is bullied at his school."

"I thought that the authorities had finally accepted that she was innocent of involvement."

"It would not matter, Mr Ian, she would be hated by one side or the other, whatever."

"Is she back at her old apartment?"

"No, she has moved to near my home at Càmara de Lobos. If you like I will give you the address."

"Thank you, I will go and see her straight after I have finished my lunch," said Vaughan picking up the menu.

***

As Vaughan sat down and started looking through the menu, police in London were entering the Hamstead home of Yakov Gorokhin.

A young police constable, the third person through the door, gagged on the smell of rotting flesh and glancing at the mutilated body in the study turned and ran out into the street, throwing up into the gutter. Even the most hardened of officers were shocked by what they had found.

The room had been ransacked, as had much of the three-storey house.

"All three computers have had their hard drives removed, Sarge."

"Oh, right," answered the sergeant, his attention focused on a grey suited man, who had suddenly appeared standing in the study doorway, holding up a badge for the sergeant's inspection. "SIS, so I presume you want to take over from here."

The man nodded, "It would be appreciated, Sergeant, with as little further contamination of the scene as your men can manage, if you don't mind."

"Stop everything," the sergeant shouted. "We are being politely asked to leave. No rush, and be careful how you do it."

Then turning back to the man in the grey suit he said, "What's the interest for SIS then?"

"If I told you I would have to kill you."

"Oh God, a bloody comic. No seriously, what's your interest?"

"I'm sorry, Sergeant, I honestly can't tell you."

"Fair enough; you heard about the hard drives."

"Yes, I did. It seems the killer was a very frustrated and angry man."

"Seems to me that the man was a bloody psychopath."

The police sergeant was not the first to pronounce Staunton as being psychopathic. The army doctor at Camp Bastion in Hellman Province had come to the same conclusion following a fight in the camp between Staunton and another Major. Tragically the recommendation for Staunton to be returned home for mental assessment and treatment following the incident had been put into a handwritten report that was destroyed the next day in a Taliban rocket attack on the base.

"Probably that as well, Sergeant, but looking at the way his search becomes more ruthless and destructive as he makes his way around the shelves in this room suggests to me that he arrived relatively calm and almost composed. I would further suggest that the victim either withheld information or in fact did not know the information that his attacker wanted."

"Well, Sir, without the hard drives I doubt if you will learn much information either," said the sergeant.

"Oh, I don't know, Sergeant, in his anger and frustration our attacker failed to take with him the three back-up units on the floor there, alongside the CD stacks."

The sergeant glared at the constable who had just pointed out that the hard drives had been taken. "Come on, bright eyes, you had better leave the scene of crime to the more observant."

The specialist team from SIS arrived twenty minutes later to discover the intricate world of a code breaker of enormous talent with a research facility worthy of the man. Yakov Gorokhin was the name given to Mikhail Dostovalov, ex Russian KGB, shortly after he crossed the Berlin Wall and walked into the British Mission then at Building Leipziger Platz 12, leaving a wife and daughter behind who he would never see again. After his arrival in England, MI5 kept a protective watch on him, which over the years was scaled down and responsibility handed over to the Metropolitan Police who were required to inform the Intelligence Services should they be asked to attend anything involving the man or his property. Agent Adam Chilton, of 'J' section, responsible for communication with Russian defectors, returned to 85 Albert Embankment late that evening, handing over the three computer back-up units and two pages of code that had been carefully cut from a notebook and hidden between the pages of a volume of Evgeny Baratynsky's poetry. After his delivery to 'K' section, he went down two floors to his desk to write a full report on what he had found at the house in Hampstead.

**

Following his lunch Vaughan returned to the hotel and using the courtesy coach went into the centre of Funchal to hire a car. The SEAT Leon FR was impressive, the two litre turbo diesel engine taking the steep inclines easily in its stride. Vaughan found the house, set high above Câmaro de Lobos looking down over the town and its small harbour. Getting out of the car, Vaughan took in the view and the sun sparkling on the ocean beyond and wondered whether Amelia would ever want to leave Madeira. *"Where the hell did that thought come from, don't get involved out of sympathy, or is it sympathy. I have to think about this a lot more and that is assuming that she has any real feelings for me. She runs a business and has a son, she wouldn't want to give up the business or uproot her son and leave this beautiful island. Why am I thinking like this, I went out of my way to avoid seeing her when I came to collect the boat, what has changed? I don't have any responsibility for her being attacked or is it that subconsciously I know that things would have gone further between us had I not been wounded and returned to the UK. I am either in love with Amelia or I am not. Is it that I still have hopes of rekindling my relationship with Sarah, or is it SIS and the work I do that is creating this fog that is preventing me from seeing such things clearly."* Walking up the steep side driveway, Vaughan stepped onto the porch and rang the doorbell, he heard voices followed by the clatter of feet and the door opened to reveal a young boy and a girl, surprised at first to see him and now rather shy at the sight of a complete stranger.

"Mama," the boy called, and immediately a young woman appeared from the kitchen.

"Your husband, Bruno, suggested I call. Is Amelia de Lima here at the moment?"

Alicia smiled, "You are Senhor Vaughan, yes?"

"Yes, I am Ian Vaughan. Please call me Ian."

"I am Alicia, Bruno's wife, Amelia is through here, please quiet, it will be good surprise for her," Alicia said softly putting a finger over her lips.

Vaughan followed Alicia to the door of the dining room where he saw Amelia sat at the table facing the window, beside her sat Zeferino, fidgeting in his chair, as he read very slowly from an English course book.

Vaughan looked at the sling covering a plaster cast on her left arm from shoulder to wrist and the stitches along her jaw line. Some of her beautiful hair had been shaved off revealing another scar, but what was so alarming to Vaughan was the sallowness of her complexion and the dullness in her voice as she spoke to her son. She moved to turn the page of the book and Vaughan saw that her right arm was bandaged.

Alicia pushed Vaughan back out of sight then said, "Amelia nós temos uma grande surpresa para ti."

As Amelia turned towards the door, Alicia pulled Vaughan into view, "Tad da!"

Vaughan saw a flash of joy in Amelia's eyes but it was only a flash. "Why did you return then sail away and not come and at least say hello?"

"Because, Amelia, I had to leave in a hurry."

"Well, I thought it was very rude of you and I am very angry with you. I am even more angry now you come back," she replied loudly.

"I am sorry, Amelia, I will leave, it was a mistake my coming, really I am so sorry."

Vaughan got as far as the front door, having passed a very distressed Alicia on the way, when he heard Amelia shout out, "No, no, Ian, please don't go, I need you to er, help me."

Vaughan was about to turn the front door knob and froze. *"Do I carry on and walk away? If I stay, will I have to tell her what I really do? She has been through hell, will knowing what I do make it much worse for her than if I just walked away? It really comes down to what I actually feel for her, and at the moment, as I have been living a lie all the time I have spent with her, I do not know."* He turned the latch and heard Alicia gasp.

Releasing the latch Vaughan turned and walked back to the dining room where he found Amelia standing now with tears streaming down her face. "I will do all I can to help you, Amelia, but I am here because on my way home to England, my yacht was attacked and sunk whilst I was at anchor on the north-west coast of Spain."

"Oh my God, were you hurt? Oh how terrible for you, Ian, your beautiful boat sunk."

She took two steps towards him and raised her right hand and touched his face gently.

"I managed to dive over the side just before the grenades went off, and swam ashore."

She gasped then frowned. "Did they know you were on board?"

"I think so, yes."

269

"Do they know that you have survived?"

"Unlikely, I saw them celebrating shortly after the attack, they seemed confident that they had completed the job."

"Who were these people?"

"Amelia, this is frightening Zeferino," said Vaughan, seeing fear in the young boy's face, "Please, let him take a break from his studies and you and I go somewhere quiet, where we can talk."

"Where do you suggest?"

"Let's go for a drive up into the hills and find a good view to look at."

"I cannot go out looking like this."

"You did this morning when you went to work," said Alicia, who was now standing in the doorway, "Go, you look fine. I will stay and keep an eye on Zef."

"Come on, you look all right to me," said Vaughan, smiling at Amelia, who was now searching in the pocket of her skirt to find a handkerchief.

"At least let me repair my make-up."

"I'll give you five minutes," said Vaughan, "Then we leave whether you are ready or not."

Amelia went to protest but Alicia stopped her. "Go, hurry."

Vaughan, smiling at Zeferino, went and sat down alongside the boy and pulled the school book towards him. "You are learning English, Zef, I am sure you are better at it than I am at learning Portuguese."

The boy smiled shyly and shook his head.

"I don't understand, tell me in English."

"I am no good learning."

"To learn a language you must listen carefully to each sound," said Vaughan, slowly putting his hands behind his ears as if hard of hearing.

Zeferino looked at Vaughan very seriously.

"Okay, Zef, close your eyes and listen to me." Zeferino closed his eyes and Vaughan selected the first sentence on the page and read it out slowly and clearly. "Now you say it back to me."

"Richard… lives in a house with his… father, mother and his two… sisters," Zeferino said haltingly.

"Now look at the book just here and say it again."

As Zeferino repeated the sentence Vaughan moved his finger along the page in time.

"Now keep repeating that sentence moving your finger along the line."

Taking the book back, Zeferino repeated the sentence again.

"Very good, now whilst your mama and I go out for a drive, you take some time off from homework, and maybe watch some television?" Vaughan said again, supporting his words with hand signals.

The boy smiled and said quietly, "Sim, er, er yes."

Standing, Vaughan smiled down at the boy, "See you later, Zef." He ruffled the boy's hair.

The plaster cast and sling on her left arm and the bandaged right arm made getting in and out of cars difficult for her. Vaughan had also noticed that she had a limp as she walked. Carefully he helped her in and fitted the seat belt.

"Are you comfortable?"

"I just need to shuffle a bit. Ah! Ooo. It is okay, I am all right now."

"While I am driving you can tell me exactly what happened to you, Amelia. I know the memory will be painful."

"With no boat, where are you staying?"

"I am staying at the Pestana Grande, I only arrived this morning. I went along to the Real Canoa to have some lunch, that was when I heard from Bruno about the attack."

Feeling slightly mollified, Amelia described what she could remember of the attack. "Had it not been for the paramedic who was with the ambulance and the wonderful Dutch couple who came to help me I may have been killed by them."

"Did they say anything, like why they were attacking you?"

"No, they just hit me and kicked me and stamped on my arm, breaking it."

She was crying now, the trauma of the last few weeks had destroyed her resolve to be brave.

"It must have been terrible for you. Did they steal anything?"

"No, they appear to have been stopped before they could. It happened so quickly, one moment I was leaving my office building and the next I am unconscious on the pavement."

Vaughan reached into his pocket and, giving her a clean handkerchief, waited until she had dried her eyes.

Whilst Amelia had been telling her story Vaughan had driven to Ribeira Bravo then north as far as the turning that led high up onto the Brian da Serra, where he had found a quiet place to park a little off the road with a view of the serra stretching out before them.

"It is very beautiful up here, Amelia."

"You have not been here before?"

"No, the previous times I have visited here I hardly moved out of Funchal."

"While you are here I hope you will take the time to see more of our island," said Amelia, in the form of a rebuke.

Vaughan was very aware now of the hurt he had caused in leaving without a goodbye. The way she sat in the car just looking forward, not turning her head when she spoke, even the tone of her voice.

He gave a much adjusted account of the attack north of Muxia and his escape, but now Vaughan was presented with the problem of giving a reason for his return to Madeira.

"You have not told me why you have returned."

"When I eventually got back to England I thought that it was all over and started to find out if my yacht insurance covered that type of loss." *"No, Vaughan, you have to come clean now, you can't keep the lies going."* "Amelia, forget what I have just said, there is something you must know and once you do know maybe you will understand. You see, I am a British Secret Intelligence Agent." She gasped looking at him eyes wide. "My cover is that of a maritime author. I was only sent here originally to make contact with Walid al Djebar in connection with the North African Unification Conference. This time however, I have been sent to track down a British rogue agent who is on the island, we think to complete an illegal arms deal. I think he was also behind that attack on me."

"No, no I don't believe you."

"Sadly, Amelia, it is the truth and I only tell you this because I really do care for you and would not want you to think that I do not. When this man is caught, I will have to leave, and after that I will probably be sent somewhere else in the world on some other little mystery, though probably still calling myself a maritime author."

"Since my husband died men have told me many lies but none have been as good as this." Vaughan could see her anger rising and hurriedly pulled his badge from his pocket.

"Here, take a look at this, Amelia." She took the leather fold from him and opened it. "Now do you believe me?"

"Oh… oh, now I see, you are who you say you are. I am sorry I accused you of lying but you must admit I would never have expected to meet a Secret Agent in my life. I think I understand now how, er, what is the word, ah yes, er, pivotal it was that you save the life of Zeferino, for had you not, we would not have met and maybe the coup would have been achieved."

Vaughan did not respond.

"Of course you would not wish me to share this information."

"It would be much better if you kept it to yourself. If it got out, I am sure the Colonel would be wanting to ask you many more questions."

She nodded. "You said that you really cared for me, yet not enough to give up this life of yours."

"I have a duty to perform, one that I must complete."

"This is the real reason that your wife left you."

"No, not exactly, Amelia. We were just starting off to deliver a yacht across to France and I saw a yacht in trouble and went to help. It was manned by a gang of terrorists who took my wife and daughters hostage and coerced me into sailing the attack section of the gang across the Atlantic. Whilst she was hostage she endured some considerable suffering. When I returned to England she held me responsible for becoming involved and listening to her so called 'best friend' and her parents she insisted that we divorce."

"That was an extreme reaction I think, Ian."

"Her suffering involved a miscarriage, Amelia, she was expecting our son. She had wanted a son so badly, then to lose him that way, well."

Amelia sat silently for a while and appeared to Vaughan to be relaxing a bit, then she asked. "When you join this SIS?"

"Shortly after the first run in with this terrorist gang they came back and by an unfortunate coincidence I got involved again. After that SIS approached me by which time the divorce was very much underway."

She had turned now to look at him, her expression one of concern, "What if he sees you first, this person you are searching for, he could kill you?"

The change of subject caught Vaughan by surprise, "He thinks he already has, I'm sure of it, so he won't be expecting to see me." Vaughan reached into the glove compartment and pulled out Staunton's photograph. "Think back to the meetings that Esteves held with his friends, did this man ever attend one?"

Amelia took several seconds looking at the picture, "No I don't think so, I'm sure it was always just the same group." She handed the photograph back, "Is this the man you are looking for?"

"Yes, that's Leonard Staunton, ex senior agent."

"He looks to be a very hard man so I am not happy that you take such risk to track him down as you say. If you find him then what?"

"I have a Special Branch Policeman working with me, he will arrest him."

"Oh yes, and you will just point to him and say arrest that man. No, I think you take too much risk, if he sees you coming you will die. I am really not happy you involve in this thing."

"And I am not happy that you are attacked and I understand abused in the street and Zeferino bullied at school," replied Vaughan wanting to switch the conversation over to his concern for her, "You deserve proper protection, you did a great service for your country and it is their duty to now keep you safe. When we get back I am going to phone the Colonel and tell him to arrange protection for you," said Vaughan wanting to take her mind away from his search for Staunton knowing that mention of the Colonel would achieve that.

"No, Ian, no no no. I do not want the army around me or my family and friends anymore, ever," she protested loudly. "It will start that Colonel Castelo-Lopez asking those same cunning questions again trying to trick me."

Vaughan went to say more, but she shouted, "No, no, I won't hear of it!"

They sat in silence for a while, "Is there anything else you want to tell me?" she asked.

"No, Amelia, there is nothing more." He waited for her to say something but when she didn't he asked, "Have you sold the old apartment yet?"

"No, I have been too busy trying to recover my health and repair the damage to my business."

"Susie and Luz still work for your?"

"Oh yes, Ian, they have both been great support to me but there are things they cannot do."

They talked for a while longer mainly about Zeferino and her fear that he would forever be cursed by the association of being related to the Esteves name and the stain associated with it. Then Vaughan drove back to Cämara de Lobos and helped her back into the house.

***

On leaving Amelia's house he drove up to Capo Giräo and, finding a quiet spot away from the crowds of tourists, sat and thought hard about his future probably for the first time since his ex-wife Sarah and daughters were kidnapped at Bosham and held hostage. So much had happened since then, his wife's reaction to the miscarriage of a son, the second run-in with Murata's wing of the Japanese Red Army, the divorce and recruitment to SIS, and the mission that had first brought him to Madeira. On the island again alone, with orders to find and bring to justice a very dangerous man who would undoubtedly kill him given the slightest chance, he now stood tempted, so so tempted, to turn away from the task and seek a normal life with the very beautiful Amelia. What he had to decide was whether it was genuine love and affection or sympathy and a sense of responsibility.

As evening approached and the tourist crowds thinned Vaughan walked out to the glass floored platform and stared down towards the thin strip of cultivated land five hundred and eighty metres below, fascinated by the scale of it all. Surrounded by deep ocean the island of Madeira is not much larger than Britain's Isle of Wight, yet in the centre the mountains rise to a little over eighteen hundred metres, just a huge volcanic plug that now provided soil for the most amazing gardens, vineyards, banana plantations and abundant fruit and vegetables. A paradise, remote in the Atlantic Ocean.

Returning to the hotel he walked through the foyer and lounge then out into the gardens, still churning over in his mind what path to follow. It was well after dark when he found Conway in the lounge bar.

"I guessed you had got held up somewhere. I was about to turn in, with only two and a half hours sleep last night I feel pretty shattered."

"Sorry about that," replied Vaughan, "But the afternoon became… very interesting shall we say, more on a personal level than business."

"Oh. I won't ask."

"We had better make a plan for tomorrow, Brian. Breakfast at seven I think, then go into town, there is a house there I think we should visit."

"Sorry I can't do that," replied Conway. "I can't start an investigation here without it being cleared with the Portuguese authorities. The CPS has issued all the request letters from London and I am here as the Case Liaison Officer under Europol arrangements. My orders are to make contact with the local police and work with them on finding this man. It's all tied up with ACPO rules, so my afternoon's reading has been 'Practice Advice on European Cross Border Investigations', just to make bloody sure that I don't make a mistake that some clever lawyer can spring him on."

"Which of his crimes are you investigating, gun running or his possible connections with the coup here?"

"The coup?"

"Yes, his little abduction operation in Gibraltar used a powerboat and apartment owned by a private banker who the Portuguese SIS think may have connections with the coup leadership. Also, Staunton did his best to deflect my interests in anything other than my mission orders when I was last here particularly when I started asking questions about a Russian named Reshetnikov and Amelia de Lima's uncle Olavo Esteves."

"I see. No, I am definitely not interested in the coup, that is a Portuguese matter, and your little den of darkness of course. I'm just here regarding the illegal arms trading and abduction of a British national."

"I'm glad we cleared that up, Brian, as I said before, this was arranged so damn quickly they had to skip my briefing in order to get me out here in the hope of finding the man before he moves on," said Vaughan. "The house I mentioned earlier is the one previously occupied by Sarkis Kasakov."

"Ah, I see, he's the arms dealer who was shot."

"The very same, currently his daughter lives there in the care of Kazakov's ex-minder. We know that Staunton has made contact with the minder and I now believe that it was in order to do a deal on any stock of weapons that Kazako had stashed away."

"Stashed on the island, here?"

"A most unlikely place possibly, Brian, but one never knows. The deal would have to be done here though, which is why I suggested the visit."

"Right, thanks for the pointer, it means that I can go to the locals with some intelligence as a basis to the man hunt."

"You've got the details of what passport Staunton is travelling under and all that?"

"Oh yes, that is all in hand," replied Conway. "Like you, London could not give me the full briefing so now I know why you came along."

"Didn't they tell you anything?"

"Not much, it was a rush to get me out here like you. In fact when you sauntered off this afternoon I was beginning to think you were here on a jolly."

CHAPTER 12

The rendezvous with the ship was days away and the arms were safe enough where they now were, so, in the meantime Staunton decided to sweet talk Alice Morgan into making a trip to London to deliver the notebook and collect the diamonds promised as payment for its recovery. He picked up his mobile and called her.

It rang several times before he heard a nervous, "Yes?"

"It's me, sweetie, where are you?"

"Oh, it is you, Leonard, I'm frightened out of my wits."

"Where are you?"

"I'm hiding in the holiday home of family friends and thinking that I am going to be arrested at any moment."

"Whereabouts is that, sweetie?"

"In Wales, and I am not your sweetie."

"In Wales, whereabouts in Wales, Alice, not too near to your parents' home I hope."

"No, it's just outside Lampeter, I'm not that stupid to be near to home when my face is on every TV News broadcast," she replied in a contemptuous tone, "It's over, Leonard, I don't want any further part in this grand plan of yours."

"Oh, Alice, now come on, this is only a little hiccup in the plan, we'll come out of it all right you will see."

"I don't want anything more to do with it, Leonard Staunton. Nothing, do you hear me."

"But, Alice, you have Vermeulen's notebook and believe me he won't like it if you don't give it back to him," Staunton said with a slight hint of menace in his voice.

"He can go hang for his sodding notebook."

"Well, Alice, don't say I didn't warn you. He will find you."

There was a silence at the other end but the threat had been realised. "You mean you will tell him where to find me, you fucking bastard."

"Now did I say that, Alice."

"You didn't bloody have to, Leonard, it's now obvious to me how your mind works, I should have woken up to you months ago."

"All right, Alice, if you want out from the prize giving so be it, all you have to do is deliver the notebook, then you will be free to hide where you want until the heat's off. SIS will give up looking in a month or two; they'll have bigger problems to deal with, but Vermeulen won't."

Again there was silence while Alice Morgan considered her options. "Oh sod you, all right, Leonard. Where do I meet him?"

"I've thought of the most public place I could think of that he would wish to go to and that is 'The Rivoli Bar' in Piccadilly, you know, on the ground floor of the Ritz," Staunton replied, trying to hide the relief he felt. "I chose it for your safety, if you dress up in that Valentino dress of yours and the blue high heels, plus of course the Ascot hat, with sun glasses and make-up you would not be recognised by the normal clods looking for you."

"And how am I to get there?"

"Train to Paddington and a taxi, Alice. I'll tell him to pay you two thousand pounds in cash which you can keep to tide you over for a bit."

"That notebook is worth more than that!" She had almost refused the money then remembered that she only had a little over one hundred pounds left in her purse and the train fare would take most of that.

"Okay I will tell him you want five thousand pounds for it. How will that do?"

"When?"

"What is the weather like?"

"Pardon?"

"I said what is the weather like, is it going to be sunny tomorrow or the next day?"

"Tomorrow I think. Why?"

"Well, Alice, that will be the day, can't have you all summery on a rainy day can we."

"What time?"

"Say midday for cocktails, he might even treat you to lunch."

"Oh, ha ha."

"Relax, Alice, it will be okay, I will tell Jan to be nice to you."

"You really are a bastard, Leonard Staunton, leading me into this hole. You owe me, you really do, but I doubt whether you will ever think of paying for what I have done for you."

"Oh, Alice sweetie, I had a really wonderful plan worked out that I am sure you would have been delighted with."

"Don't bother really, Leonard, don't. You've caused me enough problems, I really don't want any more."

"Okay, sweetie, your choice. Give my best wishes to Jan when you see him."

"Oh, go fall down a hole, Leonard."

The phone went dead and Staunton looked at it frowning. Then dialling again, a smirk spread over his face. "Put the phone down on me will you, you little tart."

"Evet," said the gruff voice of one of Turkey's finest criminals to operate in London.

"Emre Yilmaz?"

"Evet."

"Leonardo, remember me?"

"Huh, yes, what have you got to sell today?"

"Nothing, Emre, a gift in exchange for a Chilean passport."

During the next five minutes Staunton explained where the pretty Alice Morgan would be a little after midday the following day and where his new passport was to be delivered. "I will text a photograph or two, I am sure you will find her… most enjoyable."

His next call had been to Jan Vermeulen to tell him of the delivery arrangements for the notebook and promising to text over a photograph of Alice in the Valentino dress. Bringing the picture up onto the screen he looked at it and sighed, the dress looked fantastic on the stick insect of Valentino's model but not a patch on what it looked like on the more shapely form of Alice Morgan, especially in those blue high heels and looking back at him pouting. "Oh and, Jan, don't bother with the diamonds just yet, I've decided to terminate her employment after tomorrow."

"Getting a bit boring in bed is she, Leonard?"

"Something like that, Jan. Oh by the way, did I hear you say you were thinking of going to Rio?"

"No you didn't, Leonard, but that could be a good place to be for a while. Keep in touch, eh."

***

At eight o'clock the morning after his arrival, Detective Sergeant Brian Conway entered Police Headquarters in Funchal and asked to speak to their International Liaison Officer. Half an hour later, following a grilling from the desk sergeant and a detective, he was introduced to Detective Sergeant José Livramento.

"How may we help you, Sergeant Conway?"

"We are wanting to find and interview a British subject named Leonard Staunton believed to be currently on this island."

"Oh really, what crime is this man believed to be guilty of?"

"Our investigation is in connection with illegal arms trading."

"You wish to find him and would like our assistance."

"I would very much like your assistance in finding out where he is staying," replied Conway, now having seen the number of hotels in Funchal, he was well aware of the needle in a haystack task in front of him. "He could well be using two other aliases, Leonardo Giovani and Laurens Van Vuuren."

"So I think this man is a little more than someone you just wish to talk to."

"We will see when I get to meet him," replied Conway.

"At the moment, Sergeant, we do not have the formal request required for such assistance but it is early in the day and maybe by lunchtime Lisbon will have agreed to help your police. Please if you return this afternoon the situation may have been clarified."

"We are very concerned that this man will move on very soon. Would it be possible for you to contact Lisbon to see if they have received the request?"

Livramento looked at his watch, "If you come with me I will put a call through. Tell me do you have a reference number concerning the request?"

"No, it was quite a rush to get me out here you see and I have not been informed of the request number, surely there aren't many sent from the UK."

"We will see, I will phone for you."

Livramento's desk was piled high with files.

"You look busy," said Conway.

Livramento gave a deep sigh, "It seems that nearly everybody on the island is suspected of collusion with the coup so our kind security services have asked for us to investigate many people here, all of who so far have been totally innocent of any involvement. A few may have had some sympathy but not in any active way."

Conway was about to suggest that Staunton may have been involved but decided to stick to his brief and not trespass into Vaughan world.

Livramento picked up his telephone and punched in the number in Lisbon, "Fabiana? Ah bon, Livramento aqui, Funchal…"

The loud conversation went on for some considerable time before there was a pause while Fabiana went away to make further enquiries. On his return the conversation continued until shaking his head, Livramento put the phone down.

"I am sorry but Lisbon say they not received such request and remind me very strongly to wait until all is agreed before I become involved."

"May I use your phone to call London?"

Livramento hesitated, wondering whether allowing his phone to be used would be deemed as involvement, "Yeh okay, here you dial, eh."

Opening his notebook Conway flicked through the pages until he found the number he wanted, hurriedly he dialled and waited, "Good morning, DS Conway here, could you put me through to the European Cross Border Investigations section please." There was another wait, then a lady with a strong Glasgow accent came on the line.

"Good morning er, WPC Breslin? I am DS Conway speaking to you from Funchal Madeira, sorry… say again… Oh, it's sunny and rather hot here, pardon… Oh is it raining still, look I am here on an investigation searching for a man named Leonard Staunton. When I left London yesterday I was assured that a formal request had been made to the

Portuguese authorities to sanction my investigation and obtain assistance when required… Right I'll hold.

"Coffee?"

"Ah, thank you, Sergeant, white please, no sugar."

The coffees had arrived before Breslin got back and confirmed that the request had been sent to the Lisbon head of the Europol section.

"Chief Inspector Tomas Miranda you say, that's great thank you, could you do me a big favour and phone through to them to chase it up. I am very concerned that our man may move on somewhere else very soon… Oh that's magic, thanks again."

Livramento shook his head, "Chief Inspector Miranda is the boss of Fabiana, I will speak to Lisbon again but first I must explain to my boss, please enjoy your coffee."

***

After meeting Conway at breakfast Vaughan had gone for a swim in the hotel's pool and was now sat on a sun lounger drinking a black coffee. Somewhere around midnight he had made a decision and having done that was now focused. Looking at his watch he picked up his mobile and dialled DS Conway's number.

"Conway."

"Brian, it's Ian, any movement your end regards paying a visit on that house?"

"I'm with the local Liaison Officer at the moment, Ian, we've only just got full confirmation out of Lisbon."

"Oh God, bloody bureaucracy. Can you get him to check out the car hire firms to see if Staunton has hired a car?"

"Hold on."

Vaughan waited.

"He's is starting to ring round now."

"Can he check with the hire car companies against the names, Laurens Van Vuuren, Leonardo Giovani or Leonard Staunton."

"He says it will take some time. I'll call you back, Ian, as soon as we have something."

"We also need to find the hotel he is staying at."

"The sergeant here has already got someone onto that, patience Ian; we will get back to you asap."

Vaughan sat back and tried to put himself in Staunton's position. *"By now he must know that SIS are onto him and have traced him to Madeira. He would also guess that the first thing anyone searching for him would do is find the hotel or address where he is staying. I wonder whether Conway has thought about showing Staunton's picture around the taxi drivers at the airport?*

"If it were me I would try and rent an apartment, it would take ages for the police to track that down. I wonder whether they will put out a TV appeal. Now that would have me thinking of changing my appearance."

Vaughan left the poolside and went up to his room to shower and change, then sitting out on his balcony overlooking the sea his thoughts returned to Staunton. *"If the arms are here on the island how the hell would he be able to ship them out? The two ports are Machico and Funchal but surely he would not be able to use those without all the right paperwork and checks."*

"I know, I will ask Amelia, she will know how it could be done."

At last Vaughan had something to do and hurried down to his hire car, he was about to start the engine when his mobile rang.

"Ah, Brian, hang on a moment my signal is not very good here."

Getting out of the car Vaughan ran up to the road entrance of the car park where the signal was good.

"Okay, Brian, what news?"

"The car was hired under the name of Leonardo Giovani, who it turns out has hired cars from this company before, always paying in cash."

"Interesting, very unusual I would have thought to pay for car hire in cash."

"That's precisely what I thought. The full registration is now known and has been circulated throughout the island's police force, so hopefully he will be tracked down quite soon."

"How about the bureaucracy?"

"Sorted thankfully, here's the car's registration details…"

Noting the information down Vaughan stood for a moment before acknowledging. "Brian, if it were me I would have almost immediately driven away from Funchal and switched the plates."

"Good point, I'll mention it."

Ending the call Vaughan went back to his car and drove off in the direction of Cämero de Lobos.

***

It had been a very early start for Alice Morgan. Wearing jeans, a dark blouse and hooded jacket that covered her hair curlers, she slipped on her trainers and sunglasses then hurried down the track to the road carrying an overnight case containing the Valentino dress, shoes and make up. The bus to Llanrda was surprisingly almost full. At Llanrda she boarded the train for Swansea but travelled only as far as Llandeilo, occupying a toilet for almost all of the journey and applying her make-up. Leaving the train she walked to where she had left her car parked in Alan Road.

She was, however, unaware that on the day Staunton flew from Gatwick a car number recognition device on the Severn Bridge crossing had informed the authorities that the car registered in the name of Alice Morgan had entered Wales and a further motorway bridge device indicated her direction as being towards Swansea. This had brought the police and SIS officials to the home of her parents, expressing their concerns as to her disappearance. By the evening of her arrival at the holiday home hideaway, SIS had constructed a supposed CCTV footage of her apparently leaving a nightclub with friends followed by another sequence of her going through a tube station ticket barrier followed by a hooded man. This had been fronted on television late news by recent images of her with an appeal for the public to report any sightings. Dewi Morgan, a young shop assistant in a bakery at Ammanford had recognised her as the very shy woman he had served late that afternoon, and phoning in his sighting was surprised to find himself being interviewed by police at two o'clock in the morning. By lunchtime the next day her car had been found and a police tracking device fitted to it.

Now, as Alice pulled away heading for the A483 the movement was detected and reported to SIS and by the time she had reached the start of the M4 two unmarked police cars were operating a relay tailing system.

At the Marina Street car park in Swansea two plain-clothed policemen were guided in on her as she made her way to the train station where she entered the ladies pulling her overnight case behind her. Calling on a WPC they waited for ten minutes then sent the WPC into the toilet area just as a very glamorous lady walked out, her face immaculately made up and wearing sunglasses, carrying only a dark blue patent handbag that matched her expensive shoes. There were a few minutes delay in response before one of the officers commented that he had not seen the glamorous woman enter the toilet. Minutes later they saw her walking onto the platform for the 0828 London train.

Alice, having entered the cubicle, had stripped down to her underwear and slipped on the Valentino dress and the high heels, then placing her trainers by the toilet pan with toes towards the door she lowered her jeans onto them, stuffing the legs with the hooded jacket and blouse, leaving the impression, to any cursory glance under the door, that someone was sitting on the toilet. Taking a length of cotton from her handbag she tied a loop one end and slipped it over the end of the lock lever before closing her handbag and, opening the door, stepped outside holding the loose end of the cotton thread. Closing the door she carefully pulled on the thread hearing the lock secure the door closed. It would be well into the afternoon before the cleaning staff became suspicious and raised concerns.

Based on the concerns of the officers monitoring the toilets, orders to follow the glamorous lady taking the 0828 to London were given and the WPC and one of the detectives boarded the train and travelled as far as Reading, where they were to be relieved by SIS agents. In the meantime, the detective remaining in Swansea had learned that the glamorous woman had purchased a ticket that included Underground travel in London, and informed his colleagues and SIS.

The most anxious time for Alice Morgan had been her journey from the house near Lampeter to Swansea Station where she had arrived believing that she had not been identified. Even the change in the ladies had worked smoothly and she felt a little smug leaving her overnight case secure behind a locked cubicle door. In keeping with the part she was playing she had bought a copy of Vogue magazine and spent most of the journey to Paddington Station reading it. At Paddington, however, her confidence disappeared as she then realised that her dress stood out to the extent that she was attracting a lot of attention, particularly from men.

Having left her everyday street clothes at Swansea Station Alice had no alternative but to carry on and she walked as fast as her high heels would allow her to the Circle Line Underground where she caught a train as far as Notting Hill Gate. A change to the Central Line got her to Bond Street where she changed trains again, taking a Jubilee Line train to Green Park. Walking out of the station onto Piccadilly she found herself almost opposite the Ritz with five minutes to spare.

As she stood on the pavement deciding where to cross the busy road, the two agents tailing her remained just inside the station entrance calling for backup in numbers. By the time Alice Morgan had reached the junction with Berkeley Street eight SIS agents supported by police were homing in on the area at high speed with sirens and blue lights clearing the way.

As Alice waited for the traffic lights to change, Jan Vermeulen and Pieter's taxi had just crossed the lights at the top of St James Street into Albemarle Street.

"Driver, pull over please and wait whilst my colleague checks that our host is already at the restaurant, I don't want to arrive before him."

"I'll find a place, sir."

After a few yards the driver swung the cab into a gap in the street parking and Pieter leapt out and hurried back to Piccadilly. Once there he walked along to Dover Street looking for any signs that the Ritz entrance was being watched. Crossing Dover Street he saw Alice Morgan, in the dazzling dress, a picture of which Staunton had sent over, making her way towards the entrance to the Ritz Hotel but he failed to pick up the agent following her. After a final look along the pavement and a more careful look across the road he returned to the taxi.

"Your host is there, Boss."

Vermeulen paid the driver, adding a tip, then followed Pieter round the corner and along Piccadilly to Dover Street. Waiting for the lights to turn red against the traffic they crossed the road and, entering the Ritz

Hotel, made their way to the Rivoli Bar. Alice Morgan sat at a corner table studying the cocktail list.

"Alice Morgan?" asked Vermeulen.

"Yes, are you Jan Vermeulen?"

"I am, it is nice to see you at last. Leonard has been hiding you away for far too long," said Vermeulen looking down admiringly at the very pretty Alice. "Tell me what does a beautiful young lady like you see in a sour face like Leonard, eh."

"Nothing anymore," replied Alice, feeling immediately embarrassed by her honesty.

"I would be very happy if you came and worked for me, Alice, if that is how you feel."

"I am sorry, Mr Vermeulen, but Leonard has got me into enough serious trouble which I think is linked with what you do, and I do not want to get any deeper into the mess than I already am."

"I do not know what business Leonard is in that has caused you trouble, Alice. It definitely is not something that I am connected with, all I run is an import export business."

"That involves diamonds?"

"Huh, the choice is yours, my dear," Vermeulen replied, "But we are 'ere so that you can 'and over a notebook of mine but first please join me in a drink, it 'as been a long time since I 'ave 'ad the pleasure of sipping cocktails with a lady as pretty as you."

Alice almost smiled. "I can't be long, Mr Vermeulen, as I have a long way to go this afternoon."

"Call me Jan, please. Now what would you like?"

"Oh, just a dry Martini please."

Pieter, who had been standing alongside Vermeulen, his eye shifting between the two men at the bar and the doorway, went across to the bar and ordered the drinks. On his return he sat himself next to Alice but showed no interest in either her or the conversation, concentrating instead upon those now entering the bar.

"Tell me, Alice, just how did you get involved with Leonard?" Vermeulen asked, sounding genuinely interested to know.

"He approached me one day when I was stationed at Portsmouth Command, Whale Island, saying that he wanted me to apply for a communications post. Wanting to know why he had selected me, he said he had read my file and thought that I would be ideal for a position he had in mind but that it would depend on whether I got through the course. I suppose I was flattered really," she explained.

"And then?" said Vermeulen.

"I did the course and passed and the next thing I know he turns up and takes me to this garden party at a big house on the Thames, and, well, things got going a bit between us until I got posted aboard one of the new frigates. We kept in touch while I served six months with the ship, then I was ordered to report to London and we saw each other regularly."

A rather wistful expression had come across her face at that point which Vermeulen guessed was memories of a time when she was happy in the relationship.

The drinks arrived along with some nibbles.

"Your very good health, my dear," said Vermeulen, raising his glass.

Alice reached for her glass and took a sip.

"Where is Leonard now?"

"In Spain I think, said he had some things to 'cover up' whatever that means."

"Bodies knowing Leonard, he made a real job of topping my stepdaughter's nosy 'usband," said Vermeulen, thoughtlessly introducing a little too much honesty to his comments now that the job offer to Alice had been rejected.

Alice looked shocked and almost spilt her drink. "He killed someone?"

"You didn't know 'im very well obviously."

Alice put her glass down, she was feeling sick. The odd dodgy deal was bad enough but murder, no, she couldn't really handle that.

"Are you all right, Alice? You're very pale."

"Could I have some water please?"

"Pieter."

The big minder got to his feet instantly and hurried to the bar. It was as he was returning to the table with his back to the door that the four men walked in swiftly, making their way straight to where Alice and Vermeulen sat. As Pieter put the glass on the table he suddenly became aware of bodies behind him and turning, was already reaching for his gun.

"Don't even think about it," said the man in the dark navy blue suit nearest to him pointing a pistol at him.

"What is the meaning of this!" shouted Vermeulen, knocking his chair over as he got to his feet.

Smiling slightly, another man stepped forward showing his badge. "Jan Vermeulen, I am arresting you for the illegal trading in arms. You do not have to say anything but it may harm your defence if you do not mention when questioned something which you later rely on in court. Anything you do say may be given in evidence."

Thinking that his police guard's attention may have wavered a fraction Pieter made a lunge at the blue suited officer only to find himself moments later face down on the floor with his left hand pinned painfully behind his back. Alice meanwhile just put her head in her hands and wept.

Several seconds passed during which you could have heard a pin drop as the other customers in the bar stood frozen with all eyes focused on the group in the corner. Then the manager from reception came bustling in.

"What's going on here," he demanded to know.

The senior officer, Detective Inspector James Paxton, who had hung back from the rest turned and raised his badge for the manager to inspect. "It is police business, sir, if you don't mind waiting I will explain in a minute or two."

"You 'ave got the wrong man," said Vermeulen, sounding very indignant. "'ere is my passport, you will find that I am Henri Vanderkloof, now let me and my colleague go immediately."

"He is Jan Vermeulen all right and like all men lies to get his way out of anything," screamed Alice Morgan.

"Don't believe her."

"It's the truth I tell you, this will prove I am right," she said, pushing the black notebook across the table. "He was willing to pay a lot of money to get that back."

Vermeulen made a grab across the table at her but was restrained and cuffed.

Waving to three uniformed policemen who had just entered the bar, D.I Paxton said, "Take them away." Then turning to Alice he said, "Alice Morgan I am arresting you for breach of the Official Secrets Act. You do not have to say anything but it may harm your defence if you do not mention when questioned something which you later rely on in court. Anything you do say may be given in evidence."

Alice stood up shakily and walked, head bowed, with Paxton towards a waiting WPC, without saying a word. It was over now and as she walked out of the hotel entrance she felt a strange sense of relief. She would turn Queen's evidence, she was determined on that.

On seeing her leave the Ritz handcuffed to a WPC, Emre Yilmaz signalled to his two men to return to the car and put a forged Chilean passport into his pocket for burning on the barbecue later.

***

At MI6 headquarters Alex Campbell took his seat between section heads Angela Merivale-Atkin and newly appointed Michael Porter. In front of them were two clerks, one to act as a messenger and the other monitoring dual recording devices.

"Are we all ready?" asked Campbell.

The clerks nodded just as a red light showed up on the messenger's desk.

"Shall I get that, Sir?"

"Yes please, Miss Khan."

She smiled, he had remembered her name, not many senior bosses do that after a break of two or three months. Crossing the room she opened the door and received a message slip and hurried back to place it in front of the Commodore.

Looking at the message Campbell smiled, "Thank you, Miss Khan. We can proceed now, would you invite Sir Andrew Averrille to join us please."

When Sir Andrew entered he looked surprised to see the formal set-up. "If this is how it is being played, Campbell, I insist upon having legal representation."

"Sir Andrew, this is merely an enquiry to lay out the facts regarding the activities of former agent Leonard Staunton and former communications clerk, Alice Morgan." The mention of Alice Morgan made Sir Andrew's face pale noticeably. "Please take a seat," said Campbell gesturing towards a desk and chair in the centre of the room.

Campbell, noticing the change in Sir Andrew's complexion followed by the lack of a further challenge to proceedings turned to Merivale-Atkin and nodded.

"Sir Andrew, we have gone back to the initial appointment of Leonard Staunton and noted that he was recommended for recruitment by Captain Jonathan Fitzpatrick who we now understand to be your son-in-law."

"I do not like the insinuation you have just made, Madam. Jonathan, at that time, had no connection with my family at all."

"You were not aware then that at that time his London address given for all mail was your daughter's flat in the Lesson Grove area of London."

"No, I was not." Sir Andrew looked genuinely shocked at the revelation. "Were the usual checks carried out at the time?"

"Yes, they were, Sir Andrew, but please understand we believe that Staunton applied pressure in some way upon your future son-in-law in order to gain the recommendation."

"I assume that you have asked Jonathan about this?"

"He is being interviewed at the moment, Sir Andrew."

"I suppose you are enjoying this, Campbell."

"Not in the least, Sir Andrew, in fact I am extremely disappointed that this meeting is actually taking place, but a rotten apple had been allowed to be selected for work with this organisation and that person has apparently been supported in a programme of rapid promotion."

"What are you accusing Staunton and myself of?"

"Staunton's list includes murder of a fellow agent, illegal arms trading, blackmail and collusion with a political coup aimed to destabilise the government of a friendly nation and co-member of the European Union."

"Good God, that is impossible to believe."

"Two hours ago police arrested former communications clerk Alice Morgan. Under questioning she informed officers that a Jan Vermeulen told her that Leonard Staunton, I quote, 'Topped his stepdaughter's nosy husband.' Her husband was David Patterson, an agent of ours sent into Angola along with Staunton to trace illegal arms dealers, one of whom was Jan Vermeulen," said Campbell.

"Patterson was one of your DELCO group if I remember correctly."

"As you well know, Sir Andrew, DELCO is just a safe reporting location for agents who, because of their cover, would be unwise to report here except under special circumstances."

"Is this woman to be believed?"

"I would think so, Sir Andrew, after all, she is your daughter," said Campbell, as Porter got up and placed two DNA profiles in front of Sir Andrew. "Staunton, we believe, discovered your relationship to Alice Morgan and let you know of his discovery at the garden party you held shortly after your promotion to Head of Service."

There was a long silence whilst Sir Andrew stared at the profiles tracing each telltale line with a slender forefinger.

"Following a meeting I had with Mrs Patterson some months ago she willingly became an informant against her stepfather providing information that triggered an international warrant for his arrest. It appears, however, that he was tipped off and escaped Angola taking with him his wife and Patterson's widow, Anna-Maria. During their journey Mrs Patterson escaped and despite efforts to kill her made contact with our agent, Ian Vaughan, near to the Salvage Islands. She was successfully taken to Gibraltar where she was met by a member of my team for an RAF transfer to the UK," said Campbell. "Whilst they were being taken by the Navy to the airport both women were abducted and the Marine driver killed by a gang acting on behalf of someone who must have been a member of this organisation, as only someone connected with SIS would have had the time to react and arrange such an attack." Campbell looked up from his notes, but saw no reaction from Sir Andrew. "They were taken by sea to the port of Lagos, Portugal, then to a house in the town of Burgau, where they were imprisoned by an ex SAS soldier named Barry Jacobs. When a search was made for the file on Jacobs it was learnt that it had been pulled suggesting that SIS had recruited him.

Further investigation eventually revealed however that the file had been pulled by none other than Leonard Staunton acting way above his authority. We then learnt that during an attempt by Jacobs to rape Mrs Patterson she managed to kill him in an act of self defence. Shortly after this harrowing event, agent Ian Vaughan, acting on his own initiative, located both ladies and volunteered to bring them to safety. During the questioning by the Portuguese authorities of those assisting in their imprisonment, it was revealed that the mastermind behind the abduction and imprisonment was a person, known as Leonardo in Portugal, associated with the Galician Mafia. Leonard Staunton's arrival in Gibraltar and his use of SIS personnel strongly suggested that he was this mysterious Leonardo and knew of the planned abduction. A note passed to me just prior to this meeting confirms that your daughter had intercepted Vaughan's coded approach message and passed that information to Staunton who I understand was, at the time, under your orders in Madeira."

"What is all this about collusion involving a political coup?"

"My opposite number in the Portuguese Servico de Informações de Segurança, Senhor De Lacerda, has information that suggests that Leonardo and Leonard Staunton are one and the same due to a link with a Portuguese private bank, which they suspect of bankrolling the coup."

Campbell sat back in his chair watching Sir Andrew as the man took in the information he had just presented.

Realising that Campbell had finished what he had to say Sir Andrew looked up from his doodling and just stared at the three people in front of him in turn. "What happens to me now?" he said finally.

"You accept our findings then, Sir Andrew?" said Porter.

The man nodded and looked blankly at the floor. "For the record," said Merivale-Atkin, "Sir Andrew Averrille has nodded his head in agreement."

"What your future holds, Sir Andrew, is not for us to decide," said Campbell. "You are, however, to remain under suspension awaiting the outcome of further enquiries. As before you must not leave the country without permission."

"A car will take you to your home, Sir Andrew," said Merivale-Atkin, with a hint of sadness in her voice.

Sir Andrew Averrille rose and walking a little unsteadily, left the room.

"He didn't put up much of a fight," said Porter.

"Ruined all because he hid a love child," said Merivale-Atkin.

"He was relatively newly married at the time of the affair with Alice Morgan's mother and the revelation would undoubtedly have led to a divorce and the loss of a considerable fortune when his then young wife inherited. How do you think he got the Culverdon Estate and its two hundred acres, plus a villa on the French Riviera," explained Campbell.

"That will all go now surely," said Porter, "When this all comes out."

"If this all comes out, Porter, if," replied Campbell. "My betting is that he will either be shuffled onto a security committee for a year or two before requesting early retirement or some minor health issue will be used as an excuse to pension him off now."

"You know, Sir, I was really hoping you weren't going to say that," said Porter, getting up, very tight-lipped, and looking around for something to punch. "Another Westminster élite cover-up that will cost the taxpayer hundreds of thousands up until he and his wife are dead. So much for open bloody government and fairness for all. You can bet the armourer who mislaid a few boxes of HK417's in order to pay the rent will get sent down for years and branded for life."

Nobody said a word, they were all looking at Campbell. "I think we could all do with a drink," he said. "Will you join us, Miss Khan. I know Miss Standish enjoys the odd glass of red."

"Thank you, Sir, but nothing alcoholic."

"Of course. Come on people, coats on, there is a little pub across the river where Chief Inspector Brian Jackson and I would go at a time like this."

***

Staunton decided to change the identity of the car he was driving immediately after he had checked out of his hotel. No longer wishing to hang around in Funchal he drove to Camacha where he found a car of the same model and colour in a car park near the centre of the town. There was no one about and the switch of plates was straightforward thanks to the screw holes on both sets matching. He drove on to Santana where he found a car parked off the road with flat tyres, from having been left for a long period, and swopped the plates again.

By the time he had reached Ponta Delgado he was feeling more relaxed and stopped to make a call to Alice Morgan, but her phone was switched off. Checking his watch he smiled and made a call to Emre Yilmaz assuming that all had gone to plan and that Emre was by now enjoying the delights of Alice.

The call connected, "Evet."

"Emre, it is Leonardo, are you enjoying the gift?"

"No, your gift left the Ritz in handcuffs along with two men. Next time you wish to send me a gift just make it cash."

"Are you sure it was the right woman?" queried Staunton, suddenly feeling uneasy again.

"I am certain."

"What about the passport?"

"Cash only now, Leonardo. I do not like being that close to your police force when they are arresting people."

"I need it quickly, I will get the money to you as soon as I can."

"That is not how it works, Leonardo. I get the money first then I will arrange the passport."

"Emre, you know I am good for it, please just let me have the passport, you know I will pay."

"I do not know that anymore, Leonardo, you have fast become a risk."

"Emre … Emre!?" The phone was dead. "Oh go fuck yourself, you Turkish turd," Staunton yelled at his phone, before throwing it into the car's passenger footwell.

A strange sense of claustrophobia was coming over him as the realisation of his world collapsing in on him became more acutely apparent. He found himself breathing heavily as though he had run a mile and had to make a conscious effort to calm himself. Several minutes passed before he was able to analyse his situation and start to plan a way out.

Unless they had put someone very stupid on the job he knew that SIS would know that he was in Madeira. Alice would have told them that she had dropped him off at Gatwick, it would not be long before they discovered that he took the Funchal flight instead of the Madrid one. Would they link him to Kazakov and therefore Boris though? That was unlikely, but he would have to be very careful how he made contact again with the man. He assumed that they would only know about his Laurens Van Vuuren passport via the airport, so his use of the Giovanni name was he thought for him, secure.

His head felt as if it was bursting with questions and he was fearful that nothing now appeared certain. He must make contact with Boris first of all and see if he could stay at the house for at least that night. Starting the car he drove back to Funchal, parking along the Rua do Lazareto near the Jewish cemetery, then walked along to the top of the Calcada do Socorro and was just about to cross the road to the green when he saw that the gates to the rear courtyard of Kazakov's house were open and a police van parked just inside. Altering course he went into the café on the corner and ordered a coffee, taking a seat where he could watch the house. Realising that he had not eaten at all that day he added two pieces of cake to the order and sat wondering what to do next.

A police car came up the hill at high speed and two men got out and went into the courtyard. The girl behind the bar had stopped what she was doing and was looking in the same direction as Staunton, "What is going on?" he asked in Portuguese.

"They took the bully they call Boris away just now, everyone know his boss was crook but I think he not cause trouble for police so they leave him alone, eh."

"Was he dealing drugs?" asked Staunton.

"I no think so, the rumour is he handled guns," the girl replied in English, recognising immediately Staunton's natural language.

"Huh, is my Portuguese that bad?"

"No, Senhor, but the accent is er, not so good," she said, placing the coffee and cake slices in front of him.

A little while later a taxi pulled up and a middle-aged woman and young girl got out. On seeing the police van the woman cried out and hurried across the road followed more carefully by the young girl.

"Oh my, that poor Nadezhda, first her father is killed and now Boris he is arrested," said the bar girl.

"How old is she?"

"She maybe fourteen or fifteen years old, she cannot speak poor thing, but she is very sweet you know, nice. I feel so sad for her."

At that point two workmen came into the bar who were obviously regulars and the girl moved along to serve them, both gave Staunton a suspicious look before asking the bar girl about what was happening at the Kazakov house.

Finishing the cake and coffee, Staunton paid the bill and left, walking back to his car deep in thought. At least the weather was hot so sleeping rough would not be too much of a hardship, but where would be safe? Then an idea occurred to him, Sonia, or at least Reshetnikov's place across the island. He felt sure that Reshetnikov was still being held by the police and probably taken away to Lisbon for questioning, so maybe they took Sonia as well.

An hour and a half later Staunton, having stopped on the way for food supplies, was sat dining at the Orca Restaurant in Porto do Moniz staring out at the Atlantic swell crashing on the rocks, but Staunton's stare did not register the beauty and power of nature as, behind the stare, his mind was planning the approach to Reshetnikov's house. Satisfied with the approach plan he phoned the MV Verlorenvlei.

"Kallenberg."

"Leonard here, how far away are you?"

"We should be off the north-west tip of Madeira shortly after midnight in three days' time."

"Be on station one half nautical mile off Paúl do Mar at 0300 hours."

"Paúl do Mar at 0300 it is. See you then, Leonard."

CHAPTER 13

Amelia had just let Vaughan in at the front door and gone to the kitchen to make coffee when the doorbell rang.

"Are you expecting visitors, Amelia?"

She shook her head, "No, can you please go and see who it is?"

Vaughan went to the door and, looking through the moulded glass panels to the side of the door, made out an army uniform. *"Oh Jesus wept, what do they want?"*

He opened the door without releasing the security chain and stole a quick look, "Colonel, hold on while I release this chain." Opening the door fully he called. "Colonel Castelo-Lopez has come to pay you a visit, Amelia. Come in, Colonel, come on through to the lounge."

The Colonel gave a friendly smile, "Ah, Senhor Vaughan, you are here, that saves me a visit to your hotel."

Amelia appeared in the doorway her face full of rage. Vaughan quickly held up his hand and shook his head.

"What can I do for you, Colonel?"

"My colleague, the Chief of Police informed me of your return to Madeira, which he says was after you were attacked in Spain."

"That is correct, Colonel, it was believed by police on the mainland that the attack was related to my small part in exposing the coup plot. I have been working with them and British police investigators; they showed me first an identikit picture of a man, then later a photograph. They also believed that he has returned here and that is why I came back to warn Amelia."

"Quite rightly so, Senhor Vaughan." The Colonel turned to Amelia, "I have learnt today that you also have been attacked, Senhora, I have requested the Chief of Police to organise protection for you? If you are not satisfied with that I will be more than happy to offer specialist military personnel for your protection."

"Why are you now so concerned about my safety after so many accusations of my involvement in my wicked uncle's plan?"

"Senhora De Lima, please believe me when I say that we are now convinced of your innocence with regard to your uncle's plans. My only wish now is to ensure the safety of you and your son, and of course that of Senhor Vaughan here."

The Colonel's firmness of tone surprised Vaughan and appeared at first to put Amelia onto the back foot.

"I am pleased to hear that at last, Colonel." She walked to the centre of the room and turned to face Castelo-Lopez, "The delay in your decision has made life for my son, Zeferino, and myself very difficult. We are ignored in the street, people turn their backs on us, my son is abused at school and the police do not appear to have done much to find the men who attacked me and caused these injuries. Thanks to the help of Senhor Vaughan we revealed enemies of Portugal and all you did was to accuse me as if I was a leader in the coup." She went to walk away then turned back, "Why now, Colonel, what has changed your mind. Tell me, I would just love to know!"

Vaughan stood back and admired the display, she was balanced, almost calm, but one could see the anger that she held barely below the surface. *"Colonel, you had this coming, you and your grey suited secret service people. Amelia de Lima deserved the gratitude of the nation not your protracted questioning."*

"That, Senhora, is something that I cannot disclose to you, as it is a matter of national security. I hear and understand the suffering that has been caused and I assure you that steps are already being taken to rectify matters."

"What can you do now, Colonel, the hurt has been done, I will tell you now that there were many times during those endless sessions of questioning when I wished I had not divulged my suspicions concerning my uncle."

There were a few moments of silence then she said, "I would like you to leave now, Colonel, please."

"Of course, Senhora, I have no wish to cause you further distress but please remember my offer for greater protection if you have the slightest

300

concern. Here is my card with my direct number on it. Anytime, day or night, feel free to call me and I promise that I will do all I can for you."

Amelia hesitated before accepting the card then placed it on the coffee table.

As she had glanced at the card Vaughan had feared that she was about to tear it in two and was relieved when she put it down.

"Senhor Vaughan would you please come with me to my car, I would like a few words with you."

"Yes, sure."

Vaughan returned to the house half an hour later and immediately Amelia asked, "What did the Colonel want?"

"He wanted to know the full details of the attack on me and the loss of my yacht."

"Oh, is that all." Then realising how that sounded quickly added, "I did not mean that the attack on you was not important, just that it was the only subject."

It wasn't all that he and the Colonel had discussed but Vaughan was not going to tell her about what they had learnt from Reshetnikov and his mistress or the warning to not involve himself any further.

Amelia had turned away to stare out of the window and Vaughan was about to join her when she spun round her eyes blazing with anger, "Why did you invite him into this house when you know how much I hate the man!"

"I was hoping he was going to tell us that they had caught the men who attacked you and that you could get on with your lives, Amelia, instead of sitting here like bait in a trap."

She glared at him angrily her right fist clenched tightly.

"It is over, Amelia, he was doing his job, let it go, it will harm you more than it will harm him if you keep that hatred in you alive."

She stormed out of the room and Vaughan heard her climbing the stairs followed by the slam of her bedroom door. *"Not the best result, but at least she now knows for certain that she is no longer suspected. Now all that needs to be known is what the Colonel meant about rectifying matters."*

When lunchtime came and she had not appeared Vaughan took coffee and some sandwiches up to her room. "Amelia, I've brought you up some lunch." There was no reply but he could hear her moving around in the room. "I'll leave the tray outside the door."

When he returned he found the coffee and sandwiches untouched outside her bedroom. He knocked on the door and when there was no response turned the door handle.

"Go away," he heard her say.

"Stop acting like a child, Amelia," Vaughan replied, and retreated downstairs.

It was not until Alicia and Zeferino arrived that Amelia appeared downstairs again. She greeted the boy as normal then waved Alicia into the kitchen, closing the door behind them. Zeferino looked at Vaughan confused.

"It is all right, Zef, your Mama and I had small 'argumento'."

The boy frowned and shook his head, "Please, er, you and my Mama make, er, friends, please."

"Okay, Zef, I will try. What is your schoolwork for today?"

Zeferino pulled a face and took his maths book from his school bag. Chuckling at the boy's facial expression Vaughan picked up the book and was just about to ask which page to look at when his phone chirped; seeing it was Conway calling he got up and left the house by the front door.

"Brian, how's it going?"

"It has been an interesting day, Ian. Kazakov's minder has been arrested and they are holding him awaiting some guy from Lisbon who speaks Russian to come out and question him."

"He didn't give up any information voluntarily then?"

"No, not a word. I reckon your hunch is correct and he will hold out until Staunton has moved the stuff on."

"Anything on Staunton?"

"Yes, around lunchtime they found the hotel he was staying at. The reception told the local boys that he checked out this morning and was on his way to Italy."

"Oh yes, and I'm walking to the moon."

Conway chuckled, "Yes that was my reaction. They searched the room but there was nothing there of interest. He may also be onto the fact that we are here as he switched car number plates with a vehicle parked in Camacha. The lady whose car it was had a nasty shock when she got back and found the police there."

"Oh right, he has probably done that at least once more for good measure."

"Oh great."

"No sightings then."

"None."

Returning to the house, Vaughan met Alicia in the hall. "Hi, how are you today?"

"I was fine until I return here to find Amelia in such bad mood."

"I am sorry, Alicia, it is my fault for inviting Colonel Castelo-Lopez into the house. She is quite right, it was not my place to make such an invitation."

"I do not think it was that."

"Really?"

"I think she is trying hard to convince herself that she has no feelings for you, when all the time she has."

"Ah."

"Are you trying to tell me that you have no feelings for her?" Alicia took a step forward looking straight into Vaughan's eyes. "If that is so why are you here?"

"Of course I am fond of Amelia, but my life is roaming the seas, Alicia, not sat behind some desk or waiting at table in a restaurant here in Madeira. As I explained to Amelia it was the main reason for my wife, Sarah, divorcing me."

Alicia took a step back, frowning, then turned and walked away back into the kitchen, leaving Vaughan unsure where to go. *"I should never have come back here as all I have succeeded in doing is precisely the opposite of what I intended."* He dithered for a moment longer then went out and sat in his car hoping to return to the house later and persuade Amelia to help with the shipping advice.

An hour later, Alicia left the house and walked down the side driveway. Getting into her car she looked across at Vaughan who was still in his car, "I have left you some food in the oven, it's safe to go into the kitchen now; Amelia and Zef are watching television in the lounge."

Laughing, Vaughan waved her goodbye and went into the house via the back door to sit in solitude eating the pasta and smoked salmon dish that Alicia had prepared. By the time he had finished his meal and washed up the plate it was dark, so he went and checked that the upstairs shutters were locked, but left the windows open to allow some air movement. Downstairs again he returned to the kitchen and was texting a report to Campbell when Zeferino came in.

"Boa noite, Senhor."

"Boa noite, Zef, sleep well, happy dreams."

A quiet command from the hall had the boy hurrying away, leaving Vaughan thinking yet again about the harm he had done re-igniting the friendship with Amelia. Finishing the report he sent it and then considered the most likely method for an arms shipment. To bolster his cover he had previously sailed round the island looking at the smaller fishing harbours and assessing them in terms of suitability for yachts. The exercise had been interesting to a point, but revealing insofar as apart from Funchal and Machico, no vessel with ocean capability could safely enter the other harbours except maybe Quinta de Lorde which would be all right for yachts' entry only. His notes and marked up chart were in London and the more recent work at the bottom of a cove in Spain, but he had on hand an expert in shipping.

The lounge was in darkness so Vaughan climbed the stairs and gently knocked on Amelia's bedroom door, "Amelia, can I come in, I need your expert shipping advice."

"Can it wait for the morning?"

"I'm afraid it can't, it shouldn't take long."

"Oh, all right, please wait a few moments."

He heard her plaster scrape against the bedroom door and guessed that she was putting on a dressing gown. "Okay you can come in now."

He found her sat on the side of her bed, a dressing gown held tightly around her was obviously not comfortable.

"Here, stand up a moment and let me sort the dressing gown out a bit, you look as if you are in a badly fitting strait-jacket." She got up and allowed Vaughan to make the adjustments and tie the belt. "There, is that better?"

"Thank you, yes."

"The police and security services in London believe that the man I'm searching for will be shipping the arms out from here very soon. How would he do it, bearing in mind that these are illegal weapons intended for a rebel group somewhere."

"Do they know the size of the cargo?"

Vaughan took a guess, "Could be as much as one tonne if ammunition was included."

"Is that a single case or many cases?"

"Oh, it would be several boxes."

"So, say two men could lift each box." She pointed towards the dressing table stool. "Please sit on the stool, I cannot keep looking up at you all the time."

Vaughan pulled the stool near to her and sat down. "Yes, you are right, two men could do the loading."

"Most of the shipping here is from mainland Portugal and that is handled in Machico with only small amount to go from Funchal to say, Porto Santo." Amelia reached painfully across to the bedside table for her tablet and switched it on. "I have the ship arrivals list here and there does not appear to be any cargo vessel due to call for several days and only three cruise ships, so if it is to happen very soon it would not be through Machico or Funchal, and if unscheduled vessel arrive it would attract a lot of attention."

"When we did our circumnavigation of the island I didn't see any other harbour big enough to take anything larger than an inshore fishing boat."

"There isn't such a place, Ian, but if the cargo is so small as one tonne a small boat can take it out to a larger boat waiting offshore."

Vaughan looked at her, impressed by her response.

"Yes, Amelia, a very good point. That then gives us Camara de Lobos, Quinta de Lorde, Porto do Moniz and Paúl do Mar."

"You are forgetting Calheta and Seixal, Ian, surely you remember Seixal."

"Calheta maybe, but Seixal is too exposed to the Atlantic swell for that type of operation. You can't guarantee a flat calm there and that is what you would need. The same could be said for Porto do Moniz."

Both sat quietly for a time considering each location. Vaughan broke the silence, "Camara de Lobos, Calheta and Porto do Moniz are busy places with many people overlooking the quaysides so would they risk being seen. If I were doing it I would choose Paúl do Mar. The type of cargo vessel that I suspect would be involved in this type of thing would draw about nine or ten metres at the most and would therefore be able to come in quite close to the island without fear of going aground, and there are no off lying rocks, islets or reefs to worry about."

"I would say Camara de Lobos, Calheta and Paúl do Mar. Surely this would be done in the early hours of the morning when few people would be about."

"Of course, you're right, it would be then, not when there is a high risk of being seen loading heavy boxes into boats but Camara de Lobos is a busy fishing port and the harbour is overlooked from all sides."

"You think, eh. It would be a better choice than Calheta so I will keep watch for you from the window there. I can see nearly all that goes on at the quayside."

"If you want to, Amelia, but I can't ask you to get involved in this. Look, call me on this number, but only if you see a cargo ship standing offshore," said Vaughan writing his mobile number down for her. "I can't risk missing this man and letting him get away."

She looked at him and nodded, "Is there anything else, concerning shipping?"

"No, thank you, Amelia, that idea of yours was marvellous." He stood and put the stool back in its place. "I'll leave you in peace now, thanks again, and please only call me if you are sure."

"Please, don't go, Ian, not just yet." She shifted herself on the bed to get more comfortable. "Zeferino told me when I was seeing him into bed that I must again make a friend of you. He said that in English, so I take it that he wanted me to understand it was important to him."

Vaughan smiled and was about to say something when she held up her hand. "Please let me finish, Ian, as this is for me difficult to say, but Alicia, she says, I must tell you, or I will regret for the rest of my life, my silence." Vaughan sat on the stool and in the moments that passed made a decision. "Ian, when we first met I was not dazzled by you as I was with my husband Paulo, but that was because I was too concerned about Zeferino to realise anything else, but after that you did dazzle me, and when you were rushed back to England I felt as if my heart would break. Then I hear that you come and go, without even a phone call, so I start again my lonely life. Now you are back and we sit face to face, and I have to tell you that if you must leave, I would like to leave with you, wherever you go, and if you stay, I pray that it would be with me."

Her clear declaration stunned him.

"After all I have told you about what I do for a living and you still want to be with me?" Vaughan felt a strange sense of joy to be quashed by the reality of his immediate situation. "You do understand that I have to finish the task I have been sent to do, don't you."

Amelia nodded, her eyes filling with tears.

"When I come back we can make some plans."

"If you come back. This man you are chasing is, I think, a very dangerous one."

"When I find him I will call the Colonel, I think he will be more than willing to help."

"You think he will help," Amelia replied shaking her head, "I think he is too much interested in bullying innocent people to want to risk getting hurt or damaging his reputation chasing a real criminal."

***

As darkness fell, Staunton had left the restaurant and driven south to the house where Reshetnikov had been hiding out, near Achades da Cruz, and parked the car along the same track he had previously used. Again, he used cuttings from the surrounding bushes to camouflage the car, then donning the black all-in-one night camouflage suit and night goggles he carefully made his way through the trees to the clearing surrounding the house. The property in complete darkness had an atmosphere of abandonment about it that encouraged him to test the defences, so he broke cover fully expecting to be illuminated at any moment by the high wall security lights, but all remained in darkness. He circled the property then cautiously approached the front gates where he noted the padlocks and police notices before climbing over the gates and making his way towards the house, still without attracting any electronic security response. He circled round the house to the back door that accessed the utility room where he used skeleton keys on the lock and was inside in under a minute. He found the burglar alarm keypad near to the front door switched off; apparently the police had not bothered to activate it again after they had made their arrests and searched the property. A second box in the cupboard marked with a camera logo was also switched off explaining the lack of response from the equipment along the walls. Now he checked all of the rooms, finding beds unmade and stale bread in the kitchen, confirming that the house had been unoccupied for some time. In the garage he found an extending ladder, and separating the two sections, he used them to climb over the garden wall and return to the car where he sorted through his suitcase and removed just the bare essentials he would need plus the hair dye.

***

On leaving Amelia's house Vaughan drove back to the hotel, but instead of going in to join Conway he walked up to the Real Canoa for a late snack. The place was packed but after a short wait Bruno found him a balcony table from which he had a grandstand view of the pretty Latvian musician Agnese Alde playing a kokle, a delightful instrument like a horizontal harp on a sound box. The ham omelette was excellent as were the three large glasses of Quinta das Bandeiras red. He had arrived quite late and as he ate the restaurant slowly started to empty and the conversation level decreased to the point where the calming music could be clearly heard.

Vaughan was still in a state of shock at Amelia's revelation of her feelings towards him and now, sat alone, his mind was taken up trying to analyse his own feelings for her. She was without doubt very beautiful, highly intelligent with excellent English and with a sense of humour, but she had a Latin temper that erupted like a volcano in a blink of an eye, to calm again almost as quickly. Her dress sense, minimal make-up and the tidiness of her home demonstrated that she had great taste, all of those things were to Vaughan attractive, but thus far in their friendship he had hardly put his arms around her or even shared a kiss. Always it had been either the lingering love for his ex-wife Sarah or his duty to the service that had restrained him from taking the friendship onto a romance. Despite the relationship to her traitorous uncle her parents had been decent hard working people, but a life together with Amelia in Madeira would always be haunted by the ghost of Olavo Esteves hanging over them whichever side of the coup her attackers were on. If he persuaded her to move to England he had also to consider her son, Zeferino, how would he cope finishing his schooling in England when, if Amelia was to be believed, he struggled at school here being taught in his native tongue.

The thoughts surrounding a relationship with Amelia were still turning over in his mind as he left the restaurant and made his way to the hotel. It was not until he got to his room that he decided what he must do the following day.

***

Staunton had slept well and risen early, washed and was now looking in the mirror scrutinising the grey haired man looking back at him. His face still relatively unmarked by age gave him more the silver fox look than the one he had hoped for. Maybe dirt and scruffy clothing might give a better picture; he needed one more day's stubble on his chin to really achieve the image he sought. Leaving the bathroom he went into the main bedroom, noting the twin beds, and looked through Reshetnikov's wardrobe. Curiosity had him also looking through Sonia's wardrobe, nodding in appreciation at her choice of attire – Channel, Dior and two rather surprising Paco Rabanne dresses that had Staunton picturing Alice wearing. Returning to Reshetnikov's wardrobe he pulled a couple of suits out and looked at them, noting that, apart from the obvious Saville Row quality, their size put the use of any jacket or trousers out of the question. He moved to the bedrooms at the other end of the house and found where the minder Ivor slept. This was more like it, good quality yes, but not over the top for a tramp to have picked up. Moreover, the jackets were much nearer his own size and the style more uniform than executive. Trying on the trousers he found that he would have to roll up the legs a turn or two and maybe use string to hold in the waist but those adjustments were well in keeping. At the bottom of the wardrobe he found a boot, a half size too large, but with, say, two pairs of socks would be okay, the exposed plaster cast on his right foot was already looking grubby enough for a tramp.

Satisfied with his finds he returned to the kitchen and made some coffee and toast.

Finishing his breakfast he searched the house for keys, eventually finding a set hung on a hook behind a cupboard door in the utility room. The next question was whether it should be tramp or silver fox appearance, a decision which required careful consideration. Finally deciding on the tramp he changed, and letting himself out, walked towards the perimeter wall, keeping the house between him and the front gates. The ladders positioned out of sight of the road and driveway made his climb over the wall easy but as he put his good foot on the loose stones outside it slipped and his protecting boot hooked in the ladder causing it to fall sideways to crash to the ground, painfully trapping the booted foot. In agony, Staunton carefully extracted his foot and sat for several minutes waiting for the pain to subside. The fall had, however, served to dirty the suit and his face as he rolled over and began crawling through the low scrub between the wall and the trees. A tear on the back of the jacket from a thorn bush further helped the image which he completed by scuffing the shoulders of the jacket against a tree. Reaching his car he swallowed two more pain killers then drove to the forest shack where he and Boris had re-located the weapons cache. Hiding the car as best he could, Staunton unlocked the shack and got down to painting all of the boxes on the back of Boris' truck, hidden inside, in white gloss paint.

***

Vaughan was helping himself to a full English breakfast when Conway joined him.

"Morning, Ian, you had another late night?"

"Not particularly late but I have learnt a lot about potential places from where one could ship out a quantity of arms and I intend today to visit them to check out the lay of the land."

"You reckon that he will supervise the shipment himself?"

"Wouldn't you?"

"Yeh, I probably would considering that it is the only asset I would have. I assume his bank accounts have been frozen."

"Probably, or at least the bank accounts we know about, and leaving with the shipment is, by now, the only way that he will get off this island without the risk of officialdom stopping him."

"That makes sense. Are you really going to eat two eggs with all that?"

"Yep. I've got a long day ahead of me. What are you up to today, Brian?"

"Trying to trace the car is first on the schedule and trying to keep my opposite number DS José Livramento focused on this case and not wandering off to interview people who they think may have known about the coup but who in fact had no idea what was going on or actually cared."

Vaughan put down his knife and fork, "Ah, yes, I was thinking through the business of arms and shipping them out earlier, and thought that a vehicle would be required, a truck of some sort. Can you get the local boys to check on what vehicles Kazakov and Boris owned?"

"Yes, of course, he would have had access to more than just the Range Rover they found at the house."

Over breakfast, Conway gave more details about the events of the previous day in the company of his Portuguese opposite number.

"He is actually a great bloke and I suppose it's not his fault that he disappears frequently on this coup business, our little game is of no real interest to them in the great scheme of things."

"No, I don't suppose it is, though I do have the feeling that Staunton was connected with some pretty murky types in mainland Portugal. The Galician Mafia was mentioned but that was left to their SIS to deal with, and they seemed very keen to do so."

***

After Conway had been collected by Livramento, Vaughan drove to Calheta where he spent most of the morning studying the tiny harbour. Basically, a marina where there appeared to be no craft tough enough to go alongside a steel-hulled cargo vessel without risk of considerable damage even with strong fenders attached, he also noted the key operated drop posts preventing easy vehicle access to the quayside. Driving on to Paúl do Mar he found a very different situation with a couple of stout fishing boats moored up, easy access to the quay and a quietness about the place that made a night operation look highly feasible. In both locations, if the wind remained from the north east the sea state would be slight enough for a transshipment, provided that it wasn't too far off shore. Vaughan decided to cover both options, planning to put Conway at Calheta whilst he kept watch at Paúl do Mar. He had spent most of the afternoon at the port and, careful not to be seen, found a way of getting into and out of the derelict building that overlooked the harbour quay without actually coming in sight of the quay itself.

Satisfied with his plan he phoned Conway, "Hello, Brian, any news?"

"They found another car with the plates changed, you were right, he had done it again."

"What's the new number?"

Conway read it out then told Vaughan about Kazakov's minder, Boris, and the interrogation by a Russian speaking police officer sent in from Lisbon.

"The guy's been at it for bloody hours and got nowhere. I'm now convinced that this Boris character is too frightened of your man Staunton to risk shopping him by divulging any information regarding a weapons cache."

"You're probably right there, Brian, Staunton is a highly trained killer and though Boris is big and probably a hard man he would be no match, that's for sure."

"And I've been sent here to arrest him, oh, terrific."

"Don't worry, Brian, I'll hold your coat."

"Oh, thanks."

"Staunton would probably have used Kazakov's daughter's life to keep Boris in line, that's why the guy's keeping mum, then of course there is the money; he would lose that."

"What has your day been like?" asked Conway.

"I've been looking at the two most likely shipment ports. I'll explain later when I get back to the hotel. If I were you I would finish work early and get some rest."

"Ah, I sense that you have a plan."

"Something like that, see you later."

Finishing the call, Vaughan sat for a short time plucking up courage to visit Amelia again. Was he about to confirm his feelings for her or worse find that they did not share that vital spark that would bind them, and he leave her sadder than she already was. The risk of hurting her more than he had already done was something that he wanted to avoid at all costs, but regardless of the outcome with Staunton it was essential that they both knew whether their feelings for each other were deep enough for a lasting relationship. If they were, their future was something that would largely depend on where it would continue, and that was a whole new ballgame, would she leave Madeira and consider settling in England and would she allow him to continue his work with SIS.

Getting into his car he drove towards Camaro de Lobos still pondering what to do. He had parked the car on the brick-paved apron in front of Amelia's garage when an unwanted thought struck him; was this a subconscious reaction to Sarah's new romance?

Needing now more than ever to know the answer he got out of the car and made his way up to the house. Zeferino answered the door and on seeing Vaughan smiled and stepped aside to let him in.

"Hello, Zef, is your mama at home?"

"Mama! It is Senhor Vaughan."

Amelia came to the dining room door and looked down the hall at him.

"Can he watch TV for a while? You and I need to talk." She nodded. "Zef you can watch TV for a while, I need to talk to your mama, okay?"

Zef smiled, "Sim, er yes, er okay," and turned to hurry into the lounge and switch on the television.

"Have you come to ask me more questions about shipping?"

"No, I have come to talk about us," he said, quietly closing the lounge door and walking towards her.

She stood still in the doorway waiting for him. She looked tired, the scar on her jaw though was not so angry and she had combed her hair differently to hide the scab on her scalp, but it was the tiredness that struck Vaughan.

"You look all in," he said quietly looking down at her.

She frowned, "What is 'all in?' All in what?"

"Oh sorry, it is an English phrase for saying that you look tired or exhausted."

"Oh, I do not sleep so well with this," she replied raising her left arm slightly, "I will be so glad when the plaster is taken off."

Vaughan gently put his arms around her, "So will I."

As he had reached out so had she, her plaster cast clad arm resting against his right side and her bandaged right arm gently adding pressure to the embrace. The side of her head rested against his chest and he waited for her to look up but she didn't, instead, after several seconds, she took her arms away breaking the contact.

"No, Ian, I want to be sure that this is not just sympathy."

"So do I, Amelia, I also want to be sure."

"At this moment feeling tired and in pain, worried about the impact on my business, how people are treating us and you, how can I know anything for sure," she said looking at him intently, "I don't even really know who you are, do I?"

Vaughan was stopped short by her last comment, "No, Amelia, you are right, you probably don't know who I am."

"So I need to learn who this man, Ian Vaughan, really is, and if you have the time we can start now by you telling me your life story from when you were a small boy. Come, sit at the table and tell me."

Two hours later Vaughan got up to leave, "When the Staunton problem is dealt with I will come and let you know, then I will return to England and wait for your invitation to come and see you again, in what, a month, two months?"

"When I am healed and my life is more stable. I have to think of Zeferino as well as myself. Until my uncle arrived, my life was stable and my future clear, but now I cannot think beyond the next hour. I am sorry, because I said those things about my feelings without fully thinking of the consequences of what I said. Please understand that I meant those things, but now I am too confused and unsure, I am sorry, so sorry, Ian."

***

Vaughan left Amelia's house strangely more confident about his own feelings and prepared to wait for her. She was complex yes, but she was also honest and cautious and he could well understand her current dilemma.

After a hurried farewell to Zef, Vaughan had walked swiftly to the car and driven back to the hotel to enlist Brian Conway's assistance in a night-time vigil. He found the man sat in the bar taking a sip of the second beer of the day.

"Hi, Brian, how's it going?"

"Slowly, but at least we now have the details of the vehicles you were interested in." Conway reached into his jacket pocket and pulled out a piece of paper. "I was just about to spoil your cosy evening with the very lovely Amelia de Lima, then you turn up here. Has she told you that you are not rich enough or only that you are too old and ugly."

"How did you know I had visited Amelia?"

"When you left she phoned Alicia who phoned your mate Bruno who then brought a beer out to me."

"The jungle drums, eh."

"Yep, he also brought out a photograph of the lady. Wow."

"Wow she most definitely is, but sadly you are right again, Brian, one look at me in daylight was enough, she didn't even ask about the bank balance."

"Oh yeh," Conway chuckled giving Vaughan a friendly punch on the shoulder. He looked down at the piece of paper. "Right, the news is this – apart from the Range Rover there is an Isuzu two tonne truck plus a SEAT Leon both registered as belonging to Boris Kuznetsov. We took a look at the house, but could not find the truck, that was two hours ago. We are going to ask him about it in the morning, bet he'll claim that it has been stolen whilst he has been in custody."

"Wouldn't you."

"Yeh, I suppose I would in the same circumstances." Conway waved to the barman. "What are you drinking, Ian?"

"A fruit juice, that's all. I'm going a-hunting shortly to take a look at a couple of small harbours. Want to come along?"

"Yeh, all right. What's this about?"

Vaughan outlined the theory he had concerning the export of the weapons cache.

"So you're about to suggest that each of us keeps watch, one at Calheta and the other at Paúl do Mar."

"You're quick."

"Years of working with devious minds like yours. The number of senior officers I've had whose apparent aim in life has been my sleep deprivation."

"Oh good, you're in training then."

"I'll get the bar to have some sandwiches made up for us."

***

Vaughan left Conway on the flying bridge of a sport fishing fast powerboat, "I'll give you a call from Paúl do Mar as soon as I have got settled there, hopefully there'll be a mobile signal." Vaughan turned to go.

"What if there isn't, Ian?"

"I'll come back."

The road from Calheta to Jardin do Mar was the old one, narrow and very winding, but once into the new tunnel link to Paúl do Mar, Vaughan was able to travel at speed. The harbour road was immediately by the exit from the tunnel and turning down the steep incline Vaughan parked the car facing the sea wall. Getting out he strolled down to the small harbour past two late drinkers at the café on the front. The harbour wall was deserted but there was some activity in a small fishing boat moored alongside the quay. Wandering along towards it, hands in his pockets, he looked down into the boat and noted the empty crates being arranged ready to receive the early morning's catch. By the time he had walked to the end of the harbour wall and back the two fishermen had left, presumably to get a night's sleep.

Taking his mobile out of his pocket he found he had a signal and keyed in Conway's number. "Anything at your end?"

"No, mate, nothing except a lad pushing drugs on the esplanade."

"A good trade?"

"Yeh he seems to be doing all right. Just done a deal with a very pretty young thing and her boyfriend. No wonder I have bloody nightmares about my daughter."

"Are you okay there for a few hours?"

"Well it's better than waiting around all day in the police headquarters. They're doing their best but this guy Staunton has gone to ground and until he makes a move we're not going to have a chance of picking him up. I reckon you're on the best track; we better get the local guys involved though. I realised just now that if he has company it could well turn into a shooting match." Conway waited a moment or two for Vaughan's response. When there was no reply he said, "But of course you knew that."

"My plan was to call in the army; I have a direct line to the guy in charge."

"Oh, so you did have a plan, right."

For both men it was an uncomfortable and cold night and by dawn Vaughan knew that the shipment would not take place until darkness fell again. He collected Conway at six o'clock that morning having seen his fishermen put out to sea at daybreak. "Sorry, Brian, maybe we can do it again tonight if you're up for it."

"Yeh, okay, if you're sure about this. Why not bring in the local police as well?"

"Well 'a', I'm not supposed to be anything other than a maritime author and 'b' Staunton would have scouted the area for law enforcement. Also, the weapons they are likely to have available have greater range and accuracy than the police nine millimetre Glocks."

"Suddenly I'm feeling even more vulnerable."

"All you have to do is give me a call if you think anything is going down, then stay out of sight. I will call in the cavalry."

***

Vaughan arrived back at Amelia's house just as Alicia was leaving to take Zeferino to school. She gave him an odd look but other than 'Bom dia' and a wave, said nothing.

Amelia was sitting in the kitchen eating cereal as Vaughan entered.

"Bom dia, Amelia."

She smiled, "Bom dia, Ian. It is a relief to see you unharmed." She nodded towards the kitchen window, "I was surprised to receive an invitation from Colonel Castelo-Lopez very early this morning, to attend a meeting at the Presidential Residence the day after tomorrow."

"Will you go?"

"It was signed by both the President and the Colonel so I feel I must."

"Good decision."

"You think so, eh."

"Did you sleep well?"

"Yes, after I spent some hours thinking about what passed between us yesterday"

Vaughan reached for the coffee pot, "May I?"

"Please go ahead, there are cereals and fresh bread, help yourself. Then I think you go to bed, you look very tired."

A good part of Vaughan's training had been conducted alongside sleep deprivation and during his time at The Manor he had learnt to sleep whenever he had the opportunity.

"I've only just got here, Amelia."

"There is a spare room upstairs and the bed is already made up."

As he ate some breakfast he told her more about his first brush with dangerous criminals, which was the initial event that had brought him to the attention of the then Commander Campbell.

"And your poor wife she suffered a miscarriage, oh, Ian, how sad for you both."

"That had happened while I was still at sea and by the time I got to talking with her from the States she was all for me seeking revenge. So I stayed and helped a bit tracking down the gang."

"So the divorce was something else."

"No, the divorce was because her parents who, now it appears, had never liked me, and her so called best friend, persuaded her that despite her request for me to 'Go get them' that I should have returned to her side. They branded me unfeeling and dangerous and the man who had deserted her in her hour of need."

"Surely she remembered what she had said."

318

"Apparently not and if she had said those things I should have ignored her. Anyway, shortly after I got back other members of the gang were released from jail in Japan and it was thought they were coming after me."

"Did they?"

"I don't know, but by misfortune I was working at a facility they wanted to attack so I became involved again and in the meantime Sarah had hired a divorce lawyer. Much to her parents' delight."

"Where was the place they attacked?"

"I'm sorry I can't tell you."

"Oh, a secret place, eh."

Vaughan nodded, "I'll take up that offer of sleep if you don't mind."

***

When he awoke he was surprised to find that it was four o'clock in the afternoon and that alongside him in the spare bedroom lay Amelia, her head on a pillow looking at him.

"Have you been there long?"

"I brought you up some lunch," she pointed to a plate of sandwiches on the bedside table, "But you looked so peaceful I did not want to wake you. Then I thought I would keep you company."

"Thank you," he said sitting up, stretching and yawning. "I'll take a shower if that's okay with you."

"There are clean towels in the corner cupboard, help yourself."

When Vaughan returned to the bedroom he was surprised to see Amelia still lying on the bed.

"You are going searching for this man again tonight?"

"Yes, not alone though, there is this policeman I told you about from London, here to do the formal arrest, I will be working with him."

"So that is someone else you have to look after."

"Oh no, Brian is a big boy, he can look after himself."

She looked at him disbelievingly, "Huh, so you say." She rolled onto her right side and pushed herself up using her elbow. "I will be so glad when this cast is removed."

Swinging her feet off the bed she sat for a few seconds then stood up, "Alicia will be here soon and I do not want to raise her hopes if she finds me here, in a bedroom alone with you." She had made her eyes big and had a mischievous smile on her face.

Vaughan laughed. "I had better hurry downstairs then."

"Yes, you better had otherwise my reputation will be totally in ruins and I will have to leave the island forever."

***

Staunton adjusted the boot straps on his injured right foot then downed two more pain killers. Reaching for his mobile he flicked through the directory to MV Verlorenvlei and pressed the call key. The vessel's radio operator answered.

"Tell your captain that Leonard wants to speak with him." There was a few seconds delay, usual for Inmarsat communication time lag.

"He off watch."

"Well wake him up, idiot, this is urgent!"

Several minutes passed and Staunton was becoming worried about the phone preload amount running out before he got an answer.

"Kallenberg."

"Leonard. Just checking your schedule, will you be on time?"

"You said 0300, is that correct?"

"Yes, 0300 hours is good."

"We will be there."

"No lights, understood."

"Understood."

Staunton gave a sigh of relief as he ended the call and slipped the phone into his jacket pocket. Getting up he tested his weight on his injured foot, and wincing with pain reached for the walking stick. Hobbling, he made his way to Reshetnikov's study; the thought of money had crossed his mind earlier, guessing that the Russian would have been surviving on cash acquired via Sonia's business, now his bank accounts were frozen. There were two desks in the room, the larger obviously Reshetnikov's, and guessing from the diary entries the smaller one for the use of Sonia. Rifling through the large desk's drawers he noticed that

320

the second drawer depth was some fifty millimetres shallower than the exposed drawer sides. Feeling underneath he smiled, withdrawing his hand holding the latest Grach nine millimetre pistol. Slipping the magazine out, he checked that it was full then slipped the clip home and hefted the weapon for balance. A bit heavy maybe but he knew that they were hard hitters. The rest of the drawers revealed little of interest so he moved to Sonia's desk where he found two of the drawers locked. Ten minutes later, and after the destructive application of a nail bar brought in from the garage, Staunton happily counted out two thousand euros in notes. Feeling generous he left the three soiled five euro notes and the bags of coins behind.

Tipping the contents of Reshetnikov's smart leather briefcase out onto the floor he poked through the small pile with his walking stick but found nothing of value so, scattering it, he moved back to Sonia's desk and carefully put the money in the case then turned his attention to the shelves nearby, one of which held a large number of DVDs. He glanced at the labels which had girls' names written on them. Intrigued, he took a few through to the lounge and putting on the television inserted a disc into the player. After a few minutes he took the disc out and turned off the television, the content of these discs required time and careful study, he was sure that the crew of the MV Verlorenvlei would feel the same. Now, however, he had to prepare for the night's work and filling a shopping bag with the DVDs he returned to the bedroom to pack.

It was eleven o'clock at night when Staunton picked up the fishermen and drove them to the forest shack hidden down a track off the road heading north-east out of Prazeres. By the light of the car's sidelights the two fishermen watched curiously as Staunton undid the padlock on the shack doors. After a brief nod of his head towards the doors one of the men stepped forward and pulled both doors open to reveal an Isuzu truck.

Staunton held up the keys and the other fisherman took them and made his way towards the driver's door. As he did so, Staunton stepped up to the truck, pulled back the tarpaulins and pointed to the lettering on the side of the exposed box. In large red letters "Frágil Porcelana" was written on all sides.

"So make sure you drive very carefully down to the harbour."

"Sim, Senhor, we take good care."

The journey was slow but Staunton knew he had plenty of time as he followed behind Boris Kuznetsov's truck down to Paúl do Mar.

Arriving at the quayside the two men set about loading the boxes into their boat, in the fish hold of which was a loading pallet already prepared with hoisting strops. As Vaughan had anticipated Staunton had stopped short of the quay and spent time driving around looking for police or army vehicles before making his presence known at the harbour. He would have been well advised to have looked into the derelict building overlooking the quay where the weapons cache had previously been hidden and was now Vaughan's hiding place.

CHAPTER 14

Vaughan was beginning to think that again he was to be disappointed, and had already checked with Conway twice to see if there was any activity at Calheta, when the truck arrived. Checking the number plate against that given to him by Conway was enough, and the white paint and red lettering on the boxes did little to disguise what was contained within them. As he watched it became obvious that the task of transferring the boxes from the truck onto the boat by hand was a laborious one as with virtually every box there was a grave risk of it ending up at the bottom of the harbour.

Pulling his phone from his pocket Vaughan keyed in the Colonel's direct number.

"Castelo-Lopez." The voice was dull from sleep.

Vaughan gambled that the half asleep Colonel would not tie in the fact that he wasn't on the island when the attack on Amelia occurred, "It's Ian Vaughan, Colonel. I thought you should know that the man who attacked Senhora De Lima is standing on the harbour wall at Paúl do Mar with two others, and is about to leave on a fishing boat together with a shipment of illegal arms."

"How do you know this, Senhor Vaughan?" The Colonel's voice was now firm and clear.

"I am standing in a derelict building overlooking the harbour and have recognised him," replied Vaughan. *"Well, shipping illegal arms is illegal so browny points for the Colonel whichever way it goes, but will they get here on time?"*

"I will come straight away but I need time to gather some men."

"I would also suggest, Colonel, that you make contact with the Portuguese Navy and get their vessel, currently in Funchal, to put to sea and arrest a cargo vessel hovering off Paúl do Mar waiting to transship the weapons."

"You have seen this ship?"

"No, Colonel, but I know it's there, you cannot deliver, maybe one tonne, of weapons very far using a small inshore fishing boat."

"I understand, Senhor Vaughan. I will see if they can put to sea so quickly."

"Current progress on loading suggests that you have just over two hours, Colonel."

Both of the men handling the boxes appeared to be middle aged and after the initial enthusiasm Vaughan noticed that the weight of the boxes was rapidly taking its toll and pace had slackened.

With no proper lifting tackle, the task of lowering the boxes down into the boat was both strenuous and risky. Frequent rests were soon being taken; occasionally one of the men would look at his wristwatch but neither seemed to be hurried or panicking, and after a short while Vaughan estimated that he had more than enough time to collect Conway.

Slipping from his hiding place he ran back to his car and drove south to Calheta contacting Conway through the car's hands free phone link.

"It's a go, Brian, I'm on my way to collect you, can you meet me at the marina entrance."

"What's happened?"

"Boris's truck turned up with a load of heavy boxes on board. He's got two men, probably the fishermen who own the boat, to do the heavy work."

"He's there then."

"Not yet, I don't expect to see him until the last minute, he won't want to risk being close to that cargo until it's time to cast off."

"You sure about this, Ian?"

"Yep, sure enough to call in the army and the navy."

"Oh, right, mate, I'll be there waiting."

The ten kilometre drive to Calheta seemed like fifty to Vaughan that night. Not that there was much traffic about, but more that the road from Jardin do Mar was full of blind bends and steep gradients.

Arriving at the marina Vaughan saw Conway standing in the shadow of a palm tree.

"Hop in and buckle up."

"Just to let you know, I have a wife and children waiting for me back home in the UK," Conway said, as the car's acceleration induced a bit of wheel spin.

"The tarmac out here doesn't give much grip when it is cool."

"Oh is that it, I thought it was more connected to your right foot being flat on the floor."

The gearbox and two litre engine in Vaughan's Leon FR were working very hard indeed and Conway was soon admiring the driving exhibition he was experiencing. "You've done this type of thing once or twice before I gather."

"What, intercepted arms shipments?"

"No, driving like you're on a bloody rally time trial."

"We have got to get back there and into hiding before Staunton turns up, or the army, come to that."

"Oh… mind that bloody armco will you…! My whole life flashed before me just then."

"Stop moaning, my grandmother drives faster than this in her mobility scooter."

"Who built it for her, Ferrari?"

"Have you alerted your man in Funchal?"

"Yeh, shortly after you called. He wasn't very impressed, I think he was trying to create another little José Livramento at the time."

"Look on it as your part in a world population control scheme."

"It will be more like, my part in pissing off a guy who already thinks I'm a bloody nuisance."

"Cheer up, I thought you were enjoying this 'jolly'."

"I must admit it has had its bright moments, particularly around the pool."

"You included that scenery description in your postcard home of course."

"If I had I wouldn't last to tell the tale at the pub," Conway put his hand to the dashboard again as Vaughan slung the Leon into a tight left-hand bend followed immediately by a right and steep drop that had the car sideslipping with squealing tyres. "What's the set-up at the harbour?"

"We take up our position in a derelict building which has a good view. Ideally we get there without being noticed as the two fishermen, if that's who they are, will sound the alarm for sure. Once in place we watch out for Staunton to arrive and if he looks like doing a runner before the cavalry turn up we attempt to make an arrest."

"Why wait for the cavalry?"

"Because I don't want to die just yet."

"Oh yes, the guy is a trained killer. Sorry I forgot that for a moment."

On arrival at the harbour they found their luck was in as the two fishermen were down in the boat positioning a box, so they were able to slip into hiding without being seen.

"No sign of Staunton, do you honestly think he's going to show up?"

"I'm sure of it, Brian. He knows by now that every port and airport in Europe has people looking out for him, especially here in Madeira. What better than to slip away with this arms shipment."

Since the truck had arrived over one hour had passed with only four of the six long crates loaded into the boat, and there were several smaller crates and ammunition boxes still to be lowered over the quayside and down into the boat. Two o'clock came and went and still the men cautiously laboured over the boxes until nearly the last of the smaller boxes was taken off the truck and carried to the edge of the quay.

"What do you think is in those smaller metal boxes?"

"Ammunition for the assault rifles, and in the shallow ones grenades or may even be rockets. The lightweight long box they offloaded just now made me think that a shoulder launcher was included."

"How did you know one box was lightweight?"

"They loaded it much more quickly than the others."

"You don't miss much do you?"

Based on previous cycles, Vaughan estimated that the final box would be safely stowed on board in twenty minutes, and he was beginning to get concerned that Staunton had not put in an appearance.

"I have just had an unpleasant thought, Brian."

"What about?"

"What if Staunton was overseeing this loading operation from a hiding place and saw us arrive."

"Thanks for that thought, Ian. It makes me feel so much more uncomfortable."

"A pleasure. You watch our intrepid labourers while I have a quiet look round."

Ten minutes later Conway almost had a heart attack as Vaughan crouched down beside him. "Don't you ever knock."

"I didn't want to wake you."

"Cheeky bastard." Conway took another look at the fishermen on the quay, "Well, looks like they are almost done. What's that noise?"

"Sounds like a trolley of some sort. Ah, there he is pulling a couple of suitcases, I was right, he is travelling with the goods."

"What do we do?"

"Wait and hope the cavalry arrives."

Staunton reached the truck and appeared to be giving orders to the fishermen as to his personal luggage, then he hobbled back towards the seafront and the wide haul-out slipway.

"Now what's he doing?"

"I don't know, Brian, and he has dropped out of sight." Vaughan wished he had a set of night goggles with him. "With those two standing like daisies on the quayside we can't go looking for him without raising the alarm."

Both men fell quiet listening intently. A rat scurried across the room and both men tensed.

"A rat?" Conway whispered.

"Probably."

"Hey, I just saw a light flash out at sea."

"That's what Staunton's been doing, he's been signalling to a larger vessel waiting offshore. Amelia was spot on, clever girl."

The sound of the waves on the shore was drowned out by the sudden wailing of a siren.

"Oh for Christ's sake, announce your arrival with a fanfare why don't you."

"That's got Staunton heading for the hills I bet." Vaughan stood and went to leave. "Brian, are you armed?"

"No, no bloody way, that's against the rules."

"Right, you stay here and introduce yourself to Colonel Castelo-Lopez. Make sure to hold your badge up high so they don't shoot you."

Conway swallowed hard, "Thanks for the tip, where are you going to be?"

"Tracking down Staunton. Oh you might need these to get home with." Vaughan handed the car keys over.

"Are you armed?"

"Oh, Brian, that's against the rules."

Vaughan had just made it to the corner of the building as the lead police car rounded the bend onto the seafront and accelerated towards the quay where the two fishermen were scrambling down into their boat, preparing to cast off. Behind the police car, but travelling a lot slower round the bend, was an army truck loaded with soldiers.

***

Nervously, Detective Sergeant Brian Conway stepped out of the doorway onto the terrace of the derelict building and walked towards the steps. The beam of a powerful lamp blinded him and he instantly raised both hands above his head allowing his police badge to dangle from his right hand where everyone could see it. Two soldiers approached cautiously, one padding Conway down whilst the other held a gun on him. Finally satisfied, the soldier who had done the search gave Conway a shove in the back sending him down the steps towards the army truck.

"Colonel Castelo-Lopez! Colonel Castelo-Lopez!"

"Yes, Senhor, what do you want?"

"I am Detective Sergeant Conway of the Special Branch Section of the Metropolitan Police in London. I am here liaising with your local Force in finding and arresting a British subject named Leonard Staunton."

"You aren't by any chance in the company of Senhor Ian Vaughan?"

"Why, er yes, Sir, I am."

"Where is he now?"

"One of the men loading boxes onto that small boat ran off when he heard the police siren, Mr Vaughan has gone after him," replied Conway, not wanting to disclose the fact that the man he had been sent to arrest was now being pursued by maritime author Ian Vaughan instead of himself.

"Which way did they go?"

Conway pointed towards the corner of the building, "Er, that way, Sir, I think."

The Colonel turned and ordered three of his men to search.

"Stay with me please, Detective, I would like to hear what these men at the boat have to say for themselves and see what they have taken on board."

"Colonel, olhar, o mar!" shouted a sergeant standing in front of the army truck.

The Colonel turned to see a rusty cargo vessel caught in the powerful beam of the searchlight from the rapidly approaching Portuguese naval vessel, "Schultz Xavier".

"The man that ran off signalled to the ship. Vaughan and I saw the response flash, Colonel."

"Thank you, Detective Conway. If our Policia Maritima manage to secure an arrest and get the vessel into Funchal, your evidence will be most useful."

The cargo vessel's bows were pointing south-east when the "Schultz Xavier'" caught her in the searchlight and now she was trying hard to get underway and execute a sharp turn to starboard in a futile attempt to escape. It appeared that radio contact had been ignored so the naval vessel used a loudhailer and when that failed to get a response army personnel on board opened fire with automatic rifles aimed at the bridge door. Almost instantly the cargo vessel lost way allowing the "Schultz Xavier" to close and give instructions to enter the port of Funchal.

The manoeuvres at sea had held both men's full attention right up until the "Schultz Xavier" had drawn close alongside the MV Verlorenvlei.

"There will be a great deal of protesting their innocence no doubt. I am quite looking forward to this; I have never been party to an arrest of a ship at sea."

"I am more interested in our arrest on land, Senhor Conway; shall we go?"

Conway, feeling a little embarrassed, followed the Colonel onto the quay where they saw the two fishermen handcuffed and sat under armed guard. "Which one is the man Mr Vaughan identified?"

"Neither of these two, he must be the one that ran off. Damn."

The crates on board the boat were being opened and as they looked down into the boat a corporal approached the Colonel and saluting, handed him one of the assault rifles taken from the haul. The Colonel inspected it nodding his head slowly.

"Impressive, Detective Conway, very impressive. This is a Chinese Type 56 assault rifle, a variant of the Russian AK-47." He smiled, "There are not enough of them there to start a war, but enough for a guerrilla movement to cause a great deal of trouble."

Handing the weapon back to the soldier the Colonel turned to Conway, "Tell me, Detective, what is Ian Vaughan? He is not police, but he is something similar I am sure."

"All I know is that he is an author of some sort. We contacted him after he was attacked in Spain, it fitted with some enquiries we were making connected with illegal arms trading. You see we believe that some British subjects were involved and may be doing business here. My work was to assist your local Force here in any way I can with the arrest of this Leonard Staunton, who we believe to be seriously involved."

"How come you are working together?"

"After interviewing him in London we learnt that he was returning here and I was ordered to find him and warn him not to get involved, but as you see he took no notice."

"But how did you get here?"

"He phoned me at my hotel earlier and told me he had something to show me that may lead to the arrest of this Staunton character, and here I am, tired and wishing I was safely tucked up in bed."

"Did you not contact your opposite number here?"

"Oh yeh, straight away, he's standing over there." Conway pointed to a man in a black leather jacket who was talking to the fishermen. "Hey, José, can you come here a moment?"

The man turned and walked towards them. "Colonel, this is Detective Sergeant José Livramento. José, this is Colonel Castelo-Lopez." Having made the introduction Conway took two steps back breathing a sigh of relief, content at watching Livramento face questioning. The conversation between the two did not last long as it was interrupted by the three soldiers returning to report that they had not found anyone.

"Detective Conway, are you sure that the man and our friend Senhor Vaughan went away in that direction?"

"I am certain that they did."

"My men report that they could not find anyone."

Tempted to ask how hard they had tried Conway contented himself by saying, "The man on the run may well have planned a backdoor escape route. Our information is that he has had military training to a high level."

"Ah, that puts a different, how you say, er light on the situation." Castelo-Lopez turned to his Lieutenant. "O mapa por favor." Like a magician's rabbit from a hat the Lieutenant handed the Colonel a map. "Let me see, how can we quickly get troops to form a cordon."

Stabbing his finger at the area around the hotel Jardin Atlantico, the Colonel explained to his Lieutenant what he required to be done.

Soon one dozen men were climbing aboard the army truck under the command of a sergeant with orders to form a cordon along the rim of the gulley that led inland from the southern edge of the slipway. A second truckload of soldiers had arrived and similar orders were given to them to cover the rim to the north of the gulley.

"We will place a few men here just in case the man doubles back."

"What do we do?" asked Conway.

"Be patient and wait, Detective."

Conway sighed, then looking at the Colonel realised the man was about to start asking questions again and beat him to it, "Colonel, Ian Vaughan has spoken of you quite a bit in the short time I have spent with him, and it is obvious to me that you know a lot more about him than we do. When did you first meet him?"

"It was the evening after the attempted coup…"

***

When he left the derelict building, Vaughan had crossed to the steps and gained the cover of a high wall as the police car's headlights shone over the esplanade road to the quay. A ramp ran up alongside the wall leading to a pathway behind the building. It was the only way out and taking it he found himself crossing the backs of the harbour front houses. A track led off to the right which he ignored at first, running on until he found himself at a dead end. Returning to the track he started up it then stopped and searched in his trouser pocket for his keyring torch. Shining the light down onto the dusty path he picked out a set of footprints, one clear and the other scuffed as if the foot was dragged. *"Staunton, you won't get far walking like that."*

Vaughan estimated that Staunton had at most a three minute start on him and set off up the track as fast as he could at first, then found that against the cliff face the track turned sharply to the right and became narrow and very steep, leading back high above the slipway area where it turned left following the north side of the gulley. Keeping low and trying hard not to make a noise he rounded the corner, his eyes straining to see ahead in the dark and praying that the lights now on the quay did not show him up in silhouette. Moving into a shadowed area Vaughan held his breath, listening intently but nearly all small noises were being masked by the sound of rushing water from the stream in the base of the gulley. He looked up at the sky seeing a myriad of stars on that clear but moonless night; Staunton had picked his night well. He advanced some thirty metres, his night vision improving as he went. The track turned right down to the banks of the stream which it followed for some distance before coming to a fording point. Risking the torch again Vaughan checked that he was still following the lame walker, noting that Staunton had stopped and sat, crushing a small plant by the side of the stream. *"I must be close to him by now, more care required from here on. Lenny dear is a wounded animal and likely to be very dangerous if cornered."*

Crossing the stream the path started a steep climb again clinging now to the south side of the gulley. The scrub, now head high, increased the danger of just running into the man in the pitch dark. The faint sound of rock scree being disturbed some way ahead encouraged Vaughan to increase his speed but the going was getting harder with almost every step in the now almost impenetrable darkness. Suddenly he stepped out from the cover of the scrub and almost walked into the sheer rock face that formed the side of the gulley where the track turned sharply left and rose to a narrow ledge above the stream several metres below. A burst of automatic gunfire in the distance had him turning quickly and pressing himself against the rock to look back and down towards the quayside, then in the distance he saw the "Schultz Xavier" and the arrest at sea of the cargo vessel. *"That should tie up a few loose ends for the Colonel."* Back in pursuit he shortly came across the point where Staunton had nearly gone over the edge and Vaughan would have placed a foot into the same gap in the path had he not heard some more scree slippage a moment before placing his foot into the void. Taking the torch from his pocket again he pointed its beam in front; he could see where Staunton had frantically scrabbled with his hands to pull himself to safety. To clear the gap meant a jump across and the chance of a collision between his shoulder and the rock wall on landing, risking what would be a fatal fall. He studied the rock face the other side carefully. *"If I land on my right foot I should be able to pivot on it to face the rock wall and reach for a hand hold. I've got to land between the edge of the gap and that lump of rock overhanging the path, not the easiest thing to do."* Taking three paces back, Vaughan sprang forward and launched himself over the gap landing closer to the overhang than he would have liked, his left shoulder slamming into it as he pivoted. Fortunately his right hand found a crevice in which to form a fist wedge allowing him to arrest his fall backwards. After a moment or two's rest to get his breath back he cleared the overhang then followed the rock face round to the right, here again the path entered scrub, the darkness now requiring him to put both arms out in front feeling his way. Another thirty or forty metres brought Vaughan back close to the stream again and the risk of its noise masking any sound of his quarry. Hindered by caution, he had allowed Staunton to gain some distance on him, fear of pursuit and capture providing a boost to the man's energy.

The path veered right and started to climb up a side gulley taking a series of sharp zigzag bends as the climb steepened. The higher the path climbed the less dense was the scrub resulting in exposure to anyone above. In places the path had fallen away and Vaughan made a near fatal slip that took him back down one level in a cloud of dust. He would have fallen further had he not caught hold of a sapling whose roots miraculously held in the shallow topsoil. The sound brought two shots in his direction, forcing him to crawl back down the track to hide behind a rock. Hoping to make Staunton fire again and so reveal his position, Vaughan shouted out, "Oh give it up, Staunton, if you don't you'll be dead by dawn, I've got half the Portuguese army closing in, you'll never make it off the island or out of here come to that."

"Vaughan!" The voice was loud, almost a scream.

"Top marks for voice recognition, Lenny dear," Vaughan shouted back, intent now on goading Staunton into making a false move, he needed an edge to balance the scales. Between him and Staunton was a lot of open ground that would make him an easier target. "That's what Alice liked to call you wasn't it, Lenny dear. The staff in the communications room fell about laughing when they heard her."

Two more shots were fired, neither hit close enough for Vaughan to worry about.

"We have little Miss Alice Morgan and Vermeulen, Lenny dear, both are telling us an awful lot about you. My, you've been a naughty boy, Lenny."

Three shots followed and this time Vaughan just caught the muzzle flash as the bullet pinged off the rock next to him. *"Time to move I think."* As he broke cover three more shots were fired, the thwack of their impact on the vegetation close to him, making Vaughan realise that Staunton had night vision goggles.

"Shit he can see me really clearly, this makes it very tricky, too bloody tricky." One thing was certain, Staunton had not moved position and was now hidden behind a screen of undergrowth, Vaughan fired twice and was rewarded by hearing Staunton move to a position further up the path.

"How's the foot, Lenny dear? It is slowing you down a lot, Lenny, either that or you are out of shape, and you don't have your gang of executioners on the island to help you do your dirty work this time."

Vaughan moved quickly to the next rock large enough to hide behind, watching as he did for the telltale muzzle flash of Staunton's gun. *"There you are, you bastard, just to the right of that dark blob and down a bit. He's used three of his second clip, seven more and I hope he will be out of ammunition."* He squeezed the trigger twice then moved at a low run to the next bend diving flat as Staunton's return fire hit a straggly tree just behind him. *"Two shots left on that clip, Staunton, and I am sure you have been counting."* Scuffling noises indicated that Staunton was on the move again, firing twice as he did so. Vaughan moved again only to feel the left side of his light wind-cheater plucked as a bullet skimmed through it. He dived for cover feeling a burning sensation on his ribcage and a warm trickle across his chest.

"Missed again, Lenny dear, you really are an awful shot. Had you still been clean I would have recommended you went back to 'The Manor' for some training." Three shots snatched at the undergrowth around him. "Not even close, Lenny dear, you really are a bloody failure you know." The wound was stinging like mad but Vaughan's concentration was still focused on what Staunton was doing. *"That wasn't a Glock he was firing, the bastard's got hold of something else, which means the count can go as high as twenty on just one clip."* Something was digging into Vaughan's right leg and as he pulled it to get it out of the way he found it to be a long slender branch. Pulling it clear of the undergrowth he stretched out along the path and using the branch started to move a bush. Almost instantly Staunton fired a rapid six shots, sending leaves and twigs in all directions. Vaughan elbow crawled to the bush and used the branch again hoping that Staunton had run out of ammunition. When there was no response he made a crouching run to the next corner without drawing fire. *"No, Lenny dear, I wasn't born yesterday."* The corner was close to the gulley wall and there was an outcrop of rock that offered good cover.

"Campbell's got the top spot now, Lenny, I bet you are delighted to hear that, in fact it was Campbell who sent me to bring you in, Lenny, think of it, we would be sat next to each other on the flight to London, you in handcuffs of course, the full set naturally, you know, ankles and wrists with a short chain between the two. Fancy having to bend double to wipe your nose." Vaughan finished with a laugh, and using his foot waggled the stem of a branch sticking out from the outcrop whilst peering through the long grass on the top.

The next four rounds were fired individually from a position much further to the right than Vaughan had expected and from a point much closer to the top of the gully. Catching just a glimpse of muzzle flash, Vaughan guessed at Staunton's next move and fired off two shots, hearing clearly a muffled cry.

"Ooops, you moved the wrong way, Lenny dear, even without night goggles I hit you."

As Staunton moved again it was obvious that he was stumbling. "Stay alive, Lenny dear, and give it up, in your current state you won't make it to the top, you see, you are finished, Lenny, no Alice, no job, and your arms cache in the hands of the Portuguese Police Force. Oh yes and we also have Vermeulen's precious black notebook, so you can't even use that. Failed again, Lenny, just like the coup you were backing. Why is it you are always such a failure, Lenny dear?" Vaughan was about to shout further comments when four shots hit the rock he was hiding behind.

Moving as fast as he could up the track to the next corner Vaughan had been expecting Staunton to fire at any moment, but nothing happened. Instead, when he stopped now, only one dogleg away, he could hear Staunton's laboured steps and the rattle of loose stones. He had to catch up with him now and hope that the man had run out of bullets.

As Vaughan reached the top of the gulley he was aware of an increase in vision and glanced at his wristwatch. *"Quarter to four, it won't be full daylight until about seven."* He took a look around, and seeing Staunton's head silhouetted against the lighter sky, moved off in pursuit. The gradient was less arduous now but after the steep climb from the gulley floor, Vaughan's legs were not up to sprinting, anyway, he was catching Staunton and wasn't going to rush it and risk being shot. The path they were following appeared to run along the rim of the gulley and though neither man was aware of it they were both making straight towards the first batch of soldiers detailed to form a cordon.

The distance between the two men was closing rapidly and Vaughan hoped that he could catch Staunton before the man reached a low building that was being revealed as they neared the brow. His foot kicked something heavy in the grass that made a metallic chink as it landed amongst some stones and reaching down he picked up the Grach 443 and automatically freed the magazine clip. *"Empty, got you, Staunton, but who is going to want a slice of you first, Portugal, Angola or Britain."*

Vaughan was only five or six metres from Staunton now, the path had led them back towards the sea and the top of the impressive cliff that went almost sheer to the beach two hundred metres below. He was about to order him to put his hands in the air when Staunton turned, waving a knife in his left hand.

"You come any nearer, Vaughan, and I will slice you like a salami sausage. You will never take me in; you don't have the skill to deal with me."

"What did you use on David Patterson, Lenny, a machete?" A wild guess by Vaughan. "He was your colleague, someone who you were duty-bound to support and protect."

Staunton nodded and Vaughan could just make out a twisted smile, "Yeh, you should have seen the look of shocked surprise on his face when I chopped his right hand off."

Vaughan slid his pistol back into the trouser pocket holster, "And now you think a lame one-armed sick head case like you, creepy Lenny, with just a knife is a match for me, you really must be mad."

Vaughan was close now, close enough to see Staunton's eyelid movement that split second before making a lunge with the knife. The sidestep, trip and wrist grab were standard moves that normally Staunton would have avoided but faint from the pain of his right foot and wounded right arm meant that he went to the ground easily uttering a frustrated yell. Taking the left arm up high and twisting it behind Staunton's back made it easier to force the knife from his grasp. As Vaughan threw the knife clear three men stood from crouching positions at the side of the path and Vaughan sensed movements behind him. He had been concentrating so hard on Staunton he had not seen the soldiers laying in wait.

"Stop, Senhors, hands above your heads, now!"

Vaughan pulled Staunton by the collar onto his feet using the move to steal the man's wallet from his hip pocket before pushing him away towards the soldiers.

Staunton slowly raised his left arm, his right arm hanging limply at his side. "Arrest this man behind me, he is guilty of arms smuggling and is wanted by the British Government. I am a British Intelligence Agent sent here to arrest him," shouted Staunton, groping for his hip pocket.

A soldier stepped forward and shone a torch in Vaughan's face.

"Ah, Senhor Vaughan, Senhor Vaughan, how are you? You are wounded." The man speaking stepped between Vaughan and the soldier with the torch. "I Sergeant Gomes, I guard apartment you wounded at, remember!"

"Of course, Sergeant Gomes, good to see you again. That is the man you should be arresting."

The Sergeant turned to his men and ordered them to arrest Staunton who, with all eyes focused on Vaughan, had staggered several paces away hoping to find concealment in the darkness.

"Oh, give it up, Staunton, I told you, you can't escape."

As the powerful torchlight illuminated him Staunton turned to face Vaughan, then, overbalancing slightly, took two awkward paces backwards and caught the heel of his strapped boot on a tuft of grass and toppled back, arms flailing, over the cliff edge. As he started the long fall he cried out, "You baastaaaaaaaaaarrrrrrrrrrrrrrd," a cry that stopped abruptly only when his body struck the cliff face for the third time before crashing into the scrub on the sloping cliff shelf halfway between the summit and the sea far below.

The sky was a little lighter now and as Vaughan turned back to look at Sergeant Gomes he thought, *"I warned you, Staunton, I told you that if you didn't give up you would be dead by dawn."*

***

Sergeant Gomes elbow crawled his way to the cliff edge and looked down, "I can no see him he fall a long way, we will need much rope to reach him."

The sound of a car arriving heralded the appearance of Castelo-Lopez and Brian Conway, and both men were soon hurried down to the scene. Fortunately, the Colonel was distracted by the excited Sergeant Gomes, anxious to explain what had happened, allowing Conway to get to Vaughan first.

"The Colonel wants to know how it is you are carrying a gun," said Conway quietly.

Vaughan slipped him his Glock, "Look after this one for me, I have another to show the Colonel."

"Oh, okay, if you're sure about this."

"When they recover the body they will find that he has a wounded right arm." Vaughan then slipped Staunton's wallet into Conway's jacket. "You also better hang onto that until you get back to London, SIS will be delighted that it was returned unseen by the Portuguese."

"What is it?"

"Staunton's wallet and it has his SIS identity badge in it."

"Senhor Vaughan, you were wounded I hear." Castelo-Lopez strode across from his men to where Conway and Vaughan were standing.

"It is just a graze, Colonel, nothing very serious."

"I had hoped that you would leave the hunt for this man to my soldiers, who as you see were in the right place to capture him."

Aware that no soldiers had followed him up the track Vaughan said, "A couple of times I waited to see if any support was following me and had to assume that I was on my own in the chase."

"Huh, I sent some men to search for you but they obviously failed to search far enough." The Colonel replied somewhat stiffly. "We heard much shooting, Senhor Vaughan, I was not aware you carry a gun," the Colonel's voice carried a large hint of accusation and annoyance.

"The man had an injured foot and stumbled early in his scramble up the gulley back there, and dropped this," Vaughan handed the Colonel Staunton's Grach, "There were still several rounds in the clip, so as he was firing at me I returned the favour and wounded him in his right arm."

"He was carrying two pistols?"

"Bearing in mind what he was shipping out of here, I would not have been surprised had he been carrying an AK47!"

"You have a good point there, Senhor Vaughan." The Colonel glanced over Vaughan's shoulder. "Ah here is the medic, he will take a look at your wound."

Vaughan slipped off his wind-cheater and undid his shirt. Turning Vaughan round so that the torchlight illuminated the wound, the medic went down on one knee and looked at it. "Please stop still, eh."

Three hours later the Colonel, Conway and Vaughan were finishing breakfast at the Hotel Jardin Atlantico up above where Staunton and Vaughan had met. Vaughan, wearing a tee shirt and shorts purchased from the hotel shop, felt particularly conspicuous as the group were attracting a huge amount of attention from the other diners. Some of the guests had been disturbed earlier by the sound of gunfire and obviously did not fully believe the announcement that the army had been holding an exercise in the area.

A sergeant, marching smartly across the dining room, stood to attention alongside the Colonel and announced that the recovery team were ready.

"Thank God for that," Vaughan said, standing as the Colonel signed the bill. "I now know how animals must feel in a zoo."

"Even in that fashion statement you look smarter than when you arrived here."

"Gee thanks, Brian," said Vaughan, giving the detective a very sour look. "Let's get out of here shall we, I want to be absolutely sure that bastard Staunton is dead."

Back at the cliff top they found that a metal winch stand and lifting jib had been assembled and a man and stretcher were already on the way down the cliff face.

A police sergeant approached Vaughan.

"We hear that the man who attacked Senhora De Lima had accident here and that you also are here, Senhor Vaughan." The Detective Sergeant moved close to Vaughan, "Maybe you helped his accident?"

"No, not me. Go and ask Sergeant Gomes over there what happened, he'll give you the details I'm sure."

"I may wish to question you later, Senhor Vaughan, so please, you no leave."

"That is someone else who doesn't want me to leave the island; I never thought I would be this popular."

"Who were the others?" asked Conway.

"I think Staunton actually wanted me to be buried here, or rather cremated, I don't think they have burials on Madeira."

"And?"

"To my surprise, Amelia de Lima."

The radio held by the Colonel's lieutenant squawked into life and he ordered for the slack to be taken up on the winch cable. "Ah, here we go, just pray that the bullet that wounded him went straight through and out the other side, otherwise someone will work out that it didn't come from that Grach I handed over."

"Will they check?"

"Wouldn't you?"

"Yeh, you're right, we would."

The team on the winch showed little enthusiasm for the work, but eventually the head of the stretcher bearer came into view, followed by the stretcher containing the battered remains of Leonard Staunton. When the stretcher was swung in and carried a safe distance from the cliff edge, Vaughan and Conway joined the Colonel to inspect the body.

"Jesus what a mess, can you recognise him, Ian, because I'm buggered if I could."

Vaughan reached down and turned the head round to see the other side of the face, "Yes that's Staunton all right. This side isn't as smashed up and you can see the wound in the right arm. That Grach packs a punch, look, it's gone right through."

A young soldier, tempted to take a look, retched and turned away hurriedly.

Detective Sergeant Brian Conway showed remarkable professionalism in producing a pair of latex gloves from his pocket and started a search of Staunton's pockets, "Ah, that's good, his mobile phone is still in one piece, let me see what calls he has made recently." Flicking the touch screen a few times brought up the call list. "There we are, he made an Inmarsat call last night. In fact it was the last call he made."

The Colonel looked at the phone list and nodded, "That should make the arrest of the captain of that ship much easier. What else is in his pockets?"

Conway searched but revealed nothing of importance other than Staunton's Glock pistol and indicated that the body should be covered up. "He won't be travelling back with me after all," he said, straightening up and stretching and yawning. "I had better inform the Honorary Consul and start arrangements for repatriating the body." Conway turned to the Colonel, "You have no interest in holding onto this corpse for any reason I suppose?"

The Colonel crouched down again and lifted up Staunton's right arm to inspect the wound then put it back down again. "No, Detective Conway, it will not serve any purpose here. I will have it delivered to the city morgue and inform them that your Consul will be in touch."

"Did you bring the car up, Brian? I really fancy getting back to the hotel and changing out of this kit."

"Yeh, you all right to drive, Ian?"

"I'll be okay driving, it'll take my mind off the events of last night. There were moments when I thought I was coming to the end of my shift in this world."

Conway handed Vaughan the car keys, "I'll hitch a lift with the local police, if Livramento wants to talk to you any more he knows where to find you."

The Colonel had started giving orders for his men to dismantle the winch gear and return to barracks, leaving Conway and Vaughan alone.

"I'll see you at the hotel later on, Brian."

"You know, many of your guys are married and do a similar job to you, don't you. You didn't need to get this involved, the Colonel was right, he had set an ambush for Staunton, they would have got him, maybe alive."

"That, Brian, may have been a problem."

Conway looked puzzled for a moment or two, "Ah, I see what you mean."

After making his farewells Vaughan picked up the carrier bag containing his bloodstained clothes and made his way up to where his hire car was parked. It took him a few minutes to collect his thoughts and compile the sequence of actions he must now follow. Starting the car he drove a short distance away from the scene towards the hotel before pulling over, and taking his mobile from his jacket, phoned Campbell's direct contact number.

"Campbell."

"It's Vaughan, Sir. Staunton has had a rather nasty accident just as he was about to leave Madeira aboard a small cargo vessel."

"Is he in hospital?"

"No, Sir. The morgue."

"I see, use the Consul's services to send me a full report as soon as you can, then get back here. I have a job for you."

Later, as Vaughan walked up the driveway to Amelia's house the front door opened and he could see her standing in the shade waiting for him. He had changed at the hotel and carefully checked the wound dressing not wanting her to see that he had been hurt. It was the time for real honesty to himself, was he really in love with her and just as importantly, was she really in love with him.

"Are you all right, Ian? You are not hurt?" she asked, anxiously noting the darkness under his eyes.

"No, I'm fine, just very tired, I haven't had any sleep and have done a lot of walking, uphill mainly."

"Did you catch him?"

"Almost, then he fell over a cliff edge."

"Did you push him?" she asked cautiously.

Her question shocked him a little, then he realised that she needed to know that he was not an assassin. "No, no I didn't push him, he tripped."

"Is he dead?"

"Yes, Amelia, he is dead. Had he survived, however, I would have always been looking over my shoulder knowing that he wanted to kill me, but now I can get on with my life without that threat."

"Maybe I will be part of it, Ian." Her words did not sound as if they were a question, but more ones of a vague possibility that she was considering.

Vaughan sighed. "As I said earlier, I await your invitation, but in the meantime I have been ordered back to London. They have a job for me."

Lightning Source UK Ltd.
Milton Keynes UK
UKHW010639200621
385805UK00003B/383